Doktor Glass

Doktor Glass

Thomas Brennan

ACE BOOKS, NEW YORK

THE BERKLEY PUBLISHING GROUP
Published by the Penguin Group
Penguin Group (USA) Inc.
375 Hudson Street, New York, New York 10014, USA
Penguin Group (Canada), 90 Eglinton Avenue East, Suite 700, Toronto, Ontario M4P 2Y3, Canada
(a division of Pearson Penguin Canada Inc.) • Penguin Books Ltd., 80 Strand, London WC2R 0RL,
England • Penguin Ireland, 25 St. Stephen's Green, Dublin 2, Ireland (a division of Penguin
Books Ltd.) • Penguin Group (Australia), 707 Collins Street, Melbourne, Victoria 3008, Australia
(a division of Pearson Australia Group Pty. Ltd.) • Penguin Books India Pvt. Ltd., 11 Community
Centre, Panchsheel Park, New Delhi—110 017, India • Penguin Group (NZ), 67 Apollo Drive,
Rosedale, Auckland 0632, New Zealand (a division of Pearson New Zealand Ltd.) • Penguin Books,
Rosebank Office Park, 181 Jan Smuts Avenue, Parktown North 2193, South Africa • Penguin China,
B7 Jaiming Center, 27 East Third Ring Road North, Chaoyang District, Beijing 100020, China

Penguin Books Ltd., Registered Offices: 80 Strand, London WC2R 0RL, England

This is an original publication of The Berkley Publishing Group.

PUBLISHING HISTORY
Ace trade paperback edition / January 2013

Library of Congress Cataloging-in-Publication Data

Brennan, Thomas, 1965–
Doktor Glass / Thomas Brennan.—Ace trade pbk. ed.
p. cm.
ISBN 978-0-425-25817-0 (pbk.)
1. Police—England—Liverpool—Fiction. 2. Men—Crimes against—Fiction.
3. Liverpool (England)—Fiction. 4. Steampunk fiction. I. Title.
PR6102.R465D65 2012
823'.92—dc23
2012030179

For Mary and Albert

One

MATTHEW LANGTON KNELT beside his wife's grave and watched the rising sun burnish the Transatlantic Span. Far below Everton's hilltop cemetery, beneath stepped terraces of snow-bound tenement roofs, the great bridge's foundations stood anchored in the River Mersey's mist and shadows, but its soaring towers and suspended steel cables turned first red, then gold. Light slid down the pristine steel and illuminated the road deck; rail lines like silver threads dwindled to a distant vanishing point lost somewhere in the haze over Ireland.

Langton tried to imagine those new rails stretching westward across the Atlantic, all the way from Liverpool to New York. He could not; the distance was too great, America too remote. Like the hopeful thousands waiting below for the Span's inauguration, he would have to see for himself.

Now, as November cold gripped him, he stood up from the gravel path and read the headstone's angular gold letters for the hundredth time. Like Egyptian hieroglyphs from one of the recently opened tombs, they meant so much more than the simple form of the words:

SARAH JANE LANGTON

BORN FEBRUARY 2ND 1872

DIED AUGUST 17TH 1899

NEVER FORGOTTEN

Langton shed a glove and laid his hand on the smooth black marble. The icy wind racing up from the Mersey froze the droplets at the corners of his eyes, then closed them. Three months. Only three months. Langton could almost *will* his hand to register soft, warm skin, or feel the coiled hair gathered at the nape of Sarah's neck on a summer's day.

For a moment, Langton became as still as the sculpted monuments surrounding him. Frozen cherubs and angels reached up to the sky, their faces contorted with rapture, their bodies veined marble, granite, obsidian. How closely their rapture resembled agony. How unlike Sarah's final, peaceful features that Langton had discovered when he raced to the Infirmary, already too late.

He turned away, the gravel path crunching beneath his feet. Other than the sound of Langton's steps, only creaking tree branches and the ringing of small bells disturbed the silence. The bells stood above many of the graves, with cords or fine chains disappearing into the ground and into the coffins below. So many people feared being buried alive, being presumed dead rather than the doctors diagnosing narcolepsy or seizure. Langton could understand their fears: In his worst nightmares—the most recent—solid walls contained him, pressed in on him, robbed him of air; when he tried to scream, no sound came out; when he tried to move, he had no body.

Yes, he could understand those fears. In three months of daily visits, Langton had seen servants sitting beside the graves of the wealthy, waiting for signs of life from below, signs that never materialized.

Hope, Langton knew, came in many forms.

"Inspector Langton?" The cemetery gatekeeper stood in the lodge's doorway, his gaunt body silhouetted by flickering yellow light. "Have you a few minutes, sir?"

Langton hesitated, then said, "I have, Mr. Howard."

Thanks to his sleepless nights and early awakenings, Langton had almost two hours before he must report for duty. He left his coat in the hall and followed the gatekeeper into a sitting room filled with dark, heavy furniture; dusty ornaments; and a loud grandfather clock.

Howard crossed to the cluttered table. "It's uncommon cold already, sir. We've a deep winter ahead."

Langton warmed himself by the coal fire and glanced at the objects arranged on the mantelshelf. A severe woman stared back from a staged photograph; a ribbon of black velvet hung from the silver frame. A row of medals, some frayed and dulled with time, leaned against the photograph. "In all the times we've spoken outside, Mr. Howard, I never realized you were a Boer veteran."

The gatekeeper, busy at the table, stood a little taller. "Queen's Own Riflemen, sir. Togoland and Tanganyika, then the Transvaal, God's own purgatory here on earth, sir."

Langton stared into the fire and remembered the taste of South African dust, the hot-copper smell of fresh blood in the sun.

Howard continued, "That's where I picked up the taste of coffee, sir, and it stuck with me. Expensive habit, I know, but I don't smoke and I drink only to Her Majesty's health. I'd bet a shilling you're a coffee man yourself, sir."

Langton took the proffered seat beside the fire. "You'd win your wager, Mr. Howard."

He watched as the gatekeeper trickled coffee beans into a grinder, worked the handle, and then poured the fine grains into the hexagonal Italian percolator. When Howard screwed the steel percolator together it resembled an artillery shell; he placed it onto a pivoted rack and swung it over the coal flames.

Langton listened to the tick of the clock and the bubbling percolator. For two decades, many of Britain's young men had fought
the Boers, and many still lay out there beneath the baked red soil
and the unforgiving sun. But so did the Afrikaners, women and children, too. Langton had discovered how fear and desperation sounded
out the true depths of a man's soul, and that of an empire.

Coffee spluttered and bubbled and filled the room with a rich,
acrid odor. Howard produced two china mugs. Langton breathed in
the fumes for a moment before tasting the coffee. He smiled.

"Truth is, sir . . ." Howard said, then coughed and looked away.
"Truth is, I wanted to mention something."

Langton waited.

"Well, sir, I've seen you every day now since . . . since your misfor-
tune. Every morning at the same time. Not that I was spying on you,
sir. But we got to saying hallo and to passing the time of day."

"Go on."

Howard gulped coffee. "Fact is, sir, I did the same when my Maude
passed away: I couldn't say good-bye to her. The good Lord knows, I
seen plenty of dead and dying, enough to last ten men's lifetimes.
Maude was different. Like someone had reached inside and ripped a
piece of my soul right out."

Closing his eyes, Langton concentrated on the coffee in his hands
and the waves of heat from the fire.

"Sir, I just couldn't get over it. Stopping me from sleeping, eating,
everything, it was."

"Mr. Howard, I—"

"Hear me out, sir. Please." Howard topped up the mugs and said,
"Maude's sister told me about this woman over in Hamlet Street,
the other side of the park; she's a spiritualist, what some might call a
medium."

Langton stared at him. "You believe such fancies?"

"I didn't, sir, not before, but I was so desperate I paid her a visit."

So much more than a mere fad, spiritualism had erupted in every town and city in Britain. As science progressed and wars and pestilence flourished, people searched for answers, even the wrong ones. Through his fellow officers, Langton had heard of fake mediums and spirit guides defrauding anguished families of hundreds or even thousands of pounds. At the other end of the scale lay poor men like the gatekeeper.

Langton set his mug down. "I'm sorry, Mr. Howard."

"She let me say good-bye to my Maude, sir," Howard said. "She helped me and she can help you, sir, I know it. Perhaps I'm being forward, but I hate to see suffering. Especially in a comrade."

Langton looked into the man's face etched with deep lines, the eyes wide and still hopeful. "Mr. Howard, so many of these people are charlatans."

"Not this one, sir. Not Mrs. Grizedale." Howard reached into his waistcoat pocket for a small card. "If you feel able to, please call on her. You'll not regret it if you do."

Langton nodded, took the card, and slipped it into his jacket. "Perhaps I shall."

As he collected his Ulster coat and gloves from the hall, Langton wondered if the spiritualist had actually helped Howard or whether the gatekeeper simply *believed* that she had. Either way, as long as Howard felt he'd benefited, the end result must be the same.

"I hope you'll forgive me bringing this up, sir. Being forward, like."

On the front step, Langton folded his collar up against the cold and then shook the gatekeeper's hand. "I appreciate the consideration, Mr. Howard. And thank you for the coffee."

Langton looked back from the massive wrought-iron gates and saw Howard stooped in the lodge doorway. He had a sudden image of the cottage standing alone in the snow, very far from the city's bustle, with Howard guarding something neither of them understood, something quite different from the certainty of these manicured grounds. Something elemental. Then the icy wind shredded the image and brought Langton back to the city waiting below him.

He crossed Walton Lane and walked south toward the city center, dimly registering the whine of cart wheels and the snorting horses whose breath hung in clouds. Soot flecked the snow under Langton's boots and he tasted coal dust in the air; most of the roadside tenement windows glimmered with candlelight or gaslight, and smoke writhed up from myriad chimneys to join the pall that never quite left the city.

As he crossed Walton Breck Road, Langton heard a steady roar and pounding like some great beast laboring uphill. The polished brass boiler and belching smokestack of a Riley steam car wheezed up the incline. Even before the vehicle veered to his side of the road, Langton recognized the insignia of the Liverpool Exchange Division Police, his own company. He stepped back as narrow rubber tires skidded on the compacted snow and the beast halted with a belch of blue-black smoke.

The two men in leather coats and fogged goggles resembled aviators, but the vehicle itself, with its curved wooden stern and brass boiler, looked like a boat wrenched from its natural home. Indeed, one of the men gripped the shaking tiller like a helmsman. The other man peeled off his goggles and saluted Langton.

Langton nodded in return. "McBride. You've chosen a noisy companion this morning."

"She's a fine craft, sir. And all the hansom cabs were out when I asked."

Langton doubted that was true, since Sergeant McBride loved all the new machinery, all the latest advances of Queen Victoria's technological age, and needed little excuse to use them. Every week, wide-eyed, he related broadsheet stories of zeppelins and gyroplanes, warcraft and atomics, horseless carriages and landships.

"I called at your house, sir, and Elsie told me where I might find you." McBride looked away as he mentioned Langton's maid.

"Why the haste, Sergeant?"

"A bad business for us, sir, down at the docks."

Langton, already climbing aboard the steam car, said, "What sort of business?"

A hiss, a roar, a grinding of metal cogs, and the car lurched forward. McBride turned and shouted above the din, "Murder, sir. And the work of a madman."

THE DEAD MAN lay facedown on the cobbles edging Albert Dock. All around the scene, dockers and supervisors bustled, steam winches hissed and groaned, beam cranes hoisted, men clawed at bales with metal hooks. But a subdued silence encircled the corpse and its waiting attendants.

Langton knelt beside the man. Dark woolen trousers, patched, and new boots, scuffed at the toes; no jacket but a white, collarless shirt and black waistcoat. A gold Albert chain trailed from under the stomach but had no fob watch attached. The chain's last link had not been broken, as usually happened when a thief tore a watch away.

The man's arms jutted out at unnatural angles, like some collapsed scarecrow, and Langton winced at the break points above the elbow on the left arm and above the wrist on the right. The unfastened shirt sleeves revealed skin tanned to the color of teak, with faint blue tattoos struggling through.

Langton knelt a little closer to the left arm's tattoos and then focused on the head: cropped hair as black as jet, and a bald spot of pale white. The left ear had been pierced and held five gold studs of varying sizes. The head lay on its right cheek, so that the left side was exposed.

Someone had sliced off the man's face. Instead of tanned flesh was raw red bone, striated ligaments, and sagging tissue. A precise incision ran from the forehead, down the front of the ears, and under the jaw and chin. On one side of the cut lay the neck and throat, dirty tanned flesh. On the other, ruin.

As Langton stood up, he tried to remember the last time he had seen those injuries. Not since South Africa, and certainly not in Great Britain, until now. He looked around at the brick warehouses surrounding the grey water of the enclosed dock. Life continued as if nothing had happened. At every level, even the top floor a hundred feet or more in the air, men leaned out of open doors and steered roped cargoes up from the wharves below. Ships, steam and sail, lined every inch of the busy wharves; more waited at the open dock gates, impatient to unload and return to the river and sea.

And above all, towering over everything, stood the Transatlantic Span. It reduced even the enormous docks and steamships to toys.

Langton turned to the waiting circle. "Who discovered the body?"

A burly, unshaven man in a torn shirt spat into the water. "I did. First light. More's the bloody pity."

Another of the men, this one older and wearing a faded brown suit and hat, said, "You'll show some respect, Connolly."

The docker crossed his thick arms. "What for? I get paid when I work; more I stand around here, less I make."

"Mend your tone or you'll be on the street."

"That's enough, gentlemen." Langton raised a hand to stop the older man from speaking, then turned to the docker. "Tell me what happened."

Connolly nodded toward the enclosed grey water. "I was on my way to the office, to see if I could get anything for today. Healey was gang foreman last week so I didn't get a ha'penny, even though I can do the work of two of his cronies."

Langton knew that the dockers found work through Company-appointed foremen. They had to report every morning and hope they found a fair-minded man giving out the day's employment. If not, they didn't work, just as in Langton's grandfather's day. "Go on."

"Well, I was walking alongside the ramp over there, where they sometimes haul the boats out, when I saw a shape in the water. Thought it was a tarpaulin or slung cargo, but closer I got, the more it looked like a man. So I grabbed a boathook and fished it in. Gave me a turn, it did, and I don't mind admitting it."

Langton looked down at the edge of the man's face, where the flesh became raw red bone.

"Robbery, obviously," the brown-suited man said. "We get a few bodies washed up every month with their throats slit or heads bashed in."

"Nothing like this?"

The man hesitated. "Not to my knowledge."

"And you are . . ."

"Perkins, Inspector. Assistant piermaster."

Connolly spat eloquently into the dock again but said nothing. Perkins glared at him. "Of course, it could be someone inside the docks. You never know what these layabouts will get up to."

Langton did not want to get diverted, and so he told Connolly, "Give your address to Sergeant McBride here and you can go back to work. Mr. Perkins, have you any idea who the dead man might be?"

Perkins didn't look down at the body. "How could I? Besides, he wouldn't be one of our workers, not dressed like that."

"Pardon me?"

"Well, the boots, the trousers and waistcoat: They're issued by the TSC."

Langton glanced at the bridge. "The Transatlantic Span Company?"

"I'm sure of it, Inspector. You can't help but notice them, swanking about with their pockets full of silver, even though most of them are no better than navvies. That's why I'm sure it's robbery."

As if speaking to himself, Langton said, "But they didn't take his gold chain or rings."

"Pardon me?"

Langton looked up. "Where can we find you if we need you?"

"That brick cottage next to the dock gates, but—"

"Thank you, Mr. Perkins. We'll finish our work here as soon as we can."

As Perkins left, Langton checked the dead man's pockets. He found no identification, but a fine steel chain secured a key to the man's belt; triangular in shape, with the simplistic outline of a bridge engraved into the metal, it reminded Langton of keys used by watchmen to prove they had done the rounds of their assigned buildings or routes—

they would slip the key into a suitable clock that time-stamped their presence.

A guard or watchman would no doubt have unfettered access to the Span. He could identify its weak points, its vulnerabilities. And he would know that the Queen herself would inaugurate the Span in five days.

Langton waved forward the two waiting stretcher bearers. As they rolled the body onto the canvas stretcher, Langton saw the whole face in full. It grinned back at him like some gruesome effigy. Langton closed his eyes and took a deep breath; when he looked again, the bearers had loaded their cargo in their horse-drawn black wagon.

"Are you all right, sir?"

"I'm fine, Sergeant. Fine."

McBride nodded at the last man remaining, a bearded giant broad across the shoulders. "What shall I do with him, sir?"

"Who is he?"

"Olsen, sir, a stoker from the steam brigantine *Asención*. Reckoned he saw a small boat slipping through the Canning Half-Tide Dock gate around four this morning. Mind, he's been hard at the liquor."

The disheveled sailor clung to the iron lamppost like a shipwreck survivor with a piece of driftwood.

"Do you have his statement?"

"Aye, the gist of it, sir."

"Then send him to his ship. We'll talk to him tonight, after he's slept off some of the drink."

As the stoker lurched toward the King's Dock gate to the south, Langton took a final inventory of the scene. The man could have been murdered anywhere and his body dumped in the water from boat or carriage. Or simply hurled over the side of the docks.

And the motive? Langton had encountered so many in his career: greed, hatred (for as many reasons, both real and imagined, as man could devise), love, and fear. Or madness, the most difficult to fathom since it relied on its own perverse logic. Robbery was the simplest explanation but the wrong one here; the victim's thick gold watch chain, earrings, and rings would not have survived.

And thieves would have no reason to slice off the man's features.

"Sir, is there anything else?" McBride went toward the swing bridge leading to Gower Street.

"Return to the station," Langton said, "and ask Doctor Fry to check the man's body for any more tattoos and scars, especially around the chest and stomach. This is not just another murder, Sergeant."

McBride seemed about to ask a question, then nodded and walked toward the steam car parked on Gower Street well out of the lanes of passing horses and carts.

"One thing, Sergeant," Langton said. Then, as McBride turned around, "Why did we get this call? We're not on the duty roster this week."

McBride shook his head. "I never asked why, sir. I just did what the Chief told me, and came to collect you. Did I do wrong?"

"No. I'm sure he has good reason," Langton said, still wondering why Chief Inspector Purcell should want him on this case. Perhaps the Chief wanted to distract him, although Langton had never attributed compassion to the man. Perhaps he had misjudged him.

Leaving a constable at the scene, Langton crossed the east swing bridge into Salthouse Dock and walked its perimeter until he reached busy Wapping Road. The cold November air would clear his head and help him think. It might help him to remember what those tattoos signified; back in the Transvaal, he'd been adept at reading the enemy's intricate body art. No design was redundant—all had a special meaning. And he had no doubt the man was a Boer. The tattoos confirmed it.

Why would a Boer veteran, an enemy of Britain and all its dominions even after the Bloemfontein truce, work on the Transatlantic Span?

* * *

LANGTON REACHED HIS office after nine and hung his Ulster by the coal stove. He warmed his hands for a moment before peering through the sash window to the bustling traffic of Victoria Street below. A tram shouldered its way through the carts and horses, blue light arcing between its pantograph and the suspended cables. The sounds of street-organ music drifted through the fogged panes.

Although a leaning stack of paperwork awaited Langton in his tray, he ignored it and opened a new case file for the dead man. As he searched his drawer for a pen, he found a framed monochrome photograph of Sarah smiling up at him from a summer three years gone. Langton rested his fingers on the chill surface and traced her outline. He closed the drawer as if it too were made of glass.

After ten minutes of precise writing, he looked up at the sound of knuckles rapping his frosted glass door. Harry, the office boy, leaned through the gap. "Begging your pardon, sir. Chief Inspector would like a word."

As the boy went to leave, Langton called out, "Wait a moment, Harry."

He found a pad of telegraph forms and scribbled a few lines. "Send this to the Labor Department at the Transatlantic Span Company offices at the Pier Head. Urgent."

Harry pocketed the telegram and sixpence and limped down the stairs as Langton ascended.

On the third floor, Chief Inspector Purcell's personal secretary waved Langton through to the sanctum sanctorum of the Chief's office. Purcell stood at the window with his hands behind his back. Oil paintings of previous chiefs watched Langton from the walls. "You wanted to see me, sir?"

Purcell turned from the window and pointed his cigar at the visitor's chair. "You've caught a strange fish this morning."

"That's so, sir." Langton wondered how Purcell had heard about the dead man. And why.

Purcell settled into his leather chair. "What have you found?"

Langton relayed his initial impressions. After hesitating a moment, he mentioned the Boer connection.

Purcell leaned forward. "You're sure?"

"The crossed plow and sword on his left arm confirm him as Boer, sir. The windmill designs on his right arm mean a soldier from the southern battalions, if I remember correctly, perhaps one of the Graaffe-Reinert or Uitenhage companies. I'd be surprised if the examining physician doesn't find more tattoos on the body."

Purcell ground out his cigar. "So. A Boer on the Span. Could there be an innocent explanation?"

Langton considered for a few moments. "It's possible but I doubt it, sir. After the truce, some of the surviving Transvaal platoons promised revenge, and the Span is our greatest engineering achievement. It would be a great coup for them."

"If they disrupt the inauguration?"

"Or worse."

"Indeed." Purcell sighed and reached for the telephone. "I don't relish asking for help, but this is too delicate a matter. I'll inform the Home Office that there may be a Boer plot afoot."

"Must we, sir? The investigation has only just begun."

"We've no choice, Langton, not with Her Majesty's safety at risk. Keep me informed."

Langton made for the door, then hesitated. "Sir, may I ask a question?"

Purcell kept one hand on the telephone's cradle. "What is it?"

"How did you find out about the death this morning? And why send me?"

Purcell frowned. "I have to explain myself to you now, Langton?"

"Of course not, sir." Langton opened the door and was almost through it when Purcell called him back.

"My secretary prepares a summary of the night's events in all our stations," Purcell said, "and I believed you would welcome the opportunity to prove your . . . recovery. I hope I was not mistaken."

"Sir." As he closed the door and walked through the secretary's office, Langton almost stopped and asked him. It would make little difference; even if the man's death had appeared on the nightly summary report, why would Chief Inspector Purcell focus on that particular one? Unfortunately, fatalities were not uncommon: Liverpool Exchange and Central districts averaged four or five a week, sometimes more when thousands of sailors poured into the docks, flush with money and ripe for thieves.

Langton told himself to concentrate on the case. He ignored the rickety iron lift and made for the stairs down to the basement. By now, the police physician should have started his examination of the body.

He couldn't fault Purcell for informing the Home Office, since the Chief Inspector was simply protecting himself in case, God forbid, anything did happen while the Queen and the various dignitaries attended the Span's inauguration. No, Purcell had done what any other official with an eye to his future would do. Even if it disrupted Langton's investigation.

Halfway down the final set of steps, Langton staggered against the tiled wall and almost fell. He clutched the banister and struggled to stay upright as the sudden blindness made him reel.

Darkness, colloidal and greasy, choked his face and mouth, engulfed his tongue, and gushed down his throat. His chest struggled against bonds that tightened with each faltering breath. No sounds save his own gagging and a discordant ringing like the grave bells of Everton cemetery. He flailed and sank deeper, deeper.

Then he returned. On his knees on the stairs, clutching the banister like a falling man grasping a rope, Langton blinked and tried to focus his gaze. He hauled himself upright and then doubled over, retching but bringing up only acid bile. He gulped in deep breaths tainted with disinfectant and stood there, ashen, until the taste of the cloying darkness left his mouth.

He looked around, grateful that nobody had seen this latest attack, one of the worst so far. He took the last few steps clinging to the banister like an old man or an infant.

In the light of the basement's flickering gas lamp, he took out the card that gatekeeper Howard had presented. A simple pasteboard square with curled edges and copperplate printing: *Mrs. Eugenie Grizedale, 33 Hamlet Street, Everton 512. Interview by appointment only.*

Langton slipped the card back into his pocket, wiped a handkerchief across his mouth, and smoothed the front of his uniform jacket before he followed the sign and peeling black letters painted onto the white tiles: *Examination Room and Mortuary.*

Two

As LANGTON PUSHED through the outer doors, the basement's odors struck him: disinfectant, tobacco smoke, and some acrid chemical like bitter almonds. On the left lay Doctor Fry's office: an empty chair, a desk cluttered with papers and laboratory glassware, a full ashtray. On the walls, charts and illustrations of the human body fought for space with cartoons cut from *Punch Illustrated* magazine.

"Fry?"

"In here, Langton."

Another set of wooden doors opened into the examination room and mortuary, where three marble slabs faced wood-and-steel drawers as wide as a man's shoulders. A cluster of gas lamps illuminated the center of the chill, tiled room and made it resemble a Rembrandt painting. Doctor Fry's bald head glistened with sweat and yellow light as he bent over the murder victim on the first slab. Fry's assistant stood behind him, taking notes and sliding red samples onto white enamel dishes.

Langton crossed the echoing chamber until he stood at the dead man's feet. Fry, intent on exploration, did not look up but said, "Your man McBride said this was important."

"It could be." Langton shivered as he glanced at the eviscerated body now so similar to the anatomical drawings in the adjacent office.

"I hope so; I don't usually devote this much attention to a victim."

"He's an unusual victim."

"He is that." Fry raised bloody forceps up to the gaslight and examined the glistening exhibit for a moment before depositing it in a bowl. "He was a drinker. Liver's in a terrible state, distended and scarred. Surprised he made it this far."

Langton looked away.

Fry continued, "Around forty-five years old, although hard living might have aged him prematurely. Callused hands suggesting manual labor. False teeth made by a good dentist, German if I'm not mistaken."

"And the broken bones?"

"Done before death, I think." Fry pointed with the forceps. "There's bruising around the fracture points. I could be wrong, but they remind me of boot prints."

So they'd beaten him before stripping his face. "And his identity?"

Fry said, "He was a Boer, of course."

"You saw the tattoos?"

"And these." Fry peeled back the flap of skin he'd unfurled from the man's chest and stomach. "You can't see too well in this light. I've asked Lord knows how many times for some decent electroliers down here, but we never hear a thing."

The yellow gaslight made the man's naked body look like grained wood. Langton followed the trail of Fry's forceps down the abdomen and saw a network of fine silver lines. "Scars."

"Look at the shape," Fry said, and then, to his chief assistant, "Johnson, pull that mantle closer."

Langton thought he could make out a triangle, a circle, and the numbers eight and six, or zero, carved into the skin.

Fry said, "One of my old Edinburgh lecturers made a study of the South African battalions' initiation rites; they were vicious enough to their own men, never mind ours."

"I know. But this . . . I don't recognize it."

"The Orange Free State Irregulars of eighty-six," Fry said, "one of the mercenary outfits brought in by the Boers and given free rein. I believe the militia were very effective."

"Oh, they were: The mercenaries learned their craft from the British officers who first created them," Langton said, anger boiling up inside him. "No wonder the Boers hated us."

Fry glanced at his assistant. "Fetch me the Kodak, Johnson."

Then, to Langton, "Take care in what you say; some in the police might misconstrue your words. Remember, the Boers did the same to us, and sometimes worse. War draws out men's evil like water from a deep spring."

Langton had to agree with Fry. Both sides had committed atrocities in the name of war, of territory, and of nationalism. No hand had remained free of blood.

As Johnson returned with the bulky camera on its tripod, Fry moved up to the dead man's head. Langton joined him beside the fixed rictus grin of the mutilated face. The blood had darkened with the passing hours, and the edges of the skin had hardened. "Why do this? Why erase his features?"

"Obviously to remove his identity," Fry said.

Langton shook his head. "We know he worked for the Span Company unless he stole the clothes from a worker. Someone there will surely recognize the body from the tattoos and build alone. Have you his fingerprints?"

Fry pointed to the man's inked fingers. "Johnson dispatched copies to Scotland Yard. I don't hold out much hope."

"Nor do I." Langton had attended a lecture in London on the use of Magistrate Herschel's fingerprinting; he recognized their value, even their eventual necessity, but a system was only as good as the information put into it. And Scotland Yard had no more than two thousand or so records on file so far. "Did you find anything to help his identification? Other than the tattoos."

Still gazing down, Fry said, "He had nothing in his pockets, no papers or letters. Money, though: eleven pounds, five shillings and sixpence."

So, as Langton had already concluded, robbery was not the motive. "Any tailors' labels in his clothes?"

"Only those of the Company." Fry angled the gaslights, then froze. "This is something I've never encountered before."

Fry tilted the man's head on the marble block and said, "What do you make of that?"

Langton couldn't see any interruption to the tanned skin until he made out a small, square red mark high on the neck, practically in the hairline. "A bruise?"

"It reminds me more of a burn." Fry tilted the man's head again. "There's a corresponding mark on the other side in the same position."

Langton tried to imagine the sequence of events: Two quick blows to the back of the neck would take most men down. Would sandbags or blackjacks leave such a perfectly square imprint?

As his assistant set up the camera near the man's head, Fry pulled Langton back into the shadows. "With your permission, I'd like to suggest gaining a second opinion on all this. There's a professor who specializes in reconstructive surgery; you might remember him from the broadsheets, that accident with the ship's boiler in Gladstone Dock."

"When all those passengers were burned?"

"That's the one. Professor Caldwell Chivers gave most of them their own faces back. I think he can help with our friend here."

Langton glanced at the ruined features. "By all means, if you think it will help."

"I do. And I hope he might have an idea as to those bruises, or burns."

"Such as?"

Fry looked at the slab again, then said, "Leave it with me, Langton. When I've finished here I'll send the body over to Caldwell Chivers at the Infirmary, if he's amenable."

The mention of the Infirmary took Langton back three months. He forced his voice to remain calm. "May I use your telephone?"

"Of course."

Automatically, he went to shake Fry's hand, then saw the bloodied rubber gloves. Langton made for the doors, then turned and said, "You forgot to tell me one thing."

"Which is?"

"The cause of death."

"I want to study the stomach contents and blood separations before I'm sure, but I think he was poisoned. The pinhole pupils certainly suggest it."

Langton stared at him. "But those injuries—"

"Agonizing, I know, but not necessarily life-threatening. I've seen men survive worse."

So have I, Langton thought.

In Fry's office, Langton sat behind the cluttered desk and reached for the upright telephone. He took the card from his pocket, read it, returned it. He pushed the chair back. Then he remembered the episode on the stairs; if that had happened in front of his sergeant, or fellow inspectors . . .

He could see his own physician, Doctor Redfers, but what would he recommend? Drugs? Rest? No, work was the best medicine—being busy distracted him. All God's creatures needed sleep, and Langton knew he couldn't keep going without some rest, some relief from the nightmares. Howard, the cemetery gatekeeper, had sworn that Mrs. Grizedale had helped him. Langton had little to lose apart from his skepticism.

He read the number off the card and dialed for the operator. "Everton five-twelve, please."

* * *

WHEN HE RETURNED to his office after a late lunch, Langton found McBride waiting. "News, Sergeant?"

McBride stood at ease with his hands behind his back. "Sir. I took it on myself to do a little sniffing around the docks, see if anyone had spotted our man. Hope I did right, sir."

Langton nodded as he reached for the sealed telegram Harry had obviously left on his desk. "You did well. What did you discover?"

"Well, sir, not as much as I'd hoped; the dockers are a closemouthed lot, not keen on giving out answers, though it seems I wasn't the first one to go around asking questions."

Langton looked up from the telegram.

McBride leaned toward the desk like a conspirator. "A couple of fellas hung around the docks and the pubs, asking about the Span and the people working on it. They'd buy a man a pint and ask a few questions, sort of casual like, then move on to the next pub. The dockers are always on the lookout for Dock Company spies and suchlike, so they passed word to each other, kind of warning."

Langton nodded. "And one of the men asking questions was about six feet tall, with tanned skin and probably the trace of a foreign accent."

McBride looked vaguely disappointed. "So they say, sir, yes. They thought he was German."

Langton wondered why the dead man had been trawling the pubs and docks for information. A Boer would want to melt into the background; he wouldn't want to publicize his presence, especially if he had some scheme planned, some attack on the Span. It didn't make sense yet.

Langton knew he and McBride had so much to do: interview the workers at the Span, trace the dead man's identity, discover his actions leading up to the day of his death. And there were so many people who could have connected with him—not just the Span employees but the thousands waiting in the sprawling shantytown that had grown beneath the bridge's deck and arches: the immigrants from almost every country in Europe; the Caisson Widows, the protesting wives of the many navigation engineers, or "navvies," who had died in the construction of the bridge's foundations; the Mersey mudlarks and assorted scavengers, fleecers, and predators.

"McBride, I need you to interview the sailor who believed he saw a boat dumping something this morning."

"Stoker Olsen, sir."

"If he's sober, try to get descriptions, the type of boat he saw, anything you can." Langton read through the telegram sent from the TSC's Labor Department, who agreed to "make themselves available for his inquiries." "Tomorrow, we'll pay a visit to the Span Company and see if they know about our friend."

"Can I drop you somewhere, sir?"

Langton glanced to the clock on his wall: twenty minutes after four. He stood up and reached for his Ulster. "Thank you, no. I have business in Everton."

THE TERRACED HOUSE in Hamlet Street looked no different from its neighbors, or indeed from the hundreds of dwellings in the adjacent streets. Faced with yellow brick and sandstone lintels, it merged into the soot-laden smog that had descended over Liverpool. Isolated pools of yellow light glowed on either side of the road; the lines of gas lamps gave way to a sharper, whiter light farther on, where the main road electroliers stood.

Langton paused at the front-garden gate and listened to the sound of a piano coming from some front room nearby; the same hesitant notes played over, obviously by a beginner, most probably a child. This area attracted ambitious families, those wishing to advance themselves. Families not so very different from Langton's own.

He rang the bell and saw a vague shape moving behind the stained-glass door panels. The maid who opened the door came from India or one of its colonial neighbors; the spot of red dye dabbed on her forehead contrasted with the white mob cap of her uniform. "Good evening, sir."

"Matthew Langton," he said. "I have an appointment for six o'clock."

The maid stepped aside. "Please."

After Langton gave her his coat, hat, and gloves, the maid left him alone in the front sitting room, giving him time to take in the contorted furniture of teak and sandalwood, the tapestries and tassels, the vivid rugs laid one over the other. Tribal masks grinned at him from the walls. A swirl of rich odors clogged his throat: jasmine, lilies, orchids.

Langton knew he'd made a mistake. The foreign maid, the room like a theater stage set, the overpowering fumes: All signaled artifice if not fraud. He opened the door, intending to leave, and found the maid about to enter. She blocked his escape. "Please, sir. This way."

He followed the maid down the short hallway. He would apologize for wasting the spiritualist's time, perhaps give her a few shillings as compensation, then leave. This was obviously no place for him. His heart went out to gatekeeper Howard, who had found solace in all this pretense.

The maid tapped at a door and ushered Langton inside. He had expected more of the same ornate decoration. Instead he stood in a bare, almost monastic room: a plain deal table with two hard chairs, one of which was occupied; a single electric lamp; bare floorboards whose polish reflected firelight.

The woman at the table took his hand. "Inspector Langton? I'm Genny Grizedale."

"Mrs. Grizedale." Langton shook her hand but didn't sit down. "I fear I've made a mistake."

She smiled. "I'm sorry that Meera showed you into the sitting room; it gave you the wrong impression, I'm sure. You see, most of my visitors expect a certain . . . ambience. A certain spectacle. They would be disappointed if they saw this room, my real place of work. Sit, please. If only for the moment."

Langton tried to guess the woman's age. Her stocky frame and heavy black clothes and cap, so reminiscent of Queen Victoria's perpetual mourning, implied late middle age, but no lines or fatigue marked her youthful face.

She smiled and said, "You are skeptical of my work."

"How do you know?"

"By your expression and your movements, as well as your words."

"I'm not sure you can help me."

"You may be right," Mrs. Grizedale said. "Shall we find out?"

Another door opened to allow the maid in with a tray balanced in both hands. Langton caught a glimpse of a modern, gleaming kitchen bathed in electric light.

"Thank you, Meera." Mrs. Grizedale busied herself with the tea paraphernalia, the cups, saucers, pot, bowls, and trivet all in blue Chinese Willow pattern.

Langton cleared his throat and asked, "Have you practiced this . . . spiritualism for long?"

She tilted her head to one side. "I suppose I have. Ever since childhood, I could see things others could not, make certain connections others found difficult."

"If you'll forgive me saying so, it strikes me as a strange choice of career."

Her smile faded. "It has never been a question of choice, Inspector. And there are many strange aspects to all our lives. Now, in your telephone call, you mentioned Mr. Howard; you know him well?"

"A few months only."

She tended the teapot. "You share at least one thing: You have both suffered losses."

A knife twisted inside Langton's stomach. "Three months ago. My wife. Sarah."

Mrs. Grizedale nodded and clasped her hands in her lap. She waited.

The warm, quiet room had an atmosphere of tranquillity and of disconnection, as though the outside world existed but some way off. Langton found himself explaining the events of Sarah's wasting illness, the Infirmary, his arriving too late to say good-bye. He admitted his lack of rest and the nightmares that affected him when he did sleep. Because of either the spiritualist's influence or the effects of months passing, Langton surprised himself by remaining calm; his voice didn't waver.

Mrs. Grizedale listened, poured out the tea, and waited for him to finish. Then she said, "I am sorry for your loss."

When she said that, Langton actually believed her. The words were not mere platitudes.

"You say you cannot sleep."

"That's so," Langton said. "In fact, I almost fear sleep."

"The nightmares? Tell me about them."

Langton stared into the fire. "I cannot breathe. It's as though the entire weight of the world presses down on my throat and chest, and something soft and clammy fills my mouth. When I manage to make a small sound, only a whimper, I feel the atmosphere around me—not air, something thicker and more oppressive—swallow the cry."

As he remembered the dreams, the effects started to return. He closed his eyes a moment, took a deep breath, and continued, "That's not the worst; it's the sense of utter despair that grips me. Of being so alone, so bereft, so helpless."

Now that he had admitted his fears, Langton hoped that they would lessen. For a moment, he wondered why he found it so easy to talk of these things to Mrs. Grizedale when he could not tell Sarah's family or his own physician. Perhaps because the spiritualist was a stranger? That wasn't the only reason.

As if on another path, Mrs. Grizedale said, "You visit the cemetery every morning."

Had Mr. Howard told her? "I do."

"Does it help?"

"It's not a matter of helping," Langton said. "I have no choice. I find myself drawn to . . . drawn there."

Mrs. Grizedale nodded. "You cannot let your wife go, nor she you."

He stared into those calm eyes. "Must I?"

"If you are to continue with your own life, then yes, I'm afraid you must."

He went to speak, then bit back his words.

Mrs. Grizedale continued, "We live so close to death, Inspector. We are so fragile and yet so optimistic. We navigate the waters of each day without thinking of the hidden dangers, the rocks and shallows, the tides and storms. If we thought of them too often we would never accomplish anything; we might never leave our houses."

Langton looked down. "Maybe that would be better."

Mrs. Grizedale took his hand. "No, Inspector. That way lies not life but only a pale imitation of life. We cannot hide away. But these are mere words, and words do little to soften your loss. So."

With that, she took his other hand in hers and set them on the small table among the crockery. Langton's hands lay on their backs, with Mrs. Grizedale's resting on his palms, her skin soft yet cold. "Breathe softly, Inspector. Close your eyes and forget the world outside this room. Relax."

Langton listened to the crackle of the fire's coals. No sounds of traffic or people filtered through to the room. Smells drifted past: tea, coal smoke, a faint perfume like white flowers.

"Now, Inspector, think of your wife; picture her, despite the pain I know will come. Focus on her."

Sarah's image rose in Langton's mind and made his heart race and his throat tighten. Sarah. A summer's day among the crowds at New Brighton, with the warm breeze swirling her pale cotton dress. The flash of her blue, blue eyes. Her dappled skin. Laughter. Sarah.

"I see . . ." Mrs. Grizedale whispered and gripped Langton's hands a little tighter. "Sarah. Sarah. All is safe. Come to me. Come to me . . ."

Langton opened his eyes. Mrs. Grizedale rocked slightly in her chair, her eyes closed, her skin blushing. She tightened her grip on his hands. "Darkness. Cold darkness. And pressure, something pressing in from every side. Oh, the fear. The fear. Speak, Sarah. All is safe. Speak through—"

Langton winced as Mrs. Grizedale's nails bit deep into his palms and drew blood. Her body snapped taut and rigid as though every muscle simultaneously contracted. The teacups and crockery shattered against the floor.

He tried to drag his hands from Mrs. Grizedale's grip but she would not or could not let go. He said, "Meera, quickly."

As the maid rushed into the room, Mrs. Grizedale's body began to shudder; her heels drummed on the bare wooden floor. Blood trickled from her mouth.

"Grab her," Langton said, "before she falls."

Meera took the woman's shoulders as Langton pulled his bloodied hands from her clawing grip. He helped Mrs. Grizedale to the floor and tried to slide a spoon between her teeth. He could not; the woman's jaw was locked tight as though set in steel.

"Missy, oh missy." Tears rolled down Meera's cheeks as she held the spiritualist's head.

"Has this happened before?"

"Yes, sir, but not for long time. And never this bad." Meera stared at Langton. "What you do to her?"

Before he could answer, a terrible, guttural sound erupted from Mrs. Grizedale's throat. Her eyes opened to reveal dilated pupils and an expression of absolute fear. Then, as suddenly as they had started, the contractions ceased. Langton felt her body go limp; her head lolled to one side.

Fearing what he would find, Langton pressed his fingers into her neck. Her heart still beat, although erratically. As he counted, her heart gradually slowed until it seemed almost normal. Then her eyes focused on Meera and she whispered, "Brandy."

As Meera ran into the kitchen, Langton helped Mrs. Grizedale sit upright on the floor. He supported her back with his knee and dabbed at her mouth with his handkerchief. He stifled his questions and waited for her to catch her breath.

Mrs. Grizedale sipped the brandy and looked at Langton. "Never again . . . I had hoped . . ."

"Don't talk," Langton said, even though he longed to know what had brought this about and what she had discovered about Sarah. "Rest awhile."

Mrs. Grizedale shook her head. "I am sorry. So very sorry."

"What is it?"

"Your wife is lost." Mrs. Grizedale turned her bloody, frightened face to Langton. "The Jar Boys have her."

Three

A S HE WALKED home through the streets of fog and shadows, Langton went over everything he had ever heard about the so-called Jar Boys. The cold air numbed his face; pools of light, gas and electric, punctuated the gloom, but Langton stared straight ahead and remembered stories told around firesides and on midnight beats. For the Jar Boys inhabited that strange borderland between truth and fiction, or between hope and fear.

The poor believed in their existence, but he had also heard of them from time-served constables and sergeants, from apparently sane and balanced veterans. Physicians refuted them, just as they had with the Resurrectionists, but the newspapers reported Jar Boy gangs in Liverpool, London, Edinburgh, and Newcastle; in Paris and Frankfurt; in America. As far as Langton knew, that was all they were: sensationalist stories.

The stories all shared the same basic "facts": The Jar Boys stole the souls of the dying. With their bizarre apparatus, they waited at the bedsides of those close to the end and captured the soul as it left the body, trapped it in special vessels of glass or clay. Poor families, either tricked or paid a guinea or two, allowed the Jar Boys access during those final minutes.

It was madness. It had to be madness.

What if it was true?

Langton stumbled at the junction of Briar Street and Islington. He clung to a hissing gas lamp standard and pressed his face to the clammy, ridged steel. What if Sarah's soul had been captured? Trapped and alone, she could be anywhere now, beyond Langton's help. He'd sworn to shelter her, to protect her. Always.

No, it could not be true. Mrs. Grizedale must be wrong. That seizure had not been an act; Langton still had her blood on his clothes. And she'd spat out fragments of broken tooth. She had been sincere, of that he was sure.

Heavy footfalls in the fog preceded a constable in a slick black cape. He stood watching Langton for a moment, rocking on his heels.

Langton straightened up, nodded to the constable, and walked on; since Langton didn't stagger like a drunk, the constable didn't call out. That made Langton remember the array of bottles locked in the sideboard at home. Whiskey and port. Wine, brandy, Curaçao. All waiting, collecting dust for so long. Wasted for so long. He walked faster.

One question would not leave his mind. It returned again and again like a moth beating at an electrolier's glass globe: Why would anyone *want* to capture another person's soul?

And that led to another question: What would they do with it?

Elsie, the young maid, opened the door of Langton's house. The hall gaslight gave her two spots of color high in her cheeks. "Evening, sir. There's a visitor."

Slipping out of his Ulster, Langton said, "At this time of the night? Who?"

Elsie took the coat and looked away. "Sergeant McBride, sir. He said it was urgent, so I took the liberty of putting him in the front sitting room, sir. Hope I did right."

Langton couldn't help a slight smile. "That's quite all right, Elsie."

"Could I get you anything, sir? Cook made a nice pie, steak and kidney. It's in the larder."

Langton wondered why he kept a cook on his staff when he never ate anymore. Perhaps because Sarah had taken her on. Perhaps because to let Cook go would be to admit to change. "Thank you, Elsie, I'm not hungry. That will be all for tonight."

She turned away, blushing deeper. "Oh, I'll stay up for a while yet, sir, in case there's anything you and the sergeant need."

Langton found McBride standing by the fire in the front room. "I asked if I could wait, sir. Wasn't Elsie's idea."

Langton glanced at the sideboard in the corner, remembering the ranked bottles, then waved McBride to a chair. "You have news?"

"A few things, sir. Remember Olsen, the stoker on board the *Asención*, the one who said he saw a small boat in the dock just before the body washed up?"

"What did he have to say?"

"Not as much as we'd hoped, sir. He's dead."

"The drink?"

McBride shook his head. "Someone slid a knife in his back while he was asleep, sir."

Langton stared into the fire. He didn't like coincidences; he didn't trust them. "Did anyone have a grudge against him? Any of the other sailors?"

"If they do they're not saying, sir. Nice clean wound it was, too: straight through the back of the ribs and into the heart."

"The weapon?"

"Got it down at the station, sir. A narrow blade, a piece of Sheffield steel long as my forearm."

Langton tried to remember what the stoker had told McBride. If a small boat had dumped the faceless corpse into the dock, it could have come from a thousand places along the river, if not from one of the hundreds of moored ships. Langton could spend weeks searching even if the stoker had given a good description. All they had now was fog.

"Did any strangers board the *Asención?*"

McBride scratched his head. "Funny you should say that, sir. The captain put a man at the top of the gangplank, just like in every port. Third mate, sober and trusted. Seems he heard someone calling for help, splashing around, and thought it was a sailor worse for drink. So he rushes off to starboard with a life preserver in his hand."

"And found nothing."

"That's right, sir."

That would give someone time to board the ship and search for Olsen, who probably slept close to the boilers and the coal hoppers, as stokers did on most vessels. But was Langton being too fanciful? Could there really be a connection between the faceless corpse and the death of the stoker? If such a connection did exist, Olsen's killers must have learned of his sighting and his identity within hours. And then acted.

"There was something else, sir," McBride said, fishing in his jacket pocket and producing a crumpled envelope. "I found this waiting for you when I got back to the station."

Copperplate handwriting, blue ink on cream paper. In the top-right corner, embossed gilt script: *Professor H. Caldwell Chivers.* "We've been summoned, Sergeant."

"Sir?"

Langton folded the note into his pocket. "It seems that the Professor wishes to see us tonight."

SEATED WITH MCBRIDE in the rear of a jostling hansom cab, Langton thought of the few people who had known of Stoker Olsen's information. He could see the group standing around the faceless corpse at Albert Dock, could picture their faces: the docker, Connolly; Perkins, the assistant piermaster; Olsen, clutching the lamppost to keep himself upright. And McBride, of course.

With his elbow, Langton wiped a clear patch in the cab window's condensation. Lights glimmered like swollen eyes in the fog that had thickened and now clogged every street, pressed down on the city like a soporific pad over a patient's mouth. Langton envied the sleeping inhabitants. He envied the sweet ignorance of their slumber.

After the driver halted the cab at the corner of Hope Street and Hope Place, Langton paid him and stood on the snow-crusted pavement looking up at the Infirmary. A high, wide building in red brick and local sandstone, with a single electric globe burning above the side portico. A dimmer light glowed yellow in an adjacent window, no doubt the night porter's quarters.

Despite himself, Langton remembered the last time he had visited this place. Running through the stifling streets, unable to hail a cab, then stumbling up the steps to the emergency ward. All in vain.

"Sir? Is everything all right?"

Langton uncurled his fists in his pockets and made for the steps. "Come on, Sergeant."

Inside the echoing marble lobby, the old porter yawned as he slid aside the glass panel. "Emergency?"

"No, we're here—"

"We only see emergencies after ten at night, gents. Proper hours is seven till ten."

Langton retrieved his warrant card and said, "Professor Caldwell Chivers said he'd wait for us."

"Oh. Right, sir." The porter pulled on half-moon spectacles and checked his ledger. "The Professor is still signed in. You might find him in Theater, sir. Take those stairs on your left, third floor. Or he might be in Casualty."

Langton and McBride followed the directions. Their boots echoed from the white-tiled walls. They passed the open doors of long, cold

wards lit by dim electric lights, where patients became indistinct
mounds beneath grey blankets. Young nurses in white looked up from
their desks as if berating the policemen for disturbing the sick with
their steps. The reek of disinfectant flooded every corridor.

On the third floor, two sets of wooden doors with frosted glass
portholes opened into the operating theaters. Inside, Langton saw a
short corridor leading to a ward with a handful of white-shrouded
beds, each with a nurse attending. On the left, an office of dark
wooden file cabinets, bureaus, bottles behind locked glass. An empty
birdcage hung from a hook in the corner.

Langton saw the woman's hands first, in the light thrown by a lamp
of green glass: small and delicate, they moved through the lozenge
of bright light on the desk, turning pages, making small entries in
the massive ledger. Then Langton took in the dark blue dress, the
apron and cap of starched white cotton. When she looked up from her
seat, half hidden in shadow, the woman's eyes shone like stars. "Can I
help you?"

Langton stepped into the office and introduced himself and Mc-
Bride. "Professor Caldwell Chivers asked to see us."

"He did?" The woman set the pen down, rose from her seat, and
brushed an errant wisp of escaping black hair back behind her ear.
"He's just finished an operation and I hate to disturb him. He's had
perhaps four or five hours' rest in the past twenty-four."

Langton wondered if the woman had managed any more sleep
than that herself; fatigue obviously pulled at her body. "I think it's
important. Miss . . ."

"Wright. Sister Wright." She shook Langton's hand and nodded to
McBride. "I take it this is important?"

"It's part of a murder investigation."

"Ah, the faceless man that was brought in . . ."

"Exactly."

"Then please follow me, gentlemen."

She led them back the way they had come, along deserted corridors and through an unmarked door. The room beyond could have come straight from a gentlemen's club: leather armchairs, wooden paneling, newspapers and periodicals strewn over cluttered tables. The smell of cigar smoke.

An elderly man lay slumped in one of the vast armchairs with his long legs stretched out toward the fire. His posture, his crumpled white shirt and unbuttoned waistcoat, all implied drowsiness, if not sleep, but the man looked up as Sister Wright approached.

"Professor, Inspector Langton here said you'd arranged to see him."

"Of course, my dear. Thank you." Professor Caldwell Chivers stood up, smoothed his crumpled clothes, and ran a hand through sparse white hair. "Forgive my appearance, Inspector. We've had quite a day, haven't we, Sister?"

Sister Wright smiled but said nothing.

"Thank you for seeing us," Langton said. "I gather you've discovered something?"

Caldwell Chivers buttoned his waistcoat and reached for his jacket. "Perhaps we should take a look at our mutual friend together."

Sister Wright followed them after brushing dust from the Professor's shoulders. "You know you should rest, Professor."

"I'll have plenty of time for rest when I retire," Caldwell Chivers said, smiling.

"Then at least let me order you something from the kitchens."

"My dear, I promise that I will leave for home as soon as our business with the good inspector here is over."

Langton glanced at the sister as she looked to heaven and shook her head. She and the Professor had obviously worked together for quite some time: Their bond was apparent, almost like that of an affectionate, exasperated married couple. Inside Langton, a twinge of regret, almost of jealousy.

A brief walk brought them to a cold room near the Infirmary's theaters. The Professor switched on banks of electric lights that flooded the chamber. The faceless man lay on a long zinc table with upturned edges and drains leading to a floor sluice.

The Professor selected a slender knife from the surgical steel instruments arrayed in wall cabinets and approached the body. "Your Doctor Fry was quite accurate in his prognosis: We have here a middle-aged man with a failing liver, perhaps not very far from terminal cirrhosis. Caucasian, but he's obviously spent a great deal of time under the sun. A Boer, from the tattoos."

"The Orange Free State Irregulars of eighty-six," Sister Wright said.

Langton stared at her; she stared back, unflinching, but didn't volunteer an explanation of how she knew.

The Professor continued, "Cause of death was poisoning, a compound of hyosine and an opiate derivative. Slow acting. Paralysis would have set in first, followed by gradual loss of consciousness and then asphyxiation."

"So he would have been conscious but unable to move?" Langton asked.

"In my opinion, yes. For a short time."

A truly horrible image reared up in Langton's mind. "Do you think . . . Was he awake when they did this to him?"

The Professor looked down at the excised face. "It is possible. I see little motive for it, other than madness, but it is quite possible."

Langton shook his head. What kind of men were they dealing with here?

"These are the most intriguing aspects." The Professor pointed the long knife at the dark patches on the dead man's neck. "They appear to be burns. Low-voltage electrical burns unless I'm much mistaken."

"Why torture him further?"

The Professor hesitated, then said, "I don't think it was torture. I can't be sure, but . . . Inspector, have you ever heard of the Jar Boys?"

* * *

LANGTON STILL COULDN'T believe the Professor's words. Even now, sitting in the dining room of the Professor's Upper Parliament Street mansion, he refused to accept the coincidence. For that must be the case; hearing two references to the apocryphal soul snatchers must be strange accident and no more. There could not be a connection.

He glanced at the ornate clock on the mantel: two fifty in the morning. Langton had sent McBride home; Sister Wright had stayed at the Infirmary. So now the world shrank to the luxurious, eclectic dining room of the Professor. Egyptian effigies stared back from the shadows, their gilt decoration reflecting the flames.

Although he longed to ask questions, Langton waited until the Professor had finished his sandwich and poured out another glass of claret for both of them. The Professor leaned back in his chair and pushed the plate away. "Fine piece of beef. Hungrier than I realized. You get so intrigued by the day's cases that everything else is forgotten; no doubt the same happens in your line of work."

"That's true," Langton said, fighting his impatience.

"Are you a superstitious man, Inspector?"

Pushing away the memory of Mrs. Grizedale, Langton said, "Not as a rule."

"No, nor me." The Professor sipped his claret and leaned his head against the chair back. "I've lived a long life and I'm more open-minded than perhaps I once was. I've lost a great deal of my natural cynicism."

Langton waited. The clock ticked.

The Professor continued, "I first heard of the Jar Boys thirty-odd years ago. You might recall the work of Tesla, Marconi, and Hertz in the field of radio communications."

"We traveled on ships that use their equipment."

"Quite. At the time, little was known about electromagnetic emissions. Edison, the American, made extravagant claims, and Faraday showed some promising experiments, but many people mistook their work for magic or misdirection. Some still do."

Langton remembered attending Crystal Palace, where he and Sarah had marveled at the latest inventions and feats of engineering, not least of which had been the palace itself. Some of the watching crowd had jeered the Marconi Company demonstrations, calling them street magicians and worse.

"You know how their apparatus works?" the Professor asked.

"To a degree; one piece of equipment emits some kind of message while the other accepts it."

The Professor nodded. "In essence, yes. Speech, or teletype data, is reduced to electrical pulses and transmitted; the receiving station uses an 'aerial' to capture the transmitted waves and render them back into speech or information. This is the basic operation of radio."

Langton wondered how the Professor knew so much about the subject. But the Professor had only just begun; he didn't seem tired in the least. In fact, his eyes burned with a keen intensity.

"I could go into the minutiae of the matter," he said, "and tell you about the waveforms, frequencies, amplitude, and so forth, but it isn't necessary. In this instance, all you need to know is that certain people believe they can apply it to the animus, the very essence of humanity. To the soul itself."

Langton leaned forward. "How? How do they do it?"

"They locate a container of glass or clay, some material that will not conduct electricity, near the subject. Then an aerial is inserted through the jar's lid and carries a negative electrical charge. The subject is connected to a positive charge."

Langton remembered the faceless man. "The burns on his neck."

"Precisely."

"I don't see—"

"Watch." The Professor reached across the table and pulled the electric lamp within reach. He switched it off so that only the light of the fire remained; it tinted the right side of his face red. "Imagine this lamp is the dying subject. Close to the end. The soul is the light contained within, contained only by a fading shell that will soon wither."

Langton stared, hypnotized by the words, as somewhere deep inside of him began a scream; Sarah had gone through this. Sarah had withered away as he'd watched.

"Now the end comes," the Professor said. "The soul is free."

The light blinded Langton and flooded the room.

"See how it travels to every corner. The experimenters needed to isolate it." The Professor manipulated the shade until only a narrow beam of light left the lamp. The beam focused on a decanter and made the claret within glow deep red. "The subject's waveform carries the positive charge and gravitates toward the negative aerial of the waiting jar. In this way, the experimenters found, or so they said, that they could capture the final essence of a dying subject. Capture it and keep it alive."

Langton doubled over, fighting for breath. The Professor snapped on the overhead lights and knelt before him. "What is it, man?"

"My wife . . . Sarah . . ." Langton said, the words shuddering as they left him.

"Lord, forgive me." The Professor bowed his head. "Forgive me for these petty theatricals. I had no idea."

Langton grabbed his claret and swallowed it in one gulp. The wine burned his throat but helped him recover his breath. "You were not to know, Professor."

"Even so." The Professor got to his feet and swayed slightly. "Perhaps Sister was right: I need sleep."

"Before you do, please tell me something."

"Of course."

"Do they exist? The Jar Boys. Or are they mere fancy?"

The Professor sat down and poured more wine. "As a surgeon and a scientist, I should tell you that they are a fiction, and a poor one at that. I would be lying if I did; I have seen the apparatus in action. For a short time, many years ago, I assisted Professor Klaustus in Frankfurt. He experimented with near-death patients for some years."

"And you saw this work?"

"I saw *something*," the Professor said. "A charged field did leave the subject's body; Klaustus captured it in a heavy jar similar to a Leiden container. And there did seem to be some kind of Brownian motion within that jar. But his laboratory and its contents were consumed in the great winter fire of eighty-four, although the doctor himself possibly survived."

"But . . . a jar?"

The Professor shrugged. "It's not a new icon, Inspector. Consider the Holy Grail, most probably no more than a simple clay chalice. Or the Egyptian mummification process, where the organs of the deceased are transferred to canopic jars. Other civilizations have used similar containers for similar reasons."

To Langton, the story could have come straight from the pages of the penny periodicals, and the more alarmist ones at that. But to have it endorsed by a renowned professor . . .

"You actually believe this?"

"Consider the times in which we live, Inspector. We have achieved more in the past fifty years than we have in the last five hundred, or a thousand. We have come so far since Thomas Willis and the 'Oxford Circle' of philosopher-physicians back in the seventeenth century first posited the human brain as the engine of reason, passion, and insanity.

"We have pushed back the boundaries in every subject: science, engineering, medicine, manufacturing, art. Why not this? And why should there be any boundaries at all? What if all the disciplines are connected? There may be no separation between medicine and superstition, or between science and religion."

The Professor's zeal disturbed Langton. And he thought he detected a hint of hubris, maybe even of arrogance. "What good would come from capturing someone's soul?"

"Apart from proving that such a thing existed? A good question." The Professor sank down in his chair and suddenly looked old and tired. "Klaustus found a strange side effect in his experiment: He sealed the jars with copper and wax, and when he touched the metal collar, he experienced a brief image from the subject's life. For those few seconds, he relived some of the poor man's memories."

Langton didn't want to make the connection, but the Professor did it for him: "Some people, Inspector, like to vicariously replay those captured lives. They enjoy the sensation of being someone else, of plundering other minds. Some consider it a great . . . delicacy."

Langton looked around at the luxurious room and the staring Egyptian effigies. It seemed unreal, as did the city that surely existed beyond those walls. "This happens here? In Liverpool?"

Professor Caldwell Chivers nodded. "Throughout Britain, Inspector. With the Span completed, no doubt America also, soon enough."

Langton remembered Mrs. Grizedale's words, her belief that Sarah had been captured. Without realizing it, he gripped the Professor's arm. "Who? Who deals in these jars? Who?"

"Please, Inspector." The Professor pulled back. "It might be no more than hearsay. I have no proof—"

"Who?"

The old professor hesitated. "There's Springheel Bob's gang, and the Caribs, but I know of one name that my patients and their families repeat over and over again in fear, a pseudonym for Lord knows who."

"What is the name, Professor? Please."

The Professor looked into Langton's eyes and said, "Doktor Glass."

Four

L ANGTON WOKE IN his own bed and enjoyed a moment of absolute, stupefied forgetfulness. Then, when his searching hand found only crumpled bedclothes, reality returned with its burden of fresh memories. He lay there for a moment, staring at the dull grey light through heavy curtains, then threw back the tangled covers and found his robe. The bedside clock said seven.

After the shocks and excitement of the previous day, he had been afraid to go to sleep. He'd expected the same recurring nightmare, only with the added horror that it might be more than a dream. Exhaustion had silenced his demons; he could remember no nightmares this morning.

One decision remained from his interview with the Professor: to explore Sarah's final moments. Although Langton had arrived too late at the Infirmary, Redfers, their family doctor, had accompanied Sarah from home to the emergency room. Elsie had called Redfers out that night, while a case had preoccupied Langton. Now he couldn't even remember the details of the case, or perhaps he didn't want to think of that night.

He knew he must. He crossed to his bureau and jotted a note to Doctor Redfers. Not a request, but a statement: Langton would call on him that evening.

Downstairs, he found a new fire and the table laid for breakfast. Elsie hurried in with coffee and a shy smile. "Good morning, sir. Fog's cleared. We might even see some sun later."

Still half asleep, Langton let Elsie bustle about him like a mother hen. Only after his second cup of strong coffee did he say, "Elsie, I'd like to ask a question."

She set down the tray of toast and waited, her hands held loosely in front of her apron. "Sir?"

"Have you ever heard of the Jar Boys?"

The good humor left Elsie's face. "I have, sir."

"Go on, please."

Her hands tightened. "When my auntie's youngest was on her way out, sir, close to the end, a man came calling. Well dressed, he was, spoke very far back, but Auntie ran him from her house, threatened to get the priest and the coppers, begging your pardon.

"Ten years old, I was, sir, but I knew he was a wrong'un; I thought he was a Resurrectionist after the body. After he'd gone, Auntie told me about the Jar Boys, how they wait like leeches and take away your soul. I heard it from other people, too. Always planned to steer clear of them, sir, if I could help it."

Langton looked down at the table. "Thank you for telling me, Elsie."

The maid went to speak, then curtsied and left the room.

Alone for the moment, Langton wondered what he'd hoped to hear from Elsie. Perhaps some honest common sense from a girl with her feet firmly on the ground. Perhaps he'd wanted her to laugh and tell him the Jar Boys were a fanciful fairy story used to frighten children in their nurseries. She'd only confirmed the words of Mrs. Grizedale and the Professor.

Back upstairs, as he bathed and dressed, Langton still didn't want to accept the Jar Boys as truth. He told himself that he needed more information. He had a good idea where he might find it.

The front doorbell rang as Langton finished dressing. He called downstairs, "Is it McBride?"

"It is, sir," Elsie said.

As Langton came down, he saw Elsie and McBride take a step away from each other in the hall. McBride, blushing, turning his derby hat in his hands, said, "I've a hansom waiting, sir."

Turning away to grab his coat from the rack, Langton hid a smile. "I'm sure I'll be late, Elsie."

Then, almost at the door, he took an envelope from his pocket. "Elsie, will you make sure Doctor Redfers receives this?"

"I'll send a boy around with it this morning, sir."

Outside, Langton could see down the steep road to the city and a sliver of grey river. Roofs still bore slabs of snow, but the fog had receded. The Transatlantic Span reared up, immense and faintly unreal, its scale dwarfing even the steel-hulled liners and freighters at the docks.

The police driver touched his cap with the whip. "The station, sir?"

"The Pier Head first."

As they climbed into the hansom, Langton asked McBride, "Is Forbes Paterson back on duty yet?"

"I saw the inspector in the canteen yesterday, sir."

Forbes Paterson supervised the officers who investigated the various swindles in Liverpool: the false investment companies, ersatz solicitors bringing news of amazing inheritances, and art dealers selling stolen or fake works, particularly following the latest fad for all things Egyptian. His duties also included the growing problem of manipulative clairvoyants, mystics, soothsayers, tarot readers, and mediums. If any officer on the force knew about the Jar Boys, it would be Forbes Paterson.

This made Langton think of Mrs. Grizedale. "Constable, a detour; take us to Hamlet Street in Everton."

Mrs. Grizedale's house seemed asleep. Most of the curtains remained closed, while no new footsteps showed on the front garden's snow, but dark smoke drifted from the chimney. Langton looked back from the front door and saw McBride watching him from the hansom window.

After two rings on the bell, a face appeared behind the glass; the door opened just enough to show Meera's scowling face. "Missy Grizedale not seeing anyone."

"How is she?"

"Resting. Sir."

Langton hesitated. "I really do need to see her, Meera. Just for a few moments."

Meera's eyes blazed. "You hurt her bad."

Then, at some sound from within the house, Meera turned away and listened. She said something Langton couldn't hear, then glared at him and opened the door as if allowing in a muddied dog. "Missy see you."

Langton followed the maid upstairs and found Mrs. Grizedale reclining on a red chaise longue. A blanket reached up to her bosom and a shawl covered her shoulders. She looked pale, with only two spots of red high in her cheeks. "Inspector."

"I'm sorry to waken you."

"I wasn't asleep. Just resting." Mrs. Grizedale smiled at Meera and said, "It's all right, my dear. I'll be fine."

The maid glared once more at Langton as she left the room.

"I hope you've recovered," Langton said.

"I will. It's not the first time that . . ." She forced a smile, then waved to a chair. "Won't you sit?"

"Thank you, no. I have a cab downstairs. I just wanted to check that you had improved."

Mrs. Grizedale nodded. "And?"

"Pardon me?"

"Much as I appreciate your concern, Inspector, I'm sure you have something else you wish to ask me."

He hesitated, then said, "I still have difficulty believing in these . . . these Jar Boys."

"They exist," she said.

"But—"

She leaned forward, dislodging the shawl. "I am sorry to tell you this, but your wife is beyond our help."

Langton paced back and forth. "Is there no way to find her? To release her?"

"She is one of hundreds, perhaps thousands, of captured souls secreted by collectors."

He froze. "Collectors?"

"That is what they call themselves. And no one man knows the contents of all the jars, all the vessels."

"What about Doktor Glass?"

Mrs. Grizedale sank back. "You know of him?"

"Only that he is feared."

"And with good reason," she said. "Avoid him. Even fellow collectors will not talk of him."

"Why?" Langton knelt beside her. "What is so special about this Doktor Glass?"

Instead of answering, Mrs. Grizedale began to hyperventilate. She couldn't catch her breath. Meera burst into the room and pushed Langton aside. "Go."

"But—"

Meera, already opening a small phial and holding it to the medium's mouth, spat out the words, "Go, before you kill her."

Langton ran downstairs and pulled the door shut behind him. He climbed into the hansom and slumped beside McBride. As they rattled along Hamlet Street, McBride asked, "Is this part of our investigation, sir?"

Langton bit back the first words that came to him, and said instead, "Perhaps."

He realized then that McBride was right: Sarah's possible fate had distracted him from the murder case and made him neglect his duty. How could he do otherwise? His own wife. He had to know.

Perhaps there was a connection, after all: the Jar Boys. Langton could justify that to himself.

As the hansom neared the Pier Head, the driver had to weave through dense traffic. Langton saw great carts and steam wagons carrying cargoes to and from the docks: lumber from the Americas, marble from Italy, rolls of woven fabrics fresh from Manchester's mills and destined for the colonies.

A constant din filled the air, composed of iron wheels on cobbles, engines' roars, pistons pounding in their greased tracks. Over all this, the yells and curses of drivers. Like a wide, turbulent tributary, the traffic flowed toward the Mersey. And on either bank, pedestrians waited to cross; some took their chances and dived through the jostling wagons to reach the other side. Others, mainly ragged children, darted between and under the wheels, snatching what meager detritus fell from the jolted cargoes.

Langton held his breath when he saw a grimy, barefoot child of no more than six years scurry beneath the belly of an immense wagon. A blast of steam, a volley of curses, and then the child sprinted for the other side, clutching a fallen bundle. Iron-shod wheels taller than Langton missed the child by inches. Looking back from the hansom, Langton saw the child offer the scavenged bundle to a squat woman, who promptly slapped the child around the ear.

Soon the hansom rattled through vast gates of sandstone and wrought iron. Langton told the driver, "Wait here for us."

Standing with McBride, Langton looked around at the frenetic activity. The colossal entrance ramp of the Span stood half a mile away on the site of the Canning Graving Docks, the stepped dry docks long ago filled in by the TSC. The ramp swept up from the Pier Head in a great curve of iron and steel and concrete, a graceful arc joining the land to the first support tower rising from the Mersey.

A shantytown had grown beneath the ramp, and smoke from the

encampment filtered through the bridge's delicate struts and drifted toward the glass-and-wrought-iron edifice of the Span Company. Langton wondered how the Company's directors liked having the poor, complaining masses so close to their feat of engineering.

Langton checked the time on the hexagonal tower that stood a few yards away with a clock on each face. Nine forty. They still had twenty minutes before his appointment. He asked a passing foreman for directions and led McBride across Albert Dock. Another man pointed to a low brick house near the stone edge of the dock facing the Mersey. The piermaster's house, complete with small garden, seemed incongruous, more suited to a small town or village than a busy working dock. Not four yards away, steel hulls reared up like sheer, rusting cliffs.

Langton leaned inside the open top half of the door. "Mr. Perkins, please."

A clerk scuttled into a side office. Perkins appeared at the door, pulling on his suit jacket. "Inspector? You've caught the robbers?"

"Not quite, Mr. Perkins. I wanted to ask you something."

Perkins opened the bottom half of the door. "Only too pleased to help, Inspector."

Langton stepped inside. "You were one of those around the body yesterday. Can you remember the others?"

"Let me see . . . Connolly, that loudmouthed agitator; you and your sergeant, naturally; the men with the stretcher."

"And?"

"Oh, that sailor, the one who could hardly stand."

"You remember his name?"

"Olsen, I believe."

"And his ship?"

"I'm not—"

"His ship, Mr. Perkins."

Perkins looked away. "The *Asención.*"

Langton nodded. "Perhaps you've heard of another death in the docks? A stabbing?"

Perkins mumbled into his chest.

"Pardon me, Mr. Perkins?"

"I had heard something, Inspector."

Langton leaned a little closer to the assistant piermaster. "Why did you tell everyone, Perkins?"

Perkins puffed out his chest and seemed about to argue, then looked at Langton and sank in on himself. "I didn't mean anything, Inspector, I swear I didn't. We just got to talking, down the pub—I only go in for a half of bitter, maybe two, a glass of rum if the weather's nippy. People had heard something had happened, and I let slip I'd been there, so—"

"Can you remember who was there?"

"It was full, Inspector. I couldn't name everybody."

Langton could imagine Perkins standing in the pub with a glass in his hand, telling everybody who would listen about the discovery of the faceless body. So keen to impress the drinking men with his inside knowledge.

"Let me offer you some advice, Mr. Perkins: Keep your own counsel. Share no more information with your friends down the public house, or anywhere else for that matter. I have no wish to investigate your own demise."

Leaving behind Perkins's apologies and protestations, Langton and McBride made for the offices of the Transatlantic Span Company. McBride asked, "How did you know it was him, sir?"

"I didn't," Langton said. "At least, I wasn't sure. Only two men outside the force knew about Olsen: Connolly and Perkins. Only Perkins knew which ship the stoker sailed on. And I wondered whether Perkins had that type of personality which might crave attention."

Avoiding a swinging net of grain sacks, McBride said, "So there was someone in that pub who wanted to keep Olsen quiet, or who told someone else who wanted to silence any witnesses."

"Exactly." Langton didn't continue his logic: that whoever had wanted to silence Olsen, presumably the same man who had killed the

Boer, couldn't have known Perkins would go to that particular pub and repeat the valuable information; either it had been pure chance or the murderer had some kind of network of informants. That implied organization. It implied a dangerous sophistication.

Langton and McBride waited in the marble lobby of the Span Company until the receptionist allowed them into a gilt elevator. The uniformed attendant took them to the top floor, where a man in a tailcoat bowed and ushered them into a cavernous office. "Lord Salisbury, sir? Inspector Langton and, ah, associate."

"Gentlemen." The man behind the enormous desk stood up but didn't offer to shake hands. He nodded to the visitors' chairs opposite and said, "How may I be of service?"

As he sat, Langton saw that the offered chairs lay slightly below the level of the desk, giving Lord Salisbury the advantage of looking down on his visitors. "There must be some mistake, your lordship. Our appointment was with your director of labor."

Salisbury waved the point away. "This unfortunate accident affects the entire Company, Inspector, and its many shareholders. Anything that reduces public confidence in our endeavor must be dealt with quickly and tactfully. As I explained to your chief constable this morning, I hope my personal involvement will speed the process."

That gave Langton much to think about. Why would the chairman of the Span Company want to squash this investigation? Not only for the shareholders. "Forgive me, your lordship, but it was no simple accident. It was murder. The injuries to the body confirm this."

Salisbury frowned. "A modern screw propeller could have caused the lacerations. I myself have seen the terrible damage such blades can inflict."

Langton knew he was on delicate ground. "I'm sure you are correct, your lordship, but in this instance the man's face was removed carefully and precisely. And certain other . . . signs indicate a deliberate and painful death."

Salisbury stared at Langton. "You gainsay me, sir?"

Langton stared back. "I'm afraid I have no choice."

From McBride, a quick intake of breath. Langton looked into Salisbury's eyes without blinking. After what seemed like an eternity, Lord Salisbury nodded and sat back with his hands forming a steeple on his waistcoat. "What makes you think the man worked for us, Inspector?"

"His clothes, your lordship, and he carried a key of a strange design, possibly a watchman's or security guard's time key, with the outline of a bridge engraved upon it."

Lord Salisbury nodded and reached for one of the red ledgers stacked on his desk. "As usual, we're missing at least a dozen workers, men who think it right and fair to laze in their beds rather than complete an honest day's work."

He riffled pages and plucked out a handwritten sheet. "Here we are: navigators, joiners, fitters, and cablemen. And one security guard and night watchman: Abel Kepler."

"No doubt he would carry a time key like the one we discovered," Langton said.

"I presume so."

That had to be the one. "You have Kepler's address, your lordship?"

Salisbury pushed the note toward McBride and dismissed him, saying, "You'll find the director of labor on the third floor. Tell him I sent you."

After McBride had left the office, Salisbury beckoned Langton to the windows. "Look at her, Inspector: the engineering marvel of the century. The Company owns all these docks, all these piers, warehouses, and wharves, but she is the jewel."

Salisbury's plush quarters offered a superb view of the Span. Sunlight glinted on iron and steel, on the sweeping catenary support pipes strung between the vast towers, and on the delicate vertical cables holding the road and rail deck; the polished electric rails glimmered like silver threads.

Langton had never been this close to the structure. The angular bas-relief figures on the first tower's Egyptian-themed frieze dwarfed him.

From this angle, the first tower, with its crown lost in cloud, looked like a mythic pillar supporting heaven. "It's very impressive, your lordship."

"More than impressive, Inspector: stupendous." Salisbury rested one hand against the glass as if reaching out to touch his creation. "For thirty years have I dreamed of this. Thirty years. Engineer after engineer failed until the Brunels stepped forward. Whole countries were quarried to supply the foundations and facings of those towers. Those beams and cables carry steel from every foundry in the empire. The Span is more than a mere bridge, Langton; it is an emblem. A symbol. Nothing is beyond us. Nature is at our command."

Then, before Langton could ask where the various dispossessed families camped below fitted into the design, Salisbury turned to him and said, "Yet all this could fail. Those foundations rest on a mountain of pound notes and promissory papers, the deposits of hundreds of thousands of investors. Yet if one—just one—of those investors loses his nerve, the whole beautiful edifice could collapse. All because of a simple whiff of scandal. I must not let that happen, Inspector."

Salisbury stepped closer. His eyes burned. "In four days' time Her Majesty the Queen will open the Span. Nothing must prevent that. Nothing."

As HE WAITED for McBride in the lobby, Langton wondered why Lord Salisbury had taken the time and effort to warn him, indeed to threaten him. Langton would have to choose his path with care; Salisbury could prove a powerful enemy.

"They gave me the address, sir," McBride said as he descended the marble staircase and followed Langton outside. He drew a typewritten sheet from his jacket and said, "Abel Samuel John Kepler. Forty-seven years old, unmarried. Joined the Span Company almost six months ago. Currently lodging in Gloucester Road in Bootle."

The text confirmed McBride's words but also added to them. "Who's this? Peter Durham?"

"Another Span fella, sir, a daytime security guard who bunks at the same lodgings as Kepler. Seems he joined the same day as our man, too."

More coincidence. "Durham wasn't on Lord Salisbury's absentee list, so I suppose he must have arrived for work today . . ."

McBride grinned. "Happens he did, sir. He's over on pier three in the King's Dock, the clerk said. Seems that the Span owns a fair chunk of the Mersey waterfront."

As Langton followed the signs toward the King's Dock adjacent to Albert Dock, he wondered how the ship owners and liner companies regarded Lord Salisbury and the Transatlantic Span. After all, the bridge would rob them of millions of pounds of cargo and passenger revenues; it might put many of them out of business altogether. Could they be behind Kepler?

Langton considered that a remote possibility. He and McBride avoided the trundling carts laden with cargoes of sacks, timber, and bundles, and dodged between swaying towers of crates. All the while, the background bedlam of the docks assaulted them: yells, curses, the pounding of steam winches, the shrill cries of ships' whistles and horns. Even the odd flurry of song.

They crossed a narrow bridge set above stout wooden sluice gates between the docks and the river, then pushed through a crowded wharf to pier three. Langton questioned a wizened man with a clipboard, who pointed to the roadway linking one pier to the next. "That's Durham, the fella checking the bales on the way out."

Langton saw a tall, well-built man with broad shoulders, tanned skin, and an unkempt moustache. But the man saw Langton, too. Before the inspector could cross the busy pier, the security guard turned and dropped the ledger. His hand dipped into his pocket and emerged with a black pistol. The shot split the air and drove every man to the floor.

Instinct made Langton dive behind a stack of crates. He waited for another but heard instead the clatter of boots on cobbles. He saw Durham running toward the Albert Dock, back the way Langton had come.

Sprinting after Durham, Langton yelled to McBride, "Are you armed?"

McBride shook his head. Langton cursed and focused on the fleeing man; he could see his own ex-army Webley revolver still in his bedside drawer at home.

Almost at the bridge above the dock gates, Durham turned, sighted, and fired. Langton kept running, keeping his head as low as he could while simultaneously cursing his stupidity. Another shot boomed. He didn't stop.

Bells rang out in warning as a ship approached the dock gates from the River Mersey. White water roared through the open sluices. As the gates began to part, the narrow bridge crossing their apex split in the middle. The gap widened: a foot; a yard; almost two yards.

Durham raced along the left-hand gate and jumped over the gap, windmilling his arms to gain momentum. He slipped on the far gate's planks but grabbed the rail and stumbled to the opposite bank.

Langton saw the gap increase. He drove his feet into the slick cobbles and sprinted for the receding right-hand gate. A final leap, his arms outstretched, every muscle yearning. Below him, a cauldron of boiling white water.

Time slowed. He saw the gate pulling away; he would never reach it. Then the worn edge of the right-hand dock gate slammed into his stomach and drove the breath from his body. His fingers clawed the wet wood. Splinters dug into his hands until he found purchase. Inch by inch, he pulled himself up onto the planks of the right-hand gate and scrambled to his knees.

He dragged air into his lungs and looked back as the incoming ship's hull of tar-black wood and rusty steel slid past less than a foot away. He had time to see the foreign sailors' openmouthed surprise. Then he ran on. He thought he saw Durham a hundred yards or more ahead before the crowd closed in. He pushed his way through the dockers and climbed up onto the hexagonal clock tower.

Whichever direction he turned, he saw no trace of Durham. He slumped down with his back to the bricks and his arms wrapped around his aching stomach. He looked up when he heard his name called. "Here."

McBride, panting and sweating, leaned on his own knees and finally said, "No sign of him?"

Langton shook his head.

"You were lucky, sir." McBride slumped beside him, ignoring the looks of the curious dockworkers. "Another second or two and that ship would have had you."

Langton didn't answer for a minute. He concentrated instead on slowing his racing heart and easing the pain in his stomach. Then, "You have his address?"

McBride patted his coat pocket.

"When we return, take the hansom and two men with you," Langton said, "and remember that he's more than willing to fire on us."

"Oh, I'll go prepared, sir." McBride got to his feet. "You really think he'd go back there?"

"Probably not, but see what you can find. I think there's more to these two men than mere coincidence. Pass Durham's description on to the desk sergeant; I want every constable looking for him."

"Leave it to me, sir," McBride said as he helped Langton up.

Climbing into the back of the police hansom parked by the main gates, Langton wondered why Durham had run off like that. What had scared him?

Almost despite himself, Langton allowed his gaze to slip back to the Span. Salisbury's warnings sounded again in his mind, but he couldn't help the direction of his thoughts: The Span lay at the bottom of this.

Five

W HEN THE HANSOM pulled up in the courtyard at Victoria
Street headquarters, Langton left McBride with the desk
sergeant and strode through the lobby, glancing at the
hard wooden benches fixed to the walls where the ragged public sat
huddled against the chill. He didn't recognize anyone. Before he
could climb the stairs to his office, McBride called him back.

The desk sergeant leaned over the brass rail of his high wooden
desk. "Begging your pardon, sir, but Doctor Fry asked for you."

Langton descended to the basement and found Doctor Fry in the
cluttered office. "You left a message?"

Fry looked up from the Imperial typewriter balanced on his desk's
uneven plateau of papers and files. "Langton, how did you fare with
Caldwell Chivers?"

Eager to get upstairs and see Forbes Paterson, Langton said, "The
Professor was very helpful, thank you. He identified the marks on the
victim's neck as electrical burns."

"For what reason?"

Langton hesitated, then said, "He mentioned the Jar Boys."

Fry nodded and began to clean his pince-nez with a handkerchief. "I thought as much."

"You knew?" Langton crossed to the desk. "Why didn't you tell me?"

"Would you have believed me?"

"Well . . ."

"Exactly. And I couldn't be sure. Caldwell Chivers has a great deal of experience in the subject. In fact, he's quite an authority."

Again, Langton wondered how and why the Professor knew so much about the Jar Boys. But he wanted to talk with Forbes Paterson. "Was that all you wanted?"

"Not quite." Fry rummaged in desk drawers until he pulled out two crumpled sheets of yellow paper. "I queried London about the dead man's fingerprints and received these replies. Look."

Langton went to tell Fry that they had already identified the man, but he read the first telegram: *Positive match found. Details to follow.* "So?"

Fry held out the second telegram. "This arrived an hour or so after the first."

"'No match found.'" Langton read out the contents and looked at Fry. "I don't understand."

"Nor do I. Especially when I compared the senders' details."

Langton scanned the first telegram and saw the sender's address: The Home Office, Queen Anne's Gate. But the second came from the Foreign and Commonwealth Office. "Why would the FCO show interest in a criminal investigation?"

Fry smiled. "I rather hoped you could tell me."

Langton thought for a moment, then asked, "May I keep these?"

"By all means. Oh, I'm just finishing my report on your second customer, the sailor."

"Stoker Olsen?"

"That's the chap," Fry said. "Neat job: a single puncture straight through the ribs to the heart. They knew what they were doing."

"And the weapon?"

Fry unrolled a muslin bundle on his desk to reveal a sliver of brown-tinted steel perhaps ten inches long. "Sheffield steel with an edge on both sides. It's used to remove tissue or lesions from around a bone."

He picked up the weapon by the engraved handle, using the muslin as a glove. "You see, the surgeon scrapes it along the length of the bone—the tibia, say, or the fibula—and cuts the tissue, thus."

At the final lunge, Langton winced. "So, a surgeon's property."

"At one time, certainly, but who's to say how it ended up in the hands of a murderer?"

After thanking Fry, Langton climbed the stairs to his office. He had much to add to the case file, and much to consider. It was not to be; the office boy, Harry, limped up to him in the corridor. "A lady to see you, sir. I asked her to wait in your office."

"Did she give a name?" Langton asked, already thinking of Mrs. Grizedale.

"Sister Wright, sir."

Langton found her sitting in his office. "I'm sorry to keep you waiting, Sister. I had no idea you might call on me."

"That's quite all right, Inspector." Sister Wright had stood up as Langton entered the room, but she returned to her seat and set her gloves and purse on her lap. She wore a long skirt and matching coat of grey wool, and a simple hat in a darker grey. Somehow, the outfit seemed reminiscent of her uniform, as though she were not quite off-duty. "I knew you would be busy, but I hope you can spare me a few minutes."

"Of course. Are you not working today?"

"My duties begin at seven this evening," she said. "Although I usually go in a little early."

How early? Langton thought. He could see no ring on her finger, and she reminded him of the nurses in the Transvaal field hospitals and convalescent units: women, some no more than girls, who focused on their work alone. Like nuns, they saw their duties as a calling more than a vocation. Without their dedicated attention, many men would not have returned from the war. Langton was no exception.

"How may I help you?" Langton sat behind his desk slowly, wincing at the pain in his abdomen.

"Is something wrong?"

"Nothing, just a slight accident while chasing a suspect," Langton said. "Go on, please."

Sister Wright hesitated, then began, "Firstly, I must ask you not to mention my visit to the Professor. I realize I have no right to put you in this position, but the Professor hates the thought of people speaking behind his back, even if they have his best interests at heart."

Intrigued, Langton said, "You have my word: Whatever passes between us shall remain here."

Sister Wright's face broke into a smile that made her seem ten years younger. "I knew I had not misjudged you, Inspector."

"So . . ."

"So. I think the Professor might have given you the wrong impression last night, or rather this morning—hours lose their rhythm in the Infirmary. He has led a long and varied life, a life dedicated to relieving pain and helping people. I have worked with many doctors, but never have I met such a selfless surgeon as Professor Caldwell Chivers."

Langton gave no response as he wondered why she felt it necessary to defend the Professor.

Sister Wright continued, "We fight every day to save lives and snatch people back from the very brink of death. Sometimes we do not succeed. I know that hurts the Professor; he's not like those men who can inure themselves to death. You've met such men, haven't you, Inspector? And not just in your work here."

Remembering the Transvaal, Langton nodded.

Sister Wright leaned forward in her chair. "The Professor cares. Perhaps, sometimes, he cares too much. He lets himself become dis-

tracted by certain . . . ideas. Ideas that in daylight might seem gro-
tesque or even dangerous."

"The Jar Boys?"

Sister Wright looked at the floor. "I'm afraid so."

"I've heard of their existence from others," Langton said. "It seems
that many believe in them."

She smiled at him. "Many believe in fairies and other sprites and
spirits. Why, even voodoo, that bizarre belief in the undead. I wonder
sometimes if those beliefs stem from a need deep within a person, if
perhaps they simply see what they wish to see."

Langton didn't doubt her. In the Transvaal trenches and deserts, he
had witnessed the transformation of levelheaded men into wrecks des-
perately grasping at anything that would relieve their daily suffering.
They talked of ghosts, spirits, angels, the afterlife, Egyptology, religions
and sects from around the world. They had that need.

Did the Professor really live under so much strain? Strain and stress
enough to drive him to the outer fringes of belief? Langton chose his
words with care. "The Professor is obviously respectable, hardworking,
sane."

"As sane as you or I," Sister Wright said. "But he seeks so hard to
help his patients that he sometimes loses his perspective."

"But you trust him."

Sister Wright stared at him. "With my life."

Again, Langton wondered why she had come here. He had the
sense of things unsaid, of facts or suspicions behind her words. Perhaps she didn't register their existence herself. "Do you believe in the
Jar Boys?"

She thought for a moment. "I understand why people believe in
them. I understand the reason for their existence."

That didn't really answer Langton's question, but he did not want
to press the subject. "Could you tell me some of the other areas that
interest the Professor?"

Sister Wright twisted her hands in her lap. "I'm not sure that I should."

Langton waited.

Sister Wright glanced through the window to Victoria Street and then nodded. "He has a great interest in Egyptology, in the Orient and its philosophies: Buddhism, particularly Zen; Hinduism from India; the works of Confucius and Sun Yat-sen. Acupuncture, the stimulation of nerve points throughout the body, and the Chinese belief in *qi*, or the force within us."

"That is quite a list."

"It is only the tip of his knowledge," she said. "He is a true polymath."

Langton could see her respect for the Professor in her eyes, and that made him pull back from the questions he longed to ask. Instead, carefully, he said, "Have his interests ever led him astray?"

"Astray?"

"Has he ever . . . Have his interests ever affected his patients?"

"Never." The word came hard and sharp. "His patients have never suffered."

Langton saw he would get no further than that at this stage. As Sister Wright gathered her gloves and purse to leave, Langton said, "Thank you for telling me all this. I appreciate your honesty."

"I wanted you to know."

"May I ask one final thing, Sister? It isn't about the Professor."

She tilted her head to one side and waited.

Langton said, "When we saw the man's body, you seemed to recognize the tattoos."

Sister Wright stood up and set her gloves and purse down on the chair. With efficient movements, and before Langton could stop her, she unbuttoned the jet buttons at the side of her dress. The grey wool fabric fell open.

Langton raised his hand as if to stop her. His pulse raced in his

throat. The sight of her skin silenced him. For, between the edge of
the white lace bodice that covered her breasts and the slender curve
of her throat lay a network of fine scars; the wan office light turned
them silver.

"I joined the nursing corps at sixteen," Sister Wright said as she
closed her dress. "We treated the injured Boers alongside our own
brave troops, showing no aversion or favoritism. That didn't stop the
Boers and their Irregulars that overran our field hospitals from . . .
from . . ."

She turned away and rebuttoned her dress.

"I'm sorry," Langton said. "I'm so sorry."

Sister Wright turned and gave a tight smile. "We survive, Inspector.
We go on with our lives, for we have no choice."

Sarah's image filled Langton's mind.

"Inspector? I must go." Sister Wright stood at the door and waited
for Langton to open it. She held out her hand. "I hope I haven't made
a mistake today."

"I promise that you haven't."

With one final smile, she left him. Langton saw Harry giving him a
strange look. He closed the frosted door and rested his back against it.

His estimation of the sister had increased. Whatever reason she
might have had for visiting him, whether conscious or unconscious,
was unimportant, in a sense. She had revealed to him a major part of
her life, given him a glimpse of the horrors that had shaped her. He
doubted she would do that for just anybody. Why for him?

At least she seemed to have survived the experience, not just physically but mentally. Some of the survivors who returned home had
found no solace from the war, no dwindling of their memories. Unable
to resume their interrupted lives, they drank, took opium, fell into
crime or through the fabric of society to the depths below.

Yes, Sister Wright was strong. Of that Langton had no doubt.

He topped up the stove with coal and left his office, which still bore
faint odors of Sister Wright's scent, the memory of white flowers. He

found Forbes Paterson's room empty; a detective in the main office told him that Paterson would return that afternoon. Langton left a message and decided to follow McBride out to Bootle.

A Victoria Street tram took him from the city center, along Scotland Road and Stanley Road. Langton sat on the top deck among the smells of wet cloth, leather, and arcing electricity from the flexing pantograph above him. He watched the streets unfurl through smudged windows. Even though the royal procession would pass nowhere near this area, many of the houses and shops bore bunting and streamers; empire flags hung from windows next to special commemorative duotones issued by the popular newssheets, so that Queen Victoria's severe gaze watched Langton from a hundred or more vantage points.

The poorer streets seemed the most fervent; as the tram waited outside Stanley Hospital, Langton looked down the flower-themed roads opposite—Holly Street, Daisy, Rose, Ivy—and saw garlands of red, white, and blue strung between the houses. As the tram pulled away with a lurch and a crackling hiss of sparks, he saw men on ladders affixing more streamers to the gas lampposts.

Then, lulled by the soporific motion of the tram, Langton half-closed his eyes and drifted away. Images formed in his mind: the faceless man, Professor Caldwell Chivers, the mad leap over the dock gates, Sister Wright unfastening the jet buttons. Sarah.

He awoke as the tram jolted to a stop. He looked around, blinking in confusion, and recognized Trinity Church on Merton Road. He clattered down the spiral steps of the tram and jumped onto the cobbles as the conductor rang the bell. Still drowsy, Langton walked up toward the church; if he remembered correctly, Gloucester and Worcester roads lay to the left.

Most of his fellow pedestrians were reasonably well dressed, their clothes clean and pressed if a little worn. Mainly working-class families occupied the simple two-up, two-down terrace houses, which represented a foothold on the ladder of respectability. Langton's own grandfather had lived in Worcester Road until his determination and hard work in engineering had lifted his family to Everton Brow and beyond.

Langton found Durham and Kepler's address on Gloucester Road and saw a police hansom waiting outside. A sinewy woman in a blue apron opened the front door and pointed Langton upstairs, where McBride and another constable rummaged through clothes laid out on a narrow bed; two beds' legs stood in small pots of kerosene, to stop cockroaches from climbing up them in the night. The smell of the viscous fuel mixed with the smells of damp plaster and tobacco.

"Any luck, Sergeant?"

"Some, sir." McBride led him to an oak chest of drawers in the corner. Laid out on the top were two General Post Office telegram pads, each with less than half of their blank forms remaining; stubs of train tickets for the Liverpool–Southport overhead electric railway, and for the Great Western line to London Euston; copies of the *Liverpool Echo* going back four days; assorted pens and pencils.

Langton picked up the blank telegram forms and crossed to the window. Enough light came through the dusty glass to reveal indentations on the pads' surfaces. "We should be able to decipher the last message, back at the station. But people sometimes make mistakes when they compose a telegram; they rip out a page and start afresh."

McBride grinned. "I've got Constable Naylor going through the landlady's rubbish in the backyard, sir. The corporation dustmen don't come until tomorrow, so we've the best part of a week's offerings to sort through."

Langton didn't envy the constable his task, but he'd had to perform similar duties, if not worse, at the start of his own career. He looked around the room and tried to picture the men living there. Two narrow beds of pine, with chamber pots beneath and worn quilts on top. A washstand with a white china jug and bowl, both covered in fine cracks like spiders' webs. Floorboards dark with wax and age, with a threadbare rug of red and yellow in the center. Behind the door, fixed to the yellowing wallpaper with a brass tack, a framed embroidery typical of those produced by young girls as they learned to sew: *Be Thankful Unto The Lord.*

The room did not encourage much thought of gratitude, but many lived in conditions far worse than these. Far worse.

"Has the landlady much to say of her lodgers?" Langton asked.

McBride shrugged. "Said they were quiet, sir. Kept themselves to themselves, caused no trouble. The only complaint she had was the hours they kept."

"How so?"

"Well, sir, they sometimes came in three or four in the morning, and this is when they was on their day shifts and had to be up early. Stinking of ale, too, she said, although they never seemed drunk. Neighbors complained, as neighbors do. Got so she was about to throw them out, but they offered to pay a shilling each extra a week. Seems that made her a bit more tolerant."

So the two men had joined on the same date, lived in the same house, worked in identical jobs although on different shifts. One had been murdered, the other had fled. No doubt Chief Inspector Purcell would jump to the obvious conclusion, that Durham killed Kepler. And motive? That would no doubt appear as the case unfolded.

Langton mistrusted the obvious. "Did the landlady see any visitors? Any letters or telegrams?"

"Nobody called on them, sir, but they had more than a few telegrams, she said. Sometimes one a day."

Before Langton could ask more, the stairs echoed to the heavy tread of boots. Another constable appeared, saw Langton, and saluted. He carried a sheaf of stained papers. "Sir, I found these in the rubbish."

The crumpled yellow telegrams bore questionable and pungent stains but were still legible. Langton spread them out on the top of the chest of drawers. Optimistically, he'd hoped to find some of the telegrams received by Durham and Kepler; instead, the pages seemed to be unsent drafts prepared by the men. Some of the words had been crossed out and rewritten, or moved to another position.

The contents seemed banal: *Aunt Agnes well. Fever gone. Hopes to visit soon. Asks for news of Mother.*

Another: *Uncle Toby pleased with gift. Sends best. Weather bright but unsettled.*

McBride shook his head. "Just family gossip, sir. Boring."

Langton compared the different drafts of the messages. A penny a word soon added up, especially for men on poor wages, but whoever had composed the telegrams had gone to ridiculous lengths to get the text in a certain order.

He smiled. If he were a Boer plotting something, he'd take care with his communications. A straightforward code would result in gibberish being transmitted, and the GPO clerks always notified the police of any suspicious transmission. Family news would arouse no suspicions or queries.

"Sergeant, find the nearest post offices and check their ledgers against these serial numbers; obviously, we're looking for ones in the sequence. Find out the destination address. We need to know who Durham and Kepler were in contact with."

"Sir." Instead of taking the crumpled pages, McBride began noting down the serial numbers imprinted at the top of each sheet.

Langton let Naylor go downstairs to use soap and water and told the other constable to wait outside for a few minutes. Langton wanted to think for a while, to absorb the surroundings and the discovered facts. He sat on the edge of the bed beneath the window and looked around. The smell of boiling cabbage and wet laundry wafted up from below and mixed with the kerosene from the cockroach traps.

Was there really a Boer plot afoot? Langton had some difficulty believing it. Queen Victoria had the best protection in the empire, from what most agreed were the best soldiers, the best agents, the best network of informants. Still, even they could not give guarantees; everybody had an Achilles' heel. Durham had to be caught.

A scratching sound distracted Langton. He looked down and drew his legs up as a fat, glossy cockroach scurried from under the bed. It veered away from the kerosene pots and dashed across the threadbare rug, its legs silent until they rattled on bare floorboards again. The insect vanished under the chest of drawers.

Langton got up and made for the door. Where you saw one of the creatures, you knew there were many more; they never traveled alone. Then, as he opened the door, he heard the snap of sprung metal slamming shut. He paused. It had sounded like a mantrap, not some penny arcade device.

Slowly, carefully, he knelt down and looked under the chest of drawers. As his eyes adjusted, he saw a massive steel trap with the unlucky insect spiked and still wriggling. And behind that, a dark void in the wall. Langton shifted the heavy chest to one side and kicked the steel trap out of the way. At the foot of the wall, just above the skirting board, someone had peeled back the yellowing wallpaper and enlarged a hole in the plaster. The wooden square covering the hole lay on the floor beside the trap, probably dislodged by the curious insects.

Pulling on his gloves, Langton used one of the lengths of wooden kindling from beside the fire to delve into the hole. Three more insects spilled out and lay wriggling on their backs. Langton grimaced, then dug a little deeper. The hole was bigger than he had first thought.

A wad of paper tied with twine landed beside the insects. Langton saw ornate writing, watermarks, detailed etchings. He estimated at least two or three hundred pounds in bills of one, five, and ten. He knelt down and searched further. The kindling stick snagged on something; Langton moved back a little, then prized the object out. The cotton-wrapped bundle hit the floor with a metallic thud.

Inside the bundle, a revolver, heavy and black, slick with oil. A Webley, the same model as the force-issue weapon lying in Langton's bedside drawer. No doubt the same model that Durham had used to fire on McBride and Langton.

There was something about the brass cartridges as they clattered across the floorboards. Langton took one to the grimy window and held it to the light. The head of the bullet bore two incisions at right angles, a cross-shaped cut that meant the fired round would mushroom on impact. A simple modification outlawed by the Geneva Convention but still in use.

Although the Boer guerrillas and Irregulars were not the only soldiers to use dumdum bullets, Langton remembered clearly the last time he'd seen the ammunition's horrific effects: Transvaal.

Six

BEFORE HE LEFT the house in Gloucester Road, Langton and the constables checked the remainder of the room but found no more cubbyholes or compartments. The landlady, after ignoring the cockroaches and complaining about the hole in her wall ("And who's going to pay for that, I'd like to know?"), told Langton little more than she'd told McBride: The two lodgers had caused no trouble apart from coming home late; they'd had no visitors but a lot of telegrams and post. No, she couldn't remember the postmarks on the envelopes, and what did they take her for? A busybody?

Langton stood on the pavement outside the house as McBride made his way through the gaggle of children that played out in the street despite the cold. The bundle of notes and the revolver lay locked in the hansom's trunk. Langton waited until he and McBride had climbed into the cab before he said, "What did you find?"

McBride flicked through his notebook. "Busy little bees, our two lodgers were. They sent at least one telegram every day, usually to the same address. The GPO clerk showed me the ledger that him and the operators use to record everything."

Langton read the notebook page that McBride held open. "Fifty-seven, The Mall, W1. I'm sure I know that address."

"I was going to look it up, sir, but the clerk had a quicker way; they have a directory they use for the telephones and suchlike. Turns out that address belongs to a government department: Foreign and Commonwealth Office."

Langton remembered that he'd seen a similar address on the telegram that Doctor Fry had received, the one stating that the faceless man's fingerprints did not match any records. What connection did Durham and Kepler have with the FCO? He had no doubt that Kepler was a Boer; the tattoos proved that. So what kind of convoluted scheme or intrigue had Langton stumbled upon?

He glanced at McBride and considered talking though his suspicions. He decided to wait until he had something more definite. "McBride, when we get back, ask the desk sergeant if he has any news of Durham."

"Sir."

As the hansom rattled along Scotland Road, Langton realized that the Kepler case had distracted him from thinking about Sarah's passing. Torn between the two, he knew that Kepler should be his priority, yet the thought of Sarah alone and trapped and in the power of some collector . . . No, he had to be wrong. Here in the cold reality of daylight, with trams and carts crowding the streets and pedestrians bustling every way, the idea of the Jar Boys and Doktor Glass seemed like a bad dream. A fiction.

Yet that suspicion would not leave Langton: Sarah waited for him to release her.

Redfers would know. He had stayed with Sarah until the very end. Nobody could have troubled Sarah without his knowledge, and Sarah had trusted Redfers, the man who had looked after her own mother, father, sisters.

As the hansom drew into the headquarters courtyard, Langton ran up the steps and made for the detectives' room. Before he could find Forbes Paterson, he met Chief Inspector Purcell coming down the wide staircase. "Ah, Langton. I wondered when we might track you down."

"If you'll excuse me, sir, I'm a little busy—"

Purcell blocked his path. "I'm sure it can wait. My office, Inspector."

Langton bit back his reply and followed Purcell. As Purcell opened the door to his office, he said, "I want to introduce Major Fallows from the Home Office. He's closely involved with the safety of Her Majesty's visit."

A tall, elegantly dressed man stood at the window. He turned and nodded to Langton but didn't offer to shake hands. "I'd prefer it if you didn't mention my work so publicly, Purcell. We must retain some confidentiality, after all."

A flush rose from Purcell's collar. "We're in a police station, Major, not a public house."

"Even so." The major folded his body into Purcell's leather chair and adjusted his shirt cuffs. "The Chief Inspector informs me that you are in charge of the investigation, Langton. I'd appreciate a résumé of your findings so far."

As he repeated the bare facts of the case, Langton evaluated Major Fallows. The grey hair and deep-set eyes put his age around fifty years, perhaps more, but he looked attentive and alert; he sat bolt upright, the opposite of Purcell's customary slump. He did not interrupt while Langton stood and itemized the events.

Langton did not relay everything he had found; for some reason he did not yet fully understand, he kept back McBride's news of the telegrams' destination address. Nor—thanks in some part to fear of ridicule—did he mention the possible involvement of the Jar Boys. He finished his explanation and waited for the major's response.

Fallows nodded. "It's quite obvious: Kepler and Durham inveigled their way into the Span Company, with robbery as their probable motive. For some reason we don't yet know, they fell out and Durham killed Kepler. Whatever scheme they had in place is no doubt in tatters."

Purcell breathed an audible sigh. "You don't believe it to be a plot."

"Not from the evidence," Major Fallows said. "It seems no more than straightforward avarice."

Langton could see no logic to support the major's dismissal of the case. He glanced at Purcell, then said, "I don't believe it is quite so straightforward, Major."

"Really, Langton?" The major stared at him. "Do go on. Please."

Purcell, red-faced and frowning, stood between the two men. "Look here, Langton, Major Fallows is one of Her Majesty's most experienced—"

"Please, Chief Inspector. I want to hear."

Langton looked past Purcell. "Well, Major, if robbery was the motive, what did Durham and Kepler hope to gain?"

"No doubt the Span Company keeps a reasonable amount of operating capital in its offices."

"Enough to justify months of preparation and deception?"

"I would imagine the Company payroll is quite large."

"It was," Langton said, "during the main phase of the construction, when many thousands of navvies and engineers worked on the Span. But only a few hundred men maintain the structure now. Durham and Kepler missed their opportunity by months if robbery was their motive."

In contrast to Purcell, the major's expression did not change. "Go on."

Langton said, "If Durham did kill Kepler, why disfigure the body? He could have hidden it away, anchored it to the bottom of the Mersey or thrown it into one of the many disused shafts that litter the shore. Instead, the killer dumped the body in the busiest dock in the area and mutilated it in such a way as to guarantee publicity and investigation."

"Perhaps Durham is mad," Purcell said. "Without reason or logic."

Langton nodded. "Perhaps, sir, but I believe there is more to this than simple robbery. Especially since Kepler was a Boer."

"That does not exclude him from also being greedy."

"True, Major, but a possible witness was also murdered."

"This Stoker Olsen? You're quite sure his death is connected?"

Langton stared at him. "The alternative stretches coincidence, Major. I don't think either of us is that naïve."

At that, Purcell became almost apoplectic. "Now see here, Langton, I will not have you speak to—"

Major Fallows stopped the flow with a raised hand. "That's quite all right, Purcell. Inspector Langton has made some good points. Perhaps my initial opinion was too hasty. But that is all it was: an opinion. I have a duty to Her Majesty which obliges me to investigate any possible danger to her person no matter how slim the evidence."

Fallows stood up and brushed his sleeves and waistcoat. "With that in mind, Inspector, perhaps you would be good enough to show me the evidence you have collected so far?"

"Of course, Major." Langton followed him out of the office and saw by the look on Purcell's face that this matter was not closed.

Down in Langton's office, Fallows settled himself at the desk with the case file and statements laid out before him. "Don't let me keep you, Inspector. I'm sure you have many pressing duties."

As he lifted his coat from the stand, Langton smiled at the irony of being dismissed from his own office. "If there's anything you need, Major, ask Harry, the office boy."

"Thank you." Then, as Langton reached the door, "You believe I have been too swift to reach a conclusion in this case."

Langton waited. Up in Purcell's office, he had wondered why the major had wanted to reduce the case to a mere robbery. And Langton could understand why Purcell grasped so firmly at that explanation: It removed the embarrassment that a plot against Her Majesty would bring, a plot formulated in Purcell's area and under his very nose. Robbery was so much more palatable and so much easier to deal with.

The major continued, "As we discovered in Africa and South America, panic can cause almost as much damage as an actual attack. I must ensure that public confidence is not jeopardized, and that Her Majesty's visit is not unduly interrupted. I trust that you understand the situation. Until later, Inspector."

Langton stood for a moment outside his own office, going over the major's warning. He agreed with the logic but not with the end result. For Major Fallows had implied that the Queen's visit obliterated all other considerations, even the truth. As patriotic and dutiful as Langton was, he could not simply dismiss this case because it might cause panic. Chief Inspector Purcell might.

And what would Major Fallows make of the references to the Jar Boys? He was sure to find it in the file and Kepler's postmortem reports. If the public got hold of that possibility, they would create their own sensationalist theories. The more outlandish the story, the longer it ran in the newspapers.

Thinking of the Jar Boys made Langton remember Forbes Paterson and Doctor Redfers. He checked his fob watch; he still had time to see both men. But he found Paterson's room empty again.

"I gave him your message, sir," the clerk in the main office told Langton. "Is it really important?"

When Langton said it was, the clerk beckoned him closer, looked left and right like a pantomime theatrical, and lowered his voice. "I don't suppose Mr. Paterson will mind me telling you, sir: They're down in the Hole in the Wall pub, celebrating."

"Celebrating what?"

"They put some big swindler in the cells, sir. They've been after him for a year or more."

Langton thought immediately of Doktor Glass.

"You'll keep it under your hat, won't you, sir?"

Langton thanked the clerk and hurried down the stairs. He knew the small, cramped pub down a winding side alley, such a favorite among the police that it sometimes seemed like their unofficial social club. He hurried through the cold streets and pushed his way inside the pub, automatically stooping to avoid the low, dark beams hung with horse brasses. Even at this time of the afternoon, the smoke-wreathed room bustled with drinkers. Langton squeezed through the crowd, peering at faces through clouds of cigar smoke. On a cold winter's day like this, the warmth and the smell of beer and food seemed like an oasis.

Inspector Forbes Paterson sat in a red leather booth at the back of the snug, surrounded by his fellow detectives, inspectors, and sergeants, all red in the face, grinning and laughing. Glasses and bottles hid every square inch of the table in front of them. Sepia photographs of sporting heroes and prizefighters looked down from the walls, and Paterson himself resembled a pugilist: broad, heavy, with pummeled features and an exorbitant moustache waxed to points. "Langton, sit down and have a drink. I got your message, but the boy Harry said you were in Percy's office."

Langton smiled. "Percy" was one of the least insulting nicknames given to Chief Inspector Purcell. "Sorry to interrupt; do you have a minute?"

Paterson looked over the rim of his pint. "Private?"

"Please."

Paterson finished his pint and carried the empty glass to the bar. As the barmaid refilled it and poured a fresh glass for Langton, Paterson leaned over and spoke a few words. She nodded and pointed to a side door.

"This way," he said, sliding one of the pints toward Langton.

Langton paid for the drinks and followed Forbes through the crowd, trying not to spill his beer. The side door opened onto a narrow staircase that led to a second-floor function room that smelled of dust and stale beer. A fire burned in the grate behind a mesh guard.

"Bev said we could use this until they start setting up for the night," Paterson said, pulling two chairs from against the wall and placing them by the fire. He raised his glass. "Cheers."

"Cheers." Langton sipped the dark beer. "I'm sorry for interrupting your celebration."

"Oh, we'll be here awhile yet." Paterson looked away, into the flames. "How are you holding up?"

Langton knew what he meant. "Work helps; the busier I am, the less I . . ."

Paterson nodded but still stared at the fire. "People believe that time helps, too."

"Maybe so." That didn't reassure Langton; he wanted the pain to lessen but he didn't want to forget Sarah. He couldn't imagine the day when the thought of her didn't pierce his heart.

That reminded him of Doktor Glass. "I believe you had some luck today."

Paterson grinned. "A year we've been after him. Every one of my boys put in extra hours, worked themselves dry, but we got him."

Langton kept his voice level. "Who was it?"

"A determined, clever, devious little swindler by the name of Archibald David Healey. His specialty was separating recently widowed women from their wealth. And he was good at it, too. Séances, fake mediums, apparitions, the works. Most of his gang's victims were too embarrassed to testify; in the end, we had to hook him with our own little game. We used an actress from the playhouse and set her up in a fine house in Toxteth. Worked a treat."

That gave Langton a germ of an idea; he put it to one side for now.

"So what did you want to see me about?" Paterson asked.

Even now, Langton hesitated, but he had to know. "Have you ever heard of the Jar Boys?"

The smile left Paterson's face. "I've heard of them."

"Are they swindlers? Or just stories?"

Paterson cradled his pint in both hands and didn't answer for a moment. Then, "This is between us?"

"Completely."

Paterson nodded and gulped his drink. "They're real. We had a handful of cases in the past six months. They used to target the poor, who were too afraid, too cowed, or simply too superstitious to speak out. Once they started on the middle classes and the supposedly educated . . ."

"They?"

"I've heard of three local gangs, although they seem to be fighting among themselves lately," Paterson said. "There's plenty more in London, but three's enough for me. More than enough."

Langton leaned forward. "What do they do?"

Paterson spoke slowly, apparently choosing his words with care. "They used to pay the poorer families for the privilege of attaching some kind of machine to their loved ones just before they passed away. Are you sure you want me to go on?"

"Please."

"They used various stories: The machines eased the pain, or delayed the inevitable, even that they pointed the dying to heaven. This was with the poor."

"And with the others?"

Paterson reached automatically for his glass, saw it was empty, and frowned. "The gangs told these supposedly educated families another lie: that the machines could store their loved ones' souls until a new body was found. And these people actually believed it. They only came to us when the gangs disappeared with their money as well as the contents of the jars."

Langton stared at him. "The families paid them?"

"Amazing, isn't it?"

But as he thought of it, Langton could see a reason: Some families might do anything to extend the lives of their dying loved ones. They might grasp at any and every possibility. "Do you believe they trap the victims' souls?"

Paterson hesitated. "I've talked with more than a few who've witnessed the Jar Boys at work. They're convinced that something happens; they swear you can see a bright mist streaming toward the jar. But as for it being the soul . . . I don't know, Langton. I think desperate people see, and believe, what they wish to."

Langton believed that, too. "What do they do with these jars?"

"You'd have to ask them."

"Have you caught any of the gangs?"

"We had our hands on a few of the smaller fishes, but the bigger ones always swim a little deeper, out of our reach."

Langton took a chance: "Have you come across a Doktor Glass?"

Paterson turned to him. "How did you hear that name?"

"I'm investigating a body washed up in Albert Dock."

"The faceless chap?"

Langton nodded.

"You think he's connected with Glass?"

"Possibly. What do you know?"

"Only that Doktor Glass is the worst of all of 'em," Forbes said. "Springheel Bob's gang is bad enough, the Caribs no better, but nobody will speak of Doktor Glass out of fear. If he really is involved with your faceless man, you've got your work cut out for you."

At that moment, as if on purpose, a maid opened the door, saw the two men, and gave a start, almost dropping the white linen folded over her arm. "Sorry, sirs. I was told to start setting the tables."

"Give us just a minute, please," Langton said. Then, when she'd left, he asked Paterson, "You know nothing about him?"

"I wish I did. I hate cruelty, especially to the old and the weak. His arrest would comfort many, not to mention solving at least three murders, maybe more."

"How do you mean?"

Paterson said, "You can't always depend on when someone is going to die. Only the Lord himself knows that. That interferes with Glass's schedule, so he's been known to speed the course of action."

"He's murdered the victims?"

"I'm sure he has." Paterson got to his feet and reached for his empty glass. "Proving it is another thing altogether."

Langton thought for a moment, then stood and swallowed his beer.

"I can think of one way to catch him. It would be difficult, possibly immoral, and definitely dangerous."

"How?"

Langton said, "We set a trap."

BY THE TIME Langton left the public house, the streets had filled with people. Homeward-bound commuters huddled beneath the tram stop glass shelters; office workers, clerks, and secretaries hurried along with heads bowed against the cold. At street level, most of the snow had melted. Wet pavements reflected yellow gaslight.

Langton checked his watch and then searched the congested roads for a hansom cab. He walked up Castle Street and all the way to Dale Street before he could flag down a driver. "Gladstone Crescent, and hurry."

"Do the best I can, sir."

As the cab lurched away into the stream of traffic, Langton hoped Doctor Redfers would wait for him. Langton hadn't expected to spend so much time with Paterson. Had it been a waste? Paterson had confirmed what Mrs. Grizedale, Sister Wright, and the Professor had all stated: The Jar Boys existed. Now Langton had no option but to accept them as a fact.

But he'd had no right to ask Paterson to consider setting a trap. After all, the Jar Boys might play only a small part in the case of the murdered Kepler. Hand on heart, Langton knew he should not have asked Paterson to consider such a dangerous and possibly immoral trap. It might be different if the whole case pivoted on them, but Langton had to admit that it would be for Sarah's benefit and for his own peace of mind. He almost asked the driver to turn the cab around.

"Gladstone Crescent, sir."

Langton paid the driver and climbed the steps of the three-story town house set opposite a well-tended park bordered by iron railings.

He rang the brass bell and waited. Most of the house lay in darkness, with not even a glimmer in the transom above the door, but one dim light glowed in a room to the left. Redfers's consulting room.

Langton rang again. No answer. Obviously, Redfers had left for the evening or did not wish to be disturbed. That didn't explain why the maid didn't open the door. Langton hesitated, looking up and down the quiet crescent, then tried the door handle; it turned in his hand.

"Redfers? It's Langton."

The cold hallway led into darkness. Slipping inside, Langton eased the door shut and stood there, listening. The tick of the grandfather clock. No voices. No murmurs. No movement.

The narrow central strip of carpet on the parquet floor silenced Langton's steps. He tried to remember the layout of the house from his last visit. He pushed open the first door to his right and saw the waiting room. The light of a dying fire in the grate. Empty, hard wooden chairs surrounding a massive table. Pot plants.

Redfers's rooms stood opposite the waiting room. Langton put his ear to the closed door but heard only his own pulse. He reached for the handle. Every sense seemed sharper: the odors of disinfectant and tobacco smoke; the feel of the cold, smooth brass as he turned the handle. His eyes, adjusting to the meager light from under the door, scanned the receptionist's empty room in a moment. Her desk, neat and clear apart from the squat typewriter under its cover. The file cabinets closed. Nothing in disarray.

Langton crossed the room and hesitated outside Redfers's door. He knocked but heard no response. He stood to one side, turned the handle, and pushed the door open with his right foot. Nobody rushed out.

He peered around the edge of the door and saw Redfers sitting at a wide desk. The doctor's head rested back against the high leather armchair. His mouth hung slack. Langton half-expected to hear snores. An electric table lamp threw white light onto the scattered papers and files. In the corner, a bleached skeleton hung from its support.

"Redfers?"

Langton slipped inside the room. Little heat came from the fire, which had almost died down to nothing. He sniffed at the odor, something chemical akin to bitter almonds with perhaps a hint of white flowers. "Redfers?"

Another two strides brought him to the desk. The dead doctor gripped the arms of the chair like a falling man clutching a parapet; the tendons stood out like steel cables on the Span.

Langton raised the lampshade and saw Redfers's eyes wide and dilated, staring straight ahead. The light glinted on metal; below Redfers's chin, just above his necktie, jutted the snapped shaft of the spike that pinned his neck to the back of the chair. Only a trickle of blood showed around the wound.

Langton listened for a moment. He thought he'd heard floorboards creak. He reached for the telephone on the desk, then saw the cord severed and hanging. He turned to the door, then back to Redfers. By twisting the lamp slightly, he threw light onto the doctor's neck. At the sides, just under the ears, he saw two small patches of burned skin.

Standing on the top step at the front of the house, Langton put his police whistle to his lips and blew three piercing blasts. He repeated the summons at minute intervals until he heard the pounding of constables' boots from the neighboring streets.

Even as the first breathless constable arrived, Langton had hailed a cab. For, as if to deprive Langton of information or to remove witnesses, someone had killed Stoker Olsen and then Doctor Redfers. And Langton remembered someone else connected to Sarah, someone even more vulnerable than the dead men: Mrs. Grizedale.

Seven

B EFORE THE HANSOM cab stopped moving, Langton jumped out and ran to the front door of Mrs. Grizedale's house in Hamlet Street. Every window blazed with light. The constable who opened the front door stared at Langton in surprise, then stood aside at the sight of his warrant card. "The body's upstairs, sir."

Taking three stairs at a time, Langton ran up to the second floor, all the while cursing himself for allowing this to happen.

A bedroom door stood open at the head of the stairs. Instead of Mrs. Grizedale's body, Langton saw a man sprawled out on the floor beside the chaise longue like a marionette with severed strings. He was roughly dressed in torn woolen trousers, a navy jacket, and scuffed boots, and a flat cap that had slipped from his balding head and over his face as he fell; Langton wanted to raise it but left it in place until Fry's photographers arrived. Langton could see from the pale skin and tonsure of grey hair that it was not Durham.

The man's body hid his left hand, but the right clutched the edge of the rug he lay upon. A long steel knife had rolled under the chaise longue. Langton couldn't see any marks on the blade, but blood seeped from under the body and merged with the expensive carpet. Langton tried to understand how the man had died. He stood up and found Mrs. Grizedale in the doorway. "Are you all right?"

She nodded, then looked down at the body and back at Langton. "It was self-defense."

"I know."

"He forced the back window . . ."

Langton steered her out of the room, but she gripped his arm and said, "Don't let them take her away."

"Her?"

"Meera. She did it to protect me."

Langton understood. "Meera killed him?"

"She heard my shout and ran in from her own room. I didn't know she kept a gun, but I'll swear it was mine, I will . . ." Mrs. Grizedale covered her face.

As a medium, Mrs. Grizedale must surely be more sensitive than most people. Langton wondered if the man's death had affected more than her emotions; had she detected some . . . resonance? Some echo? With these thoughts, Langton realized how far he'd gone down the path of superstition and the supernatural. He had allowed talk of the paranormal to infect his perspective. That might prove dangerous.

With his arm around her shoulders, Langton guided her across the landing. He saw Meera coming upstairs with a tray holding china mugs and a bottle of brandy. She stopped when she saw Langton, then continued into her own room. She pulled Mrs. Grizedale away from Langton and sat her on the bed. "You have some tea, missy, and a little sniff of brandy."

Then Meera looked up at Langton. Her ordeal didn't appear to have upset her; on the contrary, her voice sounded calm. "Will they take me?"

"No," Langton said. "Just explain that it was self-defense. Every householder is entitled to protect themselves against burglars."

"He was no burglar."

Langton wondered how much she knew. "Have you ever seen this man before?"

"Never."

"Nobody hanging around? Perhaps watching the house?"

Meera smoothed her employer's hair and told Langton, "We get none of this before. Very quiet here. Till now."

He looked into her unblinking eyes and said, "Is there somewhere safe you and Mrs. Grizedale could stay?"

"With my family," Meera said. "They'll help us."

"Good." Langton nodded and turned to leave. "Don't worry, I'll have a word with the officer in charge. Let me know where I can find you."

"Why?"

"It might be important."

"You bring this trouble," Meera said. "This is your doing."

Langton couldn't disagree with that. He left the two women and found the constable in the hall. Meera had given the young man a mug of tea, probably laced with brandy, which he tried to hide before Langton nodded approval. "What happened?"

"Well, sir, I was up on Alder Road, doing my rounds, when I heard a woman screaming for help. I ran down and found the maid pulling the older woman back in from the upstairs window. Fair bellowing, she was. Anyway, the maid let me in and I saw the burglar stretched out on the floor. Dead as he could be."

"Where's the gun?"

The constable patted his tunic pocket. "Maid gave it me, sir. Will you take it?"

Langton wondered whether to stay and supervise, but he wanted to get back to Redfers's house. Just then, he heard the chugging of a steam car from outside. He looked through the window and saw two constables and a local sergeant climbing out of the hissing vehicle. He found his pocketbook and took out two notes. "Do something for me, constable: See that the two women leave here tonight. Take a cab and go with them, and make sure they reach the maid's family safely. I'll have a word with the sergeant."

The constable took the money. "I'll see to it, sir. And as to what happened here . . ."

"Self-defense, no doubt about it."

As the local police entered, Langton took the sergeant aside and explained his presence and what had happened. "When the photographers have finished, please have the body taken to Doctor Fry at headquarters."

With that, Langton found his waiting cab and returned to Gladstone Crescent. As with Mrs. Grizedale's house, light now poured from every window. Two police wagons stood at the door and a handful of cold, curious loafers pestered the constable on duty. Inside the house, Langton saw McBride and Doctor Fry examining the body of Redfers.

Fry, probe in hand, stood up and nodded to Langton. "This is getting to be quite an epidemic for you."

"What have you found?"

"Much as you see: death caused by a single stab wound through the trachea and spine. A very neat job."

"And the . . ." Langton rubbed his own neck, just below the ears.

"Yes, I saw those." Fry glanced at McBride, then said, "The same as on our faceless friend. I take it this is part of the same case?"

Langton didn't answer. With Redfers's murder and Mrs. Grizedale's intruder, the two divergent strands, Sarah and Kepler, seemed almost to meet. What possible connection could there be between Sarah and Kepler? On the face of it, none.

Langton told Fry, "I have another one for you."

"You're not serious."

"I'm afraid so. Hamlet Street in Everton."

For a moment, Langton thought that McBride started in surprise.

"And he's connected with this?" Fry said. "The same case again?"

"Perhaps. On the margin."

Fry started packing his instruments into his bag and signaled for the attendants to remove the body. "I don't know what you're on the trail of, Langton, but I hope you find it soon."

"So do I. Can you let me have the postmortem results as soon as possible?"

Fry checked his watch and sighed. "So much for *The Marriage of Figaro.*"

As Fry left and the attendants transferred Redfers to the stretcher, Langton thought about all the late nights he himself had worked. All those missed dinners, the evenings when he should have returned home to Sarah. If only he could have that time back.

"I called in at your house, sir," McBride said. "Elsie was kind enough to give me this address. For a moment, when I got here . . ."

"You thought they'd got me?"

McBride nodded.

That made Langton realize how much the case had developed. Already he and McBride had a vague enemy: "they," an amorphous form that seemed all the more powerful because of their ambiguity. Doktor Glass? The figure certainly had a link with the Jar Boys and therefore possibly with Sarah, but Langton couldn't yet see any connection to the Span or Kepler.

Langton called McBride into the waiting room. He shut the door. "We have a problem."

"Sir?"

"Someone knows our every move," Langton said, "almost as soon as we do. Stoker Olsen died hours after we met him. I make arrangements to see Redfers; he dies."

"And this Hamlet Street, sir? Part of the same?"

"It's beginning to look that way." Langton paced the room. "Whoever we're up against, they have an efficient network in place. They must have, unless they just happened to hear Perkins speak of Olsen in the pub."

"Sir? Like some kind of conspiracy?"

"Perhaps so." What would interest conspirators? "The Span."

"Sir?"

"From the start, Sergeant, I knew the Span lay at the root of all this. Either Kepler was part of some conspiracy or he fought against it. Each of the reasons could explain his murder."

McBride folded his arms. "I don't know, sir. Some secret conspiracy, blokes wandering around like Fenians or anarchists in big cloaks . . . Seems a bit far-fetched. And how does this Doctor Redfers and your dead man in Hamlet Street fit into it?"

That threw Langton. "I don't know. Not yet. But if someone is following us around and erasing possible witnesses, there's another they might be interested in: Professor Caldwell Chivers."

FIGHTING THE RISING panic, the belief that time was slipping away, Langton reached the Infirmary at close to midnight. He and McBride traced Professor Caldwell Chivers to an operating theater on the third floor; a yawning nurse guided them to a viewing room that jutted out above the theater, where a tiered circle of wooden seats—not unlike the stalls of a music hall—surrounded a conical glass skylight over the operating table.

At the sound of the doors opening, the sole occupant of the viewing room turned from the window. "Inspector. Sergeant. This is a surprise."

Leaving McBride near the door, Langton joined Sister Wright at the window. Perhaps eight feet below them, figures in gowns of green and white surrounded a prone patient. The surgeons and nurses moved with slow, deliberate motions, like mime artists in some silent drama. Electric light flooded the theater and glinted from surgical steel instruments, oxygen cylinders, white bone edged with red. Langton looked away.

"You came to see the Professor?" Sister Wright said.

"If possible."

"He's working on a very serious case at the moment. It could be hours before he's free." Sister Wright leaned her forehead to the window. The delicate crucifix around her neck swung out and tapped at the glass. "It's an amazing sight, the saving of a man's life. We almost take it for granted. Just think: Those instruments are nothing without the experience and judgment of the surgeon wielding them. Mere tools."

Langton forced himself to look down. "What happened?"

"A head injury, the skull shattered in three places. The poor man, a steeplejack, fell from a factory chimney. Broken legs and arms are easy to mend, but the skull demands another level of skill altogether."

As Langton watched, one of the surgeons threw back the sterile green sheet covering a tray of instruments and selected a short, gleaming saw. Under the Professor's guidance, he placed the saw against the man's skull and braced himself. Langton swallowed hard and looked instead at Sister Wright. "I came to warn the Professor."

"Warn him? About what?"

"There is a chance, only a chance, that his life might be in danger."

She turned to him. "Go on."

"It may be connected with the man we brought to the Professor."

"The faceless Boer."

"The same. A coincidental witness died; others with tenuous connections to the case have been killed or attacked."

"And you think the Professor might be next?"

Langton hesitated. Was he overreacting? "I think he should take precautions. As should you."

"Me?"

"Please. Just in case."

Sister Wright rested her hand on Langton's arm for a moment. "I'm sure he will appreciate your concern; I know I do."

Langton looked into Sister Wright's calm grey eyes and hoped the Professor realized his good fortune. "I should go. We have much to do."

"It's late."

Langton smiled. "Policemen, like nurses, can't always keep office hours. Good night, Sister."

Langton had reached the doors when he heard Sister Wright call out.

"Inspector, the Professor is holding a grand reception at his house tomorrow evening, to celebrate the inauguration of the Span. I'm sure he would want you to be there."

"Thank you for the offer, but I'm very busy."

"You might find it useful," she said. "The cream of Liverpool society is invited, from the legal, medical, and professional worlds. If you find that you can make it, it begins at eight."

"You will be there?"

She smiled. "The Professor insisted."

"Then I'll try to attend, Sister."

On the drive back to Redfers's house, Langton wondered how useful the Professor's reception might be. It would be an opportunity to meet a variety of people from the upper levels of society, and Forbes Paterson had implied that the jar collectors came from among these. But was Langton concentrating too much on Sarah again? Now he could argue that investigating the Jar Boys formed part of both cases.

He realized that he'd started considering Sarah as a case, as a mystery to be solved, yet she was so much more than that. Activity distracted him; hard work helped the pain. Langton still had a void inside him, a cold absence of joy that became a physical ache. He couldn't imagine the day that would ease. He wasn't even sure he wanted it to.

As if echoing Langton's thoughts, McBride asked, "Begging your pardon, sir, but do you think you might learn anything about Kepler or Doctor Redfers at the Professor's party?"

Langton had known McBride for years and didn't object to the question. "Possibly. I wonder if the same gang that murdered Kepler also killed Redfers, and Inspector Paterson said that they sell their particular merchandise to rich collectors. It's possible we may meet some of them there."

"But how would we recognize them, sir?"

"A good question." Langton saw Redfers's house looming up through the mist and gaslight. "Ask me at the reception."

"You want me there?"

Langton smiled. "By talking to the guests' chauffeurs, and the maids and staff, you could well learn more than I will."

A lone constable remained on the steps of Redfers's house, stamping his feet and pacing back and forth to fight the freezing cold. He saluted Langton and said, "All quiet, sir. Apart from the maid."

"Redfers's maid? She finally appeared?"

"An hour or so ago, sir. She's down in the kitchen."

Inside the house, most of the rooms lay in darkness, but a sliver of yellow light showed under the kitchen door at the rear of the house. Opening it, Langton saw a pale woman of maybe thirty years sitting at the wide pine table. She spilled her tea in surprise and jumped to her feet, dabbing at her black uniform dress.

"I'm sorry, I should have knocked," Langton said. "Sit, please. I'm Inspector Langton and this is Sergeant McBride."

"Evening, sir." The maid waited until Langton sat at the table before she settled down again. "I remember you, sir. You and your wife used to visit the doctor."

Langton wondered if she knew that Sarah had died. "You're . . . Agnes?"

She smiled. "That's right, sir. Been with the doctor four years last September."

Langton remembered her not only from his and Sarah's appointments but also from a handful of dinners with Redfers. An efficient, smiling woman.

"Would you like some tea, sir?" Agnes asked, reaching for cups. "I brewed a pot for the shock."

"Thank you, no. Can you tell me what happened today?" Langton glanced at the kitchen clock over the dresser. "I mean yesterday."

She sipped tea. "Just after lunch, sir, a GPO boy knocked with a telegram from my mother in Chester. Doctor Redfers was very kind, gave me money for the train fare and said not to worry, he and Mrs. Dunne would manage."

"Mrs. Dunne?"

"The doctor's receptionist, sir. She arranges his diary and looks after the patients."

Langton dimly remembered a tall, sour woman with severe hair. "Go on, Agnes."

"Well, sir, I rushed to Chester fast as I could, but Mum was right as rain. Swore she hadn't sent any such telegram. We didn't have a clue who'd spend good money to play a joke on us like that, but what could we do? So I stayed and had supper, then caught the train back. Your man on the door told me about the poor doctor."

At this, Agnes dabbed at her eyes.

Langton saw that someone had wanted Agnes out of the way. What had happened to Mrs. Dunne and Redfers's patients in the waiting room? "Mrs. Dunne lives close by?"

"No, sir, she moved up to Southport when she got married last year." Agnes sniffed. "Quite the madam, she is now."

Langton glanced at McBride, who nodded and wrote in his notebook. Then Langton asked Agnes, "Did Doctor Redfers have any enemies?"

"Not that I know of, sir. The opposite, I'd say."

"How do you mean?"

"Well, sir, he used to have lots of visitors. My room's at the top of the stairs and I heard the bell going all times of the night. Some were patients, asking for a home visit, but plenty of them were social calls."

"Did you see any of his visitors?"

Agnes blushed. "Why, sir, you take me for a nosy parker?"

Langton smiled and leaned closer. "Not at all, but it would help us if we knew his habits, and perhaps you happened to notice some of his visitors—purely by chance, of course . . ."

Agnes sipped her tea and looked down at the table. "I have to admit I did, sir. Strange bunch, I'd say. Men in top hats and fine tails, like they'd just come from the opera; navvies still covered in mud and dust; women in fine dresses that could have stepped out of the window of Bon Marché. Got all sorts, did the doctor. I couldn't hear what they was up to once they went down to the basement."

If the investigation had started in some other way, Langton might have suspected sexual or narcotic motives for Redfers's nocturnal guests. Both Langton and Forbes Paterson knew of cases where some of Liverpool's highest citizens had shown a regular, unhealthy interest in its lowest. The trade in drugs and bodies still thrived. Now Langton wondered what those frequent guests had wanted from Redfers.

As Agnes hid a yawn behind her hand, Langton said, "Go and get some sleep. We can continue in the morning."

"You're sure, sir?"

"I'm sure." Langton checked his watch: almost two o'clock. He and McBride had much still to do. "Agnes, if you could tell us where you keep the coffee, before you go—"

"You leave it to me, sir," Agnes said, already reaching into the cupboard.

Langton returned to Redfers's consulting room with McBride. The desk lamp illuminated the empty chair where the body had lain; the chair's padding leaked out where the surgical knife had been embedded. In the grate, the fire had died to ashes.

"What are we looking for, sir?" McBride asked.

"Names. I want to know all about Redfers's circle; who he saw, who he dined with."

"Who visited him late at night, sir?"

"Exactly."

"You think it's drugs, sir? Or maybe he liked a bit of variety . . ."

Langton didn't want to discuss his suspicions, or the involvement of the Jar Boys. "Let's see what we find. You check Mrs. Dunne's room next door."

Langton looked around for a starting point. Against one wall, under an oil painting of Redfers's stern father, stood a bureau next to white enamel cabinets with glass fronts. First, Langton opened the desk drawers and rummaged through the contents: old fountain pens, coins, prescription pads, rubber bands, keys of all sizes. The usual detritus of a busy man's desk.

On the desk itself stood the vandalized telephone, a blood-pressure gauge filled with mercury, patients' files, a heavy glass inkstand, and a blotter busy with scrawled fragments of words and doodles. Langton couldn't make any sense of the doctor's writing, but he easily imagined him sitting there with the phone in one hand and a pen in the other, scribbling as he talked.

After checking under the desk, Langton sat in Redfers's chair and remembered the position of the body. Head pinned back. Hands clutching the chair's arms. No, not just clutching: fastened onto the padded leather, like claws, with every tendon raised. And his wide-open eyes staring at the door. Who had come into the room? Who had scared Redfers so much, and then killed him?

As the door swung open, Langton jumped up, ready.

Agnes nearly dropped the tray. "Oh, sir, you gave me a start."

Langton put a hand over his racing heart. "Sorry, Agnes."

"I'll leave this here for you." Agnes slid the tray onto Redfers's desk. "There's two mugs and a Dewar flask that'll keep the coffee warm a good while. I gave a cup to your constable, too; must be frozen out there. If there's anything else you need, sir . . ."

"No, thank you, Agnes. You go off to bed."

Agnes paused at the door. "I don't mind saying, sir, I'm a little nervous about staying here. It's not in my nature, but the thought of the poor doctor lying there, and the person that did it still wandering the streets—"

"Don't worry. McBride and I will be here another few hours, and there's a constable out front." He tried to inject assurance into his voice. "We'll look after you."

Langton walked Agnes through Mrs. Dunne's office and saw her climb the stairs. As he returned, he looked over McBride's shoulder as the sergeant riffled through a cabinet of file-index cards.

"Hope it's not one of his patient's that done him, sir."

"Why not, Sergeant?"

"There must be three, four hundred of them, sir. Take us until next summer to question all these."

"If we must, Sergeant, we must. Now, come and have some coffee."

As they sipped their drinks in the consulting room, Langton thought aloud: "Agnes gets a false telegram, calling her away from the house. Someone wanted Redfers alone. So what happened to Mrs. Dunne and any patients waiting to see him?"

"I can ask her in the morning, sir."

"Do that. Let's presume they left Redfers alive and well. Did someone break in, or did he let them in?"

"There's no jimmy signs on the doors or windows, sir. Front or back."

Langton leaned against the couch and looked around the room. "Then Redfers let his killers into the house. Perhaps he was expecting them. Either way, I can see no signs of any struggle."

"Nor me, sir."

"So why would Redfers simply sit there and let someone drive a spike through his throat?" Again, Langton looked to the chair and asked himself why Redfers would allow someone to connect an electrical apparatus to his neck. Did he know what to expect?

"Maybe he was drugged, sir," McBride said, "like the Boer chappie."

"Maybe so. We'll have to ask Fry." Langton drained his mug and set it on the desk. He tried to remember the last time he'd eaten. It wasn't important. "Let's crack on, Sergeant."

While McBride returned to the receptionist's room, Langton searched the bureau. At first, he found only bills and receipts, pharmaceutical catalogs, and copies of old physicians' periodicals. The bottom drawer would not open. Langton tried the keys he'd found in the desk, but they were much too large. He cursed himself for not checking Redfers's body for his set of keys. Maybe he was more fatigued than he realized.

Then he remembered an old trick. He slid out the two drawers above the locked one; they stuck a little, then came out completely from the bureau to give him access to the inside. Langton reached through the bureau carcass and drew out the contents of the bottom drawer.

A heavy cash box, locked. A diary. Three checkbooks. Putting the box to one side, Langton flicked through the diary. Against certain dates, initials, a number, and a sum in pounds—no shillings or pence. *April seventh, AC, 21, £10. August twelfth, DH, 3, £25. October eleventh, SP, 16, £30.* The last entry appeared on November the fifteenth. Ten days ago.

Blackmail? Payment for drugs? The clandestine notation implied as much. Perhaps.

Langton pocketed the diary and opened the checkbooks. Redfers had an account at St. Martin's Bank on Victoria Street, and the stubs recorded small amounts to tailors and tradesmen, nothing remarkable. The regular transactions of a comfortably settled bachelor. The final stub left a balance of seven hundred pounds and some.

The other two checkbooks implied something quite different. The second book, for an account with the Banque Credite Zurich, showed a balance of more than six thousand pounds. The final checkbook had been issued by a New York institution and showed a balance of almost twenty thousand dollars. If the accounts really did hold as much as the books implied, Redfers had been close to rich. Certainly more comfortably off than a hardworking bachelor doctor might hope for. An honest one, anyway.

Of course, Redfers might have inherited money. He might have won it through gambling, or the stock market. Langton hoped so. He didn't welcome the alternative possibilities. This man had looked after Sarah in her final hours, for God's sake.

The locked cabinets beside the bureau had steel mesh woven through their glass. On the shelves, row after row of bottles, phials, solutions, and powders. Langton recognized some of the drugs as those that had crowded Sarah's bedside table before the end. Langton caught a reflection in the glass and saw the skeleton hanging in the corner. What an exhibit to have in a doctor's office. Enough to frighten off your patients.

White, white bone. Glossy and smooth under the electric light. All that was left after the flesh broke down and melted away.

Langton couldn't help it: He thought of Sarah, lying alone under the cold earth. Still. Silent. Nightmare images crowded his mind. He clutched the edge of Redfers's desk like a drowning man clinging to driftwood. He swallowed, fighting the urge to vomit.

Another image. Pick something else to focus on. Anything.

The thick, braided cables of an electrical cord sprouted from the skirting by the fireplace. Heavy with dust, the cord led from a brass socket and into the cupboard beneath one of the bookcases beside the chimney breast.

The cupboard door opened to reveal a squat apparatus of brass, steel, and shellac or bois durci. A small box, a cylinder of wound copper wire, a slender vertical tube, all on a wooden base. The whole machine could fit into a Disraeli bag. But when Langton tried to lift it, he found it heavier than it appeared. It gave off the familiar electrical odor of burned dust, and another, sweeter floral smell, like patent ointments.

Langton knelt down. The box hummed as if taking current. Wires trailed from the cylinder and terminated in two small copper squares tinted with verdigris. Traces of skin and a few hairs still clung to the metal.

"McBride," Langton called, already at the door. "To the basement."

McBride looked up from Mrs. Dunne's ledger. "Sir?"

Langton waited until they had dropped down the stairs at the rear of the entrance hall. "Agnes said Redfers's midnight visitors went to the basement. We need to discover why."

In the harsh electric light, the basement door looked stout enough to defend a bank vault. Thick strips of iron braced the heavy wood. Bolt heads as broad as farthings. And everything painted white, even the massive lock.

"I could ask the maid if she has a key," McBride said.

Langton shook his head. He doubted Agnes went into this room or knew of a key. He left McBride and ran up to Redfers's consulting room. In the top left-hand drawer of the desk, a selection of iron keys. Langton grabbed the largest and ran back to the basement. He slotted key after key in the lock, then threw them to the stone floor with a clang.

The penultimate key fitted, then turned. The great door swung back into darkness. The smell of damp and stale air seeped into the passage. Langton groped around the edge of the inner wall until his hand found a switch. Cold white light flooded the basement chamber.

Empty. Empty shelves against the white tile walls. Empty tables in the center. Langton and McBride paced the room, their footsteps echoing. Cages covered the two electric globes. The windows, like the fireplace, had been bricked up. The whole room had an air of enclosure, of constriction, as though the walls themselves pressed in. Unhealthy.

"Whatever was down here has flown, sir," said McBride, slapping the steel table with his hand.

"But dust carries its own message, Sergeant. Look." Langton pointed to the shelves standing against the walls. The falling dust had outlined large, circular rings in the white-painted wood. "Something stood here not so long ago."

"Jars or canisters, I'd say, sir."

Langton didn't reply. He looked along the rows of shelves. Circular dust rings as far as he could see. And on the shelf in front of each ring, a stenciled number. Langton remembered Redfers's diary entries: *April seventh, AC, 21, £10. August twelfth, DH, 3, £25. October eleventh, SP, 16, £30.*

"It doesn't make any sense, sir," McBride said.

But a whole section of the case had slotted into place in Langton's mind. "I'm very much afraid that it does, Sergeant."

Eight

AS HE WALKED along Church Street toward headquarters, Langton went over the evidence from Redfers's house. The tide of jostling workers hurrying to offices and jobs carried him along. In the distance, factory whistles announced the start of shifts. The cold morning sunlight gilded the grimy city center buildings, but Langton saw again the dim consulting room and the basement with its empty shelves.

Langton's rage had subsided to a dull, constant ache, like embers flickering and ready to erupt. He'd trusted Redfers, just as Sarah's family had trusted the man, their doctor for almost three decades. Redfers had betrayed them all by involving himself in the illicit trade. There could be little doubt of his guilt: the strange electrical apparatus, the imprints of the ranks of jars hurriedly spirited away, the excessive sums of money, the midnight callers. Even worse, the evidence supported the existence of the Jar Boys. Langton knew now that he could fight it no longer—they existed.

For a moment, Langton had wondered if Redfers and Doktor Glass were one and the same. That suspicion had passed. Instead, Langton saw the hands of Doktor Glass behind the murders, directing them, orchestrating them for his own ends. And not without help, since the shelves had spaces for one hundred forty-two jars and the transfer could have taken an hour or more. Langton had asked McBride to question the neighbors; someone must have seen Glass's men taking the jars away.

As headquarters drew near, Langton wondered how he would break the news of Redfers's duplicity to Sarah's parents. He'd interrogated murderers and molesters, anarchists, thieves, and arsonists. Those interviews would be nothing compared to the pain of telling Mr. and Mrs. Cavell that Sarah might have suffered even more than they'd realized. Might still be suffering.

Langton stopped at the foot of the headquarters steps, closed his eyes a moment, and drew a breath. He would do what he had to do. He had no choice.

Inside the building, the desk sergeant called Langton across. "McBride told us to look out for this man of yours, sir. Durham."

"You have him?"

"We have *sight* of him, sir. Maybe."

"Where? And how recent?"

Like a clerk in an accountant's office, the desk sergeant consulted the massive ledger. "Yesterday evening, sir. Around ten o'clock near the encampment. The constable chased after him but the fella disappeared into the crowd by the gatehouse."

Ten the night before. Durham could be anywhere by now. If it had been Durham at all. Still, a cold trail was better than no trail at all. "Thank you, Sergeant. I'll visit the encampment myself."

"I wouldn't go alone, sir."

Langton turned back to the high desk. "Why not?"

"It's an unruly place, that encampment. They don't like police or anyone from the Span Company going in there. Especially the closer they get to the bridge's opening. You might want to take a guide in with you."

"A guide?" Langton said, smiling. "This is Liverpool, not Africa."

The sergeant blushed slightly. "Even so, sir, I'd advise it. I drink with a bloke from the Corporation who knows his way around the camp. They don't mind him so much, sir, seeing as how the Corpy helps with food and shelter."

Langton hesitated. "Can your friend take me over this morning?"

"I'll send a lad to ask him, sir," the desk sergeant said, already waving over one of the yawning office boys.

Upstairs, in his office, Langton wondered about the encampment. As far as he knew, it had started as a few tents and rough shelters to hold the families of laborers working on the Span, men who might be away for weeks at a time as the Span stretched across the Atlantic. The camp had grown as the Span grew. How had it become such a thorn in the Span Company's side, and a place where policemen feared to patrol? Perhaps the man from the Corporation, Liverpool's city council, would know.

Langton had almost finished adding Redfers's details to the case file when he heard a hesitant knocking at the door. "Come in."

A constable slid into the room, his helmet under his arm. He stood straight and looked past Langton, to the view of Victoria Street. "Inspector."

Langton struggled to remember the man's face. He'd seen so many people over the past few days. "You're . . ."

"Constable Eames, sir. I was at Hamlet Street. The dead burglar."

"I remember. How is Mrs. Grizedale?"

Eames blushed. "I have to tell you, sir . . . I mean, I have to say . . ."

"Go on, man."

"Well, you asked me to look after the two women, sir, this Mrs. Grizedale and her maid."

Langton's heart jumped. "And?"

"I hailed a hansom, sir, and went along with the two women. The maid told the driver to take us to Toxteth, Upper Parliament Street. I was sitting beside her and noticed how she kept looking back through the window. Then, as we got to Canning Place, she dug her claws into my arm and swore someone was following us. I told the cab to stop, got out, and—"

"They drove on without you."

Constable Eames looked at the floor. "They did, sir."

Langton smiled with relief. He'd expected to hear much worse from the constable. "I don't suppose you took a note of the cab's number."

"I'm sorry, sir. What with all the excitement, the dead man and everything . . . I remember what company it was, sir: Tate and Sampson."

The largest cab company in the city. "Leave it with me, Eames."

"I'm sorry for letting you down, sir."

"You did right to tell me."

Alone again, Langton leaned back and rubbed his eyes. He hadn't returned home until after four in the morning. Three hours' fitful dozing had left him more exhausted than before. As he'd shaved, he'd seen Sarah's medicines in the cabinet: morphine, opiates, tinctures, preparations. And a small brown glass bottle of white pills. Benzedrine, for Sarah's failing energy.

Tempted to take one, Langton had even opened the bottle. He worried that once he started, he'd never stop. Coffee seemed a less harmful choice. He'd pocketed the pills just in case.

Now, after sending Harry for a flask of coffee, he added the constable's comments to the file. He didn't panic about Mrs. Grizedale and Meera; the maid had simply outfoxed Constable Eames since she obviously didn't trust anybody at the moment. Perhaps that was wise.

Sipping coffee, Langton tried to remember what Meera had said the night before, something about going to her family. Where could she have taken Mrs. Grizedale? Hopefully somewhere beyond the reach of the man who'd sent the killer. Was that same man Doktor Glass?

Another knock at the door, this time a small, wiry man in a faded brown suit and derby hat. "Inspector Langton? The name's Dowden, sir, Herbert Dowden, from the Corporation. Ted said you needed someone to show you around the camp."

Ted must be the desk sergeant. Langton shook the man's hand. "Thank you for coming over, Mr. Dowden. I hope I haven't interrupted your work."

"Glad to get out of the office, sir, and into the fresh air. Shall we go over there now?"

Langton grabbed his Ulster coat and went to lock away the case file. Inside his coat pocket, the angular bulk of his force-issue Webley revolver, which he'd taken from his bedside cabinet. As he and Dowden took Victoria Street and then Dale Street toward the Pier Head, Langton said, "I'm surprised that I should need a guide, Mr. Dowden."

"Oh, I think it's wise, sir. They've taken against the police, just as they took against the Span Company."

"Who exactly are 'they'?"

Dowden waited until a tram had trundled past, hissing sparks. "There's a fair mix of people now, sir. Started out with a few families, wives and children of the men building the bridge. Navvies, masons, metalworkers, drillers, carpenters; the Company needed them all, and more besides."

As Dale Street became Water Street, the Span emerged from between the buildings like a mountain suddenly appearing between foothills. The rising sun coated the towers and steel cables with gold.

Dowden continued, "She's a hungry beast, that Span. A lot of the men that worked on her never came back home. The families they left behind felt badly done to: no compensation from the Company, nothing from the government. So they stayed put. The camp grew and grew."

Langton could see the encampment now as he and Dowden reached the foot of Water Street. Across four wide lanes of traffic, past the pillars and girders of the elevated electric railway—the so-called dockers' umbrella—lay the camp's fringes. Tents, many of them ex-military sand-colored cotton, clustered around smoking fires. A rough barricade of recycled wood, metal, and masonry marked the boundary between the temporary shelters and the respectable world outside.

"If you don't mind, Inspector, we'll walk along the front toward the Pier Head," Dowden said, looking for a break in the traffic. "These tents belong to the new folks, the ones just arrived. The old sections are the most important. That's where the decisions get made."

Dowden spoke as if the camp existed as an entity in its own right, a city within a city. And the structures behind the barricade, not to say the barricade itself, became more solid, more permanent as Langton and Dowden approached the Pier Head: Wooden shanties replaced tents; cabins of reclaimed driftwood were covered with patchwork tar-paper roofs; even bricks and chiseled blocks of sandstone and granite supported makeshift buildings.

Behind the barricades, burly men with cudgels at their waists patrolled back and forth. Watching. Waiting.

The shantytown camp stood to Langton's right. To his left, the incomplete shell of the Liver Guaranty Building, a smaller version of a Chicago newspaper office and already a recognizable monument. Steam cranes hauled granite, brick, and steel a hundred feet into the air to the waiting men working so precariously above.

"They reckon half of the Liver Building ended up as walls and roofs in the camp," Dowden said. "They should have finished months ago."

Langton had never before realized the full extent of the "temporary" camp. It stretched from Prince's Dock, to the north, all the way along the Mersey's banks to the Pier Head and farther south, all along George's Parade and the Chester Basin, almost to the office of the Span Company. To the west, it seemed to wash up against the foundations of the Span's massive first tower. It filled the stinking wasteland between the river's high-tide mark and the busy streets. Tram cars and steam buses wheeled around their terminus yards from the barricades.

Opposite the fine buildings of the Customs House and the Mersey Docks and Harbor Board, the barricades bent inward to form a rough

entrance complete with gatehouse. Concrete blocks, set in a complicated pattern and separated by movable iron railings like portcullises,
allowed in carts and pedestrians under the scrutiny of gatekeepers.

Here, the immense curving roadway of the Span's entrance ramp
swept above the camp and threw the gatehouse and half of the cabins
below into shadow. Langton looked up at the suspended deck of concrete and steel less than a hundred feet above him; it seemed too
solid, too massive to remain up there. Logic demanded that gravity
pull it to the ground. But engineering defied both gravity and Langton's eyes; the graceful arc swept up from the Span Company's concourse and merged with the stone tower. Pigeons and gulls wheeled
about the undersides, raucous specks of grey and white against the
stone and steel.

And the itinerant camp had erupted beneath this great feat of
engineering. "Why doesn't the Span Company simply get rid of them?"

Dowden stopped near one of the lunch wagons next to the tram
stops. "You've asked a good one there, Inspector. For one thing, the
land they're on is mostly derelict or common land, or nobody's sure
who owns it. For another, a lot of the families had loved ones who died
on the Span; it wouldn't look too good for the Company if they perse-
cuted them, too. It'd take the shine off the Ninth Wonder of the Industrial World."

Remembering his meeting with Lord Salisbury, Langton understood. The Company wanted to avoid bad publicity; they didn't want
to alarm their investors or the general public. At least not until the
Span opened. "And what happens after the inauguration?"

Dowden stared out across the camp. "I give the poor buggers two,
three weeks. Then the Company will send in the troops. Come back
then and you'll see nothing here but rubble and blood."

That reminded Langton too much of the Transvaal, where the
scorched-earth policy had been just that. Villages and farms reduced
to embers. Foundations jutting from the black soil like broken teeth.
Smoke and rubble and blood.

"Are you all right, Inspector?"

"Just a little tired, Mr. Dowden."

Dowden led him to the gatehouse, a rough cabin of wood set beside the concrete blocks. A squat, red-bearded man moved away from the group of guards manning the gate. "Mr. Dowden."

"Mr. Lloyd. You're well, I trust?"

"As can be expected." Lloyd looked Langton up and down. "I wouldn't have thought to see you keeping company with coppers, Mr. Dowden. Disappointed, I am. Fair disappointed."

"This is Inspector Langton," Dowden said. "He's looking for a man wanted for murder. You've heard of that fella with his face missing?"

"I have." Lloyd didn't change his expression, the same hard, set features as the guards watching the exchange.

"I've no interest in the workings of the camp, Mr. Lloyd," Langton said. "I'm after one man and one man only. If he isn't here, someone might remember him."

"We don't like talking to the police. Almost as bad as the Span bastards."

"I need your help, Mr. Lloyd. Three men are dead. I don't want any more on my conscience."

Lloyd thought for a moment. He looked at Dowden, back to the guards, then told Langton, "Wait here."

As the man disappeared into the gatehouse, Langton wondered what Purcell or Major Fallows would expect him to do. Probably to burst into the camp with a squad of mounted police. Bash some skulls; break a few bones. And learn exactly nothing. Violence was seldom the best answer although often the first resort.

A booming echoed down as the ramp above him reverberated, sending echoes like distant thunder.

"One of their electric trains," Dowden said. "Imagine what it'll be like when the Company's sending out one every fifteen minutes, fully loaded instead of empty."

Lloyd appeared from the gatehouse. "I had a word with the committee and if Mr. Dowden vouches for you, you're to come in. But I'll be by your side. Agreed?"

"Agreed, Mr. Lloyd." Langton followed Lloyd and Dowden through the zigzag gates of concrete and iron. As he passed the gang of guards, one of them spat onto the ground a few inches from Langton's boots. He ignored the taunt and walked on, scanning the face of every man.

The camp's entrance opened up into a main central street running north–south. Here stood buildings of wood and brick, snug with glass windows and smoking chimneys. Ragged children ran splashing through the mud, their bare feet cracking the ice at the edges of puddles. Women wrapped in shawls watched from doorways or windows. Loafing men leaned against the jury-rigged walls.

It reminded Langton of the old slums in Bootle and Wavertree: families packed together, compressed into a small space, rife with the smells of cooking, laundry, and coal smoke. But whereas the old brick-built slums were a maze of narrow alleys, fetid lanes, and leaning buildings, this camp lay open and horizontal, and perhaps slightly cleaner. Almost as if planned.

"So, this man you're after," Lloyd said.

Langton gave a brief description of Durham. Lloyd called over some of the watching men and gave them instructions. As they strode off in different directions, Lloyd said, "They'll ask around, find out if anyone's seen him. If he has friends in the camp they're not likely to admit he's here."

"I understand," Langton said, already wondering if he'd wasted his time. "Durham worked as a guard for the Span Company—he wouldn't be welcome here, would he?"

When Lloyd didn't answer, Dowden said, "The people here have to get by, Inspector. Even the young comb the banks of the Mersey, every one of them a little *ragazzi* mudlark. The adults get to know people, friends of friends you might say, and sometimes the odd bit of cargo might slip out of the docks unnoticed."

Langton understood. Some of the security guards, as badly paid as the dockers, might look the other way or even supply "unnoticed cargo" themselves.

"The Corporation does what it can to help," Dowden said. "We donate food; we try to supply clean water stand pipes and even basic sewer facilities. We can only do so much."

"Tell him why," Lloyd said, then offered the answer himself: "The Span Company fights everyone who tries to help us. Even the charities. If they had their way, we'd have no water, no coal, no food, nothing. We'd be sitting here rotting in our own filth."

Langton could understand the Span's attitude even if he didn't agree with it. They wanted the camp closed down. He imagined Lord Salisbury looking down from that fine office and seeing this rash of humanity like a blemish on a fine painting.

"This here's the oldest part of the camp: Bell Lane," Lloyd said, pointing left down a wide alley. "The Caisson Widows."

Beyond a rough painted sign fixed to a wall, Langton saw neat houses of wood, tar, and glass. "Caisson Widows?"

"They were the first," Dowden said. "Their husbands worked on the most dangerous part of the construction: sinking the towers' foundations."

"Imagine it," Lloyd said, skirting a wide scummy puddle. "One thousand and twenty-four towers between here and New York. And for every tower, at least three men dead. At least."

"What happened?"

Lloyd explained how teams of men plummeted down to the seabed inside immense caissons of wood and steel, like bells a hundred feet across. Above them, the support ships pumped down compressed air to keep out the seawater and allow the men to breathe.

"Hard men, they were," Lloyd said. "I couldn't do it: hundreds of yards down, with your blood pounding in your ears, hardly able to take a breath. Half in darkness, with only a few electric lights lit. And you're digging and digging, with the cold sea up to your waist.

"And sometimes the sea would break in; either the pumps would fail or the caisson would tip to one side. Or strange sicknesses would get them; I've heard stories of men's hearts exploding on the way back up to the surface, of blood running from eyes and ears. Or dying days or weeks later, after cramps and seizures that bent them double."

Lloyd paused and looked back at Bell Lane. "The Company said it wasn't their fault. Nothing to do with them. The widows got no compensation. Some of them even had to pay for the bodies to be brought back. That's why they never left here. To shame the Company."

From what he'd seen and read, Langton doubted that the Span Company suffered much from shame or guilt. Bad publicity, yes; adverse news that might affect shareholders or public confidence, certainly. Not shame.

Even as he thought this, and as he listened to Lloyd's explanation, Langton searched the faces of the men around him. Some of the men did resemble the fugitive security guard, but Durham had no doubt moved on. His trail had cooled.

A quick shower of hail sent the children cowering into doorways or under eaves. Langton joined Lloyd and Dowden under the tilting porch of a house where a piebald dog watched them from the open door. A man ran along the side of the muddy street, holding his cap on with one hand while the other gathered his sodden jacket closed. He saw Lloyd, veered toward him, and whispered in his ear.

"Any luck?" Langton asked.

Lloyd sent the man away and turned to Langton. "Nothing yet. We get hundreds of new people every week. Mostly steerage."

Before Langton could ask, Dowden said, "Families waiting to emigrate to America. If they can't get on the boats, they hope to buy fourth-class steerage on the trains."

Hope. The foundation of the entire camp, Langton realized. The Caisson Widows and their fractured families hoped for compensation or apology; the newcomers wanted a better life. Langton looked across the muddy, potholed street, through the curtains of hail, and wondered if any of the inhabitants' hopes would ever be fulfilled.

He focused on a window. A face watching him through the grime, wide-eyed with surprise.

Meera.

Langton took a step forward, then stopped.

"What is it, Inspector?" Dowden said. "You've spotted him?"

Langton saw the face pull away from the window. "No. It was nothing. Shall we go on?"

"We'll try the Bull and Run," Lloyd said, testing the lessening hail with one outstretched hand.

"Pardon me?"

"It's their pub," Dowden said, smiling. "They named it after the Company."

"Aye, 'cos that's all we get from them," Lloyd said. "Bullshit and the runalong."

As he followed Lloyd and Dowden along a side alley, Langton wondered why Meera had brought Mrs. Grizedale to the camp. Did she have family here waiting to emigrate? Obviously she thought it safe. Either way, he didn't want to cause them any further trouble or draw attention to them.

A vast groaning and creaking made Langton stop and look up. The complaining echoes of metal under stress sounded like a beast in pain. Langton stared at the underside of the ramp, sure it was about to fall and already bracing his body for the impact.

Dowden touched his arm and said, "She's just settling on her haunches, Inspector."

Lloyd said, "It's worse when the bridge starts singing."

"Singing?"

"Oh, aye." Lloyd shielded his eyes and looked upriver. "When the wind comes down the Mersey and hits the Span just right, the whole thing starts wailing and groaning. Restless, she is."

Langton wondered why men always called large vessels or structures *she*; perhaps it made them think they could control them more easily.

"See those wires," Lloyd continued, pointing up to the vertical steel cables linking the road and rail deck to the curving support pipes. "Look like the strings of a harp, don't they? Sounds like one too, sometimes."

The Span's strange "song" accompanied them to the door of the pub, where a surprisingly ornate painted sign swung over the door. Inside, a fug of smoke, coal, and tobacco gripped Langton's throat. Behind the counter, a thick-armed barmaid in a red shawl smoked a clay pipe. A pyramid of barrels faced a stove that looked as though it had started life as a ship's boiler, and a horseshoe of morose men sat facing the flames, clay mugs clasped in their hands. They made room for Lloyd and his charges.

Langton warmed himself and accepted a mug of warm ale tasting of cloves. He wondered where the beer barrels had come from. Probably best not to ask. Eyes heavy, he let the heat settle through him as Lloyd and Dowden discussed life in the camp. He sat up when he heard them speak of ghosts.

"It's just superstition," Lloyd said, signaling for more ale. "You pack enough people into a space small as this camp, you're bound to get rumors and strange talk. Bound to."

Dowden shook his head. "I don't know, Mr. Lloyd. I wonder if there might be something behind the stories."

"What stories?" Langton asked, leaning closer.

Lloyd swapped an empty mug for a full one from the barmaid's tray. "Fantasies, no more. Too many folk with too much time on their hands and too many hopes."

Langton turned to Dowden, who said, "Some claim to have seen lights around the Span. Like mist or slow steam, but colored yellow, gold, red, or orange. And they reckon they've heard children singing in the cables, and crying."

Lloyd shook his head and smiled. "Oh, Mr. Dowden, Mr. Dowden. You've been listening to fancies, tales spun by people a little empty in the head, or by those who see what they wants to. They think the lights

are the spirits of their dead husbands come back to see them. They're
nothing like that."

"So the lights do exist?" Langton said.

Lloyd reconsidered his words. "Well, you see a glimmer or two
some nights, I'll grant you that. It'll be no more than marsh gas or dust
from the uranium docks."

"I'm not so sure," Dowden said. "I've no wish to gainsay you, Mr.
Lloyd, but my mother's mother was a wise woman back in Donegal and
I wonder sometimes if I see a little more than I should. There's an air
to this camp; a feeling of things a little out of kilter."

Lloyd glanced at Langton, then looked at Dowden as if seeing the
Corporation man for the first time. Before he could say anything, the
door burst open in a blast of icy air. A gaunt man rushed up to Lloyd
and spoke in a hoarse whisper.

"We might have your man, Langton," Lloyd said, downing his pint
and making for the door. "Bob here reckons there's a newcomer over
by the tower shanties that fits your account."

"You stay here, Mr. Dowden," Langton said, rising. "I thank you for
your help but I don't want you harmed if this is the man I'm looking
for. He's too keen to use his revolver."

Dowden plucked at Langton's sleeve. He checked that Lloyd was
out of hearing before he said, "One thing, Inspector. This talk of lights
and voices in the night; it's not the only strange occurrence."

Langton hesitated, torn between wanting to follow Lloyd and wanting to hear Dowden. "Go on."

"People disappear," Dowden said. "The young, the old, even full-
grown men. Some say that gangs come for them in dead of night. Most
won't talk about it, but—"

From outside, Lloyd called out, "Langton."

"I'd like to hear more," Langton said. "Later?"

Dowden nodded.

Langton left Dowden in the pub and followed Lloyd down the

alley, heading west. Water ran down the middle of the muddy track as if drawn to the river glimpsed between leaning shacks; the surface of the Mersey looked like hammered pewter. On either side of Langton, the poorer shacks leaned at disjointed angles, propping one another up like wooden drunks. Wan faces looked out from glassless windows.

Langton checked the comforting weight of the Webley in his pocket. He didn't want to use it, not with so many people packed tight. In truth, he'd fired a weapon only three times since returning from Africa, but Durham seemed to have no compunction about using his.

"Another old section," Lloyd said, breathless. "Almost as old as the Caisson Widows' cabins."

The ground dropped away as it neared the high-tide mark. The original quay's sandstone bank, where once boats had docked, fell away to an expanse of foul silt. Here, a rough framework of embedded timbers reached out across the void; lashed together with whatever the camp could scavenge, the precarious roadway connected the shore with the first of the Span's towers, that immense column jutting from the river. Each stone block of the tower looked larger than a tram.

"We thought the Company wouldn't dare touch us if we clung onto the tower," Lloyd said. "But it isn't the favorite place to stay."

Langton could understand why; the stench of the river drove straight up through the open timbers. As he walked along the shifting, creaking platform, Langton looked back to shore; a dozen pipes jutted from the bank and spewed sewage and bloodred industrial waste into the water. The reek caught the back of his throat and made him gag. How could anyone live here?

But they did. As he strode after Lloyd, Langton heard babies crying from within the homes built onto and into the framework. Some of the hovels were no more than open wooden boxes nailed to the timbers, while others had doors, windows, chimneys. And the quarters continued right up to the very stonework of the Span tower itself. Up close, the scale of the bridge overwhelmed Langton. Despite logic, he couldn't escape the certainty it would sink down and crush him. He could almost feel the weight and mass of that thundering concrete and steel above his head.

Bob halted and pointed to a shack perched half on the framework, half over the water. "Mrs. Naylor's place, boss. The bloke came over yesterday."

"Stay back," Langton said. "If it is Durham, he's dangerous."

"You're welcome to him," Lloyd said. "Only remember that—"

The rough plank door to the shack swung open. Langton pushed Lloyd back and reached for the Webley. Instead of Durham, a ragged woman emerged from the shack and emptied a basin of dirty water over the side. Only as she turned to go back inside did she spot Langton. She yelled once.

Langton crossed the distance in seconds. He shielded the woman and looked around the edge of the door. Bunk beds, no more than planks covered with patched blankets. A woodstove perched on bricks. A wriggling baby, its crib an old drawer. And next to the fire, a man's muddied jacket that could have been Durham's.

The wind blew the trailing edges of a dirty curtain through the hole that passed for a window. Langton hesitated before leaning out. The cold river churned and surged fifty feet below him. As he turned to question the woman, Langton heard the clatter of boots on wood; when he ran from the shack he saw Lloyd and Bob but no Durham. Still, the sound of boots on wood, as if someone ran along the length of the framework.

"What's underneath us?" Langton asked.

"Why, the timber struts of this here platform," Lloyd said, "with planks running the whole length, unless they've ripped them up for firewood. Wait, man."

Langton had already climbed out over the edge. He hung there for a moment. His hands clutched the splintered wood. Between his swaying feet, the sheer drop to the cold water so far below.

He swung his body like a pendulum until his legs twined about the nearest strut. He let go above and clung to the structure. Like a bridge built by a drunken carpenter, the underside of the platform stretched on either side of him in a jigsaw of mismatched timbers. He ignored the stench from the encrusted pigeon droppings and ducked inside the platform. Disturbed birds flailed and shrieked.

Just as Lloyd had said, a collection of planks ran beneath the bowed underside. Langton batted away the panicking birds and saw the back of a man, crouched running. "Durham. Stop!"

The figure didn't even look back. Langton sprinted after him, keeping his head down to avoid the crossbeams and jagged nails. He jumped from plank to plank, skidding on the guano.

Then, as Durham reached the end of the platform, the fugitive slipped; an unsecured plank spun away and hit the water with a silent splash, leaving Durham clinging to a crossbeam.

That slowed Langton. He looked to see if the next plank beneath his feet looked secure or loose. "Durham, wait. You'll never make it."

Durham ignored him and ran on, then seemed to fall again before he caught himself. He clambered back onto a beam and jumped across a gap. Another few yards and he'd reach the sandstone bank.

Langton raised his Webley. He sighted on Durham and pulled the hammer back, the trigger cold and slippery under his finger. "Durham. I'll fire. Durham!"

The man square in the Webley's sight didn't stop. He reached the sandstone wall of the riverbank and started to climb it.

Langton swore and eased the hammer down. Even though Durham had fired on him, he couldn't shoot him down like a dog. Instead, he sprinted after him and jumped over the gap left by the fallen plank. He reached the sandstone bank just as Durham clambered up its face not ten yards away. Langton followed him, clinging to the slimy sandstone.

Voices from above as Lloyd and a group of men lowered a rope down the bank.

Durham looked up, then back to Langton. His unwashed, unshaven face contorted with pain or anger, or both. He started to move across the face of the rock like a mountain climber following a seam.

Langton wanted to yell at him, but he needed to concentrate on every move. He tried to find ledges for his boots, crevices or holes for his hands. He pressed his face into rock that stank of sewage. And it seemed that Durham was aiming for one of those sewage pipes nearby; he angled up until the plume of brown water arced out less than a yard away.

Where could he go? Surely he couldn't climb up a sewer pipe in full spate?

As Langton risked calling out, Durham disappeared. Langton stared at the plume of sewage, then down at the water below. Durham hadn't fallen. So where had he gone?

Trying to search the spot, Langton leaned out too far. He lost his balance and scrabbled at the rock. His boots skidded and lost purchase. He began to fall. The rope appeared in front of his eyes like a mirage; he clung to it and flinched as the weight of his falling body dragged his hands down the splintered hemp. The burning became cold, raw pain. His blood smeared the rope.

Lloyd and the others dragged Langton up the face of the bank. Despite the pain, despite his body slamming into the riverbank's uneven surface, Langton stretched out and searched the plume of sewage. And he saw, beneath the gushing jet, a tunnel big enough to swallow a man. From the tunnel's mouth scuttled a disturbed colony of cockroaches unused to daylight, with almost translucent carapaces.

The edge of the bank drew near. Langton felt himself pulled over the top and onto the cobbles. He lay gasping at Lloyd's feet. Every muscle screamed out. He stared at his hands, at the stiff hemp fibers embedded in his bloody palms.

"You trying to kill yourself?" Lloyd said. "Suicide, that was."

As soon as Langton got his breath back, he said, "Thank you."

"Yes, well. I suppose." Lloyd waved away the throng of onlookers, saying, "Get on with you, go on. Leave the man alone."

Langton got to his feet and looked over the edge. "He got away. He climbed into a tunnel down there."

Lloyd joined him and spat over the side. "Good luck to him, then. I wouldn't fancy it."

"Where might it lead?"

"Who knows? Riddled with old workings and tunnels, the riverbank is. Shafts go up, down, across, and inland. He could come out anywhere. If he survives."

Nine

I T DIDN'T MATTER how hard Langton had braced himself, how much he expected it; the pain cut through his palms like scalding blades. As his hands curled into reflexive fists, he winced and bit back the curse that came to his lips.

"I did warn you," Nurse Milne said. "Come on—let me see those hands."

Like a reluctant child, Langton forced his hands open. The raw flesh on his palms, scoured by the hemp rope, bore stripes of purple iodine. He looked away as Nurse Milne brought the pungent swab closer. She leaned over and brushed his wounds with delicate movements. This time around, the pain receded a little, not as though every nerve ending screamed.

Nurse Milne sealed the brown bottle and dropped the dirty swab into a bin. "All done. Just leave them there to dry."

"Thank you."

Langton sat at an old scavenged school desk, with the back of his forearms and his knuckles flat against the scrubbed wood. The reek of disinfecting iodine drifted through the small room and mixed with Nurse Milne's odors of hospital carbolic and sweat.

Mr. Lloyd had guided Langton to this small sick bay, a room set back off the shanty camp's main street. With its canvas stretcher leaning against the wall, its scavenged couch and table, its smells of mud and chemicals, it reminded Langton of Transvaal dressing stations. The nurses out there had used whatever they could find, too.

Nurse Milne reminded Langton more of Sister Wright. She wore the same uniform as the Infirmary staff: dark blue tunic, white apron, white straps crisscrossing her broad back. She even hung the same type of inverted watch at her breast, next to a silver pin with an ornate head.

Langton tried to remember where he'd seen that pin before. "Nurse, do you work at the Infirmary?"

She turned from washing her hands in the porcelain basin. "Why, yes I do."

"As well as here at the camp?"

"Oh, this is voluntary. Quite a number of us give a few hours each week."

Seeing her hide a yawn, Langton said, "You come here after your shift?"

"When we can." She checked the time on her apron watch. "Soon be home in bed, God willing."

Again, the pin glinted in the light of the oil lamp. The head, smaller than a sixpence, looked like a convoluted letter *A*.

"May I ask what that means?"

"This? It's from the Guild," Nurse Milne said, touching the pin and blushing.

"The Guild?"

"Of Asclepiadae. I joined it in nursing school. We try to donate some of our free time and experience to the needy, to people who can't afford doctors or hospitals. Some don't even like coming to the Infirmary. We do what we can."

Langton understood. The Guild must be one of the many charitable organizations set up by philanthropists or religious groups. In the rush of industrial progress and the expansion of the empire and trade, little thought was given to the poor. Bodies like the Guild helped fill the void, despite the protestations from Reverend Malthus, who said that poverty, disease, and death were all part of the Divine Plan.

Langton remembered where he'd seen that type of pin before. "Tell me, does Sister Wright visit the camp?"

"She's one of our regulars," Nurse Milne said, smiling. "She's down here three, four times a week. Considering how hard she works at the Infirmary every day, I don't know how she does it. The people here swear by her."

Langton hesitated, then took a gamble. "I suppose the Infirmary doctors are much too busy to help . . . I mean, people like Professor Caldwell Chivers couldn't involve themselves with something like the camp, could they?"

"You'd think so." Nurse Milne's smile widened, and she looked behind her as though checking for eavesdroppers. "I shouldn't tell you this—the Infirmary Board wouldn't like it—but the Professor has been known to take on a case or two. Only the most serious, mind you. I think he does it as a favor to Sister Wright."

With this, she took Langton's hands in her own and held them up to the light. "Just about dry. We'll soon have you on your way."

As she wound clean cotton bandages around his hands, Langton wondered how her news fitted in with the other facts. So Sister Wright and the Professor helped out at the camp; it was not a crime. Quite the opposite.

"There you are, Inspector. All done." Nurse Milne smiled again, rumpling her pale, tired features. She brushed escaping blond hair back beneath her cap, then reached out her thumb and pulled down the skin under Langton's eyes. "You should eat more, Inspector. And sleep. I've seen healthier people here in the camp."

"I've been a little . . . busy, lately."

"That's no excuse," she said, but she still smiled. "You must take care of yourself. We have a duty to God."

What could he tell her? That his life meant nothing? That each day's struggle seemed harder than the day before? Instead, he returned her smile. "Thank you. I appreciate the advice."

As he reached for the door, he asked, "Have you ever seen anyone in the camp with small burns under each ear?"

Nurse Milne thought for a moment. "I can't remember exactly when, but I'm sure I have. Small, square burns about this big?"

"That's it. Can you remember what happened to them? Did you treat them?"

"Well, no, I wouldn't have. By the time I reached them, a young girl and a boy, I think, it was already too late."

OUTSIDE, ON THE main street, Langton found Lloyd leaning under an eave and smoking a long-stemmed clay pipe. "Nurse sorted you out all right?"

"She did." Langton held up his bandaged hands as proof.

Lloyd nodded. "She's a good sort. Come on, I'll walk you back to the gate."

"Where's Mr. Dowden?"

"Had to go back to the Corpy."

An uneven layer of white hail hid the muddy street, although the grey clouds overhead had started to rip apart, exposing blue sky between ragged edges. Langton's footsteps crunched. He buried his tingling hands in his pockets and said, "I need to ask a favor, Mr. Lloyd: Will you and your men keep an eye out for Durham?"

"Your man in the tunnel? I don't know." Lloyd hawked and spat on the cold ground. "I don't like murder, but I don't much like helping the coppers neither. Nothing personal, mind; you don't seem like the worst of them."

Langton smiled.

As they stopped where the main street met the entrance gate, Langton said, "I don't know if Durham killed Kepler and cut off his face, but if he didn't, he knows who did. I'm sure of it. Just as I'm sure there's more to the deaths than mere coincidence."

Lloyd glanced at the watching guards. "I'd be surprised if he comes out of them tunnels. A rats' warren, they are; nobody knows where they lead. He's probably lying at the bottom of some shaft or sluice. Or under the river."

"Maybe so. But if he has killed—perhaps more than once—there's a chance that the people inside this camp might be in danger."

Lloyd nodded. "We'll watch out for him."

Langton stuck out his hand; after a moment's hesitation, Lloyd shook it. As he walked back along the front of the Pier Head, past the incomplete Liver Guaranty Building, Langton wondered if Durham still struggled along tunnels somewhere below those very same cobbles. Dark, cold, slimy, silent save for the scurrying of rats and cockroaches. Langton shuddered.

Perhaps he should save his sympathy. If Durham had nothing to do with Kepler's murder, why did he flee? Langton didn't like the phrase *No smoke without fire,* but surely there must be some guilt or blame behind Durham's repeated escapes?

He could have another motive: fear. Fear of the same fate from the same murderer.

The deep thunder of an electric train made Langton look up at the elevated railway overhead, the dockers' umbrella. From where he stood, close to the Captain's Cabin tobacconist kiosk that seemed to grow out of a support pillar, he could also see the Span. How far the engineers had come; how quickly life changed. Then, as the train faded, the music of a military band drifted from the south.

"That'll be the Brigade of Guards over at the Span offices. Saw them marching up this morning."

Langton turned and saw the proprietor of the kiosk leaning from the hatchway framed by cigars, cigarettes, pipes, and glass jars of dark tobacco.

The old woman drew her shawl tighter and continued, "Going to be a fine sight and no mistake, all them fine uniforms, the horses with their leathers and brass shined up. Been serving more soldiers and officers in the past two days than I have all year. Demons for tobacco, they are. They'll look a treat for Her Majesty."

"I'm sure they will," Langton said, smiling and turning to go. Then he froze.

"Get you something, sir?"

In front of Langton, on the wall of the kiosk, stood an advertisement for Capstan Full Strength cigarettes. The salt air had eaten away some of the etched mirror background, but enough remained to show Langton the reflected view behind him. Hadn't he seen that man before? Squat, stocky, with black laborers' jacket and cloth cap pulled down tight. He stood at the iron stairs leading up to the railway ticket office, seemingly studying the posted timetable.

"Sir?"

"A pack of . . . Capstan, please."

"Caps it is, sir. One and six."

Langton fumbled in his pockets for money and dropped coins onto the counter. The woman saw his bandaged hands and glanced up at him, but didn't say anything other than, "And sixpence change, sir."

Sliding the unwanted pack of cigarettes into his pocket, Langton crossed the road to Water Street. He fought the urge to look back. Water Street led to bustling Dale Street, where shop windows offered fragments of reflections, pedestrians' faces reduced to shards. Langton pushed through the tide of people and stared at the windows' images.

There, in the angled bow window of a confectioner's shop, the reflection of the man in black coat and grey cloth cap. Langton stopped and looked at the cakes and sweets in the window; the man slowed, then merged with the press of bodies waiting at the tram stop. He seemed to disappear like a lizard slinking between rocks in the hot Transvaal sun.

Ahead lay the junction of Dale Street and Sir Thomas Street, then Victoria Street. Langton turned the corner and stepped back into a side door. With one hand on the Webley revolver, he waited. He watched the pedestrians streaming past. Was he overreacting? Plenty of men dressed like his supposed pursuer—it was almost a uniform— but Langton could have sworn he'd seen the man standing at the tram stop outside the camp gatehouse.

Five minutes became ten. Fifteen. Langton stepped out of the doorway. As he climbed the steps of headquarters, he wondered who might want him followed. Lloyd? Doktor Glass? Or had fatigue finally brought paranoia?

"Was Bert any help, Inspector?"

Langton looked around the lobby and saw the desk sergeant peering over the shoulders of constables gathered around the counter. "Bert? You mean Mr. Dowden. Yes, a great help, thank you."

Langton made for the stairs, then remembered his conversation with Dowden just before he'd left the Bull and Run. He'd spoken of people disappearing, of gangs coming for them in the night. "Sergeant, when next you see Mr. Dowden, will you tell him I'd like to speak to him again?"

Back in his office, Langton eased off his coat and slumped down in his seat. His hands throbbed. He tried adding the day's events to Kepler's case file, but the bandages made him clumsy. He gave up and slumped back in his chair, staring at the ceiling. His eyes closed.

He woke up at a knock on the door. "Come in."

Harry, the office boy, glanced at Langton's hands and said, "Chief would like to see you, sir. Been asking."

Using the closet's water basin and jug, Langton dabbed a wet flannel on his face. Again, he thought of the Benzedrine tablets. "Harry, fetch me a jug of coffee, would you?"

"Anything to eat, sir?"

Langton started to say no, then remembered Nurse Milne's advice. "Something light, Harry."

Upstairs, the secretary waved Langton through to the Chief Inspector's room, where Purcell sat at the wide desk. Major Fallows stood at the window, looking down on the Victoria Street traffic; his cigar sent writhing trails of blue smoke up to the ceiling to join the strata already waiting there.

"We need news, Langton," Purcell said. "The clock is ticking and you seem to be out of your office every time I visit."

With difficulty, Langton bit back the first comment that came to mind. Instead he gave Purcell and Fallows a brief résumé of recent events, from the murder of Redfers to the dead burglar at Mrs. Grizedale's house. When he related Durham's escape, he saw Fallows turn from the window.

"You let him escape a second time?" Fallows said.

"Not out of choice, Major."

"Surely this proves that Durham murdered this man Kepler?" Purcell said.

Langton hesitated. "Perhaps, sir."

"He flees every time you try to apprehend him. What more do you need?"

Proof, Langton said to himself. And aloud: "The motive troubles me. I cannot yet see why Durham would kill his partner, mutilate the body to guarantee publicity, then calmly return to work on the docks. Then there's the money we found at their lodgings, and the many telegrams they sent. They were part of something much larger."

The florid coloring left Purcell's face. "A Boer conspiracy?"

Before Langton could reply, Fallows said, "I wonder whether Inspector Langton is allowing himself to be distracted."

Langton waited. He longed to itch the burning palms of his hands.

Fallows continued, "Bearing in mind what I found in the case file, I can see that you actually have two separate cases here: Kepler with

Stoker Olsen, and now this Doctor Redfers. Where the dead burglar in Everton fits in is another issue, and probably incidental at that."

"I don't think it's quite that straightforward, Major," Langton said. "I believe they may be linked."

"How?" Purcell asked.

"They have certain characteristics in common." Langton really did not want to bring up the connection.

Fallows did it for him. "You mean the Jar Boys, Langton?"

Purcell straightened in his seat. "What have they to do with this?"

Now, Langton had no choice but to explain. "Certain marks were found on Kepler and Redfers. Expert opinion suggests these were made by an electrical procedure just before death."

"You make it sound almost scientific," Fallows said. "This is mere superstition from desperate families."

How could Langton argue? He'd seen the paraphernalia in Redfers's house, the transmitter, and the room that had recently held jars; he'd spoken with Forbes Paterson, with Mrs. Grizedale, with Professor Caldwell Chivers, and with Doctor Fry. "Superstition or not, Major, I believe there is a connection. That is why I'd like to send search teams down after Durham."

Purcell stared at him. "Have you any idea of what you're asking for? The cost alone would make me think twice, but with every man needed for the Queen's visit, there is no way—"

"Arrange it, Chief Inspector," Fallows said. When both Purcell and Langton looked at him, he continued, "This man Durham may pose a threat to Her Majesty. We must find him."

Purcell said, "But . . . the cost, Major."

Fallows waved that away. "Can you put a price on Her Majesty's life? Exactly. As for the manpower, you can use one of the underground search teams you put at my disposal. This is more important than checking the Span's foundations."

Purcell looked at Fallows, then Langton. "Very well. I'll arrange it myself. Mark my words, Langton: I will not have you wasting valuable police time."

The color had returned to Purcell's face as he spoke. "The Queen herself arrives in three days and you chase phantoms like some backward peasant just off the boat. You are to concentrate on Kepler and Durham—do you understand? No more ghosts or specters. This case owes nothing to the supernatural. Nothing, Langton. Remember that."

As Langton reached for the door, about to leave, Purcell added, "I thought you were ready to return to duty. Don't prove me wrong, or I might have to assign another inspector to this case. At the very least."

Langton strode past the secretary and down to his office. He paused at the landing and took deep breaths. Slowly his hands uncurled. He forced himself to look at the case from Purcell's perspective. The Jar Boys *did* sound ridiculous. Superstition. Fireside ghost stories. He couldn't really blame Purcell for being skeptical, even if the man's anger did seem an overreaction. Then again, the Queen's visit offered Purcell the greatest opportunity to advance his career. And also the opportunity for the most embarrassment.

"Inspector."

Langton looked up the staircase and saw Major Fallows descending.

"Inspector, I wanted to say . . ." Fallows waited until two clerks had walked past them. "I'm sorry to hear of your loss. Don't give my words the wrong meaning; when I talked of mere superstition—"

"I know, Major." Langton raised one bandaged hand. "You've no need to explain. I agree; it does look like superstition. Or madness. And perhaps I am allowing Sarah's . . . allowing what happened to influence me. Maybe Purcell should replace me."

Fallows shook his head. "I know of your record, and not just in the police force. I doubt that Purcell could find a more dedicated officer. Her Majesty's visit must take precedence. It will be difficult, but try to concentrate on finding Durham, for the sooner this man is captured, the better. Whether by your constables or my men is unimportant."

"Your men?"

"I brought with me from London a number of free agents," Fallows said. "They are concerned solely with Her Majesty's visit. I've assigned several of them to hunt for Durham. That's why I need you to inform me of any developments in the case as soon as possible."

Free agents. Langton wondered about the man who had followed him, or who he'd *thought* might be following him. "Major, how will we know who these men are?"

"You don't need to. They will not interfere with your investigation. Indeed, I'm sure they will help it."

Langton carried on alone toward his office. Why hadn't Fallows told him about these agents before? And why was he so keen to find Durham? Langton realized that Fallows occupied a delicate position between the Queen's staff, the Liverpool police, the Span Company, and his own superiors. So where did his real sympathies lie?

Seeing Harry coming out of another office, Langton said, "The coffee, Harry?"

"On your desk, sir, with some cheese sandwiches. If Sergeant Mc-Bride has left any for you."

Langton smiled and walked on, then called out, "Harry, who keeps details of government departments? Telephone numbers and the like."

"Miss Martin on the switchboard, sir. What can I get for you?"

"Information on the Home Office—some kind of directory if she has it."

As the office boy's heels clattered down the stairs, Langton pushed open his door. McBride, sandwich in hand, rose from a chair.

Langton waved him down. "Sit. What did you find?"

McBride chewed and swallowed, then said, "Quite a lot, sir, but I don't know if much of it is any good."

Langton poured out coffee from the flask and took a sandwich from the pile. He lifted a corner to reveal pungent orange cheese, then set the sandwich down. "Go on."

McBride wiped his hands and took out his notebook. "Firstly, sir,

Mrs. Dunne, the doctor's receptionist. She turned up for work same as usual this morning. Seemed very surprised at the doctor's murder but not that upset. Cold fish, that one. Anyway, seems that Doctor Redfers sent her home early the night before. He had a waiting room full of patients and he sent them home, too. You can imagine how happy they were at that. Half of them arrived this morning for their appointments and they were still hanging around the gates when I left. The constable is having a hell of a time moving them on."

Langton refilled his cup and asked, "Did Redfers tell Mrs. Dunne why he sent her home early?"

"No, sir, but she said he had a telephone call a few minutes before; she heard the bell ringing."

"We need to know who called him."

"I've got a man at the exchange," McBride said. "The operator is going through the records with him."

"Good. What next?"

"The neighbors, sir. The ones next door and the ones opposite across the park saw a wagon pull up around six. They didn't think anything much of it. Said that the doctor regularly had deliveries at odd times."

"Deliveries of what?"

McBride shrugged. "They didn't know, sir. Didn't much care. Seems like one of them streets where everyone keeps to themselves, or at least they say they do. But one of the kitchen maids next door, as she was doing the washing up, reckons she saw burly men carrying big jugs or bottles up from the basement."

Langton's heart jumped. "Bottles? Or jars?"

"Could have been jars, I suppose. I looked out from the window over her sink, and you can see a bit of the doctor's garden and the top of the basement steps. Even in daylight it wasn't much of a view, sir, but she reckons she heard them cursing after they dropped one."

Langton cursed himself, too. He should have checked the outside of the basement. Then a thought gripped him: That broken jar could have been Sarah's; she might be free. He saw McBride reach for a canvas sack stowed beneath the coatrack. "You searched the area?"

"I did, sir." McBride pushed the sandwiches and coffee to one side and laid out the contents of the sack. "Not much, is it?"

Curved fragments of thick brown clay. Glazed on both sides. One smooth lip bordered with green wax.

Almost afraid to touch the debris, Langton reached out and picked up a shard. From the curve of the base fragments, he guessed the container had been at least a foot in diameter. The same as the dust rings left on the empty shelves.

"What do you think he was up to, sir?" McBride asked. "Drugs or liquor? Haven't found any liquor still, though."

Instead of answering, Langton weighed the largest fragment in his hand. Nothing. No strange visions in his mind. No echoes of the dead and dying. No echoes of Sarah.

Had he really expected that to happen? After all, what were the chances of such a coincidence? He held only inert clay, dead splinters, but sharp enough to draw blood; he dabbed at his cut finger. "Anything else from Redfers's house?"

"The maid, Agnes, has moved out and gone back to her family in Chester. She asked if it was all right and I couldn't see any reason why not, sir."

Still inspecting the shards, Langton nodded his agreement. He could see the inside of the dead doctor's basement, with its rows of dusty shelves, its white tiled walls like some infirmary ward or theater. Clinical.

"I heard you ran into Durham, sir," McBride said, looking at Langton's hands.

"He eluded me again, Sergeant. He's resourceful, I have to give him that."

"I don't get it, sir."

Langton looked up.

"Why's he still here?" McBride said. "I mean, there are docks full of ships going all over the world. He could sign on any one of them, no questions asked. Why's he staying put?"

Langton had to agree. "Something is keeping him here. Some bond or commitment."

"A woman?"

Langton remembered the camp. "The woman who shielded Durham admitted that they knew each other but not to the point of any great romance, although she obviously liked him and could be lying. She said he had no visitors and seemed to be waiting for something. Or someone."

Both men fell silent. The sound of traffic drifted up from Victoria Street: horses' hooves, steam cars, the arc and whine of trams.

"Maybe it really is some kind of Boer conspiracy, sir," McBride said. "Maybe he's waiting for the Queen's visit. Him and Kepler might have had a bit of business planned."

Langton hoped not, but what else could Durham want? "Revenge."

"Sir?"

"Supposing Durham did not kill Kepler—he could be waiting to repay the murderer. That suggests he knows who the murderer is and cannot reach him, or he's waiting for us to unearth the man." Unbidden, the name of Doktor Glass appeared in Langton's mind.

McBride considered the theory. "Could be, sir."

It still didn't answer why the two men had signed up to the Span Company and what their intentions had been.

A knock at the door preceded Harry, who bore a thick, dog-eared ledger bound in blue, and a newspaper. "The Home Office directory, sir. Miss Martin wants it back soon as you've finished with it."

Langton passed the directory to McBride, saying, "Look for Major Fallows."

Then, to Harry, "Is the paper for me, too?"

"The sergeant on the front desk thought you'd want to see this, sir." Harry laid the local tabloid on the desk and backed away as if afraid it might combust.

Banner headlines across the front: *Faceless Corpse Case—More Murders*. And a subheading: *Police Baffled*.

The article continued with news of Stoker Olsen and Doctor Redfers, quoting liberally from a "confidential source" who stated the three deaths were part of a Boer plot against "Her Illustrious Majesty and the Engineering Marvel of the Transatlantic Span." The journalist knew about Kepler's disfigurement and his tattoos, as well as Redfers's money hidden away. The final sentence berated the police for not breaking up the plot and for allowing Kepler's accomplice, Durham, to escape.

Langton saw McBride and Harry staring at him, obviously waiting. Keeping his voice level, Langton told McBride, "Go to the newspaper offices on Old Hall Street and ask them how they found out all these details. They must have someone inside our office; only a few people knew about the tattoos and the money."

McBride made for the door. "What will the Chief Inspector and the major say when they read that?"

"I'll deal with them," Langton said, folding the newspaper very carefully. Despite his calm confidence, he had no idea what he'd say to Purcell and Fallows. He could imagine their reactions when they found out.

Harry stood at the door. "You need anything, sir?"

"You can get me the next edition of the paper. The evening issue, when it comes out."

Langton stowed the newspaper in his desk and turned around the Home Office directory that McBride had opened. Arranged alphabetically, and then by department and section, the directory listed every member of staff in the Home Office. Langton flicked through the pages.

No entry for Major Fallows. Nothing in the alphabetic section; nothing by department. So much for finding out who Fallows worked for. Then Langton found a name he recognized: Peter Doran. He remembered him as a big, bluff Irishman who'd worked his way up through the Liverpool police to become the liaison between the civilian police authority and the force. Promotion, the year before, had taken him to London.

Langton scribbled a telegram and searched the corridor for Harry, who ran off downstairs with the message. The office boy almost collided with someone coming up the stairs.

"Whoa, Harry."

"Sorry, Inspector."

Forbes Paterson shook his head as Harry clattered down the steps. "Keen, that boy of yours."

Langton smiled. "He dreams of solving a case all by himself."

"As do we all." Paterson approached Langton and said, "We must talk."

Langton led him into the office, closed the door, and waited.

Forbes Paterson didn't sit down; he paced behind the desk for a minute, then stared at Langton. "You're still searching for the Jar Boys? For Doktor Glass?"

Even with Purcell's warning clear in his memory, Langton said, "I am."

"Then I might have a proposition for you." Forbes Paterson took a deep breath before he said, "You wondered if we could set a trap for them. But a trap needs bait. It seems that the good Lord has provided us with exactly that."

Ten

As HE DRESSED at home in preparation for the reception at the Professor's house, Langton thought of Forbes Paterson, who had poured out his plan's details while pacing the floor of Langton's office like a bear in a cage.

It seemed that a woman had complained to the police, and her story had reached Paterson. The widowed woman, Mrs. Barker, reasonably well off and living in Wavertree with her close family, had a seventeen-year-old niece suffering from Bright's disease, a degenerative, terminal condition that caused immense suffering. The doctors could only ease the poor girl's pain while the family waited for the inevitable.

Then, late in the evening two days before, a man had visited Mrs. Barker. Well spoken, very smart, and polite, he came with a bizarre offer: to attach an apparatus to the fading niece's body to both ease her pain and save her soul. His explanations sounded persuasive and straightforward; he had "saved" many people in this way. The fee would be moderate.

The family, devout Catholics all, had thrown the man out of their house. The whole idea reeked of heresy. First thing the next day, Mrs. Barker had stormed around to her local police station, seething with anger and determined to report the man.

"Of course, we had to explain he'd committed no crime," Paterson had said. "We could only arrest him for assault if he laid hands on Mrs. Barker's poor niece."

Now, remembering the look of distaste on Paterson's face, Langton paused in dressing. He looked in the full-length mirror at his smart dinner suit, white silk waistcoat, and gaunt features. Nurse Milne was right; he did not look healthy. Not like Forbes Paterson with his stout frame and ruddy complexion. But those features had darkened with anger as Paterson talked of Mrs. Barker's dilemma.

"It sickened her," Paterson had said, "just as it sickens me. God knows how many poor families these men have swindled. Or worse. And they get away scot-free. That's when Mrs. Barker suggested a plan . . ."

Paterson swore that Mrs. Barker suggested entrapment, not he. She offered to contact the man, via the telephone number on the card he had left, and arrange for him to return with his apparatus. The police could wait close by or in the room itself, and arrest the man and his accomplices as they connected their machine.

Paterson didn't like it but he wanted to catch these men, and he knew that Langton wanted them, so he had agreed. And he wanted Langton there.

Langton glanced at the sheet of notepaper on the dresser. He had Mrs. Barker's address and had promised to meet Forbes Paterson there at midnight. The Jar Boys were due to arrive at one in the morning. And what would Langton do when he met them? Demand news of Sarah? Of Redfers? Or try to find the trail back to Doktor Glass?

That part of his work did not trouble him. No, he most feared meeting Mrs. Barker's dying niece. He looked around his bedroom. Not enough time had passed since he had sat on the side of that very bed, there, and held Sarah's hand while the drugs had struggled to do their work. He didn't know if he could trust himself. He felt like one of the Span's great cables wound too tight. Even braided steel snapped under enough strain.

Langton rested his head against the cool glass of the mirror. He had a job to do; he must concentrate. For Sarah.

He reached for his bow tie and tried to fasten it. Sarah had always helped him when they had to dress for functions or dinners. After minutes of fumbling with the white silk tie, Langton gave up. He slid Mrs. Barker's address into his pocket and swapped the Webley from his Ulster to his dress coat. Downstairs, he found Elsie tidying the sitting room.

"Let me, sir." She wiped her hands on her apron and reached up to Langton's neck for the bow tie. A few quick passes of her hands, then, "There we are, sir. You look very smart, if you don't mind me saying so."

"Why don't you take the rest of the evening off? I won't be back until late. Very late."

"Thank you, sir, but I'll wait in. Just in case anyone calls." Elsie made herself busy, plumping cushions and adjusting ornaments that didn't need adjusting. As if in passing, she asked, "Would Sergeant McBride be going with you this evening, sir?"

Langton paused at the doorway and smiled. "He is. In fact—"

The horse and carriage that Langton had heard drew up outside. The front door bell chimed. Langton stood aside as Elsie let in McBride, and said, "Sergeant, I'll be a minute or two. I left something upstairs."

It wasn't a complete lie; as well as giving McBride and Elsie a moment to themselves, Langton had remembered Redfers's diary. He transferred it from the pocket of his Ulster to the locked drawer of his bureau. He made plenty of noise coming down the stairs and found Elsie and McBride standing apart in the hall, both blushing like children. "Don't wait for me, Elsie. And make sure you lock up."

Outside, Langton found that a heavy, colloidal fog had descended. The vapor tasted of coal smoke and brine, with perhaps the hint of white flowers. The oil lamps on the hansom cab burned like inflamed eyes. Langton climbed up and waited until the cab had pulled away before he asked, "What happened at the newspaper?"

"No luck, sir," McBride said. "The editor wouldn't say where he got the article from. Wouldn't budge, no matter what I said. He swore he trusted the facts."

"Then it's someone on the inside." Langton stared out at darkness interspersed with white and yellow smears. "Someone who knew about Kepler's tattoos and what they meant; someone who knew about the money in Redfers's various accounts."

For a brief moment, Langton wondered about McBride, then scolded himself. He trusted his sergeant completely; the man had joined the police as a cadet at fourteen, and the force was his life.

"I've other news, sir," McBride said. "When I went back to the station I found a telegram from the Martin's Bank on Victoria Street, the one checking the serial numbers of the notes we found in Gloucester Road."

Kepler's and Durham's hidden funds. "They traced them?"

"Some of them, sir. The banks don't record what happens to pound notes, but they do with the fives and tens. Seems that the notes we found were issued in London seven months ago, part of a cash transfer—two thousand pounds—made to the paymaster general."

Langton stared at the indistinct figure of the sergeant. "Government money?"

"So it seems, sir."

Kepler and Durham had sent many telegrams to the Foreign and Commonwealth Office. Their money came from the government. The connection was obvious, but had they worked directly for the FCO or had they been paid mercenaries? Kepler's history would imply the latter, but Langton had known several Boers who had turned and become Queen's agents during the conflict. And some of them had turned back again to the Boer cause. Off the battlefield, away from straightforward combat between recognizable enemies, the fight became more complex, more convoluted.

If Durham did work for Her Majesty's government, why did he insist on fleeing?

The hatch in the cab ceiling opened and the driver called down, "Upper Parliament Street, sir."

Through the misted window, a constellation of blurred lights. Illumination poured from every window of the Professor's mansion. More lights decorated the iron railings and gates, giving the appearance of some enchanted festivities quite separate from everyday existence. Indeed, the mansion seemed almost to float in the darkness. As the cab threaded its way between the lines of carriages and cars lining the curved gravel drive, Langton heard a distant melody, violins and piano.

"Find what you can from the drivers and maids," Langton told McBride as the cab pulled up in front of the portico. "Be discreet but sound them out about any visits to Redfers, or about Kepler."

"Should be easy, sir, what with them being in the news. Should I wait for you?"

Langton paused, his hand on the cab door. He hadn't told McBride about Forbes Paterson and the trap in Wavertree. "No, you go home when you've found what you can. I won't expect you in the office early."

Even as he climbed the mansion steps and heard the cab's iron-shod wheels crunching gravel as it turned, Langton knew that McBride would probably be in the station before him the next morning. He looked up and saw a stout, balding butler in black tailcoat. The figure stood framed by the hallway's yellow light.

As Langton reached the threshold, the waiting butler bowed. "May I see your invitation, sir?"

"Sister Wright invited me."

"I see. Would you mind waiting a moment, sir?"

Langton gave up his coat and hat and waited in the hallway while the butler disappeared. Music spilled from open doors. A crystal electrolier scattered shards of blue-white light. The air, warmed by the latest central heating radiators, carried the odors of floral perfumes and cigar smoke. Two ladies in fine gowns, one of yellow, the other of cerise, came down the stairs giggling and whispering to each other; they nodded to Langton as they passed. He gave a little bow in return and hid the splinter of pain inside; the carefree young women couldn't know of the memories they had set free.

A door opened to reveal Professor Caldwell Chivers. "My dear Inspector. Welcome."

"I hope I'm not intruding."

"Not at all, sir, not at all." The Professor pumped Langton's hands and noticed the fresh bandage. "What's this? Nothing serious, I hope."

"Just a scrape." Langton followed the Professor down the hall. "You seem to have a full house."

"Indeed we have. I invited the most important members of Liverpool society here to celebrate the inauguration of the Span." The Professor smiled as he threw open the wide double doors and said, "Although my definition of importance might not correspond with my peers' opinions."

In the main drawing room, Langton saw perhaps thirty people milling among the dark furniture, admiring the modern art on the walls, chatting in clusters. The men in evening dress, the women in pastel gowns and shawls. Young, middle-aged, old.

"I'll introduce you to a few of my guests," the Professor said, guiding Langton by the arm. "I don't want to throw a host of names at you. Ah, this is Jefferson, one of our leading poets—you might have read his tribute to the Span. Jefferson, Inspector Langton of the Liverpool police."

A nod from a cadaverous man with a monocle.

"And this is MacIver, one of the chief engineers working on the Span."

A brief, knuckle-crunching handshake from a squat man with bristling red hair and side whiskers.

"And this is . . ."

Despite the Professor's promise, the faces and names came one after the other, a flurry of greetings and handshakes. Engineers, doctors, painters, academics, scientists, writers, atomicists, musicians, actors: The Professor had eclectic tastes.

When one of the newly introduced guests began talking with the Professor, Langton took the opportunity to break away and find a glass of wine. A maid passed with a tray of glasses. "Vouvray, sir."

Langton had taken no more than a sip when a voice sounded close behind him. "I see you had the whirlwind tour."

He turned. "Sister Wright."

She returned his smile. "The Professor sometimes forgets that we mere mortals aren't as quick as he. Like an enthusiastic child, he wants to be everywhere and talking to everyone at once."

A good comparison, Langton realized as he watched the Professor dart from group to group, from conversation to conversation. As Langton's gaze returned to Sister Wright, he took in her long gown of palest blue, her arms and slender neck free of jewelry save for the crucifix on its chain and the silver Guild pin at her breast. Unlike most of the women's gowns, her dress covered the skin between her bosom and her throat. Someone had coiled her long hair up in a complicated plait.

She began to blush. "It's too much, isn't it?"

"I'm sorry?"

"I'm not used to . . . to clothes like this, but I knew I should make an effort for the Professor." The blush deepened. "A friend in the Infirmary offered to help me, but I think she went too far."

Langton said, "Not at all. You look beautiful."

Realizing what he had said, he took a gulp of wine and coughed.

"Are you all right?" Sister Wright patted his back.

He swallowed hard. "I'm not used to alcohol anymore."

"Nor I to compliments," Sister Wright said. Then she took his free hand and turned it over in her own. "Who tied these fresh bandages?"

"My maid, Elsie."

"She did well."

For a moment, with his hand clasped in hers, Langton didn't know what to say.

Sister Wright helped him. She collected her shawl and said, "It's a little warm in here. Shall we go out onto the terrace?"

He followed her through another room, larger than the drawing room although still crowded with guests, and out onto a stone-flagged terrace. By the light of electric lanterns suspended from trellises, he could see the outline of a neat lawn beneath the snow, and shrubs and trees that merged into gradual darkness and yellow fog. The smell of damp earth and bark.

"The Professor knows many people," Langton said.

"He has numerous interests and a keen curiosity. He craves knowledge."

"Of what?"

"Of life itself," Sister Wright said, glancing back to the crowded rooms. "All those people in there, the artists and scientists and experts, the Professor can hold detailed conversations with all of them. He is an avid collector of people and facts."

That word troubled Langton. "Collectors tend to focus on one field, one interest. Sometimes obsessively, in my experience."

"Not the Professor. His specialty is . . . everything." As she said this, Sister Wright spread one arm wide as if to encompass the garden, the city, the whole world waiting beyond the seeping fog. Light from the French windows caught the silver pin at her breast.

"The Guild must take up much of your time," Langton said.

She glanced down at the pin. "You recognize it?"

"I saw its companion on the uniform of another: Nurse Milne at the encampment."

"I know her well, a good and hardworking girl." A moment's hesitation, then, "Your work took you to the camp?"

"I had reports of a fugitive."

"In connection with Kepler?"

"His colleague. Perhaps also his accomplice."

"I hope you found him."

Langton looked away. "Unfortunately not. I would be surprised to see him again."

"He perished?"

"He escaped into the network of tunnels beneath the Pier Head. Those at the camp doubted he would survive."

Sister Wright shivered. "I'm sure they are correct. I have heard stories—hopefully fanciful—of those tunnels. Foul and dark, home to pests and insects and vermin, yet still attractive to certain people who prefer to avoid the light of day."

Langton wondered if she had heard the ghost stories hinted at by Mr. Dowden. She did not seem a superstitious sort, and the Infirmary no doubt kept her firmly grounded in reality.

Sister Wright continued, "The thought of that confined space, all those tons of earth pressing down . . . I abhor confinement, Inspector. I hate to see anything trapped."

"Is that why you keep an empty cage in your office at the Infirmary?"

"You noticed that?" Then, before Langton spoke, she continued, "It belonged to my predecessor, a fine nursing sister who nevertheless insisted on keeping a caged songbird nearby. When she left, I immediately released the poor creature and watched it fly above Liverpool's rooftops. I kept the cage as a reminder."

In all that Sister Wright said, Langton detected a fine sensibility, an empathy that touched him and reminded him of Sarah.

"Nurse Milne mentioned that you regularly help the camp's inhabitants," Langton said.

"When I can, Inspector. And they do need our help. Undernourished, cold and neglected, many of them rely on charity to survive."

Looking through the glass to the warm, privileged world inside the mansion, Langton said, "So very different from all this."

"I would not take you for a socialist reformer, Inspector."

He met her gaze. "I'm not. I simply acknowledge the difference between the fortunate families at the top of society and those at the base."

"Some do not even see that," she said. "I'm glad that you are not one of them. We have a duty to the less fortunate, the poor and the forgotten."

"Does the Professor feel the same way?" Langton said, choosing his words carefully because of his uncertain ground. "Is that why he operated on some of the camp's patients?"

Sister Wright thought for a moment, looking out at the garden. "I believe he sees his duty and responsibility now. It was not always so. The medical profession is rife with arrogance, the hubris of men from good families and privileged backgrounds, men who hold life and death in their hands every day. I may be guilty of pride myself when I say that perhaps I influenced the Professor for the better."

Langton could easily imagine Sister Wright as a benign influence on the Professor. A constant presence, calm and sympathetic, leading by her own example. Her next sentence confirmed this humility.

"I admit that I feel a fraud," she said, drawing her shawl around her shoulders.

"In what way?"

"Oh, this dress, my hair, being here at all. To be honest, I'd feel more at home in my uniform. It's a second skin to me."

Langton agreed. His clothes defined him, just as Sister Wright's uniform defined her. He said, "I was never comfortable at parties or dinners, especially in evening dress; I always felt like an actor playing a part. But Sarah . . ."

A moment's pause, then, "Your wife?"

"She grew up in houses like this, with parties, balls, receptions. Her family expected it of her."

Sister Wright touched his arm. "I don't wish to pry."

"You aren't prying," Langton said, surprised at how easy he felt in her company. For the first time in months, he actually *wanted* to talk.

"Sarah used to tell me stories about the parties she'd attended, about the little tricks she and her friends knew to avoid chaperones and guardians, or to steal a taste of wine as a young girl. I'd always thought of the richer families as staid, hidebound, but Sarah opened my eyes. She never had an ounce of snobbery or disdain in her body. She thought nothing of marrying beneath her."

"Surely nobody would consider a police inspector with a distinguished war record beneath them?"

"Some might."

"I'm sure she had a good life," Sister Wright said.

"With her family? Yes, she did."

"I didn't mean with her family."

Langton looked into Sister Wright's open, smiling face and eyes. He felt as if he'd known her for years, not days. He went to speak.

"Ah, there you are." Professor Caldwell Chivers strode out onto the terrace.

Sister Wright broke away from Langton, still smiling, and drew tight her shawl.

The Professor sniffed the air. "Bit chilly out here, Langton. I wanted to ask you about that chap Kepler's case."

"It becomes more complex with each day, Professor." Langton hesitated, then said, "At least one other murder is a result of the first, and another two deaths may have a connection."

The Professor moved closer. "And the Jar Boys?"

"They play a part, I'm sure." Langton didn't know how much to tell the Professor, who might not appreciate being considered as a possible suspect. Then again, he might have enjoyed the contradiction with the same enthusiasm he showed for everything else.

Langton said, "The strange neck burns appeared on Doctor Redfers's body as well as on Kepler's."

The Professor clasped his hands in front as if ready to pray. "Ah, yes. Poor Redfers."

"You knew him?"

"Very well. We met many times at the Infirmary, at symposiums, or over difficult cases he referred to us, and he must have dined at my house a score of times. A most sociable man; he seemed to know everybody."

Another connection, but perhaps an innocent one. Redfers might have used the Professor to increase his group of contacts and the number of men who might buy his wares. For Langton couldn't believe that women would want to collect the contents of Redfers's jars; more likely, as with opiates and prostitutes, it would be the men who showed an interest. Men with too much time, too much money, and too little self-control.

As he thought this, Langton realized how far he'd traveled beyond disbelief. At the start of his investigation, the idea of souls trapped in containers of glass or clay had seemed impossible, risible, but too many people had died. Too much information supported the trade in jars. That meant that somewhere out there, Sarah's essence lay trapped. Alone. Defenseless.

"Are you all right, Inspector?" Sister Wright asked.

"Just a chill," he said, wondering if any of the Professor's fine guests appeared in Redfers's diary. One of those well-dressed, urbane men chatting and laughing. Did they have a secret basement room lined with innocuous-seeming containers? Perhaps one of them might return home that very evening and select Sarah's jar to paw over, to lay his hands on the slick copper strips and—

Langton's glass shattered on the terrace. "I'm sorry."

The Professor waved over one of his maids. "Think nothing of it, Inspector. But perhaps we should return to the others."

Sister Wright took Langton's arm and stared up into his eyes. She didn't speak. Just for a moment, Langton felt his own soul stripped bare and laid out for examination, as though Sister Wright could see every facet of his life, his memories. The thought did not scare him. Instead, he felt strangely comforted.

As they followed the Professor through the French doors and into the drawing room, Langton said, "I feel guilty for monopolizing your company."

She removed her hand from his arm. "You'd rather I bothered someone else?"

Langton, blushing, said, "No, not at all. It's just that—"

"Don't worry, Inspector," she said, smiling. "I'll return later. I'm sure you'll want to meet as many of the Professor's guests as you can. After all, that's the main reason you're here, isn't it?"

Langton watched Sister Wright make her way through the groups clustered around the room. How much had she guessed? More than guessed; perhaps she *knew* that some of these men present were collectors. With her experience and position within the Infirmary, she must have watched over many final scenes and seen so much suffering. And seen those who might show too much interest in that suffering, just as the Resurrectionists showed an unhealthy interest in the dying.

Across the room, the smiling Professor moved from group to group, handshake to handshake. Sister Wright respected her mentor absolutely, Langton knew. And what if Professor Caldwell Chivers really was Doktor Glass? Would Sister Wright betray him?

Langton hoped she would never face that dilemma.

Now, as more and more guests poured into the room, Langton found himself pushed to the outer edges. Like a piece of beached driftwood carried on the tide, he settled near the flocked wall, between an enormous potted palm and a bookcase. He took another glass of wine from a passing tray and watched the movement of people, the black-and-white dinner suits, the pastel gowns. The scene resembled one of the Professor's modern paintings hanging on the walls, a Manet or a Degas.

"Critical mass."

Langton turned to the tall, stooped man who'd appeared beside him. "Pardon me?"

The man waved a hand toward the guests. "Watch them; a group of three becomes four, then five, then six, whatever. Eventually, the group—unable to support itself—reaches its critical mass, explodes, and scatters its individuals like atoms, which, in turn, form their own compounds."

Langton stared at his strange companion. The front of the man's dinner jacket bore a collection of dotted food stains. His tie hung lopsided, and he'd shaved badly, leaving small clumps of grey beard beneath his jaw.

"You're a scientist?"

"An atomicist, sir. And happy to celebrate the Span."

"I'm sorry, I don't see the connection."

The atomicist stared at Langton like a teacher with an obtuse pupil. "No connection? No connection, sir?"

"I just—"

"How do you think the Span's trains will journey all the way to America, sir?"

"I meant that—"

"How do you imagine that electricity appears? By magic?"

"If you let me—"

"The power of the atom, sir." The scientist drew himself up. "Without the generators of the Llandudno station, without the mighty turbines driven by the precise fractioning of base atoms, there could be no electric trains to America. Why, steam trains would have no room for passengers—every carriage would have to carry coal for the journey. No connection indeed."

Langton watched the atomicist stride away into the crowd. He shook his head and wondered if all scientists were so sensitive.

As more people entered the room, the press of bodies thickened. Langton eased along the wall and slipped through a door into a narrow passage. Cool and dim, lit by electric globes fixed to the old gaslight brackets, the passage seemed to descend. As Langton followed it he could hear music and conversation through the walls, or from behind closed doors. He paused a moment and sniffed. Hot dust and white flowers.

A door opened behind him to allow the sounds of laughter and a piano melody in, then slammed shut. Langton set his empty glass on a side table and continued down the passage. Ahead, golden light fanned out from under a door. Langton hesitated, listened, but heard only the echoes of the party behind him. The brass handle, cold and slick, turned in his hand. He threw the door wide.

A blaze of color: reds, blues, yellows, but above all, gold. Gold in the pharaohs' headdresses, in the artifacts displayed within glass cases, in the chairs and statues, the ceremonial caskets. The electrolier overhead glinted off the precious metal and made the air shimmer.

The man standing in the center of the room turned from examining a glass display case and smiled. "I see you've discovered the Professor's Egyptian obsession."

Langton stepped forward. The room stretched at least half the width of the house; pillars of brick and steel supported the upper floors and opened up the space beneath. Against one wall stood the inner wooden covers of sarcophagi, richly painted with the stern faces of ancient pharaohs. Against another, glass display cases just like those in the center of the room, and just like those of a museum. Another wall contained brilliant hieroglyphs, apparently fresh and as yet unfinished.

The fourth wall held Langton's attention. On deep shelves, row after row of squat clay jars: some decorated with faded colors, some inlaid with angular designs, some plain.

"He has an amazing collection," the man said. "I haven't seen pieces of this quality outside the British Museum."

Approaching the man, Langton guessed his age at late thirties; quite short in stature but broad across the shoulders, with deep-set eyes and a jutting jaw. More than anything, he looked tired.

The man extended his hand. "Henry Marc Brunel."

That explained the obvious fatigue: The Brunel partnership—grandfather Marc, father Isambard Kingdom, and son Henry Marc—had designed the Span and worked on it from its inception. Their family had practically built the bridge and invented the vast floating city-ships that had enabled its construction.

Langton shook hands. "It's an honor to meet you."

Brunel smiled and waved away the compliment. He turned to the exhibits. "Truly remarkable, aren't they? To think that craftsmen's hands worked on these millennia ago. Look at the detail on these brooches."

To Langton, the black-and-gold scarab brooches in the glass case looked too much like the cockroaches he'd found in Gloucester Road, or the translucent creatures that had spilled from the sewer tunnels.

Brunel leaned close to the artifacts behind the glass. "I can imagine those clay oil lamps flickering in some workman's mud house by the Nile, while the same design in gold might have illuminated a pharaoh's chamber or thrown their light onto a priest's holy book at Karnak."

Artifact after artifact lay behind glass on padded velvet. Worked in clay, gold, wood, bone. Some seemed almost recent, some so old they could have disintegrated under Langton's gaze.

Langton realized that the Brunels shared the recent public fascination with all things Egyptian. Ever since Professor Maspero, young Howard Carter, and his colleagues had unearthed the Valley of the Kings, the great temple at Karnak, Thebes, and the Upper Nile Valley, Egypt had entered the public's imagination. Touring exhibitions, readings, lantern shows, and many popular books had started a craze that showed no signs of abating.

When Brunel paused, Langton said, "I suppose I shouldn't be surprised at your interest; the designs on the Span give it away."

"You mean the bas-reliefs?" Brunel smiled. "They take the temple of Amun-Ra at Thebes as their inspiration. Hopefully the Span will last almost as long as the great temples; we like to imagine our descendants poring over the motifs just as we pore over the work of the ancients."

As they spoke, Langton guided Brunel closer to the fourth wall.

He stopped before the shelves of jars and said, "I wonder what use these had."

Brunel reached out to touch one of the clay jars but stopped at the last moment. "Canopic jars: the most sacred containers. During the mummification process, physicians removed the intestines, stomach, and liver and decanted them into these jars, then filled the body cavity with linen and cotton. Strangely enough, they did not remove the heart, which they believed housed the soul. They inserted a hook up the nose and pulled the subject's brains out, again decanting them into jars.

"As the process continued, and attendants prepared the body with strips of linen soaked in embalming fluid, the sealed jars were placed within the final tomb, alongside the sarcophagi. They believed that through this process, the body would be reborn, complete, in the afterlife."

Seeing the expression on Langton's face, Brunel said, "Is it any more brutal than our own methods of interment? Whereas they used resins, we use formaldehyde. Just as they removed the organs, so do we, in the name of science or research. They treated their dead with as much dignity as we do. More, in fact."

Langton closed his eyes and pushed down the scream that rose inside him. Brunel could not know his words cut deep.

"I say, are you all right?"

"Pardon me," Langton said, forcing a smile. "I'm a little . . . tired. Overwork."

Brunel stared at him. "You should take care, my friend. One must not concentrate so much on one's work that it obscures all else. For proof of that, I need look no further than my own grandfather and father; their zeal almost finished them off."

A fragment of a headline returned to Langton, and before he could stop himself, he said, "The Thames Tunneling Company."

Brunel looked away. "Exactly. My father and grandfather almost died during the Rotherhithe tunnel's excavation. But their work on caissons, and Grandfather's tunneling shield, gave us the knowledge we needed to build the Span. Sometimes I wonder if the sacrifice is worth it."

Langton knew that almost the whole country, if not the world, believed that the Transatlantic Span would be a great monument; he went to reassure Brunel but at that moment another door opened beside the leaning sarcophagi. Professor Caldwell Chivers entered, preceded by two laughing girls in taffeta gowns. Upon seeing Brunel and Langton, the women stopped and gave tentative smiles.

The Professor stepped forward. "Brunel. I wondered where you might be hiding. You too, Langton. You've discovered my secret vice."

Langton made a point of not looking at the shelves of jars. "You have quite a collection, Professor."

"A passing fancy," the Professor said, nevertheless smiling at the compliment. "Although I must admit I had a fascination with Egyptology even before the current fad started. To think that the ancients had such a well-developed society thousands of years before ours."

Brunel said, "They set a fine example, Professor, but I have to thank you for your help on the Span's bas-reliefs."

The Professor bowed slightly. "It was nothing, sir. A pleasure. I'm honored to contribute even a minuscule part."

Langton turned to Brunel. "The Professor helped in the design?"

"On the British side, we used his motifs on several of the towers, including the very first. They are very striking."

"What do they show?"

"*Pet Ta Tuat,*" the Professor said, biting the words hard. "The Egyptian heaven, earth, and hell. The cycle of life, in fact. Panels show life in the fields, then the ceremony of death and mummification—without too much graphic detail, naturally—and then daily rejuvenation in the afterlife. All as an allegory, of course."

Then, seeing the young girls restless, the Professor added, "If you gentlemen will excuse us, I promised these ladies a tour of the treasures."

Langton and Brunel bowed and left the Professor to guide his guests around the Egyptian room. They followed the passage that the Professor had used and found themselves toward the rear of the house, once again overlooking the gardens. The fog had deepened, now all but obliterating the neat foliage.

Brunel acknowledged the greeting of several guests and asked Langton, "Do you believe in the power of imagery?"

"In what way?"

"That perhaps certain designs have inherent meaning and power?" Then, before Langton interrupted, Brunel went on, "You see remarkably similar recurring themes in the architecture of the ancient Greeks, the Romans, Incas, Aztecs and Minoans, and the Egyptians. Not so much in the buildings themselves as in the ornamentation guarding them."

"Guarding them? From what?"

Brunel smiled. "Oh, I don't know. Fate, maybe. Chaos or entropy."

"You mean like the gargoyles that guard cathedrals?"

"They're a primitive example, but yes, I suppose so. Many engineers and architects today are still using the Gothic vernacular, gargoyles and the medieval decoration of some lost Romantic ideal more suited to King Arthur. It's not really architecture, of course, more that half-world between building and statuary, or art . . ." Brunel rubbed at his eyes. "I'm sorry. I must be boring you. I'm afraid that fatigue is catching up with me."

As Brunel went to turn away, Langton said, "Is that why you chose Egyptian motifs for the Span? To protect it?"

"In a way. Of course, the Professor's designs are attractive in their own right, but we felt it would do no harm to have an element of positive significance."

When the greatest feat of Victorian engineering adopted the superstitions of an ancient civilization, Langton thought, what hope was there for the rest of society? Even hardheaded engineers like the Brunels, men used to dealing in precise figures, quantifiable certainties, and scientific laws, had fallen for the mythology. Was all lost?

"I think," said Langton, "that any image has power if people *believe* it has."

Brunel thought for a moment, then nodded. "A good summation."

"I hope the Span benefits from the designs."

"So do I," Brunel said, shaking Langton's hand. "It will carry the hopes and dreams of millions."

Langton watched Brunel merge with the crowd and realized that the Span, although not yet open, had already become a symbol. Of freedom? Perhaps. More of optimism. The promise of a new life. A new start.

He checked his fob watch. Just before eleven. He didn't want to arrive late at Wavertree. Good manners required Langton to say good night to the Professor and thank him for being invited, but good manners could hardly apply when your host became one of your chief suspects. There was, however, one person that Langton wanted to wish good night. He pushed through the crowds, through the perfume, French wine, cigarettes and cigars, until he saw Sister Wright standing before one of the Professor's paintings in the drawing room.

"Sister? I must wish you good night."

She turned to him and smiled. "Is it so late?"

Langton hesitated. He looked into her calm eyes and almost confessed. "I have work that cannot wait."

"Our work never can, Inspector. We care too much, you and I." She took his arm and pulled him closer, then nodded to the painting before them. "I'm not keen on some of the Professor's purchases—his taste is a little modern for me—but this holds my gaze."

The painting in oils, perhaps a yard high by half a yard wide, showed a weary traveler trudging through snow and about to collapse into a small glade of sparse, bare trees. In the distance, the silver towers of a city the poor man would never reach. Every brushstroke, every hue, reinforced the cold atmosphere of the work.

"It draws you in," Langton said. "Although it is a little melancholy."

"You think so?" Sister Wright did not turn from the painting. "I find it reassuring."

Langton waited.

"The traveler has a goal," Sister Wright said. "Not the earthly one, which is beyond him, but another. Soon he will reach it. Soon he will be free and find peace."

Perhaps she was right, but Langton wondered why so many of the Professor's paintings and artifacts spoke of death. Was that usual in a man dedicated to saving life?

"I must go," he said. "I wanted to thank you for inviting me here tonight."

"Did you find what you searched for?"

How could he tell her? She respected the Professor so much. "I learned a great deal."

"If there is anything I can do, Inspector, simply ask."

From the hallway, Langton looked back and saw Sister Wright still standing in front of the snowy painting like a child staring out a window.

He took his hat and coat and tipped a footman, who waved forward a hansom cab. Once inside, Langton let his thoughts range over the evening. Images and conversations jumbled together, overlapping: the Egyptian artifacts, Brunel, the Professor, Sister Wright. How would she react if she knew Langton's suspicions? With anger? Sadness? Disbelief?

Perhaps Langton's suspicions had no foundation; perhaps the Professor's interests and tastes were no more than that. If they really did indicate a morbid fascination with death and rebirth, they might identify him as Doktor Glass. Proving it would take courage.

In the passing haze of gas lamps, Langton checked his fob watch again: eleven thirty. As he thought of what awaited him, a knot tightened in his stomach. He knew he had to do this. For Sarah.

Eleven

BEFORE THE HANSOM cab reached Plimsoll Street, Langton asked the driver to halt. Although he doubted that the Jar Boys would keep watch on Mrs. Barker's house, he didn't want to take even that small chance. He got out on Martensen Street, a handful of roads to the west of Plimsoll, and watched the cab drive away; fog swallowed the rear red light that glowed like a single burning eye.

As Langton headed east, looking up at the black-and-white street, his footsteps echoed along the empty pavement and joined in his thoughts with the fading echoes of music from the Professor's reception. The fog closed in on him, damp and cold and cloying, a fog that tasted of smoke from Edge Hill's rail shunting yards nearby.

He could have been the only person in the city; no sounds of traffic or humanity penetrated the fog, and no lights shone in any of the terraced houses. Then, as Langton turned into Plimsoll Street, he saw a white glow among the yellow streetlamps. Double-fronted houses here, more spacious and imposing than the terraces: high sash windows, fine railings, three steps up to the front door. Langton headed for the white lantern and climbed the steps of number forty-two.

The door opened to reveal a petite figure dressed in black. Inside the hallway, the pale glow of old-fashioned oil lamps turned low; their soft light reflected from the rope of pearls fastened about the woman's neck.

Langton waited until the door clicked shut, then said, "Mrs. Barker?"

"You must be Inspector Langton." She gripped his hand for a moment before picking up one of the glass oil lamps from the hall stand. Her metal-tipped walking stick tapped on the parquet floor as she made for the stairs. "Mr. Paterson is in with Edith now."

Farther down the hallway, close to the foot of the stairs, another door stood open. Langton had the impression of two faces peering through the gap, pallid and silent. Before the circle of light from Mrs. Barker's lamp illuminated them, the figures withdrew into the dark room with a rustle of cloth. The door closed without a sound.

As he climbed the carpeted stairs behind Mrs. Barker, Langton caught the odors of disinfectant and enclosed air, the almost tangible atmosphere of long-term sickness. The mixture took Langton back six months or more to his own house, to Sarah in that big bed. He stumbled, almost fell, gripped the banister, and continued up the stairs.

At the first landing, Mrs. Barker turned. She rested on her walking stick. The oil lamp in her hand threw yellow light on half of her face but set the rest in shadow.

Langton kept his voice low. "How is she?"

"Fading, Inspector. Fading." Mrs. Barker turned to the door, head bowed. "May God guide her."

As Mrs. Barker reached for the door, Langton hesitated. The whole atmosphere of the house weighed down on him and constricted his throat. The thought of the dying girl inside the room turned his limbs to lead.

"Inspector?"

Langton forced himself to approach the bedroom. How right the modern French writers were: how powerful a reaction came from a simple aroma. It made him want to run down those stairs and into the night, to escape this suffocating place.

He remembered Mrs. Grizedale's belief, her *certainty* that Sarah lay imprisoned, alone and vulnerable. Langton stepped forward.

Inside the bedroom, two more lamps gave out pale light. In the corner, the black-leaded surround of a small coal fire now glowed orange with banked embers. The room's enormous mahogany bed made the emaciated girl huddled in its center seem like a child. Blankets, sheets, and a quilt engulfed her. On one of the bedside tables, brown glass bottles, medicines, tinctures, pills, powders. The saccharine smell of liquid morphine.

Langton took another two steps and saw the girl's eyes shut, her lips open slightly, her skin greasy and yellow beneath the lamp light. At her neck, the frill of a high nightdress.

Forbes Paterson rose from the armchair in the corner. "Are you sure you can do this?"

Looking back to the bed, then to Mrs. Barker, Langton said, "I must."

Paterson drew him farther into the corner. His voice never rose above a whisper. "All is arranged. I have constables in the surrounding streets and a carriage waiting."

"I saw no one."

"That's exactly how it should be."

The girl in the bed murmured. Langton watched Mrs. Barker set the lamp down and reach for an enamel basin; she wrung out the cloth and wiped her niece's face with slow, careful strokes. Langton's eyes clouded over.

"I'll be waiting in the room next door," Paterson said, nodding toward another door. "I don't want to risk the Jar Boys recognizing me."

"Where shall I wait?"

"Here."

"Alone?"

"With Mrs. Barker."

"You'll be my brother George, from London, Inspector," Mrs. Barker said, turning from the bed. "That'll explain your fine suit."

Langton cursed himself; he should have remembered a change of clothes. Mrs. Barker no doubt believed he'd just come from a party, which, in fact, he had. "Do you have anything I might borrow?"

"I don't think so, Inspector. My poor Alfred's clothes, God rest his soul, wouldn't go near you. And there's only Maisie and Lily in the house besides us."

"You'll do," Paterson said. "It's too late to change."

Twelve ten by Langton's watch. "They're due at one?"

"If all goes well."

Langton stared at his colleague. "Is there a problem?"

Paterson glanced at the two women, then told Langton, "I've tried for so long to catch these men. Not just these, but all the Jar Boys. I have a pessimistic voice inside me that wonders if we can succeed this time. I hope we can."

"So do I, Inspector," Mrs. Barker said, without looking up from her niece. "Parasites, these devils are. It was bad enough when they tried to fasten themselves onto poor Alfred, but when I think of Edith . . ."

She stroked her niece's face with a simple gesture so natural and touching that Langton had to turn away.

"You're a credit, Mrs. Barker," Paterson said.

"It's my duty."

With time running out, Langton helped Paterson set the scene. They moved the armchair away from the other door, to give Paterson room to rush in when called. Sitting there, Langton had a good view of Edith and of the door leading to the landing. The two lamps, moved slightly and turned up, threw light on the bed and on Edith's inert face, making her look like a statue.

Leaving the communicating door slightly ajar, Paterson sat on a cabin trunk in the adjacent box room. Behind him stood dusty luggage, boxes, and towers of yellowing periodicals.

Langton set his fob watch on the arm of the chair and sat back. The house creaked as it settled in the cold night. The water in the enamel basin splashed as Mrs. Barker anointed Edith's face.

Would they come? Or would something or someone warn them off? Langton hadn't told any of his own staff about this trap; too much information had already left his office. The newspapers knew of his movements, for one, but more important so did the murderers of Kepler, Stoker Olsen, and Redfers. Langton had to consider the possibility of an inside informer, but once he began to suspect his own colleagues the ground beneath him turned to quicksand.

Twelve thirty. Langton's eyes became heavy. He blinked awake and tried to concentrate. Edith began to moan in pain, softly at first, then louder. Each cry pierced Langton and made the intervening months disappear.

"There, there, flower. It's all right. All right." Mrs. Barker's soothing words seemed to calm Edith for a few minutes. "It's all right, sweetheart."

Then the girl gasped and sat up in bed clutching her stomach. She stared at Langton in pure terror, her eyes wide like an animal's.

The cry had pulled Langton to his feet. Now he wanted to run, to flee this room.

Mrs. Barker stopped him, saying, "Pass me the tall brown bottle. Quick."

While Mrs. Barker eased Edith back down beneath the covers, Langton fumbled on the bedside table. The tallest brown bottle stood half empty. He removed the ground-glass stopper and smelled morphine.

"There, now, drink this." Mrs. Barker decanted some of the liquid into a clean glass and held it to Edith's lips.

Edith sank down onto the bed. Her body relaxed. Her eyes closed and her hands uncurled on the bedclothes.

Mrs. Barker stood up with her head bowed. "I can't go on. God forgive me, I can't take this."

Langton set the bottle down and held Mrs. Barker's shoulders. The woman leaned against him like an athlete exhausted after a long race.

"I love her so," she said, her voice muffled by Langton's jacket, "but sometimes I feel so . . . so angry at having to look after her. That's not right, is it?"

Langton knew exactly what Mrs. Barker meant. He remembered pacing the floor of his bedroom over and over and railing against life, against fate and God, and sometimes even against Sarah herself for leaving him alone. And he remembered the guilt that filled him after those thoughts. "We can only do so much, Mrs. Barker, before we break."

She pulled away and gave him a shadow of a smile that did not reach her eyes. "God tests us, doesn't he, Inspector?"

What could he tell her? He glanced at Forbes Paterson watching from the doorway, then back to Mrs. Barker. Langton couldn't repeat the trite sentiments and platitudes offered to him after Sarah's passing, no matter how well-meaning the phrases. He couldn't lie.

Mrs. Barker didn't ask him to; she turned back to Edith and held her thin hand.

Langton picked up his watch from the rug and saw Paterson check the time on his own piece. Twelve forty-seven. Returning to the chair, Langton felt in his pocket the solid weight of the Webley. Would he use it if he had to? He thought about Kepler's mutilated body, the features pared down to the bone. And he looked at the wasted form of Edith lying close by.

Yes, he'd use his revolver.

Mrs. Barker left the bedside for a moment and tipped coal from the brass bucket onto the dying fire. A plume of bright sparks fled up the chimney. As she returned to the bed, she glanced at Langton but didn't have to speak. Both knew that the time approached.

Twelve fifty-five. Langton strained to hear the sound of horses' hooves or footsteps on the cold street outside. Nothing disturbed the calm. He resisted the urge to part the curtains and look down. The waiting drew him out like a cable on a winch drum, stretched tighter and tighter; each passing minute sounded like another click of the drum's ratchet.

One o'clock became five past, then ten past. Langton glanced at Paterson, who held his gaze. Still no sound from the street, no knock at the door. The fire crackled in the grate. Edith stirred in the big mahogany bed.

One fifteen. One twenty-five. The pressure built up inside Langton, made each beat of his heart reverberate like a steam piston. The Jar Boys would not call, not this late. They had suspected the trap. Or been told of it.

There. Horses' hooves, faint but getting closer. Stopping in the street outside.

Forbes Paterson nodded to Langton and closed the communicating door. Mrs. Barker stood up, smoothed her dress, and made for the stairs. Alone for the moment with Edith, Langton stood by the bedroom door and listened.

A gentle knock at the front door. The murmur of voices, then footsteps on the stairs. At least two others accompanied Mrs. Barker, Langton guessed. He took his seat and tried to hide his tension.

Mrs. Barker opened the door. ". . . and this is my brother George, sir, come up from London this very evening to be with Edith at the end."

The first man behind Mrs. Barker hesitated a moment, looked around the room, then advanced with his gloved hand outstretched. "A most sad occasion, sir. You have my sympathy."

Langton forced himself to shake the man's hand but didn't speak. His face set into a mask.

"And this must be your dear niece, madam." The man leaned over the bed. "So very sad."

Examining the man, Langton guessed his age around fifty: neat grey beard and hair; dark, well-cut clothes in a slightly old-fashioned style. He could have been a physician with a patient. No doubt he hoped to create that impression.

The second man could have been his clerk were it not for the immense shoulders and impassive features like granite. Dressed in an ill-fitting dark suit and high white collar with a tie like butcher's string, he looked like a suspect waiting to see the magistrate. Hands like shovels reached almost to his knees.

One of those massive hands held a capacious leather Gladstone bag. At a nod from the first man, he set the bag down beside the bed and opened the clasp. Light glinted from metal.

"You're sure this will help her?" Mrs. Barker said, playing her part well.

"I have absolute faith in the procedure, madam. I could show you many families who would testify in support if it were not for our absolute devotion to privacy and confidentiality."

Hearing the man, and seeing his confident, skillful words, Langton recognized the consummate professional, the type of trickster who could extract money from old widows or sell false stocks to naïve businessmen. The easy smile and the way he stared at Mrs. Barker intently as he spoke almost hypnotized her.

Then the man turned to Langton. "Perhaps your brother, unfamiliar with the procedure, would like me to explain?"

"Please."

The man launched into an obviously practiced speech. "It's really quite simple, sir, and most beautiful; our scientific apparatus will save the departing essence of this poor, suffering girl as she takes her leave of the world of man. Instead of dispersing into the very ether and merging with the lost particles of every confused soul, instead of struggling through the foul atmosphere of this polluted world, she will be gathered into this vessel."

At this, the other man reached into the leather bag and drew out a cylindrical jar of brown glazed clay with a band of gleaming copper and green wax at its neck. It looked so ordinary. So commonplace. But Langton remembered the clay burial vessels in the Professor's Egyptian room; those canopic jars were not so dissimilar to these containers.

"It doesn't look much," Mrs. Barker said.

"Indeed, madam, but the jars are like people; the exterior is unimportant. What is inside us is the most important."

Mrs. Barker stared at the jar. "I don't know . . . To think of poor Edith trapped inside that thing—"

"Rather than trapped," the man said, "we prefer to think of the subjects as 'protected.' Safe."

Confined, Langton thought. *Prisoners. No more, no less.*

"Set it over there, Jake," the first man said, pointing to the small table across the room.

The immense Jake carried the jar in both hands as if afraid to drop it. He set it on the table and returned to the leather bag.

The question rose to Langton's lips before he could stop it: "What will you do with her?"

"Why, sir, keep her safe. Within the jar, she will feel no pain, no suffering. And should the time come . . ."

"Yes?"

The bearded man glanced at Mrs. Barker, then said, "Should the time come when science allows us to transfer the essence back into a living host, into a healthy body, then the dear child might live again. I can make no promises, sir, but you have only to think of the great strides science has made in the past few years. Who knows what the new millennium will bring."

With great difficulty, Langton controlled his anger and kept his face in its blank mask. How many families had these Jar Boys tricked? How many distraught parents, brothers, sisters had heard that slick speech and honestly believed the charlatan's words?

A new life. That was the hope these swindlers offered. A new life in a new body, God forbid.

Langton wondered what Paterson made of all this. Perhaps he'd heard it before. No wonder he wanted to capture these people.

"Now, sir, if we may continue," the man said, motioning to his accomplice. "The generator."

Jake once again reached into the leather bag and brought out an instrument of brass, wood, and shellac or bois durci. He set the machine on the bedside table beside Edith. Lamplight glinted off the generator's squat cube of metal, its cylinder wound with copper wire, its polished sphere, and its wooden base. Jake unraveled a coil of black wire and left it close to Edith but not touching her body. The two wires emerged from the machine's sphere and ended in two small copper squares.

To Langton, the generator resembled the apparatus in Redfers's house but seemed newer, perhaps more modern.

"This won't hurt her, will it?" Mrs. Barker asked, leaning close to Edith.

"Madam, I can assure you, as a doctor, that your dear niece will feel no pain."

Langton's heart jumped. "You're a doctor?"

"I am, sir."

"Your name?"

He stared at Langton for a few seconds. "That is unimportant."

Could this be Doktor Glass? Langton doubted it. These were probably no more than Glass's subordinates, foot soldiers who carried out his orders.

Langton watched Jake unwind another coil of wire from the generator. This ran along the floor of the bedroom and connected to the copper neck of the jar. Then Jake removed the final component from the bag, a delicate arc of metal that opened like a fan; he inserted this into the jar's neck, making sure it connected with the wire.

"You see the aerial fixed and ready," the doctor explained as he fixed the copper squares and trailing wires to Edith's neck. "I will not trouble you with the scientific principles behind the procedure, but the machine charges the subject's emerging essence while the aerial captures it and directs it into the vessel. So the poor soul is not lost to the elements. Jake."

Jake reached out and flicked a brass switch on the machine. Nothing happened. Langton glanced at Mrs. Barker, then at the communicating door.

"It takes a moment," the doctor said.

A slight buzzing appeared, as from a fly trapped somewhere in the room. The buzzing grew until Langton felt it at the back of his head. He smelled a faint burning.

The doctor leaned closer to Edith. "Ah, she's fading. Fading quickly."

Langton hadn't seen any change in the girl's condition. He glanced to Mrs. Barker, who seemed intent on her niece's face. The whole scene, with the warm lamplight and the figures huddled over the patient, resembled an old oil painting.

The doctor reached into his coat and drew out a flat silver case. Inside, a syringe lay on a green velvet base.

Mrs. Barker said, "What are you doing?"

"A little something to ease her final moments," the doctor said, and before Langton could leap forward, he'd jammed the syringe deep into Edith's carotid artery.

Mrs. Barker screamed. Langton slapped the syringe from the doctor's hand, then thrust the Webley into the man's chest. "Police. You are under arrest."

Jake took a step toward Langton, his enormous fists raised, then saw Forbes Paterson advancing from the next room with a revolver ready. Jake froze.

"Oh Edith, Edith." Mrs. Barker stroked her niece's face but didn't cry.

"What's he done?" Paterson said.

Langton stared into the doctor's eyes. "Murder."

The doctor licked his lips and looked between the two inspectors. "I swear I knew nothing. I was told to administer the drug."

"By whom?"

The doctor shook his head.

"Langton, look." Paterson stared at the bed.

Mrs. Barker drew back. "Edith?"

"It's beginning," the doctor said.

As Langton watched, a fine mist drifted from Edith's body. Hardly a mist, in fact; the particles seemed so small, so delicate, that it looked like a mere suggestion of vapor, like the last strands of dawn haze before the rising sun. It seeped from Edith's half-open mouth, her eyes, from her very pores.

Then the mist thickened. It twisted in a lazy spiral above Edith's head. Still transparent yet tinged with violet and pink hues. As the strange machine whined, the mist hesitated in its motion, then stretched out toward the fan-shaped aerial. Within the mist, small specks of brilliant light, gold and silver.

Langton stared, hypnotized by the stream of bright particles. The mist had its own beauty. Even the course it took, a slender arc, seemed perfect. The first wisps brushed the aerial like pollen settling on a flower.

The jar shattered under Mrs. Barker's heavy walking stick. She swung it again like a club and reduced the jar to fractured shards. Then, before any of the men could move, she brought the stick up above her head and slammed it down onto the generator like an ax.

Sparks erupted from the machine. The smell of burning metal and insulation.

Jake chose his moment. He charged at Langton and knocked him to the floor. In seconds, the doctor jumped over the two struggling men, yanked open the door, and clattered down the stairs.

Under a shower of blows, Langton clubbed Jake in the side of the head with the Webley and tried to roll out from under him. The thug's weight pressed Langton to the floor.

Then Forbes Paterson kicked Jake off Langton and jammed his

own revolver into the man's throat. "After the doctor, Langton. I've got this one."

Langton rolled to his feet and pounded down the stairs. The front door stood open. As Langton jumped to the pavement, two constables ran up to him. One of the men pointed. "We heard someone running, sir."

Langton led the way. The thick fog destroyed all idea of direction. Gas lamps glowed like isolated pools of yellow gauze. Only the pounding of boots against pavement broke the night's hush. Crosswise at the top of Plimsoll Street lay the wider thoroughfare of Durning Road. Langton stopped and listened. Silence. Fog rolled in waves.

"What's that way?" he asked, pointing.

"Wavertree Road, sir. There's more constables waiting there."

"And the other end?"

"Edge Hill Road, sir. Again, Inspector Paterson put men on that junction."

The doctor must have gone straight on. "This way."

As Langton and the two constables crossed the deserted Durning Road, a police whistle cut through the stillness. Another echoed the first. Straight ahead. Langton ran toward the alarms, through the warren of narrow streets east of Durning. Near a streetlamp, a constable stood above the prone body of another officer.

Langton knelt beside the body on the pavement. One of the constables offered him a small lantern; in its light, he saw a diagonal gash running from the prone man's shoulder down to his hip. Blood seeped from the wound and onto the pavement. As Langton found a pulse, the constable opened his eyes and tried to sit up.

"Don't move," Langton said.

"He came at me out of the fog," the constable said. "I didn't see the sword until it was too late."

Langton remembered the doctor's stout cane. Many men, even respectable ones, carried sword canes. "Just relax, man. Help will soon arrive."

"I know, sir. But it's so cold."

As Langton tore off his own coat and tucked it around the injured man, he turned to the waiting constables. "One of you fetch a doctor. The other two carry this man inside the nearest house and keep him warm. The wound looks shallow but needs attention."

Even as the constables hammered at doors, Langton ran off up the street. The fleeing doctor had gained valuable time by attacking the constable. He could be half a mile away. Farther, if he'd found a carriage.

A cold wind shredded the fog for a moment. Langton hesitated at the top of the street. Opposite him, across Botanic Road, stood a sandstone wall five feet high. Police whistles sounded again, left and right. Another whistle, deeper and more powerful, sounded straight ahead. As the ground rumbled beneath his feet, black smoke billowed over the wall and joined the yellow fog. Langton could even hear the rattle of the early-morning steam train's carriages.

He ran to the wall. He still carried the constable's lantern. He played the beam over the sandstone blocks and saw fresh scuff marks. A smudge of black polish from a leather shoe.

Stowing the lantern in a pocket, Langton scaled the wall, following the same route as the doctor. At the top, he hesitated, sitting astride the wide coping stone. The Edge Hill sidings lay spread below him, a broad, deep basin of darkness dotted with lamps, the red and green track signals like animals' eyes.

He had no idea of the drop below him. Those lights seemed a good eighty or hundred feet below the level of the road. And he knew that the Liverpool-bound trains disappeared into tunnels bored deep underground only to reappear at Lime Street miles away. But the doctor had gone this way.

With the wind cutting through him, Langton shivered and eased himself down the dark side of the wall, feet first. His arms ached. He felt for ground beneath him but found nothing. Then, with his toecaps scraping the wall, he touched solid ground. He let go of the top of the wall and dropped down.

The ground crumbled beneath him. He flailed out, trying to save himself; unseen thorns and rocks dug into his hands, but still he fell, rolling and tumbling down the steep embankment. Frozen branches cracked under him. Stones slammed the breath from his body. He curled into a ball and tucked his head tight to his chest. The fall seemed to last for minutes.

Then, with one final impact that stunned him, Langton sprawled at the foot of the slope. He lay there, dazed and battered. He tasted blood, but when he tried to move nothing seemed broken. Nothing except the shattered lantern in his pocket. He checked his other pockets and found the Webley. He held it ready in his right hand and looked around.

He was level with the gleaming rails now. The wall and streets stood a hundred feet above him. A swaying, snorting steam train appeared out of the fog not twenty yards away, its single lantern eye bearing down on him. Then it turned and plunged into a tunnel, its exhaled smoke flattening over its cargo trucks.

As the sound died away, Langton started out across the tracks. The doctor could be anywhere. If he'd fallen just as Langton had fallen, where would he make for? What chance of escape would he find?

Langton stepped over metal rails and wooden sleepers. Gravel crunched beneath his feet. Down here, in this basin scooped out from the earth, it seemed much colder. Langton drew his thin dress jacket tighter with his bloodied left hand. His right held the Webley ready at his side.

More rails. More sleepers. How many tracks intersected here? How many points and sidings and switchbacks converged at this point? And which track had the doctor taken?

Langton stood beneath a wooden signal pole and listened. Far off, the blast of a train's whistle. The wind snapping. From above him, the whirr and click of a signal dropping its arm, changing from red to green. A corresponding whirr and click as nearby points realigned themselves.

Then, close by, the crunch of gravel.

It could be a rat. No doubt the tunnels held thousands of the vermin. Rats would not make that much noise.

Langton stepped forward, taking care to choose sleepers and not gravel. The footsteps grew louder. The fog swirled around everything, its density varying: sometimes solid, sometimes no more than wisps. Langton stared at where he thought the sound originated. He held the gun ready.

A rush of wind shredded the fog. The doctor stood less than ten yards away, the sword naked in his hand. He stared at Langton, open-mouthed. Then he ran.

"Halt or I fire," Langton said, raising the Webley. "Halt, Doctor."

The man kept running. Over the rails, over sleepers, with the sword loose at his side.

Langton fired once into the air. The man stumbled but kept running. Langton cursed and followed.

From behind him, the roar and shriek of a train as it erupted from a tunnel. The ground shook. Clouds of steam rolled against the fog. Langton concentrated on the fleeing man. Ahead, the doctor stumbled and slipped on the greasy sleepers. He looked back and saw Langton, then ran faster.

Looking up, Langton saw the doctor's destination: the signal box. A spiral metal staircase rose from the yards' floor and joined a wooden hut built into the sheer sandstone face of the basin's sides. Another series of switchback stairs led up from the signal box to the roadway above. The chance of escape.

Before the fog rolled in again, Langton saw electric lights inside the signal box, lights reflecting from rows of gleaming metal levers. As he watched, a man stepped forward, gripped a lever, and eased it back. Then the fog obliterated the view.

Langton could still make out the doctor. Not fifteen yards away, just where the tracks wove a complex knot of intersecting rails.

"Doctor, halt."

Langton sighted along the barrel and fired again. The shot whined off a rail a few feet from the doctor's legs. The doctor froze.

"Drop your sword," Langton said, stepping forward. "Now."

The dropped sword rang as it struck the rails. The doctor turned to face Langton. The front of his torn suit bore streaks of soil, just like Langton's. His collar had sprung open and now flapped in the wind. He'd lost one shoe.

"Walk toward me," Langton said.

The doctor shook his head.

Langton repeated his order, but the doctor still refused. Langton looked at the interwoven mesh of rails between him and the doctor. Above him, the whirr and click of a signal changing. "Doctor, it's all over. Come here."

Still the man shook his head. "I can't."

"You have no choice." Langton looked up as another signal changed from red to green. The rails began to hum. "Please."

From Langton's left, out of the east, came a brief whistle. A single yellow eye appeared in the fog. "For God's sake, man. Don't just stand there."

The doctor looked down the tracks, then back to Langton. "I'm sorry."

Another blast on another whistle, this one deep and brash. Another lamp appeared in the fog, running alongside the first. Langton wanted to yell at the doctor. He took a step onto the first set of rails, then drew back. Which of the tracks would the engines use?

As the ground trembled under him, Langton said, "Run, man, before it's too late."

The doctor turned to face the approaching locomotives. He had to shout above the hoarse pounding of the steam pistons. "There are worse things than death, sir."

The points clicked as they changed. The stressed rails moaned under the oncoming weight. The ground shook.

Langton glanced at the two trains thundering from the east, their lanterns side by side. He thrust the Webley into his pocket, took a breath, and sprinted across the tracks toward the doctor.

Too late. An express erupted from the tunnel behind Langton. The eastbound train screamed down the central rails, its gleaming black body slick with steam. Its fender took the doctor in the small of the back and broke him like a rag doll. The enormous wheels chewed him, one after the other. First the engine, then the tender, then the glowing passenger carriages.

Langton pulled up only feet away. He had time to see the open-mouthed driver, with red firelight reflected from the man's greasy face. Then the express roared past.

Langton looked left. The two westbound trains bore down on him. He threw himself off the rails and down onto the gravel verge. Hands clamped over his ears, he saw the sparking wheels bend the rails less than a foot from his head. A banshee wind tore at his clothes. Coal smoke filled his lungs and eyes.

He couldn't move. Like an animal transfixed, he lay motionless on the gravel as the tunnels in the sandstone walls swallowed the two westbound trains. Only their brake-wagon lanterns glowed through the fog for a moment, then were gone.

Slowly, so slowly, Langton sat up. The trains' roar still filled his ears. He blinked the smoke from his eyes and saw a fragment of torn black cloth by his feet. A hand poked from the bloodied cuff. A dozen feet away, another hand, close by a leg, more fragments of cloth, a starched collar curling like a red leaf.

Langton got to his feet and stared at the remnants of the fugitive doctor. He looked up to the signal box, where two men pressed their faces to the glass, watching him. Then Langton bent double and vomited onto the cold, stained gravel.

Twelve

THE OPEN COAL fire sent waves of heat out across Forbes Paterson's office. Langton stretched out his legs and upturned hands to the warmth, trying to drive out the chill that gripped him. His torn dinner suit bore dark streaks of mud and grease; ocher stains of dried blood flecked his cuffs and shoes.

Langton focused on the flames within the grate. From behind him, the sounds of desk drawers opening and closing, a cork pulled from a bottle, the clink of glass on glass.

"Drink this." Paterson held out a glass of amber liquor. "My emergency supply."

Langton didn't refuse. He breathed in fumes of peat and heather, then took a deep draft of whiskey that burned all the way down his throat. He took another drink and cradled the glass on his stomach.

Paterson pulled a rickety chair closer to the fire and rested his own glass on his knee. After a minute's silence, he said, "Why didn't he save himself? What drove him to stay on the tracks?"

Without looking away from the flames, Langton said, "Fear."

"Surely fear would make him jump? With trains coming at me, I know I would."

"'There are worse things than death,'" Langton said. "Those were his words. He feared something so much that he preferred a quick death."

"Something?" Paterson said. "Or someone?"

Langton nodded. The man who had died on the rails at Edge Hill had been a lieutenant working for another, a man he feared above all else. "Doktor Glass."

"It must be," said Paterson. "Proving it is another thing. At least we have Reefer Jake."

"Where is he?"

"In the basement cells." Paterson drained his glass and stood up. "Will you sit in on the interview?"

Langton looked down at his soiled clothes. He knew he should go home and change. He cared nothing for his appearance but he could smell the trains' smoke in his suit, and the blood reminded him of that final collision.

He gulped the last of his whiskey. "I'll sit in."

Langton followed Paterson downstairs. At this time of the morning, just before five, headquarters belonged to the few night shift officers and to the cleaners; the stooped women paused in their mopping as Langton and Forbes Paterson descended, and told them to watch their step on the wet stairs.

"Why do you call him Reefer Jake?" Langton asked.

"He used to be a seaman and the nickname seems to have stuck. I've never spoken to him although we've been after him for close on a year now."

"And you're sure he works for Doktor Glass?"

"Sure as I can be." Forbes Paterson glanced at Langton. "Informers will turn belly-up soon as they see half a crown or a pound note, or sniff another stretch in Walton Jail. Usually. Mention Doktor Glass and they lose their voices."

The sergeant on the basement cells saw the inspectors approaching and unlocked the barred door. "You've sent us a right devil, sir, and no mistake."

"He's giving you trouble?" Paterson said.

The sergeant rubbed a rapidly forming bruise on his chin. "Not anymore. He's in the blockhouse out back."

Stout black metal doors lined an echoing corridor of white tile. The sergeant slid back the viewing panel on the last door and twisted his key in the lock. "Call out if you need us, sir."

Inside the bare-brick cell, Langton saw two massive, bullnecked constables sitting on one-legged stools either side of a stone table. Across their knees, dark wooden cudgels the size of cricket bats. They stood up and set their stools against the wall. "He's quiet for now, sirs."

From above the table, a single electric bulb in a recessed metal cage threw light onto the broad neck and shoulders of Reefer Jake. He raised his shaven head and stared with dull, swollen eyes at Langton and Forbes Paterson. The skin around his jaw and cheekbones had already started to darken into bruising. Dried blood encrusted the knuckles of his enormous hands locked tight to the stone table by steel manacles.

Jake's ankles had been shackled to the table's brick piers. A dented steel bucket stood between his legs; a stale, acrid smell caught the back of Langton's throat.

When the sergeant appeared with two chairs, Paterson sat opposite Jake and motioned Langton to do the same. The door slammed shut. The two constables stood either side of the table, the cudgels at their sides. Paterson drew a typewritten sheet from his pocket and held it to the light.

"Jacob Samuel Ignatius Conroy," he said. "Better known as Reefer Jake. Joined the merchant navy at thirteen. Discharged at twenty-five for bodily harm against an officer of the line. Sailed on various ships that we know of—and plenty that we don't, I've no doubt. Served sentences in Macau, Alabama, Philadelphia, Buenos Aires . . ."

He dropped the sheet and smiled at Jake. "I could go on, but what would be the point? You're wanted right across the world, Jake. Your jaunt is over."

Jake stared at the table as if he could read the stone.

"What have you to say?" Paterson asked. "Nothing? I've got you down for grievous bodily harm and attempted murder. Remember old Silas Ashton? Pierrot Tony? That little business over in Rock Ferry? Bad enough, all of them. But last night's little escapade . . . well, you're looking at the noose, Jake. That was murder."

Still nothing. Jake gave no sign of even hearing the inspector's words.

Langton said, "Your accomplice is dead, Jake. Dead under the wheels of a train at Edge Hill."

At that, Jake looked at the stains on Langton's suit, the blood and oil. The words rumbled out like stones from a deep quarry. "That's his lookout."

"It means that you'll take all the blame," Paterson said. "You'll swing for the girl's death."

"Nothing to do with me," Jake said. "He stuck her with the needle. I just carried his bags."

Langton glanced at Forbes Paterson. Jake had a point; if he stuck to that defense, he might escape with a year or two in Walton Jail.

Paterson said, "What about all your other efforts, Jake? I reckon I've got enough to keep you inside for the rest of your natural life. Maybe enough to put a rope around your neck even if the poor girl's murder doesn't."

The enormous man shrugged, making his chains clink. "I'll take me chances."

"What are you afraid of?" Langton asked. "Why don't you tell us about the men who put you up to this?"

"Nothing to say."

"What about the name Redfers? Doctor Redfers?"

No reply.

"Cooperate and we'll think about a lesser charge," Paterson said. "Don't be a fool."

Langton and Forbes Paterson hammered the man with questions until dawn started to show through the barred window set high above the prisoner's stone shelf bed. Jake would not budge. He would not tell them who had sent him and the dead man to Wavertree.

Exhausted, Langton slumped in his chair. He could see that Paterson felt the same way. Even the two constables wilted. Only Jake seemed unchanged. Like a statue, or one of the Professor's Egyptian carved figures, he simply sat there as if waiting.

Paterson stretched his back and asked, for the fiftieth or hundredth time, "Who do you work for, Jake? Come on, man: Who are you protecting?"

Nothing.

Langton said, "Is Doktor Glass really that powerful?"

A quick glance from under Jake's thick brow, but no answer.

"We could protect you," Paterson said. "Tell us all about Doktor Glass and we'll put you somewhere safe."

No reply.

Langton looked at Paterson, who shook his head and stood up, saying, "We're wasting our time, Langton. Let him swing. God knows he deserves it."

Langton tried one last name. "How about Professor Caldwell Chivers, Jake? Do you know him?"

A shake of the massive head. "I'm not talking. Doktor Glass will look after me."

"Doktor Glass will kill you, if he has the chance. You're a liability, Jake. You know too much."

Jake rested his head on his manacled arms and said no more.

"Chain him to the bunk until later," Forbes Paterson told the constables as he hammered on the inside of the thick door. Then, outside the cell, he said, "I nearly lost my patience in there, Langton. It's difficult to hold back sometimes."

"I don't think it would have helped," Langton said. "Jake won't talk. I watched his accomplice die on the rails rather than betray Glass."

"What hold does Glass have over these men? What can be worse than death?"

Langton had the beginnings of an idea, but he didn't want to share it with Paterson, not yet.

At the barred gate, the sergeant gave Forbes Paterson a brown paper bag. "That's all we found in his pockets, sir, along with his bootlaces and belt."

"Good. Nobody's to see him, Sergeant. Not without my permission."

As the barred door slammed shut behind them, Langton followed Paterson upstairs. Headquarters had come alive by now: Inspectors headed for their offices, constables accompanied shackled prisoners, yawning office boys scurried along with messages and telegrams clutched in their hands.

At the door to Paterson's office, Langton said, "Is Jake safe down there?"

"In the blockhouse? I'll say. Even Jake couldn't fight his way out."

"I'm thinking more of someone getting in."

Paterson stared at Langton. "You really believe Glass will try to silence Jake?"

"Either silence him or save him."

"Don't worry. Jake's going nowhere."

Langton shook hands and turned for his own office, but paused when Paterson said, "Why did you mention this Professor? You think he's our man?"

Langton hesitated. "Give me some time."

As he walked on, he realized that time was a luxury he could not afford. The Queen would soon arrive. Durham, if still living, wandered the streets of the city. And the killer of Kepler, Stoker Olsen, and

Redfers still enjoyed his freedom. And Langton himself? He'd uncovered threads and connections, a network of illicit trade in souls, a trade he didn't want to believe.

When he saw the distorted figure through his office's frosted glass, Langton presumed that Purcell wanted a report on the case. Langton smoothed his rumpled, soiled clothes, combed back his hair with his fingers, and opened the door.

Harry, the office boy, almost dropped the cup from his hand. "Oh, you made me jump, sir."

"What are you doing?"

"Bringing you a pot of coffee, sir," Harry said, already pouring from the Dewar flask on the steel tray. "Billy, Inspector Paterson's boy, told me you'd had a night of it and were down in the cells, so I thought . . ."

Langton smiled and accepted a cup. "Thank you, Harry. You're a good lad."

He closed his eyes for a moment as he sipped coffee. Then, "Any sign of Sergeant McBride yet?"

"No, sir. Shall I send him in when he gets here?"

"Please. And bring me the newspapers."

Harry paused at the door. "Which ones, sir?"

"All the local sheets."

Langton sat at his desk and slid the tray to one side. He must have left out some of the papers from the Kepler case the night before; they lay spread out across his desk. He returned them to the case file and added the events of Edge Hill and Plimsoll Street. As he wrote, the image of the dying girl, Mrs. Barker's niece, rose up again in his mind. The shadowed bedroom with its odors of medication and sickness. The lamplight flickering on the rose-patterned wallpaper.

He hesitated when it came to describing the moment of death and transfer. It seemed so unlikely, so removed from the usual sordid entries in most police reports. How could he describe the mist that radiated from the poor girl's body? The tiny points of light glittering within; the change in the quality of the air, as though the strange machine had charged every particle in the room?

Langton reached down into his desk drawer and took out the canvas sack containing the remains of the machine that Jake had carried into Plimsoll Street. Mrs. Barker's heavy walking stick had shattered the thick resin sphere to shards and dented the squat cube of metal. Copper wires uncurled from the damaged cylinder. Langton laid out the individual pieces on his desk like a museum curator with a strange exhibit.

Someone had created this machine. Skilled hands had wound copper wire around that cylinder and fashioned that cube of steel. Even the wooden base seemed as highly polished as a fine cabinet. Had one workshop—perhaps even one man—built the machine? Or had Doktor Glass and his accomplices created the final mechanism?

With care, Langton sorted through the components, searching for identification marks. The dented cube contained solid resin like amber that sealed the contents inside; on one side, in Gothic Germanic script, the letters A and F, and the numbers 174, but no maker's mark. The remnants of the sphere gave no clue as to their origin. The base of the copper cylinder, however, was more revealing; when Langton held the heavy coil up to the light, he saw a small, oval brass label fixed to the metal. *Mssrs Irving and Long, Mfctrs.*

He locked the components in his desk drawer after jotting down the name. The manufacturer might have produced hundreds or thousands of these coils and sent them across the globe, but it had to be checked.

After a brief knock, the office door opened to reveal Doctor Fry. "Am I interrupting?"

"Not at all." Langton closed the file. "Come in."

Fry carried two buff folders to the desk. He examined Langton's clothes and face and said, "An eventful night?"

"Very. What do you have for me?"

"The postmortem reports on Redfers and the burglar at Hamlet Drive. I'm sorry for the delay; you've given us more work in these past few days than the past month."

"It's not out of choice, believe me." Langton opened the first report and read down the findings. The man who had tried to attack Mrs. Grizedale, the so-called burglar from Hamlet Drive, had died from a single gunshot to the chest. Aged around fifty, with the calluses and musculature of a man used to physical labor. "No tattoos?"

"Only a simple anchor on the forearm," Fry said, "probably from the merchant service. Certainly nothing like the intricate patterns on Kepler's body."

"Nothing in the pockets?"

"A few coins, a pencil, a watch chain but no watch. Nothing of interest."

"And nothing to identify him?"

"I'm afraid not, Langton."

Disappointed, Langton set the burglar's report down and opened the one for Redfers. A single stab wound through the trachea and spine. The weapon a surgical steel blade similar to that carried by Mrs. Grizedale's attacker. Mild burn marks either side of Redfers's neck. "What's this? *Rigor extremis.*"

"Contraction of the muscles," Fry said. "Something like rigor mortis but occurring before death rather than after. Almost every muscle in the man's body had seized."

Langton remembered the contorted rictus grin on Redfers. "What would cause that?"

Fry hesitated. "I'm not sure, to be honest. I imagined it was drugs; that's why the report was delayed, to give me time to analyze the blood and tissue. But I found nothing. No arsenicals. No strychnine."

"And you're quite sure it happened before death?"

"Either just before or at the very moment of death."

Langton wondered what had happened to Redfers in his final few moments. That look of absolute terror. The electrical leads connected to his neck. The machine waiting to capture the dying man's soul, just as with Mrs. Barker's niece Edith in Wavertree. And who held that soul, that captured essence, now? It had to be Doktor Glass.

The office door behind Fry opened. Harry deposited an armful of newspapers on the desk and held out a sealed telegram for Langton. "Just came in for you, sir."

"Thank you, Harry. Oh, one more thing . . ." Langton retrieved the card with the name of the machine coil's manufacturers. "Find me the address of this company."

As Harry limped out, Fry leafed through the newspapers and said, "These journalists have very good sources."

"Too good." Langton reached for his letter opener.

"You suspect someone is indiscreet? Someone here?"

Before Langton could reply, the door opened again and McBride leaned inside. "Busy, sir?"

Langton waved the sergeant in and slit open the GPO envelope. Inside, block capitals were printed on the yellow telegram sheet. He read the message and then passed it to McBride.

Fry edged to the door. "If you don't need me . . ."

"Thank you for the reports," Langton said. "I'm afraid I have two more subjects for you."

"The young girl and the train victim? I know; I've seen them downstairs." Fry paused at the door and asked, "What's going on, Langton? Are all these deaths connected?"

"They are, but we've some way to go yet. Still some way." Langton waited for the door to close, then turned to McBride. "What do you make of that?"

McBride returned the telegram. "Rum, sir. Very rum."

Peter Doran, Langton's ex-colleague who now worked for the Home Office, stated in the telegram that no Major Fallows worked at the Queen Anne's Gate headquarters. Through friends of friends, however, Doran had discovered that the Foreign and Commonwealth Office had a senior-ranking official of that name. He could not discover the man's duties.

"Why would Fallows lie about his department?" Langton said, leaning back in his chair and sipping coffee. "Why hide the fact that he works for the Foreign Office?"

McBride said, "Maybe it's security, sir. Since he's looking after the Queen's visit and all. Maybe he doesn't want anybody to know."

"Not even us? Or the Chief Inspector?" Langton fought a yawn and said, "Any luck at the reception last night?"

McBride pulled a notebook from his pocket. "Nothing much to report, sir. Most of the drivers and footmen had heard of Redfers and Kepler through the newspapers. But five thought they remembered Redfers from previous visits by their employers."

Langton read down McBride's list but didn't recognize any of the names. They could simply be patients of Redfers. Or they could have a more disturbing motive. As he copied the names into the case file, he said, "Compare these names with the list of patients on Redfers's books. Ask his receptionist—what was her name?"

"Mrs. Dunne, sir."

"Ask her if these families consulted Redfers as patients, and ask his maid, Agnes, if they visited as friends. Either are possibilities."

"And if they're neither, sir?"

"Then there's a chance they visited the good doctor for a less innocent reason. Which means we might have to pay them a visit."

McBride pocketed his notebook and glanced at Langton's disheveled suit. "Would you like me to call by your house on the way back, sir? I could bring in some fresh clothes . . ."

Langton considered for a moment. He had much to do, but maybe he should return home to bathe and change. "Thank you, I'll see to it myself."

McBride turned back at the door. "I almost forgot, sir. You remember that Mrs. Dunne said Doctor Redfers got a call just before he sent her home? Well, the constable we left at the telephone exchange went through the records with the operators and found an entry, a call coming in to the doctor's number. I don't know if it's the one we're looking for—"

"Where was it from?"

McBride smiled. "From here, sir. From headquarters."

Thirteen

A FTER MCBRIDE HAD left, Langton took out Redfers's diary and compared the names from the sergeant's list with the clients' abbreviations. He found three possibilities: Arthur Cameron, David Hemplemann, Stephen Powell. If they were the same as AC, DH, and SP in the diary, they would have to explain to Langton what exactly they had received from Redfers. Even though they were important men, men of influence in Liverpool society.

Langton thought back to the day Redfers had died. Who in headquarters had called Redfers? Langton would have given a great deal to know the contents of that call. Whatever the message, Redfers had sent his receptionist home and cleared his house of patients. And then he'd waited. He hadn't expected to die; that final, terrified look on his face said as much.

As he locked away the case files and prepared to leave for home, Langton recalled some of the threads still hanging loose: He still had to identify Mrs. Grizedale's attacker and the "doctor" who'd died on the Edge Hill rails; he awaited news of Durham from the tunnels' search teams; he wanted to interrogate Reefer Jake again. There was Mr. Dowden to see, and also Mrs. Barker; Langton wanted to check on her, ensure she had recovered.

So much to do. So many possible connections and interconnections.

Langton switched off the office lights and started down the stairs. He stopped and looked up at the sound of his name and saw Purcell striding down the steps, coattails flapping.

"I want a word with you." Purcell strode past Langton and made for his office; he halted when he realized that Langton hadn't followed. "What is it, man?"

"Sir, I've worked all last night, I've had no sleep, and I need to go home and clean myself up at the very least. Now, what can I do for you?"

Purcell's face reddened. "I'd adjust my tone if I were you, *Inspector.*"

Langton took a breath and controlled his impatience. "Sir, we're very busy and—"

"Too busy to update Major Fallows and me," Purcell said. "People dying left and right, bodies mutilated, and citizens murdered in their own homes, and you fail to keep me informed. It's just not good enough, Langton. Now, what news have you for me?"

"The investigation proceeds, sir." Langton shifted to one side to allow people past. "Would you like me to brief you now?"

"On the stairs? I think not. No, you can tell Major Fallows the latest news. He's out at the Span, supervising the arrangements."

"Sir, I—"

"To the Span, Langton. I will not have Fallows accuse me—us, rather—of not cooperating."

Langton bit back his reply. He supposed he could use the opportunity to check on the progress of the tunnel search teams. He gave a slight bow to Purcell and descended the stairs. He slowed as he passed Forbes Paterson's department, wondering what he might have found in Reefer Jake's personal possessions. It could wait until later, when they interviewed Jake again.

Outside, Langton shielded his eyes against the sun. After the dark night in Wavertree and Edge Hill, and his hours spent in the cells and his office, daylight seemed almost painful. He stood blinking at the top of the steps until he got used to the glare. Then he submerged himself in the tide of people sweeping down Victoria Street toward the Pier Head.

The city seemed to have erupted in a patriotic fervor for the Queen's imminent visit: Many of the Dale Street shops and offices now bore banners of red, white, and blue; Union Jack flags hung from windows; Corporation workmen on tapering ladders looped bright garlands between the iron lampposts. Langton wondered how much she would see as her carriage made its way through the crowds that were sure to throng these streets. Probably very little. But perhaps the city's inhabitants welcomed the Span as much as, if not more than, the monarch. The Span promised freedom.

And as Langton turned the corner of Water Street and faced the Pier Head, he saw the Span rear up like a colossus, a physical steel echo of some ancient Grecian tale. The Span diminished with perspective until it showed as no more than a narrow thread of light over distant Ireland. Here it dwarfed every other structure, even the immense ventilator shafts for the new Mersey Tunnel. It reduced men to no more than dots, specks against the stone and steel.

"Oy! Watch your step."

At the shouted warning, Langton stepped back onto the pavement. He raised a hand in apology to the cart driver who'd almost run him down. Either side of Langton, pedestrians waited to cross the Strand; they glanced at Langton as if he were drunk.

Drunk with fatigue, Langton thought. His hand found the bottle of Benzedrine tablets in his pocket. Not yet.

As he passed the tobacconist's cabin under the overhead railway, Langton remembered the man who'd followed him from the camp. Or rather, who he *thought* had followed him. Langton saw it now for an overactive imagination. Or perhaps the atmosphere of the murder cases was affecting him. He'd have to keep a balanced perspective no matter down what strange roads the Jar Boys led him.

At the Span's Pier Head entrance, the guards at the first set of barriers asked Langton to wait. He could see the camp less than a hundred yards away, but the Queen would not; teams of Span workmen busied themselves all along the Pier Head, erecting tall hoardings to block all sight of the shanties. Lines of constables patrolled the construction, intervening where the camp's inhabitants argued with the builders working so hard to hide them away.

"This way, sir."

Langton followed a plainclothes guard through the first barrier and then a turnstile, one of a series built for the inauguration's guests. He could see how the barriers would funnel people through in single file, delay them so the various police and guards and the Queen's own officers could monitor them and spot any troublemakers. A good plan if it worked.

"Are you armed, sir?"

"I am," Langton said, already reaching for the Webley.

The guard stopped him. "You can keep it today, sir, but no weapons will be allowed as of tomorrow. This way, please."

Through a set of ornate steel gates, past tiered wooden seats beneath awnings still being erected by shirt-sleeved workmen. Beyond the guarded perimeter, the life of the docks continued: Langton could see cranes hoisting cargo, men scurrying over ships, carts, and steam wagons laden with bales. Here, within the radius of the site of the inauguration ceremony, an air of calm and comparative quiet reigned.

On one side of the concourse stood the offices of the Span Company, where Langton had spoken with Lord Salisbury. On the other stood temporary, tiered seating for perhaps two or three hundred guests. And there, at the very start of the Span's great access ramp, two massive gilt chairs, plush and red, squatted inside an ornate pavilion. The man in front of the pavilion watched Langton approach, then waved away the guard. "Langton."

"Major Fallows." Langton didn't know whether to salute or shake hands, since he didn't know who Fallows really was. "The Chief Inspector said you wanted to see me."

Instead of acknowledging that, Fallows waved his right arm to encompass the site of the inauguration and the Span itself. "We've taken every precaution we can, Langton. Every guest will be searched, even the ladies. Teams have scoured the docks and sewers and found no devices or assassins. We'll have a man in every office of the Span's headquarters there, in every window. The Span itself will be crawling with policemen, army specialists, guards, and marksmen. But all to no avail."

Langton waited.

"If you cannot find Durham," Fallows said, staring at Langton, "then all our preparations mean nothing."

"We don't know he's part of any plot."

"We cannot discard it, Langton. Now, tell me the progress of your investigations."

Langton told Fallows about Redfers and Mrs. Grizedale's attacker, and the results of their postmortems.

Fallows interrupted him with a wave of the hand. "Tell me of Durham."

"Of him I have no news. I hope to question the head of the tunnel search teams as soon as I can."

Fallows gazed at the docks beyond the temporary fences. "So he's still out there."

Langton hesitated before asking, "Who is this man Durham?"

For a moment, Fallows seemed about to answer. Then his face set into its usual impassive alignment. "You have a task, Langton. I am not the only one interested in finding Durham. You don't want to answer to Her Majesty herself, do you?"

With this, Fallows turned away to end the discussion. But Langton said, "You must have worked at the Home Office for some years, Major. I find it surprising that your name doesn't appear in any of the directories."

Slowly, Fallows turned back to Langton. "You've spent some of your valuable time investigating me?"

"You have no office at Queen Anne's Gate," Langton said. "I can find no record of you there. There is, however, a Major Fallows at the Foreign Office."

Fallows took a step forward. His eyes had become very small and bright. "Concentrate on finding Durham, Langton."

Langton stood his ground. "I need to know, Major."

Another moment's hesitation, then Fallows said, "If I wished it, I could call myself Captain, General, Commodore, or Lord. I can be whoever or whatever my duties demand of me. And I answer to one person and one person alone. I hope you understand that."

Langton nodded. "Now I understand."

"Good. Then find Durham. Before it's too late."

As Fallows strode away toward the Span, Langton followed the guard back to the entrance gates. At least one of his questions had been answered: Fallows belonged to one of Her Majesty's confidential agencies. That explained his duties, his power, and his reticence. It might also explain his interest in Durham.

Where exactly did Kepler's accomplice—and perhaps his killer—fit into all this?

Outside the Span entrance, to the north, workmen had erected hoardings around the Liver Guaranty Building site and were now busy painting the bare wood. The Queen would see little of the real Pier Head when she arrived; perhaps she never saw anything of the real Britain wherever she traveled, since everything would be cleaned, painted, or hidden for her visit. Buildings, streets, whole towns might be renovated just for her.

In front of the half-built Liver Building, around raised iron access covers, Langton found the police search squad. A chugging steam lorry leaked water and smoke. Tubes led from the wagon's pumps and down the subterranean access shaft's steps into darkness. A slim boy sat on the pavement with his legs swinging over the shaft; putrid, stinking brown filth covered him from head to foot but didn't prevent him from gnawing at a sandwich.

"Is Sapper George down there?" Langton asked, keeping upwind of the boy.

"He is, sir. And you're . . ."

"Inspector Langton."

"Right-o, sir. One minute." The boy bolted the last of his sandwich and disappeared down the access shaft like a rat down a drainpipe.

Langton waited five minutes, then ten. The pumps, driven by the steam engine, pulsed, wheezed, and gulped like a straining beast. Just as Langton thought about yelling down the shaft, a slender head and shoulders squeezed into view. The smell made Langton step back and cough.

"Quite a fragrance, isn't it, Inspector, till you get used to it." Sapper George slid from the shaft like an eel from a rock and cast a bundle of oilcloth up to rest beside the steam wagon's wheel. He grabbed a flask of water, gargled, then spat a streak of black bile onto the pavement. "Some sweet perfumes down there, sir, I can tell you."

As Sapper George climbed up to street level, Langton saw that his filthy overalls had grab handles sewn onto the shoulders, waist, and calves, so that his mates could pull him out of danger. A leather strap fastened an electric lamp to his bald head and made him resemble some strange, one-eyed underground creature. Thick brown and black sludge dripped from his limbs.

Langton took a step back. How could anyone get used to working in conditions like that? The search squad went where no one else would go: lakes, sewers, pits, quarries. They dragged lime pits and cesspools. They found the bodies that murderers thought, and hoped, lost.

"Any sign of our man Durham?"

"Plenty, sir. We went in where you described, just below the sewer outfall. Ripe, that was."

Langton remembered the translucent cockroaches. "Go on."

Sapper George took another gulp of water before he continued. "Well, he stumbled around a bit, as you would in the dark, then headed inland. Footsteps easy to follow, except when he had to cross the sewer courses. But he's persistent, sir, I'll give him that; he didn't give up. It's a rats' warren down there, what with the old smugglers' tunnels, the boreholes, the ventilation shafts and waste sluices. This Durham fella just kept going."

Langton peered into the darkness waiting at the bottom of the access shaft and tried to imagine the network of tunnels down there. Damp, crumbling brickwork. No light. The scurrying of rats and God knew what else. He shuddered. "I didn't think he'd survive."

Sapper George smiled. "Oh, you'd be surprised, sir. We've found whole families living down there. Like Swiss cheese, the sandstone underneath Liverpool. Like another city. Why, when the navvies were digging for the Mersey Tunnel, they found bedrooms and living rooms, kitchens and all kinds; twelve skeletons sitting around a dinner table a hundred feet under the Trinity Church. Rooms stacked full of bones, neat as you like. Devilish signs and bottomless shafts leading Lord knows where. Some strange souls have lived down there."

Even though the stories were no doubt embellished, Langton had to close his eyes and grip the side of the wagon for support. The thought of deep, oppressive darkness disoriented him. Too many resonances.

"Are you all right, sir?" Sapper George asked. "I didn't mean nothing by them tales. My missus is always saying I talk too much."

Langton shook his head. "I'm just tired. But I don't have any great desire to follow you down there."

"I hopes you don't have to, sir. Now, your man Durham: As I said, he headed inland, probably finding his way by the direction of the waters. Either way, it looks like he come up by Parliament Street."

"Toxteth? He made it all that way?"

Sapper George scratched his head. "I know it's strange, sir, but distance doesn't mean the same down there. Sometimes, you think you've been crawling for days and you've only made a few hundred yards. Other times, it feels like you've been down there an hour or two and you'll suddenly pop up the other side of the city, miles away. Short-cuts, like."

Toxteth. Langton remembered that Professor Caldwell Chivers lived in a luxurious mansion not far from Upper Parliament Street.

"You're sure it was Durham?"

"Sure as we can be, sir. His boot prints were nice and clear, easy to spot. And he left this jacket by the sewer exit next to the cathedral crypt." Sapper George unwrapped the bundle of oilcloth and laid out the sodden jacket. He brushed away the albino cockroach that crawled from the pocket and pointed to labels along the inner seams. "Property of the Span Company, sir."

"Thank you."

"You want us to keep looking, sir?"

"No, call your men back. I'm sure that Major Fallows has a few jobs for you."

Sapper George grinned, revealing gold teeth. "I bet he has, sir."

Langton started walking toward the rank of hansom cabs waiting on the Goree, then turned back to Sapper George. "Do these tunnels burrow underneath the Span?"

Already halfway down the shaft, Sapper George stuck his head up above street level and said, "Some of them do, sir, but the Span Company bricked them up. Wouldn't want someone laying a charge down there, would they?"

No, they wouldn't, Langton thought. If plotters, Boer or otherwise, did exist, then where would they strike? And how?

LANGTON FELL ASLEEP in the hansom cab taking him home. He woke at some bump in the road, unsure for a moment who or where he was. Then he recognized familiar streets, gardens, his own trim house. "Just here, driver."

He saw the front door open as he climbed down from the cab. Elsie took his hat and coat. "We were worried about you, sir."

"We?"

"Me and Sergeant McBride, sir." Elsie turned away as a faint blush colored her neck and cheeks. "He just came over to check I was all right."

Langton smiled but didn't comment. He could see McBride and Elsie happy together. He wished it for them.

"This came for you, sir. Yesterday evening."

Langton broke the envelope's seal and read three short sentences of precise copperplate writing. His smile faded. He folded the letter into his pocket and stared into space.

Elsie waited a moment, then said, "Can I get you some coffee, sir? Something to eat?"

"I'm not hungry, Elsie."

"Please, sir, you should eat. Cook said she could whip you up some eggs, bacon, toast, anything you fancy. Or a proper dinner if you like."

Langton knew she was right. He needed fuel. "Thank you, Elsie. Give me half an hour. Just something light. And plenty of coffee."

As he undressed in his room and ran a quick bath, Langton glanced at the letter on the washstand. Why did Sarah's parents want to see him now? Why this particular moment? The brief text requested—almost demanded—him to call on them, but gave no hint about the reason.

Cold water opened Langton's eyes and reminded him of cemetery rain, and the last time he had seen Sarah's parents: her father glancing at him from under the wide black umbrella and silk top hat; her mother staring at the intricate rain patterns on the curving mahogany casket as if she could decode them. They had spoken only a few words to him that day. And nothing since.

So why now? What did they want from him?

Shaved and dressed, Langton entered the drawing room and

found a new fire in the grate. Weak sunlight filtered through the curtains, glowed from polished wood, and showed a single place laid at the table. Elsie really did her best to take care of the house. And of Langton.

"There you are, sir. Bacon and eggs, and some good thick toast. Careful of the hot plate." Elsie slid the willow-patterned plate before Langton and poured coffee from the silver pot. "Set you up for the day, even though it's a bit late for breakfast."

Langton smiled as the comfortable atmosphere of home relaxed him. Perhaps time had started its healing. He only had to look down the table, to the empty chair, to know that wasn't so. He forced himself to eat while Elsie fussed around the room; her chatter washed over him like the gentle warmth of the fire.

Then, as he pushed away his empty plate, Langton touched the letter in his pocket. He should call Sarah's parents and arrange a time to visit, even though he wanted to return to the interrogation of Reefer Jake. And he had so many other tasks. "I think it'll be another late night tonight, Elsie."

"Is there anything I can do, sir?"

"There is something." Langton drained his cup and left the table. He remembered Mrs. Grizedale's attacker, and Redfers. Doktor Glass obviously didn't like loose ends. Or perhaps he was simply vindictive. "Elsie, I want you to be careful."

"Sir?"

"Lock the house up tight. If someone calls, check who they are before you let them in. Even better, don't let anyone inside the house. Shout for help if someone tries to force their way in; before I go back to work, I'll ask next door's footmen to keep an eye on you."

Elsie's eyes opened wide. "Why, sir, whatever for? You don't think—"

"I just want to make sure." Langton took his coat and hat from the hall stand and turned at the front door. "Remember, Elsie: Take care."

"I promise, sir, but I've got Sergeant McBride to look after me."

Again, she blushed. "I mean, if he's not too busy, sir. I don't want you to think he's ignoring his job or anything . . ."

"I know, Elsie. He's a good man."

That made Elsie's face even redder. Langton put her out of her misery by standing on the top step while he buttoned his coat. He waited until he heard the mortise lock click into place behind him, then looked up at the solid façade and wondered if Doktor Glass would want to harm Elsie. Perhaps not, but she might get in the way when Glass targeted Langton.

Langton didn't want that on his conscience. In life, there was only so much guilt that one man could bear.

LANGTON CLIMBED THE stairs to Forbes Paterson's office just after two in the afternoon and found it empty. Presuming that he had gone down to the basement cells without him, Langton almost collided with Paterson on the stairs.

"I've been looking for you," Paterson said. He held the brown envelope containing Reefer Jake's personal possessions.

"Sorry I'm late."

Paterson grinned. "I don't think our friend Jake is going to complain. No, I wanted you to take a look at these before we question him again."

Back in his office, Forbes Paterson laid out the contents of Jake's envelope: clay pipe, pigskin pouch of dark tobacco, a few coins of various sizes, an ivory-handled lock knife. The last item caught Langton's eye: a brand-new key with the outline of a bridge stamped into the metal. Langton had seen that design before, on the key found with Kepler's mutilated body.

"It's to do with the Span, isn't it?" Paterson said.

"It is." Langton held it up to the light. A complex design, all jagged teeth and notches. "What interest would Jake have in the Span?"

"Has he any connection with your murders?"

"Let's ask him." Langton pocketed the key and followed Forbes Paterson down to the basement cells.

Another duty sergeant opened the barred doors. "Here to see the big fella, sirs?"

"Has he given you any more trouble?"

"Not after we chained him to his bunk. Quiet as a lamb."

Something troubled Langton. He rubbed the key in his waistcoat pocket.

The sergeant swung open the heavy door and called inside, "All right, you. Sit yourself up."

Enough light seeped through the barred slit of dirty glass to show a body lying on the stone shelf bed. As the sergeant flicked on the electric light, Langton caught a strange smell, so out of place that he had trouble identifying it. White flowers.

"Come on, you. You got company." The sergeant prodded Jake in the stomach with the bunch of keys.

Jake didn't move. He didn't open his eyes.

Then Langton saw a small pane of glass missing from the window. A breeze carried in cold air from outside. Cold enough to make the cell feel like a tomb.

"Get Doctor Fry," Langton said, dropping to his knees beside the bunk. He jabbed his fingers into the massive neck but knew it was too late. He found no pulse behind the cooling grey skin. He looked up at Paterson and shook his head.

Paterson looked at the missing pane and down at the lifeless body. "How? How did they get to him?"

"He let them," Langton said. "He could have called out to the sergeant; he could have struggled. Look at his body—he didn't resist."

Jake's massive frame lay on the bed as if in sleep, with his hands clasped over his stomach, his face relaxed. Langton checked the man's neck, just below the ears. In the harsh electric light, two small square burns. Just as Langton had expected.

Doctor Fry rushed into the cell, his coat flapping, his hands already opening his bag. As Langton and Forbes Paterson stepped back, Fry examined Reefer Jake. It took only a few moments. Fry set down the stethoscope and closed his bag with a metallic click. "Dead no more than thirty minutes, gentlemen."

"From what cause?" Langton asked.

"I think from this." Fry pointed to a red dot on Jake's inner wrist. "They probably injected something to stop his heart, but I can be more precise after the postmortem. Thanks to your investigations I'm becoming quite practiced at them."

Forbes Paterson turned to the sergeant standing in the doorway. "I want the area outside the window examined. They must have dropped over the walls on Victoria Street or Crosshall Street; have constables question anyone whose windows overlook the area . . ."

As Paterson continued to give instructions to the sergeant, Langton fought the sense of futility that rose within him. He had no doubt that Doktor Glass had planned this, and that Jake had willingly participated in his own murder, but Langton doubted that Glass had left much evidence. The man had begun to take on almost supernatural qualities for Langton. What could the police do against such a complex, organized entity?

"I'll send O'Neill down with a gurney to collect the body," Fry said, making for the door. "I suppose you want the results as soon as possible?"

Langton forced himself to reply, "Whenever you can, Fry. This is enough to overwhelm anybody."

Paterson seemed about to speak but waited until they were upstairs. "What is it, Langton? What's wrong, man?"

Langton shook his head. "Everything we do is known. This Doktor Glass seems no more than a step behind us, maybe even one ahead."

"You think he has informers inside headquarters?"

"I don't know. Perhaps." It would make sense. How many people had access to the most important information, to Langton's own case files? McBride and Purcell. Harry, the office boy, at a pinch. All equally ridiculous suspects.

"You're getting tired," Forbes Paterson said. "Sometimes we get too close to a case. Draw back a little."

How? Langton felt the Queen's imminent visit as a weight pressing down on him. Purcell and Fallows wanted answers. Answers Langton could not yet provide.

He thanked Paterson and climbed the stairs to his own office, so deep in thought he hardly noticed the constables and clerks milling around him. He retrieved the case files from the safe and added news of Reefer Jake's death. Now they would never have the chance to ask Jake about that Span key. Or about Sarah.

Langton pulled the key from his waistcoat pocket and traced the bridge motif with his thumb. Just like Kepler's key. What locks or doors did Jake's complex key open? What connection did Jake have with the Span?

At the sound of a knock at his door, Langton closed the files and slipped the key into his pocket. He waved McBride into the visitor's chair and asked, "What did Mrs. Dunne have to say?"

"Well, sir, I went through Doctor Redfers's files with her and none of the three gentlemen seem to be patients. She seems a thorough woman, too."

Langton read down McBride's notebook again. Arthur Cameron, David Hemplemann, Stephen Powell. Now these men would have to explain to Langton what exactly they had received from Redfers. He didn't look forward to the interviews but they had to be done. He glanced at the clock—half past three. He still had to visit Sarah's parents.

Langton sat back and rested his head against the chair. So many avenues to check. Jake and Kepler led back to the Span, as did Durham. Redfers led to the Jar Boys and possibly to Professor Caldwell Chivers at the Infirmary. The man who'd died on the Edge Hill rails led to Doktor Glass; did the dead man also have some connection to the Infirmary? He'd claimed to be a physician.

"Come on, McBride," Langton said as he locked away the case files. "Let's see what we can find in the dead men's possessions."

Downstairs, in the basement, Langton saw two shapes huddled beneath white sheets. Fry's office stood empty, but O'Neill, his second assistant, worked with test tubes and phials of colored liquids at a wooden bench. "Doctor Fry's just stepped out for a moment, sir. He had a call from home."

"Do you still have the belongings from the man who died on the rails last night?"

"Over there, sir. Third box from the left."

Langton found the cardboard box and laid out the contents on a spare table. Expensive watch and chain, fountain pen, almost a hundred pounds in notes and coins, cigar humidor, matches, penknife, and handkerchiefs. At the bottom of the box, the silver syringe case with the remains of the drug that had killed Mrs. Barker's niece Edith. And, on the reverse of the hinged case, precise words etched into the metal: *Property of Liverpool Infirmary.*

"Found something, sir?" McBride asked.

"Our man here had a connection to the Infirmary."

McBride read the text. "He could have stolen it, sir. Or got it from someone there."

"Maybe so," Langton said, doubting it. Too many coincidences; too many connections leading back to the Infirmary and perhaps to the Professor.

The door to the main entrance slammed and made Langton, Mc-Bride, and O'Neill look up. Langton found Fry red-faced in the cluttered office, muttering to himself. "What is it?"

"Some idiot's idea of a bloody joke," Fry said. "A sick joke, at that. Someone reported my house on fire. I rushed home to find absolutely nothing wrong. And they pick just this moment, when I've never been busier—"

"Where's Reefer Jake?" Langton said, already through the doorway.
"Wait, Langton."

Langton rushed up to O'Neill. "Where Jake's body?"

"The big fellow? The one I brought up from the cells?"

"Where is he?"

"Why, the men came for him, Inspector. They said Doctor Fry here had arranged it all."

"I arranged nothing," Fry said.

Langton nodded. "The hoax call took you out of the way. They must have been waiting to collect Jake. What did they look like?"

"Just the usual, sir," O'Neill said. "About my height, clean shaven, slim build . . . Just like the other orderlies that come here. White coats, stretcher, a private ambulance wagon parked outside. I didn't think there was anything wrong, so—"

"Do you remember anything that might identify them?" Langton asked. "Anything. Accents, tattoos, scars. Think, man."

O'Neill wrung his hands. "I'm sorry, sir, I was so busy . . . They had Liverpool accents, soft spoken and quiet. They handled the body as if they were used to the job. But I remember one thing about the ambulance."

"What?"

"As it turned in the yard, I saw the letters *L.C.C.H.* on the back, next to the red lamp. I thought it a bit odd."

Langton turned to Fry, who said, "Liverpool Corporation City Hospital. It's the old name for the Infirmary."

Fourteen

LANGTON SAT WAITING in the front drawing room of the town
house in Abercrombie Square. On the mantel, a clock of or-
molu and gilt chimed six. A fire crackled in the grate and threw
red and gold light onto tiered book spines, polished wood, ornate
chairs. From the other side of the square came the clatter of hooves
on cobbles. Langton shifted in his seat, crossing and uncrossing his
legs. He pulled at his too-tight collar and glanced again at the clock.
He rose to his feet as the door opened.

Mrs. Cavell, Sarah's mother, hesitated at the threshold for a moment before advancing toward Langton. "Matthew. How are you?"

Langton shook her hand and struggled to speak. So much had
happened so quickly. So many questions left unanswered.

"Arthur will be down in a moment," she said, waving Langton back
to his seat. "He's just . . . He won't be long."

She sat on the edge of the French sofa, black crepe gown against
the red plush, and folded her hands on her knees. With her slim fig-

ure, gathered hair, and slender, elfin features, Mrs. Cavell looked enough like her daughter to make Langton's heart heavy.

"Would you like some tea? Coffee?" Mrs. Cavell reached for the bell pull but drew back when Langton shook his head.

He took a deep breath. "I was surprised to receive your note."

"I hope you don't see it as a summons. We know how busy you are at the moment. We had to speak to you."

Langton waited in vain for her to continue. He saw her glance at the closed door and then clasp her hands together in her lap until the knuckles turned white.

Five minutes crawled by like hours before the door opened and Arthur Cavell entered the room. The aroma of whiskey drifted along in his wake. He nodded to Langton but didn't offer to shake hands. "Langton. Good of you to come over."

On his feet now, Langton looked between Sarah's parents and wondered what had scared them so deeply. Arthur's ruddy face and moist eyes hinted at an afternoon with the bottle; Mrs. Cavell stared down at the rug in front of the fire and seemed to shrink in on herself.

"You wanted to see me."

Sarah's parents looked at each other before Mrs. Cavell said, "We must tell you about Sarah."

No surprises now, Langton thought. *Please, not now. I could not bear it.*

Mrs. Cavell continued, "We know what she went through. We know how she suffered. How both of you suffered."

Langton sat down and closed his eyes. "Please."

"Even toward the end, we refused to give up hope. Every week, science seems to produce some wonderful treatment or drug, some miracle almost within reach."

"You were not alone in hoping for a miracle."

"I know, Matthew. But—"

"Tell him, Louise. Tell him."

"I will, Arthur." Mrs. Cavell leaned toward Langton's chair and looked into his tortured eyes. "We wanted to do everything we could.

You were blind with grief, oblivious to everything. So when Doctor Redfers came to us—"

"Redfers?" Langton stared at her. His body turned to ice. "What did he say?"

"We'd known him for years," Arthur said. "His father had treated my own father, myself, and—"

"What did Redfers say?"

Mrs. Cavell laid a hand on Langton's arm. "We thought only of Sarah's best interests, Matthew. Our only intention was to help her."

"What did Redfers say?" With difficulty, Langton kept his voice calm. "Tell me."

Again, Mrs. Cavell glanced up at her husband, then said, "Redfers swore he could save her soul."

LANGTON PACED THE drawing room like a tiger caught in a pit. He kept his clenched fists behind his back. "You let this charlatan touch Sarah? This . . . swindler, thief, molester . . . What in God's name were you thinking? Were you insane?"

Arthur took an unsteady step forward but stopped at his wife's up-raised hand. Mrs. Cavell said, "Yes, Matthew, we were insane. With grief. I know you suffered, but think of us for a moment: We watched Sarah grow up; we cared for her, loved her, missed the sound of her voice, her laughter. I remember so much. So much."

That stopped Langton. He saw Mrs. Cavell's head sink down, and Arthur's hand settle on her shoulder.

"But to let Redfers do that to her . . ."

"We trusted him," Arthur said. "He was her doctor, and we trusted him. We had no choice."

Slowly, Langton uncurled his fists. He had sunk so deep into his own pain that he hadn't considered how much Sarah's parents had suffered. Nor how desperate they might have become. "Tell me what happened. Please."

Arthur Cavell related the story. It seemed that Redfers had approached Sarah's parents three weeks before her death. The drugs
could do no more; surgery was impossible. They must face the inevitable conclusion. But not all hope was gone: Redfers could offer them
a new procedure. A *scientific* procedure. In his persuasive explanation,
Sarah's very essence—her animus—could survive, could live on until
another host could be found.

"A host? He said that?" Langton asked.

Mrs. Cavell nodded. "He said that the scientists had already transferred captured souls."

"Into what? Other bodies? And did he say what happened to these
hosts' original souls?"

Arthur looked down. "We did not ask."

I'm sure you didn't, Langton thought. Even if this truly insane procedure did work—which Langton doubted with all his heart—it would
need an "empty" host. After witnessing Edith's casual murder, Langton knew that the Jar Boys would stop at nothing. "Go on."

It had seemed so logical to the Cavells, or perhaps they allowed
Redfers to persuade them. His scientific words meant little to them but
the principle seemed simple: Sarah's departing soul would be captured in a suitable container. Later, it would be decanted to another
living body. In the meantime, Redfers would ensure its safety at his
own house.

Langton remembered his own skepticism upon first hearing of the
Jar Boys and their method. "I'm still surprised you believed him so
readily."

Arthur hesitated, then said, "I have to admit that I'd heard of this
before."

"Where?"

"At the lodge. There were rumors, hearsay, about visits to certain
houses in Kensington, Toxteth, and Bootle."

"What did these rumors say?"

Arthur glanced at his wife. "That you could experience another person's sensations, just for the brief moment you held on to the jar's connectors. Like a snippet from a dream or a sudden flash of memory."

Langton wondered if Arthur had ever visited those houses himself; something in his words, the way he looked at his wife, suggested it was more than hearsay. Even so, Langton had no wish to embarrass Arthur in front of Mrs. Cavell. He didn't want to cause Sarah's parents any more pain. That particular question could wait until later. "Did many of your fellow lodge members sample this?"

"More than a few," Arthur said. "Men tire of drink, gambling, the same old stories and jokes. They look for novelties, new experiences. For a while it was quite a fad."

"Was?"

"Well, perhaps it still is, for some."

Langton could imagine the jaded old men, the lodge's apparently respectable pillars of Liverpool society, slipping into dark doorways to try out illicit pleasures. But was it a pleasure? Forbes Paterson said the Jar Boys captured the souls of the dying; Langton himself had witnessed it with Mrs. Barker's niece Edith. What pleasure could men have in reliving those final moments of some poor creature's life? Had the men—the so-called collectors and their clients—become so cynical that they'd actually enjoy it?

Langton recoiled from the thought, but he knew it would not leave him. He swore he'd ask Doktor Glass when he tracked him down.

"So you arranged for Redfers to be present at Sarah's bedside."

"We did not have to arrange anything," Mrs. Cavell said. "Redfers seemed to have his own contacts at the Infirmary. He asked us to leave everything to him. Which we did."

Langton resumed pacing. "Why didn't he come to me?"

"Because you're a policeman," Arthur said. "And Redfers knew the procedure was not yet legal. And we knew that you would refuse."

Would I have refused? Langton asked himself. *If someone had offered me the chance, even the smallest chance, to prolong Sarah's life . . . ?*

No. Artificial existence inside some cold clay jar was not life. It was no more and no less than cruelty. Still, that doubt gnawed at Langton and prevented him from blaming Sarah's parents too much. "Afterward, did you visit Sarah? Did you try to connect to her?"

Mrs. Cavell looked up at her husband, who said, "Three times. I went to Redfers's house—"

"The basement?"

"Exactly. He set a jar on the table before me, and . . ." Arthur closed his eyes and gripped the mantelpiece for support. "I couldn't do it. Each time, I panicked and ran from the room. I was afraid that Sarah wouldn't be there, and yet more afraid that she would."

"So you don't know if he tricked you or not?"

Mrs. Cavell answered, "No, Matthew, we don't."

Mrs. Grizedale knows, Langton thought. *She believes that Sarah still exists.* He hesitated a moment, unsure whether to tell the Cavells about the medium and her visions of Sarah. He decided to leave it until later, when he had proof.

"So now you know," said Mrs. Cavell as she got to her feet. She smoothed the front of her mourning gown and clasped her hands together. "We're ready to face up to our responsibility. We know we've broken the law. As soon as we learned of Redfers's death, we realized we must tell you. So."

Langton looked at Sarah's parents standing there, waiting for retribution. Perhaps that might help ease the guilt they so obviously suffered. Would prosecuting them bring about any kind of catharsis? Langton doubted it.

"I should go," he said, making for the door.

"But—"

"I might have done the same," Langton said. "If Redfers had appeared on one of Sarah's worst nights, when I could see . . . I might have listened to him. I know enough now to be glad he didn't, but all the same, I can see how he persuaded you. How easy it would be to clutch at hope. Any hope."

Mrs. Cavell stepped forward and held Langton's hand in her own. Her eyes glistened. "We miss her so much."

Langton bowed his head and took a deep breath. Then he left the warm, quiet drawing room and reached for his coat. Standing at the front door, he asked, "Arthur, where are these houses that your friends visited?"

Arthur glanced at his wife before reaching into a drawer of the hall stand. He held out a small card engraved in fine gilt writing. "One rings this number and makes an appointment for the establishment in Toxteth. I believe this is the only house still open."

Langton glanced at the telephone number and slid the card into his waistcoat pocket. "Did anyone at the lodge ever mention Doktor Glass?"

"No, not that I recall."

Langton opened the door and then turned back a moment. "How about Caldwell Chivers? Professor Caldwell Chivers?"

"Why, yes," Arthur said, staring at him in surprise. "The Professor is one of the lodge's most respected Grand Masters."

THE EMPTY, ECHOING streets gave Langton space to think, room to consider the Cavells' admissions. He walked on icy pavements beneath hissing gas lamps and a cloudless sky brilliant with stars. His exhaled breath solidified in front of him as he walked; its pale mist resembled that which had fled Edith's body in the Plimsoll Street bedroom and gravitated toward the Jar Boys' strange apparatus.

As he strode toward home, ignoring the occasional hansom cab for hire, Langton could hardly believe the news. The Cavells had always seemed so sensible, so respectable: churchgoers, philanthropists, members of school governing boards and poorhouse committees. If they could involve themselves in such bizarre, occult experiences, whom could Langton trust?

He looked up at the silent town houses on either side of Brewster

Street. Warm lights glowed behind blinds and curtains. From one parlor, a hesitant phrase of Chopin from a family piano. What really went on behind those neat façades? What secrets did they hide from the world?

Thinking like that would lead to paranoia. Probably any and every street had its own secrets. Nothing on earth was as complex as the human heart, no matter what the scientists might say. Langton found this strangely comforting as he neared home. Then he thought of Sarah. Arthur Cavell had confirmed what Langton already knew: Redfers had taken his callers down to the basement room to sample the contents of the shelved jars. Arthur said he hadn't touched her jar, but what of the other "clients"? How many men had communed with Sarah's captured essence?

Langton forced himself to breathe deeply, to slow his racing heart. And by concentrating on his own body he realized for the first time that other steps echoed his own. He didn't turn around; he didn't look back. He kept his pace steady and listened to the footsteps behind him.

Almost in step with his own tread but different enough for Langton to notice. He unbuttoned his Ulster and slipped one hand inside to find the crosscut grip of the Webley. All the while, he looked for a good place to make his stand. It might be innocent, no more than somebody out for a late constitutional on a cold evening. Then again it might not.

The road branched ahead. A night tram cut across the junction, sparks trailing from its pantograph arms. The blue-white arcs showed tall black railings, chiaroscuro trees and shrubs. Langton leaped sideways through the garden gate left ajar. He crouched on the brick path with the Webley ready at his side.

The pursuing footsteps halted on the dark street. Silence. Langton heard his own breath, his beating heart. Had he imagined it?

No. The man turned and walked away, back the way he had come, his steps heavy but regular and unhurried. Langton inched forward and risked peering around the gatepost. The man, bundled in drab colors, slid through successive pools of gaslight; in their glow, before the shadows swallowed him, the massive, stooped figure could almost be mistaken for Reefer Jake.

LANGTON CLIMBED THE steps to his own house and looked back for a moment at the empty street. Fatigue and too much disturbing news could so easily distract the mind. They could lead to paranoia if not outright delusion. Langton knew he'd have to take care.

He tried his key in the lock but the front door didn't move. Langton made sure he had the right key, tried again, then looked up at the dark windows before pressing the bell. He rang again. Panic made him hammer at the wood.

Then, from inside the house, a faint voice: "Who is it?"

"It's me, Elsie. Are you all right?"

The sound of bolts drawn back. The click of the mortise lock. Then a wedge of yellow light as Elsie opened the door. "You said I should be careful, sir, so I made sure—"

"Are you safe? Has anything happened?" With one hand inside his coat, Langton checked the hall, the stairs, the open doors.

"Everything's fine, sir." Elsie closed and locked the door and stood with her back to it. "You said to lock the house up tight, so I did."

Langton let out the breath he'd been holding. He felt more than a little ridiculous now. How easily that paranoia set in. "I'm sorry, Elsie. I'm just tired."

"Would you like anything, sir? Something from the larder? I'm not as good as Cook, but—"

"Thank you, no. I'll retire soon."

"Well, good night, sir."

"Good night, Elsie." Langton opened the door to the living room, then turned back a moment. "Did Sergeant McBride call tonight?"

"No, sir. Not tonight."

Langton thought he heard a note of regret in her voice. Perhaps he imagined it. Either way, it was really none of his business. He warmed himself at the dying fire and retrieved the small card from his waistcoat pocket, the card that Arthur Cavell had slipped into Langton's hand as they stood in the hall of Abercrombie Square.

No name or address on the card, just a telephone number: Exchange five-seven. Although tempted to call it right at that moment, Langton knew he should wait; he didn't want to tip the hand of the Jar Boys. Besides, perhaps McBride could discover the address that belonged to that number. Then Forbes Paterson and Langton could descend on Doktor Glass without warning.

Settling back in the leather armchair, Langton wondered if Professor Caldwell Chivers and Doktor Glass really were one and the same person. Although circumstances hinted at it, and the Professor's name kept appearing in so many different areas and from the lips of different witnesses, Langton would need more than hints and suggestions. He'd need irrefutable evidence.

Perhaps the Professor had a secret room just like Redfers had? Shelves of ceramic jars sealed tight. Copper lids sealed with wax glinting under electric light. The smell of dust and charged particles . . .

Sleep caught Langton. In that state of semiawareness, where he knew that he dreamed and could almost guide his thoughts, he floated above his own body. He saw the dwindling fire but felt no heat. The tall grandfather clock ticked. Then the room twisted on its axis and became his bedroom. A shape under the bedclothes. Not him.

Terror pulled at Langton. He willed himself to wake, but his dreaming body drifted closer to the shape under the blankets. It lay on its side. The covers rose and fell, inhale and exhale. A voice called his name.

Now an odor: white flowers. Sickly sweet. Cloying. Then morphine, sticky and dark and acrid. The aromas grew stronger as the dreaming

Langton reached the side of the bed. Despite himself, he saw his own hand reach out. He could feel the soft blanket in his grip. Slowly, so slowly, he pulled down the covers.

Langton reared up in the living room chair. His clenched fingers dug into the soft leather. His mouth opened as if in the middle of a scream but he heard no echoes, no sound of Elsie's footsteps hurrying to see what had happened. In the grate, the fire had died to black ashes. The clock still ticked.

And in the opposite chair, with a black revolver resting across his muddied knees, sat Durham.

LANGTON DIDN'T MOVE. His own Webley lay in the pocket of his Ulster in the hall. The heavy poker and brass coal tongs lay almost within reach on the tiled grate, but Langton knew he would never have the chance to use them. He sniffed the air; the mixture of stale smells took him back to the tunnels beneath the Pier Head.

"I was tempted to wake you," Durham said, his deep voice slurred with fatigue, "but I remembered that you should never interrupt someone having a nightmare."

"You're thinking of sleepwalkers," Langton said, surprised by his own calm voice.

Durham nodded. "My mistake. It's unnerving to wake up staring into the barrel of a gun. I know."

So many conflicting thoughts ran through Langton's mind: How had Durham gained entry? How had he survived? What did he want with Langton?

Durham scratched at the bloodied scabs on his face and said, "Have you any liquor in the house?"

"In the sideboard."

"Would you pour me a glass? Whatever you have." Durham said. The barrel of the revolver eased around until its dark eye tracked Langton. "And please don't do anything that might make me shoot you."

With slow, careful movements, Langton rose from the chair and crossed to the sideboard. He opened the drawers and took out a bottle of Laphroaig whiskey and two glasses. He poured a small measure for himself and a larger one for Durham. His limbs felt as if they belonged to an automaton. He sensed the barrel of the revolver square in his back.

"Thank you." Durham took the glass and drained half of it in one gulp, coughing a little. He waved Langton to the chair again.

Langton stood where he was. "Have you harmed Elsie?"

"Your maid? No, she's sleeping soundly in her bed. Snoring like a corporal."

Langton sat down and sipped the strong drink. His eyes took in every detail of Durham's clothing, from the scuffed boots to the ragged, filthy trousers, dirty collarless shirt, and relatively clean jacket. He guessed that Durham had stolen that to replace the one he'd left at the Toxteth tunnel exit.

Durham's dirty face with its collection of scrapes, scabs, and cuts bore testimony to his escape through the tunnels, and perhaps to worse ordeals since then; a clotted bandage enclosed the hand clasped around the whiskey glass.

"Who is Sarah?" Durham asked.

Langton froze. "My wife. Why?"

"You called her name in your sleep."

Langton hesitated. "She passed away recently."

Durham glanced at him and then back to the fire's embers. "You are working on Kepler's case. I need to know what you've found."

"Why?"

"I have my reasons."

"You know I can't tell you," Langton said.

Durham turned slightly to face Langton. The revolver remained on his knees. "I need to know, Inspector."

Langton knew he was on delicate ground. He took a sip of whiskey. "How can I give valuable information to one of my main suspects?"

"I did not kill Abel."

"You know who did?"

"I have some idea of it, yes."

"Then tell me," Langton said.

Durham stared at him for a moment as if weighing up options. Then he said, "Abel discovered a plot against the Span. The man behind that plot lured Abel to a meeting and then . . . Well, you know the result. I believe I know who did it."

Doktor Glass? Langton thought. *Or the Professor?* Aloud, he said, "I know you and Abel Kepler were sent here to investigate a possible plot. I even know who sent you: Major Fallows."

Durham stared at him.

Langton continued, "Fallows admitted to me that he works for one of Her Majesty's confidential agencies. I don't know whether you and Kepler were agents or mercenaries."

"We've been called both at different times."

"So . . ."

Durham finished his drink. "You're well informed, Inspector. Fallows arranged for us to work on the Span. We heard plenty of rumors about a Boer conspiracy but saw little hard evidence. Obviously Abel dug deeper than I did. His reward was death and mutilation."

Langton leaned forward. "Do you know what he found?"

"Why should I tell you? Why should I trust you?"

"A good question but one that you've already answered. Why else would you break into my house and question me? You could have killed me in my sleep."

"True. But perhaps I needed information before I killed you . . ."

Langton glanced down at the revolver. His heart beat a little faster. "I suppose I must take that chance."

Durham smiled and held out his glass for a refill. When Langton returned with another measure, Durham said, "I know only that Abel discovered an address off the Dock Road, some warehouse he thought belonged to the plotters. It looks as if he was right."

"You don't know the address?"

"I'd hoped to find it from the same pub contacts that Abel did, but you chased me off the camp before I had the chance."

Langton remembered the tunnels, the smell and the translucent cockroaches. "I'm amazed that you survived."

Durham stared at him. "I've endured worse."

Langton realized then that Kepler hadn't been the only agent with experience of the Transvaal. Something in Durham's eyes spoke of the same horrors. "You thought the Boers threatened the Span?"

"At the start, yes," Durham said.

"And now?"

"I'm not sure. It could still be Brother Boer, playing a complicated game of double-bluff, but that doesn't smell right. Someone else wants the Span destroyed. There's another hand at work behind this."

With what motive? Langton wondered. At least the Boers had their own reasons, misguided though they might be.

Could he believe anything that Durham told him? The agent might be playing his own complicated game for God knew what motive. Langton considered all he knew about Durham, Kepler, and Fallows. "I don't understand; why didn't you just contact Major Fallows? Or tell me the truth instead of fleeing?"

"Because I don't know who I can trust," Durham said. "Somebody knew about Abel and me and decided to silence us. That address off the Dock Road was a trap—they expected both of us to go. If I had, you'd be looking for my face, too."

Durham echoed what Langton had sensed: the hand of a clever, deranged puppeteer at work behind the façade; someone who knew more than the police and victims. "Do you know Doktor Glass?"

Durham gave him a sharp look. "I know him, yes. Most people in the camp have heard rumors."

"Is he your plotter? Is he the one behind all this?"

Instead of answering directly, Durham said, "Me and Abel were staked out like goats in a clearing, waiting for the tiger. We were bait. Or a useful distraction."

"Would Fallows really do that to you?"

Durham rubbed his forehead. "I don't know. Maybe. If he thought he had to."

Even as Langton saw his moment to pounce, it had passed. Durham looked at him from eyes red from fatigue or fever or both. "As soon as I heard about the tattooed body in Albert Dock, I knew. Abel hadn't come back to our digs the night before. And then you appeared."

And you ran, Langton thought. *Perhaps I would have done the same.* "Come back to the station with me. I'll keep you from Fallows if that's what you wish, at least until we discover whose side he's on. You have my word."

Durham smiled. "Words are easily given."

"I don't lie."

The smile slipped. Durham stared at Langton and said, "I almost believe you, Inspector. But if I walk into a police station I'll come out the other side in a box. Fallows isn't the only one with a secret network."

Langton thought of the information leaking from his office, and of Reefer Jake. Headquarters, the one place in Liverpool that should be safe, offered no guarantees.

Durham got to his feet in one quick movement and made for the door. The revolver hung at his side.

"Wait," Langton said, rising from his chair. "Who is Doktor Glass? Tell me."

Durham hesitated, then shook his head.

"I believe I know," Langton said.

"I don't think you know any more than I do," Durham said as he opened the door to the hall. "When I'm sure, you can collect the Doktor's faceless body from the Mersey. And maybe Fallows's, too."

With that, Durham disappeared. Langton ran into the hall. Icy air poured in through the open front door. Langton pulled his Webley from his coat and ran down the front steps.

The street lay empty. Snow and ice gleamed under yellow gaslight. No sound of footsteps or carriage wheels. Nothing except the wind bending the bare tree branches.

Fifteen

L ANGTON WOKE AS though no time had passed between closing his eyes and first light arriving. He lay there in the wide mahogany bed with every muscle clenched in fear; he could not remember his second nightmare, but a residue of indistinct, amorphous dread remained, like the afterimage of the sun on the retina.

He forced his heart to slow down and sat up with the sheets wrapped around him. He remembered Durham—or had he dreamed that also? No, the man had been here. The smell of the tunnels still remained.

The luminous hands of the Swiss clock on the bedside table read six twenty. Langton shuffled to the bathroom with the sheets still around his shoulders like a Roman toga. He started running a bath but turned at the sound of knocking from his bedroom door.

"Begging your pardon, sir." Elsie saw the crumpled sheets and made a point of looking in the other direction, away from Langton. "There's a visitor."

"At this time?"

Still looking away, Elsie held out a card: *Professor Caldwell Chivers*. "I put him in the sitting room, sir. Shall I start the coffee?"

"Give me ten minutes, Elsie."

As he scrambled to bathe and get dressed, Langton wondered what the Professor wanted and how he should treat him. As a suspect? As his main suspect? Would Langton's reaction tip the man's hand?

Still buttoning his waistcoat and combing his hair with one hand, Langton clattered down the stairs and into the sitting room.

"Inspector. Forgive the early intrusion." The Professor set down his coffee cup, stood up, and held out his hand.

After a moment's hesitation, Langton shook it. "Professor. You're an early riser."

"Always, Inspector. I find there are not enough hours in the day to do everything I want. That's no excuse for waking you."

The Professor stood before the grate where a new fire threw out little heat; the room still retained its night chill and the traces of stale, stagnant water from Durham's clothing.

"I must say, your maid looked after me very well," the Professor said. "She's obviously a pleasant girl."

"Elsie is a great help."

"You have no other staff?"

"Only Cook," Langton said, wondering why the Professor should be interested in his household.

"Just the one assistant? In such a large, sheltered house?" The Professor sipped his coffee and smiled. "I don't know where I would be without my staff, the footmen and maids, gardeners and cooks. We get to rely on them, don't we?"

"I suppose we do." Langton poured himself a coffee and looked his early visitor over. The Professor, although well dressed and freshly shaved, still exuded that aura of impatient motion, as though caught between two or more important tasks. His body never seemed to be still. His bright eyes reflected the electric light.

Could this really be Doktor Glass? The Professor had the attributes: intelligent, certainly; scientifically adept, definitely. And the eclectic collection at his mansion confirmed his passionate curiosity.

Had the Professor crossed the line between science and murder?

"You left my reception so suddenly," the Professor said. "I wondered if we'd upset you."

"We?"

The Professor smiled. "My friends and acquaintances have their own particular subjects, their own hobbyhorses if you will, and can sometimes be quite . . . intense."

"I found your guests very interesting," Langton said, wondering what the Professor's real motive might be; he surely hadn't come to apologize. "I would have stayed longer but police business called me away."

The Professor hesitated, then said, "The Jar Boys?"

"The same."

The Professor crossed to the fire and set his cup on the mantel. He watched the flames for a moment. "I fear that Doktor Glass might have been at the Reception."

Langton stared at him. "Why do you say that?"

"Because of this." The Professor reached into his jacket pocket and drew out a folded piece of colored paper.

Langton examined the sheet: thick, expensive paper with three symbols drawn on in precise black ink. They seemed to be the images of a dog's head, a field of wheat or corn, and a boat. "Egyptian?"

The Professor nodded. "The first is the glyph of Osiris, the god of the dead and the resurrected; the second a ripe field of corn; the third is the barque of Amun-Ra, a symbol of rebirth and renewal."

Langton returned the sheet. "What connects this to Doktor Glass?"

"He is supposed to have a keen interest in Egyptology."

"You never told me that."

"I did not think it important. But when I found this in my display case after the reception—"

"One of the cases in your basement room?"

"Indeed," the Professor said. "Someone had placed it among the scarab brooches, in plain sight. Obviously for me to see."

Why? Langton thought. If the Professor was Doktor Glass, why would he concoct such a story? If he wasn't, why would the real Glass leave the message?

"Do the symbols have any meaning?" Langton said.

"Individually, no more than their basic references to the gods and the afterlife."

"And together?"

The Professor sagged as though the passing years had suddenly surprised him. "I may be wrong, I hope I am, but together they suggest a great reaping. A harvest of souls."

LANGTON PACED THE manager's office of the firm of Irving and Long in Liverpool's Jamaica Street. He had reached headquarters before eight and given McBride his instructions for the day, without mentioning Durham's late visit. Then he had taken a hansom cab south through the city's poorer neighborhoods, where the air had gradually thickened with smoke from dense slum quarters and a myriad of chimneys. A score of factories lined Jamaica Street; heavy steam wagons and carts clattered over the busy cobbles and added their din to the workshops' roaring and pounding. On his way through the main shop's flickering, strident red glow, Langton remembered Children's Bible illustrations of Hades from Sunday school so long ago.

Now, in the cluttered office high above the shop floor, the factory's activity came through the cracked windows as muffled yells and thuds, the whine of steam-driven belts, the smells of hot metal and burning coal. As he waited, Langton wondered who McBride had started with; which of the three men who had visited Redfers would he question first? And would they admit to anything?

"Here we are, sir, here we are." The plump manager bustled into the office with an open ledger in his hand. He settled behind his desk and beamed at Langton. "Took me a few minutes, but we found it."

Langton looked down the various columns: orders taken, monies paid, goods delivered. "Where is it?"

"Here, sir." The manager rested a blunt forefinger against an entry. "I thought I recognized the coil as soon as you showed me. It's not often we're asked for something of such a high specification."

Langton read the name—Mr. De Verre—thought for a moment, and then almost smiled. *Verre*: the French for "glass."

The address next to the name was Falkner Square in Liverpool, a select area just off Grove Street in Toxteth. Not too far from the Professor's mansion. Langton nodded when he saw the telephone number: Exchange five-seven.

The manager continued, "We usually specialize in ships' equipment and heavy-lifting tackle, but lately we branched out into electric motors, solenoids, and the like. Why, we've even supplied some of the switchgear for the Span. Quite a feather in our cap, I may say."

Langton looked up from the ledger. "The Span?"

"Indeed, sir. Even they didn't ask for such high-quality wire, nor for the exact tolerances that Mr. De Verre requested. Well, demanded, to be honest. It was all we could do to fulfill his last order."

"What last order?"

The manager puffed out his chest and smiled. "The biggest induction coil we've made so far, sir. Biggest in Liverpool as far as I know."

Almost afraid to ask, Langton said, "How big?"

"As tall as you or I, sir, and heavy with it. Lord knows what Mr. De Verre plans to use it for."

Langton glanced at the coil on the manager's table; part of the machine destroyed by Mrs. Barker, it stood no more than four inches high. If the new coil was intended for a larger version, and the rest of the machine followed the same scale . . .

It might not be too late. "Can I see it? This new coil?"

"I'm afraid not, sir," the manager said. "Mr. De Verre collected it a week ago. Even the big hulking fella on the steam cart had trouble lifting it."

That had to be Jake. "Did De Verre order anything else?"

The manager read down the ledger. "Five hundred feet of braided copper cable . . . ten of our largest copper spade connectors . . . and twenty sections of four-foot copper rod. All collected and paid for."

"But no more coils?"

"No, sir." The manager closed the ledger with a dusty thud. "Mr. De Verre's last letter said they wouldn't need any more."

As THE JOSTLING cab carried Langton back to headquarters, he stared out the window and asked himself what Doktor Glass could want with the enormous machine. If the smaller versions—the ones Langton knew from the houses of Redfers and of Mrs. Barker—transferred the soul of an individual, then logic dictated that this new, immense apparatus must be intended for a host of souls. A harvest of souls.

As the cab left Jamaica Street and joined the Dock Road traffic, cutting under the dockers' umbrella elevated railway, the Transatlantic Span reared up from the Mersey. Flags trailed from the towers, waiting for a breeze. Even at this distance the bridge seemed out of place, impossibly huge. Langton tried to imagine the crowds that would converge on the Span the next day. Thousands upon thousands. All packed into one small area.

And he remembered Reefer Jake's key, the complex design stamped with the Span's motif. If Doktor Glass really had a plot against the Span, how would he carry it out? Major Fallows said every precaution had been taken: His teams had searched for explosives; river traffic would be halted for the inauguration; even the commercial dirigibles would be grounded. And Fallows's men would check every visitor, search every man, observe every movement.

Still, Langton worried. If Doktor Glass was involved, then the usual precautions might not suffice. A madman adept with the new, extreme science might have more imaginative plans. But surely Glass would have to place the immense machine close to his victims? Close to the Span? That would not go unnoticed.

Langton willed the cab forward. The house in Falkner Square must hold the key. He would have telephoned Forbes Paterson from Jamaica Street, but he remembered how easily information leaked from headquarters. A call from there had warned Redfers; others had briefed the newspapers. No, he had to see Forbes Paterson in person to arrange the raid.

As the cab finally wound its way through the streets packed with crowds, and bunting and streamers in cascades of red, white, and blue, Langton hurried up to his office and found McBride waiting. The sergeant looked up from the note he'd been writing. "Just leaving you a message, sir. Didn't have much luck with the three blokes."

"You can tell me in a minute," Langton said, throwing his coat onto the stand. "Come on."

They found Forbes Paterson downstairs. As succinctly as he could, Langton explained about the house in Falkner Square.

"You've caught me out," Paterson said. "Purcell commandeered all my spare officers for the Queen's visit."

"Then we'll go now, just the three of us." Langton made for the door, pushing McBride ahead of him.

"Wait. I know Falkner Square. You could hide a regiment in those big old houses. We'll need men out the back, in the alleys, all around the square."

"But you said—"

"Give me an hour." Paterson reached for the phone. "I'll call in some favors."

Langton hesitated. He could feel the minutes ticking away. And every moment gave Doktor Glass another chance.

As if he saw this, Forbes Paterson placed a hand over the receiver and said, "Trust me, Langton. If you go there now you'll only warn

Glass off. And I don't want to risk that; he's caught us out too many times in the past."

Langton nodded his assent and stood outside the office with McBride. He knew Paterson was right, but apprehension churned inside him.

"Where to now, sir?"

Langton weighed options. "The Infirmary, and hopefully news of the ambulance that collected Reefer Jake."

"Can you give me a minute, sir?"

"I'll see you downstairs." Langton collected his coat and searched for Harry, to check for messages. He couldn't find the office boy, so he dropped down to the front desk and waited for McBride.

"Sorry to keep you, sir." McBride, red in the face, hailed a hansom outside headquarters and held the door open for Langton to climb in.

"The Infirmary," Langton called up to the driver, then turned to McBride. "So. The three men who visited Redfers."

"Not very talkative, sir." McBride opened his notebook and struggled to read it as the hansom rattled up Dale Street. "I called on Arthur Cameron first: a solicitor with a firm in Harrop Chambers. Unmarried. His maid said he left suddenly, took yesterday's steamer for Canada. No idea when he's coming back."

"A planned trip?"

"All last minute, according to the maid."

Langton nodded. Something had scared the solicitor. Or someone had warned him. "Go on."

"I tried David Hemplemann next," McBride said, staring intently at his own writing. "Businessman, something to do with import and export. Very fine house. Married with two children; wife's one of those big women, like a ship in full sail. Anyway, he wouldn't talk. Wouldn't even admit to knowing Redfers. You could tell he was scared, sir. Kept rubbing his hands together like he was washing something off. Pale as a ghost."

"What about the third man?"

"Stephen Powell, sir." McBride grinned. "Ran me out of his house like a common salesman. Said he knew his rights, didn't have to talk to the police, he'd call his solicitor, blah, blah . . . But he was just as scared as the other fella, sir. Maybe more. And I saw two big trunks in his hall."

So someone else had details of all Redfers's "clients," Langton realized. Doktor Glass. Perhaps Redfers had worked for Glass, acting as a contact between respectable society and the Jar Boys. And Redfers had also collected the souls of the dying. Just as he had with Sarah.

Langton screwed his eyes shut and clasped his hands tight together.

The hansom halted in front of the Infirmary steps. Langton waited at the open door to allow a stooped old woman to shuffle inside the lobby. Then he crossed to the porter's hatch and asked who dealt with the Infirmary's ambulances.

"Why, that would be the people in administration, sir. Left corridor, down a floor, and look out for room number six. No, sorry, seven, it is."

Langton pulled McBride to one side, out of the milling crowd of patients and relatives. "You ask administration about the wagon. Find out what they do with their old ambulances; maybe they keep a record of who buys them when they're sold on."

"Sir. Where should I find you when I'm finished?"

Langton looked away, feeling an obscure sense of guilt that surprised him. "Sister Wright's office."

SISTER WRIGHT SAT behind her desk and listened without interrupting. Langton told her about the man who'd died at Edge Hill, Reefer Jake's murder and removal, and Durham's survival. He drew back from telling her about the house in Falkner Square and the evidence building up around Professor Caldwell Chivers.

As he explained, one part of his mind remained separate, and marveled at how easy it was to talk to Sister Wright. She gave off an air of calm, of infinite patience. No doubt some of that came from her duties with the sick, developed as a good bedside manner. It must also come from her own nature; like Sarah, she had a natural, comforting empathy.

When Langton had finished, Sister Wright shook her head. "It's hard to believe that all this has happened in such a short time. And that you've discovered so much. You've done well."

"Me? No. Durham is still free, as are Kepler's murderers. And Doktor Glass can walk into police headquarters and calmly remove his accomplice's body."

He retrieved the dead man's silver syringe case from his pocket and slid it across the table. "I wonder if you've seen this before?"

While Sister Wright examined the case, Langton glanced to his right; the frosted-glass partition distorted the figures of the nurses working in the inner ward, made them seem like strange, slow fish drifting underwater. The clink of metal against glass or porcelain came through.

"It's not that common," Sister Wright said, closing the syringe case and returning it to Langton. "The larger medical companies, the ones who bid to supply surgical implements or equipment, produce these and give them to the more influential doctors."

"Such as . . ."

"The consultants, I suppose. And the surgeons."

Langton hesitated. "Would the Professor have one?"

"Possibly. I don't remember seeing it."

"Where is he now?"

Sister Wright glanced at the upturned watch on her tunic. "In theater. Would you like me to ask him, when he comes out?"

That might tip off the Professor. "No, thank you. It's not that important."

As if defending the Professor, Sister Wright said, "I wouldn't want you to think the Professor accepts bribes. Many of the staff here receive gifts from the medical companies and suppliers. It's common practice."

To deflect her, Langton said, "No doubt that the man who died at Edge Hill received this case just as you say, as a gift. If not indirectly through Doktor Glass."

Sister Wright leaned forward. "You're sure you're dealing with this 'Doktor Glass'?"

"I think so. He seems to be everywhere, manipulating, arranging, controlling. Like some dexterous puppeteer with real people for marionettes. A very clever, ruthless puppeteer."

"You sound almost as if you admire him . . ."

"Admire? No, not that. But I can't afford to underestimate his abilities. No matter who he is."

At that, Langton wondered how Sister Wright would react if the Professor really was Doktor Glass. She obviously revered the Professor. Even though she had survived the Transvaal, even despite the strength apparent within her, she would take it hard. Langton didn't want to destroy possibly her last illusion of decency, altruism, and humanity. He knew he might have no choice.

Now, staring at him, she said, "You know who he is, don't you?"

"I'm not yet sure."

"But—"

"Please. Soon we'll have enough proof." Langton stood up, glancing again at the empty birdcage in the corner. He shook Sister Wright's hand and said, "Perhaps tomorrow I can be less reticent."

She seemed about to ask again, but instead nodded and said, "I look forward to seeing you. And take care."

After he left Sister Wright, Langton found McBride waiting in the outer corridor, out of place among the starched uniforms, bedraggled patients, and gleaming white tiles. "Any news?"

McBride shook his head. "Sorry, sir. Seems they don't keep any records of who they pass the old wagons and carts on to. Could be rag-and-bone men, they said. Could be tradesmen."

Langton didn't enjoy the thought that some of his food might be transported on carts that had once carried bodies. Still, what the eye didn't see . . .

Returning to the main lobby, Langton showed his warrant card and borrowed the porter's telephone. He got through to Forbes Paterson and listened, nodding, to the inspector's message. When he set the phone down, his eyes burned a little brighter. "It's on, Sergeant. We move tonight."

Sixteen

L ANGTON STRODE THROUGH the falling snow with Forbes Paterson at his side and McBride and three of Paterson's own detectives behind. All bundled against the cold in heavy coats and gloves, neck scarves reaching almost to their hat brims, just like the few pedestrians that hurried along Huskisson Street in the failing light. None of the policemen spoke. Ahead lay Falkner Square.

Forbes Paterson had told the cabdrivers to halt at Catharine Street, a good half mile from their destination. Langton thought it overcautious but then remembered how the Jar Boys had slipped away so many times before. Now, glancing at Paterson, he saw the set of the inspector's shoulders, the eyes gleaming hard.

At the junction with Bedford Street, two other plainclothesmen left the shadows of doorways and joined the advancing party without comment. Langton wondered if Doktor Glass had lookouts posted in the area, lookouts that would notice eight stocky men marching toward the square. But the snow helped them here; its gusts and swirls shielded them and made passing pedestrians bow their heads and concentrate on getting home.

Now, through the snow, a sign on a brick wall: *Back Sandon Street.* Almost there.

Forbes Paterson raised his hand to halt the men. Ahead lay Sandon Street, then the square with its fine, four-story houses. On the opposite bank of Sandon Street, a handful of ragged loafers held out their bare hands to a glowing brazier. Red embers and black smoke against white snow. One of the men left the group, dodged the few hansoms and carts on Sandon Street, and ambled toward the policemen. He'd almost passed them by when he darted into a doorway, followed by Forbes Paterson.

"No one has been in or out of there for the past hour, sir," the man said. He blew on his chapped hands and shuffled from foot to foot, shivering in his thin jacket. "They had a cart drive up maybe half an hour ago; small fella in a hooded cloak went inside but hasn't come out again."

"No other visitors?"

The plainclothesman shook his head. "There's plenty of life in there, sir. Most of the lights are on, and there's music from the parlor."

"Then we have them." Forbes Paterson smiled at Langton, then told the shivering observer, "You go home and thaw out, Jenkins."

"Begging your pardon, sir, but I'd like to stick around for the end."

"Good man." Paterson looked at each man in his team, then led the way across Sandon Street toward Falkner Square.

Langton wondered how many favors Paterson had called in. "You've had men watching the house?"

"For the past two hours. Jenkins out front, Simpson around the back." Forbes hesitated to allow a coal merchant's wagon past, then hurried on. "By now, we should have another five men waiting at the back doors and yard. We've got Doktor Glass like a rat down a drain. There's nowhere for him to go."

"How do you know he'll be there?"

"The small man in the hooded cloak," Forbes said. "I think that's our man. This time we have him."

Langton hoped he was right.

Falkner Square opened out before them. Indistinct in the gusts of snow, the black exclamation marks of iron railings, skeletal trees. Windows glowed yellow and white in the tall houses. Langton hurried after Paterson, who stopped at the bottom step of a looming redbrick town house. Every window glowed. Subdued piano music drifted from a downstairs room. The black front door looked heavy and solid.

Forbes Paterson stood aside to let through two detectives. The first man took an enormous chisel from his pocket and placed it over the door's lock. Langton, amazed, saw the second detective produce a sledgehammer from his capacious greatcoat. The men waited, poised.

Paterson checked his watch, put a police whistle to his lips, and gave three short blasts that pierced the cold air.

The first sledgehammer blow sent the chisel through the lock. The second took the door from its hinges. The detectives poured into the hall, pistols in their hands. "Police!"

Langton rushed to the stairs, looking for a way to the basement. All around him, doors slammed open, boots pounded on parquet floors. His heart raced. The Webley in his hand seemed weightless.

Down a few steps, a white door. The handle turned. Langton sensed someone behind him; he turned and nodded to McBride. Then he led the way along a passageway. A bare electric bulb burned overhead. More open doors revealed scullery, kitchen, washroom, larders. Not a living soul.

Down another three steps into a cold brick corridor. The smell of damp earth. At the end, a massive door of oak bound with wide bands of steel. But the padlocks hung open in their hasps. With his Webley raised, Langton inched forward and gripped the iron handle. It took all his strength to haul the door back on its complaining hinges. Its momentum slammed it into the passage's brick wall.

Darkness. The smell of white flowers and damp. Pressed back against the passage wall, Langton reached into the dark basement room. His hand searched for a light switch. When he found it, pure white light seared the room.

Empty. Every shelf bare save for the round imprints of recently removed jars. White tiles, whitewashed walls, white ceiling. And a multitude of fresh muddy footprints on the tiled floor.

"They knew," Langton said. "Someone told Doktor Glass to expect us. Just like Redfers."

McBride said nothing. He stood aside as Forbes Paterson rushed into the room. The inspector froze, like a marionette jerked back on its wires.

Langton slid his Webley into his pocket and said, "The house is empty, isn't it?"

Forbes Paterson nodded. "Not a soul."

Langton followed Paterson through the house, through deserted rooms and echoing passageways. In the kitchen, a stew still bubbled on the stove; vegetables lay chopped on the pine table, knives scattered beside them. In the front parlor, an electric gramophone played the same Chopin melody over and over; the music washed over empty chairs, half-drained glasses of whiskey, cigar butts still smoking in ashtrays.

The evidence of hurried flight lay everywhere: clothes half-dragged from wardrobes; bureau drawers tugged open or even upturned on bedroom floors; lamps still burning in rooms where cigarette smoke clung to the ceiling. Every room seemed to wait for occupants who had just slipped out for a moment and would soon return.

"How?" Paterson asked. "How did they escape? My men fore and back swore nobody left the house."

Langton glanced up. "The attic? Maybe it runs the length of the terrace?"

Paterson rushed through the door and started calling for ladders.

Listless, as if going through the motions, Langton looked around the upper floors. Doktor Glass had spent a great deal of money on the house. Furniture of mahogany and oak. Fine silks and velvets. Persian carpets, tapestries, comfortable beds. And beside each bed, low tables whose wooden surfaces bore the imprint of some heavy, round object. Imprints that the jars from the basement shelves might have made.

Langton could imagine the scene: the "client" lying back on that comfortable bed. The jar of his choice placed on the table beside him. The man's grubby, thick fingers reaching out for the connectors . . .

Langton's hands became fists. Something began to burn inside him and spread through his body until its roaring obliterated everything else. He tried to restrain it, but the house itself seemed to challenge him: every open cupboard and door a laughing mouth, every vacant room a sign of how close he'd been to Doktor Glass. Of how he'd failed.

Had he really expected to find Sarah here? Had he been so naïve? Or so desperate?

He kicked over piles of clothes, yanked drawers from their rails, and hurled the contents onto disheveled beds or floors. The acts of petty destruction felt good, but he wanted more. He wanted to rip the house apart, brick by brick, until nothing remained but its bare skeleton.

McBride watched the increasing mess. "Sir, maybe we should—"

"I'll find him, Sergeant. There's a clue here. Something to identify him without question." Langton tore through handfuls of men's clothes, searching the pockets before casting them aside.

McBride edged toward the door. "Maybe I should get Inspector Paterson . . ."

Langton forced open a locked bureau and hauled papers out only to strew them on the floor.

"Langton." Forbes Paterson stood in the doorway, with McBride peering over his shoulder. "Langton, please. This isn't the way."

Langton turned, his mouth already open to argue. He took a deep breath and held it, eyes closed, until the pounding and roaring faded.

"They didn't use the attic," Forbes said. "We found no doorways, no hatches. And the snow on the roof is untouched, so they didn't go over the top."

Exhausted, Langton forced himself to concentrate. There could be only so many ways to escape this house. He remembered the smells from the lower floors of the house. "The basement."

He led the way downstairs, glancing at the detectives patiently searching each deserted floor. He stopped at the entrance to the basement, where harsh light gleamed on empty shelves. "Look: muddy footprints on the floor."

"So?"

"So Doktor Glass and his men carried the contents of the shelves to some other location, some safe house or storeroom."

"My men saw nothing."

"Exactly." Langton stalked the room, trying to follow logically the direction of the prints. They led from shelf to shelf, to the zinc table in the room's center, and to the walls. Curiously, they didn't head for the doorway that led upstairs. "The answer lies in this room."

All three detectives searched the walls for hidden doors. They looked for seams, the narrow border between door and jamb. They found nothing.

"I don't understand," Langton said. "It *has* to be here. There's no other way."

With his anger returning, he thought about ripping the shelves from the walls; he even stepped forward and gripped the nearest section. His boots echoed on the tiled floor. He looked down. "Sergeant, bring me the sledgehammer."

Langton dropped to his knees and rapped the tiles with the butt of his Webley. He fanned out across the floor, listening, with Forbes Paterson silent behind him. The echoes did sound different. There. And there. At the foot of the wall farthest from the door, the tiles gave back a deeper, longer echo.

Langton looked up at Paterson and grabbed the sledgehammer

from McBride. As Langton went to raise it, Paterson said, "Wait. If they used some kind of trapdoor, there must be a switch or mechanism."

"Can you see one in here? We've searched every crevice."

"What about the passageway, sir?" McBride said. "Or the kitchen?"

Langton hesitated. He knew he wanted to use the sledgehammer on the house; he wanted to see those tiles chip and fly. He wanted to destroy. But Paterson and McBride had a point. He set the sledgehammer aside.

They found the recessed lever in the brick-lined passageway. While Langton and McBride stood ready with revolvers drawn, Forbes Paterson reached into the slot beside the massive door. On silent hinges a section of tiled floor rose to reveal a square, dark pit. Dank air rushed out from the shaft and carried the odor of wet earth, brick, and decay. No sounds save the rush of distant water.

Langton looked over the edge of the shaft and saw the head of a ladder. Before Paterson could stop him, he swung over the side and grasped the rusting metal rungs. His right hand still held the Webley, but the darkness gave no target.

Almost by accident, he brushed against the resin switch set next to the ladder. Electric bulbs encased in caged globes flickered to life and showed a circular brick tunnel stretching left and right. The sudden illumination sent fat rats scurrying along the wet floor.

"What do you see?" Paterson called down, his head framed by the square trapdoor above.

"An escape route," said Langton. "It must stretch right under the square."

To his left, the tunnel dwindled with distance; the lights, strung up every ten yards or so, showed crumbling brickwork and slimy walls. The sound of distant rushing water came from that direction. To his right, the tunnel curved slightly until it bent out of sight.

"I should have known," Paterson said, splashing down beside Langton. "Doktor Glass wouldn't leave himself without a back door."

"We couldn't foresee everything," Langton said. But he wondered if Sapper George knew about these tunnels. If only Langton had realized. He blamed himself. Doktor Glass was always one step ahead. At least.

"Which way does it lead, sir?" asked McBride.

Paterson looked up and along the tunnel, trying to orientate himself. "Southwest, as far as I can gauge. Toward Toxteth."

"Come on." Langton led Paterson and McBride along the cold tunnel, heading right. No sound came from ahead; no draft carried rank odors. Upon turning the bend, Langton saw why: The crumbling brick roof had collapsed, blocking the path.

No, not collapsed. Langton saw thick wooden staves—like coal mine pit-props—among the rubble. Ropes showed where Doktor Glass and his men had pulled the staves from ahead, bringing down the tunnel roof already weakened by age or by their deliberate erosion.

Either way, the tunnel lay blocked.

"I'll get my men down here with picks and shovels," Forbes Paterson said. "We'll soon get this out of the way."

Langton didn't comment. He pocketed his revolver and returned to the rusting ladder. His muddied feet made fresh outlines on the basement room's white tiles. Head bowed, shoulders slumped, he pushed through the busy detectives and sank into a leather chair in the front parlor. He stared ahead.

Doktor Glass had won. Again. He'd outmaneuvered the police as usual, probably with help from informants within the force. How else could he know what to expect?

Langton let his head sink back against the chair. His body's adrenaline rush had faded, leaving only exhaustion and futility. What was the point? Why not simply admit that they were up against an opponent too intelligent, too cunning, too adept. They might as well try to catch fog in a net.

Without focusing on any one object, Langton let his gaze travel around the parlor. An eclectic mix of furniture and ornaments: on the walls, oil paintings and etchings of Italy, France, the Mediterranean. Indian figurines raised their multiple arms to heaven. The electric gramophone, now silent, stood on a table next to cigar boxes and decanters. In the corner, an upright automatic piano with its scrolled music spewing from the front like a drunk's shirt bib. And, standing next to the piano, a slender statue in chipped wood. No more than four feet tall, with patches of blue and gold still as bright as the day the Egyptian artisans painted her. Kohl-rimmed eyes and an enigmatic smile.

Langton remembered where he had seen the twin of that statue. The house of Professor Caldwell Chivers.

The Professor: the man who had shown such a keen interest in Langton's home when he'd visited it, and who had been surprised at Langton having only one servant in "such a large, sheltered house."

His lethargy gone, Langton jumped from the chair and ran into the hall, almost knocking over McBride.

"Sir? Where are you—"

"Protect Elsie," Langton said. "She's in danger."

"Sir, what do you . . ."

McBride's voice faded as Langton ran down the steps and skidded on the pavement outside. He sprinted across Falkner Square, down Sandon Street, and onto busy Upper Parliament Street. Swirling snow clogged his mouth, nose, eyes. He slipped and dodged between huddled pedestrians. As he ran across the main road, his feet went from under him; his hip slammed into the compacted ice and shot jagged pain up his spine. He rolled aside, ignored the cart drivers' yells, and stumbled toward the mansion.

He could imagine the tunnel beneath his feet, beneath the roadway. A direct link between the Professor and his clients. So convenient. Langton thought of all those jars removed from the Falkner Square address and now standing in the Professor's rooms. Enough evidence to link him to the trade.

On one level, Langton knew he couldn't barge into the Professor's mansion without a magistrate's warrant. But rage obliterated logic. And rage made him hammer at the front door with the butt of his gun. Even as the door began to open, he pushed past the butler. "Where is he?"

"Sir, you cannot just—" Then the butler saw the gun. "I'll call the police."

"I am the police." Langton didn't know if he'd shouted the words at the butler; a roaring filled his head like a waterfall pounding rocks.

He ran through the hall, through the drawing room, trying to remember how to get down to the Egyptian room. Frightened maids stumbled out of his way. A footman ran to him, then saw the gun and pulled back. The pounding in Langton's head grew louder.

There. He remembered that passage. He ran down the descending floor and kicked open the door. Light glinted off trophies of gold and ebony, jet and silver. Impassive sarcophagi stared back at him. The shelved jars waited.

"Caldwell Chivers."

Langton found another door and a spiral staircase leading down. Then, between two upright coffin slabs, a narrow panel left open an inch or two.

Not stopping to wonder why the panel stood open, Langton thrust it back and smelled that familiar odor of dank earth. Caged lights glowed white. Stone steps led down; Langton followed them with the Webley pointing the way. He knew he was close. Soon it would be over.

Then, at the bottom of the stairs, he sensed a movement behind him. A hand slid from the darkness and closed over his mouth. Another gripped the Webley. Immense hands like shovels, pale white against the black.

Instead of struggling, Langton stepped back and drove his weight into the attacker. He rebounded as if from a brick wall. He jabbed his free left arm into the man's ribs, pounding the chest with his elbow over and over. No response. Nothing.

The hand over his mouth moved to his throat. Fingers like clammy steel dug into his flesh. Langton struggled to breathe, to force air past the constriction. Panic made him fire the Webley. Two shots ricocheted from the basement walls. Then the attacker threw the gun into the shadows, releasing his second hand to join his first around Langton's neck.

As the man's grip tightened, Langton managed to turn. He kicked and punched and butted and scratched. But his attacker, invisible beyond the edge of light, didn't react. His hands closed around Langton's throat like a snare around a fox.

Langton's eyes bulged. His bloated tongue jutted from his mouth. An obscene, wet gurgle erupted from his throat. He heard it as if from very far away.

As the pounding in his head obliterated all sensation and his body slumped in the man's grip, Langton accepted his own death. He pictured Sarah and tried to fix the image of her face as his last thought. Then, just as Langton's vision faded, his attacker leaned forward into the light.

Langton's scream began and ended in his own head. He carried the final image of Reefer Jake's cold, blank face into unconsciousness.

Seventeen

WHITE FLOWERS. THE smell of lilies, orchids, freesia. Overpowering and oppressive. Sweet decay.

Langton blinked up at a rough timber ceiling, crisscross beams. Firelight flickered up there, orange and yellow twisting among darker shadows. Lethargic, he watched the elongated reflections for a while; the shapes they made reminded him of childhood evenings with his family. The memory comforted him. Even the overwhelming smell of flowers didn't seem too harsh now. Death didn't seem too bad.

He forced his heavy eyes open. Whatever this was, it was not death. This hurt too much.

Like a drunk unsure and suspicious of his surroundings, he worked outward from his own body: a soft material under him, velvet or plush. Warm. No shackles at his wrists or legs. He shifted position to ease the weight on his hip and side and touched his tender throat. With that came the memory of Reefer Jake, a man already dead. And with that came the name of Doktor Glass.

Langton jerked upright on the couch, eyes wide open, hands ready for attack or defense.

"Inspector. How are you?" Sister Wright, sitting across from him, poured tea into two white china cups. She replaced the pot on the low table separating her and Langton, then offered him a cup. "Milk? Sugar?"

Habit made Langton accept the cup. This had to be a dream or a delusion. It seemed so real; he could feel the heat of the tea through the thin bone china, smell the dark leaves.

Sister Wright saw him wince as he swallowed. "I applied ointment for the bruising and inflammation, but I'm afraid you'll have to let time take its course."

Langton had so many questions. How had Sister Wright rescued him? Where was he? How could Jake still walk with the living? All he could manage was, "Where am I?"

"A warehouse on Blundell Street, close to Gladstone Dock," Sister Wright said, sipping her tea.

The room didn't match her explanation. Apart from the lack of windows, it could have been a respectable front parlor with its dark dressers and bureau, its rugs, red velvet couch and chairs, its many vases of fresh flowers. But Langton thought he could detect the trace aroma of salt water. Perhaps he imagined it.

Sister Wright could have stepped in here straight from the Infirmary. Starched white apron over navy blue dress; black stockings and flat black shoes; upturned watch and Guild pin at her breast. Smiling slightly, she watched Langton like a nanny with a dim child.

"How did you get me out of the Professor's house?"

"His mansion lies over a network of old tunnels; in fact, it used to belong to one of Liverpool's most notorious slavers and smugglers."

"How . . . I mean . . ."

"You're still a little groggy, Inspector. I asked Jake to be careful, but he really has no idea of his own strength."

Ice formed in the pit of Langton's stomach. He set down the teacup as if it might shatter at any moment. He had to concentrate on every movement. "You're Doktor Glass."

Sister Wright set her hands on her lap. "I am."

It made horrible sense: the connections and clues to the Infirmary; her knowledge of the Jar Boys; her work at the encampment giving her ready access to victims. At the center of the investigation. Watching. Waiting.

"But . . ." Langton still couldn't believe it. "I thought the Professor . . ."

"He's quite innocent," Sister Wright said. "I respect him completely and I've learned so much from him."

Now Langton remembered Sister Wright watching the Professor at work in the Infirmary. He remembered her intense expression as she'd gazed down on the exposed skull and brain of the injured steeplejack on the operating table below her.

"Why, Sister? You're a nurse—you save lives."

She nodded. "With God's grace."

"Then how can you involve yourself with the Jar Boys?"

Sister Wright looked into the open fire. She waited perhaps a minute before she said, "It started in the Transvaal. I'd always shown an interest in the medical profession, a tradition in my family; my grandfather had been a missionary physician in India. Naturally I could not hope to become a doctor, since women are barred from the profession, so I joined the nursing sisters. And, in Africa, God granted me a vision of hell."

Langton remembered battlefields strewn with the dead and dying; limbs and bloody remnants under the baking red sun. Men struggling to breathe as the corrosive green gas swept along the plains and seeped into the trenches, into eyes and throats and finally lungs.

"I tended the sick," Sister Wright continued, "and believed I was helping. I was part of some plan that I did not yet understand. And I tended the Boers as well as I tended the British boys; I showed no favoritism. I could even sympathize with the Boers' cause. I didn't agree with their methods, but I tried to put myself in their position. And that's what made it so hard to understand . . ."

She looked up at Langton with wide, glistening eyes and said no more than, "Bloemfontein."

Langton looked away. He didn't want to imagine Sister Wright in that place. Not after the stories he'd heard.

The British had left only a score of men to defend the field hospital at Bloemfontein. They said the crudely painted Red Cross on its white tin roof would offer protection. The hundred Boer irregulars had ignored the cross as they'd swept down in the night. The most fortunate soldiers had died quickly. Some had taken days, staked out under the sun, sport for knives and dogs and imaginations fed by years of bloodshed.

Some of the nurses had survived, but their treatment had caused even the Boers' rebel commanders to disown the Orange Free State Irregulars.

Then Langton remembered the tattoos on the faceless man's body. "Kepler?"

"He must have been one of them," Sister Wright said. "I didn't remember him but I knew those tattoos. And half of the time we were blindfolded while they . . . Good sport, they called it."

Langton fought the nausea that rose within him. He'd heard what had happened in that place, but it made it somehow more immediate, more *real*, to hear it from someone who'd survived.

"I'm sorry," he said, ashamed of the pitiful emptiness of his words. "How did that drive you to become Doktor Glass?"

"We worked under Doctor Klaustus," she said. "A brilliant man with extreme ideas. Extreme to his colleagues, that is. At the time I believed that they couldn't see the extent of his genius, his imagination. I helped him willingly."

Langton caught the same note in her voice as when she spoke of the Professor.

She continued, "Klaustus had seen so much; he couldn't believe that human life ended with the decay of simple flesh. The spirit—so complex, so *aware*—cannot simply disappear. But Klaustus said he could never capture the final essence. Not until he read of the work of Tesla and Marconi."

Langton had to concentrate on her words. The atmosphere of the room, with the crackling fire and the everyday surroundings, contradicted Sister Wright's bizarre explanation.

"Even before the war, Klaustus had experimented with glass carboys, then clay, with different aerials and capacitors, different induction coils. The war itself gave him plenty of opportunity to perfect his machine; he called it an attractor."

When Langton shook his head, Sister Wright leaned forward and stared into his eyes as if willing his belief. "I saw it, Inspector. I did not believe it at first, either, but I watched as Klaustus connected the attractor to a dying soldier in a Natal dressing station. Afterward, I held the jar's copper connectors and for a brief moment I *became* that soldier whose body no longer breathed. His spirit lived on. The technique worked, and works still, whether for good or evil."

His mind whirling, Langton looked into Sister Wright's open, intense gaze and wondered if she was really insane. He had seen Edith's essence in that house in Plimsoll Street. He had seen the strange machine, the so-called attractor, and he knew he had to believe, though logic rebelled.

As if sensing this, Sister Wright stood up and said, "Come."

"Where?"

"You must see," she said. "And then perhaps you'll understand."

Langton followed her to the door. Fatigue or confusion made him light-headed; he stumbled and almost fell. Sister Wright held out her hand, but Langton refused it. She went to speak, then took a lamp from a side table.

The door opened out onto a wide passage. The windowless sitting room's normality gave way here to the building's real form. Old wood and bare brick. Creaking floorboards gouged with decades or more of nailed boots and trolley wheels. The smell of the Mersey close by. Langton could believe he was in a warehouse now.

He watched out for Reefer Jake, half expecting the lumbering attacker to shuffle from the darkness. He remembered those blank eyes, the fingers digging into his throat.

To his left and right lay empty rooms, caverns of brick with steel hooks hanging from the ceiling. The temperature dropped. Langton pulled his coat tight and found an empty pocket instead of the Webley. He fought the panic that started deep in his stomach and threatened to overwhelm him. This weird journey through the cold warehouse, with the lamp throwing distorted shadows of Sister Wright against the leaning walls, reminded Langton of nightmares. It had that quality of unreality, of imminent horror. He longed to wake up.

Sister Wright led him down a ramp that ended at a solid steel door that showed no signs of rust. She unlocked the two padlocks and slid back the horizontal locking bars. She turned to Langton for a moment, then pushed open the door and waved him inside.

The lamp threw a semicircle of light into the room, but Langton sensed a much larger void beyond the border. Then he heard the click of a switch behind him.

White electric light flooded the space. Langton shielded his eyes. When he blinked them open he saw a square room at least twelve yards high by fifteen square. Caged electric bulbs hung from the ceiling on chains. The light they threw reflected from white walls, white ceiling, white tiled floor. And row after row of white shelving.

And on every shelf, stretching up to the ceiling, stood glazed clay jars. Langton gave up counting. Six, seven hundred? He pulled his jacket tight against the chill.

"We have to keep the storeroom cold," Sister Wright said, "for the jars. Have you heard of Brownian motion? It's the agitation of particles, and the essences within these jars become slower at low temperatures. And that means they survive for longer, since they waste less energy."

She could have been speaking of a simple case at the Infirmary, not of transient souls caught in cold jars. "How many . . ."

"Almost a thousand, but not all are here," Sister Wright said. She brushed past Langton and stood at the zinc table in the room's center. A single brown glazed jar, as apparently unremarkable as the others, waited on that table. "My own collection stood at over six hundred, but Doctor Redfers added another three."

Langton nodded. "You killed Redfers."

"I'm afraid I had no choice," she said, and her sorrow appeared genuine. "When you asked about him at the Infirmary, I realized that he would lead you back to me, and I wasn't ready then. Besides, I'd already suspected Redfers of deceit; I thought I'd turned him to my cause, but he had started working again for one of the criminal gangs that used the jars for profit."

"And that's quite different from you, I suppose."

Sister Wright shook her head. "Please don't say that. I gained nothing from the trade in jars. Every penny from my network was used for research."

That made Langton pause. "Network?"

"Redfers was only one of several doctors who introduced the . . . clients to the captured essences. And I was not the only supplier. Fortunately, over the past few weeks, I've managed to eliminate most of the criminal gangs."

And therefore most of the competition, Langton thought. But he still had difficulty picturing Sister Wright as a villain. "If you aren't in this for profit, then what?"

"The end of suffering," Sister Wright said, smiling. "It could be even more important than that. Science has now proven the existence of a soul. Instead of fighting against religion, science can bolster it, reinforce it. Science is the tool of God."

As she said this, her eyes burned just a little brighter. Her hands clasped together almost in prayer.

Carefully, Langton said, "You justify cruelty in the name of God? I suppose you're not the first."

For a moment, he thought he'd gone too far: Sister Wright blushed red and her hands tightened into fists. Then she took a breath and let it out slowly. "I can understand your sentiment. I was not happy with the thought of bored old men pawing over the souls of the lost. And then, when I realized that the essences were themselves aware of their condition and of their molesters' actions . . . No, I did not enjoy that thought."

"Then why do it? Why continue?"

"In order to destroy the practice," she said. "When I have every last jar in my possession, every poor trapped soul, and they have fulfilled their final destiny, I shall release them unto the ether and into His hands."

Langton recognized the tone of the True Believer. He knew then that Sister Wright would be capable of anything in her pursuit of what she thought right and just. With some, that goal was religious. With her, it was a bizarre mixture of science and theology. But what did she mean by "final destiny"?

Sister Wright continued, "I honestly believed it was our duty to capture their quintessence, their very soul, and relieve their pain."

The image of Sarah rocked Langton on his heels. He could almost hear her voice. "I can think of nothing more cruel—if it's possible— than trapping a person's spirit."

"I can understand that, Matthew," Sister Wright said. "In time I came to that same realization. But perhaps we should consider your poor wife's wishes."

Langton, almost whispering, said, "She would never have agreed to this . . . imprisonment."

Sister Wright smiled and rested a hand on the jar standing on the zinc table. "Why don't you ask her?"

* * *

SURPRISE ROBBED LANGTON of words. He stared at the jar, at Sister Wright. His heart froze, and his throat tightened as if Reefer Jake once again gripped it.

"Redfers had her," Sister Wright said. "He performed the transfer at the Infirmary. I knew of it then, but I had not yet met you. When I discovered that Redfers had been lending her out, as well as other souls, well . . . he gave me no choice."

Langton hardly heard her voice. He took one slow step toward the table, then another. Could that plain earthenware jar really contain Sarah's essence, her soul?

Sister Wright stepped away from the table. "You simply grasp the two copper connectors, one in each hand."

He saw the smooth copper connectors jutting from the lid. Some of the wax that sealed the lid had dribbled down the jar's side and set in place like dried green blood. Langton took another step. He stood at the table's edge, his hands open at his sides. His heart raced.

Could he do this? For months, he had dreamed about talking to Sarah one last time; he could say all the things he should have said when she was alive. And all the things he would have said as she slipped away from him. He should have been there at the end, instead of Redfers with his apparatus, his machine. Now he had his chance.

Sarah's passing had left a void that screamed out inside Langton, urging him to grasp those connectors. No more guilt; no more pain; no more loneliness. He would be complete again.

He looked at Sister Wright, still unable to call her Doktor Glass, and saw no outward signs of manipulation. She watched him with a look of sadness, perhaps even of tenderness, like a protective mother prompting her child.

He reached out trembling hands. He could almost feel those smooth, cold connectors. Remembering young Edith's essence, he imagined the bright mist inside the jar rushing to complete the circuit. The charged particles streaming through the darkness. The surge as they clung to the submerged metal. Sarah's essence.

His hands moved closer. Closer.

Langton fell to his knees on the cold tiled floor. He wrapped his arms around his body and bowed his head. "I can't. I can't do it."

"It's all right, Matthew." Sister Wright stroked his head. "It's all right. Don't worry."

"I'm scared."

"I know. I know."

As Sister Wright pressed his head into her skirts, Langton breathed in the comforting Infirmary smells of disinfectant, flowers, freshly laundered clothes. He closed his eyes as tears trickled down his face.

Sister Wright continued stroking his hair, soothing him as she'd probably soothed so many patients. Then, very quietly, she said, "There is another way I can help you . . ."

Langton pulled away from her and looked up. After so many shocks, so many surprises, he really had no idea what to expect.

"Your wife is not yet lost," Sister Wright said, smiling. "I can bring her back. A new life, Matthew. A new life in a new body."

THE COLD OF the jars' storeroom had eaten into Langton's bones. He sat huddled in the sitting room before the stoked fire. He watched the flames dancing in the grate, blue and yellow, as Sister Wright calmly spoke of madness.

"You saw it yourself with Reefer Jake," she said. "We broke a small pane in his cell window and lowered the connectors and a syringe. After he injected the poison, we caught his essence in an attractor and retreated. Later, two of my men took his body from your morgue and brought him here. The transfer was straightforward: Within three hours of his 'death' he was sitting in this room."

Langton started, and almost looked around as if expecting to see Jake lurch from the shadows.

Sister Wright continued, "It seems so long ago, that first crude attempt I witnessed with Klaustus: He stored a soldier's essence for an hour while the poor man's lacerated body effectively died. Klaustus repaired the damage and restarted the heart with an electric shock, then transferred the essence back into the host. I saw it myself. Although the poor ruined soldier later told me he wished he had passed away on the table, the procedure itself worked."

Procedure. Host. Essence. Calm, ordered words disguising absolute madness.

"Jake was not the first," Sister Wright said. "I know of three people in Liverpool who walk and live and laugh, giving no signs that they once inhabited other bodies. So many die too early, unnecessarily, unfairly."

Langton stared at her. He wanted to make her stop, but her intense gaze pinned him down like an Indian mongoose with a snake. He didn't have the energy or the courage to argue with her.

"I can bring her back to you, Langton. Not just for a few days or weeks or months. For a lifetime."

He managed to whisper, "No."

Sister Wright leaned forward. "Think of it: your wife, alive again, to hold and touch. In your arms. You could hear her voice—"

"It wouldn't be her voice."

"It would be *her* speaking. You would know. You could look inside the eyes of her new . . . host, and know. It's within your reach."

"And where would you find this poor host?" he said. "Murder some poor girl? Compound Sarah's death with another crime?"

"There would be no need." Sister Wright looked away. "The Infirmary has a ward that most people never visit. Patients who will never see the outside world again; patients whose wits have left them. Although physically sound, they stare at the world like poor dumb animals. There is nothing inside. Whether through injury, through disease or dementia, they will forever be no more than vessels. Imperfect, empty vessels."

Her words spiraled around inside Langton's head. He curled up on himself, wanting to disappear, to hear no more. The image of Sarah's body lying in its silk-lined coffin would not leave him.

It wasn't fair; it wasn't right. She had been too young. They'd had their whole lives to live.

Still, Sister Wright continued, her voice soft and steady: "Inside the jar, her essence will fade. The particles lose their energy. Eventually, they cease. There is nothing I—or anyone else on this earth—can do then. It will be too late."

Langton shook his head. He forced out the words, "It's not right."

She touched his knee. "Not right? Is it right for an innocent young woman to lie gently rotting in a wooden box while her family grieves?"

"Please . . ."

"Is it right for fate to choose *her* rather than the old, the already sick, the criminal, and the insane? You know it isn't."

"But . . ." Langton struggled for arguments. He remembered the crucifix around Sister Wright's neck. "You believe in God; how can you do this?"

She rested a finger against Langton's forehead. "Because God gave us intelligence. He gave us knowledge. It is our choice how we use that knowledge. I see no contradiction. Our work bolsters faith in God, since we can now prove the existence of the soul. There is no need for us to continue the use of jars save as temporary refuges. Until a new host comes forward."

Exhaustion drained Langton. He couldn't fight her. Was she insane? Or did she speak the truth?

To hold Sarah again. To relieve the utter loneliness, the guilt and pain. To live again.

"I'm a policeman."

Sister Wright smiled as if she knew she'd won. "You're also a husband. And your wife needs you. Will you let her down?"

Langton stared into the fire a few moments, then sat straighter on the couch. He smoothed the front of his waistcoat and let out a breath. "What do you want of me?"

"Nothing," Sister Wright said. "Simply nothing."

"But—"

"Leave Kepler's death unsolved," Sister Wright said, rising and crossing the room to a bureau. "Go through the motions of the inquiry but no more."

"You killed him."

"I did, and I would do it again."

"Why?"

"Because as well as being an Irregular, he discovered certain . . . Let us say he unearthed too much."

"About the jars?"

"Perhaps."

"Then why did you cut off his face?" Langton asked.

"Publicity and distraction," said Sister Wright. "I had to misdirect attention toward Brother Boer. In the Transvaal, as you know, they did that to their own traitors. And I wanted the British public to remember what such men were capable of."

Before Langton could continue, Sister Wright returned from the bureau with the Webley in her hand. She held it out to him.

Langton checked the revolver. Every chamber loaded. He rested it across his knee. "I could arrest you. I should arrest you. And not just for Kepler's murder."

"I know." She stood there with her hands crossed in front of her nurse's apron.

"Then why give this back to me?"

"Because I trust you."

Because I'm an accomplice now, Langton thought. He stared down at the gun. *If I do Sister Wright's bidding, I might see Sarah again. Or some re-created version of her. Oh God, forgive me.*

He pocketed the Webley and stood up.

"You must deflect Major Fallows from me, from our network," Sister Wright said, and the way she said "our" made Langton wince.

"You know about Fallows?"

"I do. I don't want him interfering in our work."

Langton nodded. "I'll do what I can."

She rested a hand on his arm for a moment. "I know you will. And I will fulfill my part of the contract. I promise."

Sister Wright led the way down through the echoing warehouse. On the ground floor, the smell of tobacco drifted from a side room. Langton looked inside and saw three men, two at a table, one lying on a camp bed reading a yellowback novel. Smoke drifted around the bare bulb. As the men at the table saw Sister Wright, they threw down their cards and jumped to their feet.

Sister Wright waved them down. "It's all right. I'll see the inspector to the door myself. Where's Jake?"

"Here, Doctor."

Langton turned at the deep voice and saw Reefer Jake standing behind him and Sister Wright. The stocky man had made no sound as he'd approached. Langton looked into his eyes and tried to see some sign of the man he'd interrogated in the cells. He saw a brief spark before Jake's impassive features turned to Sister Wright.

"Inspector Langton has agreed to help us, gentlemen," she said. "Make sure you look out for him again."

"Again?" Langton said.

Sister Wright smiled. "My boys here have saved your life at least once. With Redfers's investigation, you got too close to the criminal jar gangs, or what was left of them. They wanted you removed."

"Then I suppose I should thank you," Langton said, but he wondered why Sister Wright had kept him alive then. Had she already accounted for his complicity?

With Jake lumbering after them, she led Langton down to a heavy wooden door bound with iron. "Jake could drive you home."

"I'd like to walk," Langton said, reluctant to be the passenger of a man he'd so recently pronounced dead.

The door swung open to allow in the rich, sour smell of the Mersey. Langton stepped out onto a wooden pier and saw the lights of Birkenhead and New Brighton flickering on the opposite shore of the river. In the darkness, warehouses showed as blocky silhouettes against the stars.

"Go left," Sister Wright said, "and you'll find stone steps up to the street. Be careful."

Langton didn't know what to say in farewell. *Thank you? Go to hell?* He shook his head and made for the street.

"One final thing, Matthew."

He turned and saw Sister Wright standing in the wedge of light thrown from the open door.

"Today is the day of the Span's inauguration," she said. "Do not attend."

"Why not?"

"Please do as I ask. If you wish to see your wife again, keep away from the Span."

Langton ran back, but the door slammed shut. He raised his fist to hammer on it, then drew back. Making for the steps up to the street, he tried to pin down all that he'd learned from Sister Wright, or Doktor Glass. Too much information. Too many surprises. One question stood above the others: Why warn him away from the Span?

Eighteen

A S HE WALKED along the Dock Road through encrusted snow, head down, left hand clutching his thin jacket closed, Langton tried to think logically, to order the barrage of information. He couldn't make sense of Sister Wright's plans; she'd involved herself in the trade of souls but implied that had ended. So why had she recently ordered the immense component from Irving and Long, as if for some enormous attractor? And why had she warned Langton away from the Span?

The few pedestrians on the streets—drunks, dockers, or men walking to workshops' early shifts—stared at Langton as they passed by, and he wondered if he'd been talking to himself again. Hardly surprising, given all that had happened over the past few days. Enough to unhinge any man. His clothes reinforced the image of lunacy: torn and disheveled, with streaks of mud and what looked like blood.

Up ahead stood a tea wagon, warm light spilling from its interior. Langton crossed the street and leaned on the wooden counter. "Have you any coffee?"

"We got Italian or Dutch."

"Italian, please. Very strong."

As the fat proprietor turned to a gleaming brass percolator, Langton glanced at the workers beside him eating sandwiches and drinking from chipped mugs of tea and coffee. Had Sister Wright sent one of her crew to follow him? Could one of these men work for her? Perhaps it was that laborer over there, or the tilting drunk under that lamppost.

Langton gulped coffee and tried to silence his paranoia. It didn't matter, in the end. He had no control over Sister Wright. The reverse, in fact: She owned him, at least for now, until they'd completed their transaction. And that realization brought images of Sarah. Alone, trapped, waiting. Wondering where she was and why nobody came to help her. Langton closed his eyes and clutched at the counter.

"Here, mate, are you all right? Had a drop too much last night?"

Langton forced a smile. "Just tired. Another coffee, please."

Feeling more alert, Langton began to take note of his surroundings. Even here, where the royal party would probably never visit, bunting and streamers fluttered in the predawn breeze. The streets seemed cleaner than usual, without the heaped pyramids of horse dung. Today, the day of the inauguration, Fallows would no doubt already be at the Span to check any last-minute hitches.

Again, the Span. Would Sister Wright, or Doktor Glass, want to target the Queen? Surely not. She had spoken of hatred for the Boers, and her scars gave her reason enough, but Langton couldn't think of any reason for her to hate the royal family. No, it had to be the Span. Jake had carried a complex key stamped with the bridge's logo. Kepler and Durham had been connected to it. So why would Sister Wright target that great metal structure?

Langton looked south, along the Dock Road and over the roofs of factories and warehouses, to where the Span glowed in the darkness, its form picked out in electric arc lights. At the head of each tower, and all along the support pipes carrying the vertical steel cables, glowed bright red dots, the sleepless eyes of electric lights set there to warn low-flying dirigible captains. The combination of lights, steel skeleton, and mist gave the Span an ethereal aura.

"How much do I owe you?"

"One and tuppence, mate."

Trying not to look behind him, Langton continued along the Dock Road. He thought about hailing a hansom, but the walk and the coffee helped clear his head. He kept on walking, heading for home.

So many questions ran through his mind. Why had Kepler died? Because he'd gotten too close, Sister Wright said, but not necessarily to the jars. Kepler and Durham had been asking around the dockers' pubs, looking for hints of a Boer plot. Could that be part of it? Had they stumbled upon another of Sister Wright's—or Doktor Glass's—activities there? Sister Wright would surely never help the Boers. It didn't yet make sense.

One question returned: What had happened to Kepler's face? What had Sister Wright done with the grisly object? Langton could not imagine her keeping it as a barbaric trophy, but then he had to accept that he did not really know her at all; she might be capable of anything if she felt threatened or if her conviction drove her to it. Langton only had to remember the fate of the criminal Jar Boy gangs and the reputation that Sister Wright—as Doktor Glass—enjoyed.

Sister Wright knew too much. She had known Langton's movements, his discoveries and suspicions. And she had known about Fallows. Someone within headquarters kept her informed, obviously, but who? Harry? He had no access to Langton's case files, other than quick glimpses of any left open on the desk. Forbes Paterson? No. Impossible. Langton had no illusion about the strength of Paterson's feelings about the Jar Boys.

In his mind, Langton went through every officer who had access to his cases, however incidentally. By the time he reached Waterloo Road, he had to face the only logical conclusion: Sergeant McBride.

No one else had access to every fact. No one else had accompanied

Langton at every major junction in the investigations. And no one else enjoyed Langton's absolute trust.

Anger flared inside Langton but quickly died. He stood at the railings overlooking Trafalgar Dock and watched a Royal Navy steamship slide into its berth under a dark sky streaked with pearl to the east. Langton had no right to blame McBride. Perhaps Sister Wright had made the sergeant a similar promise or offer; perhaps McBride had a loved one waiting among those shelves of jars.

Elsie. Langton remembered his instructions to McBride: *Go home and protect Elsie.* But if McBride really worked for Doktor Glass . . .

Langton began to run. At the junction of Bath Street and New Quay, he tried to flag a hansom. The driver saw his dirty clothes and wild waving and drove on. Langton hurried up Leeds Street, heading north toward home. He half-walked, half-ran, slithering on the pavement's compacted ice and snow. His breath erupted in white clouds and his lungs burned.

As Langton neared familiar streets, he clutched the Webley and slowed his pace a little, trying to take deep breaths. He kept to the crumbling slush at the pavement's edge, where his footsteps would make less noise. Only a handful of pedestrians passed by, servants on their way to work. Langton ignored them. He paused at the corner of his street and looked around the black iron railings. No coach or cart outside his door; no constables or loafers. All seemed quiet.

With the revolver in plain sight now, held down close to his side, Langton approached his own house. No lights burned. No smoke came from the chimney. And as he reached the steps, he saw his front door ajar.

Slowly, step by step, he climbed to the door, moved to the right, and pushed it open with his foot. Nobody shot at him. Nobody rushed out. The still silence of an empty house.

"Elsie?"

No reply. Langton slipped inside the hall and listened. Only the ticking of the grandfather clock in the sitting room. Then, from the back stairs, a shuffling sound like clothes dragged across a stone floor.

Langton made for the noise. Every nerve in his body seemed stretched tight. Every sensation seemed stronger: the cold, cross-hatched wooden handle of the revolver in his hands; the squeak of his boot heels across the parquet floor; the smells of beeswax and food and cordite.

Silent now, Langton crept down the back steps to the kitchen and scullery rooms. He peered into the kitchen and saw smashed plates, pots and pans lying on the floor, a dark pool of dried coffee or tea. And there, next to the central pine table, a body.

The man, heavy and wide, lay on his back staring at the ceiling. A knife was close to his outstretched right hand. A gunshot had exploded his chest. He must have died before he had even hit the ground.

Langton crossed the red-tiled floor, cursing as his left foot caught a shard of china plate and sent it ringing into a corner. In two strides he reached the scullery door and flung it open. He had just enough time to throw himself to one side before the bullet hammered into the door frame next to his head. The wood shattered.

"Elsie, don't shoot. It's me." Langton pressed his back flat against the kitchen wall and felt his heart thudding an irregular rhythm. Something burned his cheek; he touched the spot and pulled out a small bloody splinter. "It's all right, Elsie."

From inside the scullery, a weary voice, "Sir? Is it really you?"

"Don't shoot." Langton took one slow step around the edge of the door, then another. "It's all right, Elsie."

With McBride's revolver clutched in both shaking hands, Elsie sat on the cold scullery floor with the body of the sergeant sprawled across her legs. Wide-eyed and white with shock and cold, she stared at Langton for maybe half a minute before lowering the gun. "They would have done for me, sir, if it hadn't been for him. He saved me, sir."

Langton knelt beside Elsie and took the gun from her. He felt at McBride's neck and found a weak pulse. Blood, still wet, trickled from at least two chest wounds that Langton could see. The man's face looked grey and slack. More blood trickled from his scalp.

On Elsie's face, cuts and swollen skin that would soon turn to bruises. Straggling hair hung down over her bloodshot eyes.

"We need to move McBride, Elsie. Are you ready? Elsie?"

She blinked up at him, then nodded. Langton set the guns down and took McBride's weight to allow Elsie to slide out from beneath. Afraid to turn him over or move him too much, Langton lowered McBride to the cold floor, then helped Elsie to her feet. "Elsie, listen to me. Run next door and tell them to phone for a doctor and ambulance. Elsie? Quickly, girl. There's still time."

With an almost visible effort, Elsie seemed to pull herself out of shock. She started to walk, then run, through the kitchen. Her feet clattered on the stairs.

Langton slid out of his jacket and laid it over McBride. He slumped down on the floor beside him and pulled the guns closer. He didn't know who had attacked the house, or whether they might return, so he stared through the scullery entrance at the back door. He listened for furtive steps or the sound of forced entry. Instead of those, he heard a groan and a wet cough. He leaned over McBride. "Don't move, man. The doctor will soon be here."

"So cold . . ." McBride said, his voice a whisper.

Langton pulled down aprons and towels from the scullery shelves and packed them around McBride's body. "Don't talk. Save your strength."

"No time . . ." One red eye focused on Langton. "They burst in . . . three o'clock . . . too many . . ."

"Save your strength, McBride," Langton said, even though one part of him wanted to hear the story while another part wanted to blame the sergeant.

McBride wouldn't rest. "It was Springheel Bob's gang, sir. They took me for you—"

A fit of wet red coughing interrupted him. Langton looked on, helpless yet rapt.

"I winged one of them, sir, but they got me front and back. Me and

Elsie stumbled down here and made a stand. She's a plucky one, Elsie is. A fine girl . . ."

Langton wanted to ask so many questions: Why had the remnants of the other Jar Boy gang targeted him? Why had McBride joined Doktor Glass? McBride wouldn't have the strength to answer; the sweat stood out of his forehead and fresh blood stained the white towels.

Instead of questions, Langton said, "I know about Doktor Glass."

McBride's eye opened wide.

"I know you informed on me," Langton said. "I'm glad you were here to save Elsie's life, but you betrayed me."

"I did, sir. And I'm . . . I'm sorry."

Langton leaned closer. "Why, man? Why do it?"

A crooked smile. "He promised me promotion, sir."

He? Not *she*? "But . . . you worked for Doktor Glass."

"I never met Doktor Glass, sir. Never."

From the hall above, the sounds of voices, footsteps on the polished wooden floor.

"Then who did you tell?" Langton said, his face almost touching McBride's. "Who was it?"

As the two white-clad orderlies rushed into the kitchen, followed by a doctor, McBride whispered. "The Chief, sir . . . Purcell . . ."

COLD GRIPPED THE house. Alone in the sitting room, Langton sat staring at last night's ashes in the grate. The orderlies had taken McBride away, with the doctor shaking his head as he followed them. Langton had sent Elsie—accompanied by his neighbor's maid—home to her mother's. The doctor had given her a sedative for the shock, but Langton knew it would be a long time before she recovered her usual nature. If ever.

Exhaustion sapped Langton's will. He wanted nothing more than to sleep. He couldn't even summon anger for Purcell, not after that first reflex reaction at hearing McBride's admission.

Could it be true? It made a kind of sense: McBride would pass on Langton's movements and discoveries to Purcell, who would then pass them on to Doktor Glass, or Sister Wright, as the world knew her. And Purcell had access to Fallows, indeed to every aspect of life at headquarters. He would know where Jake was being held, and where the supposedly dead body would be transferred. There could be no more useful informer than the Chief Inspector himself.

Why would he betray them all? What hold could Doktor Glass have over Purcell?

The jars. Langton remembered the shelves of jars in the dockside warehouse. All those jars that must have once packed the shelves in Redfers's basement. Society's most respectable people—male and female—had paid good money to vicariously enjoy the sensations of the dead or dying. The great and the good of Liverpool had sampled the illicit trade. Perhaps some of them had formed a habit.

The thought sickened Langton. He could see Purcell grasping the jars in his fat fingers, his mouth slightly open as he plundered the memories of some poor, trapped soul. Maybe even of Sarah.

That drove Langton to his feet and almost to the front door. Then he froze. Sister Wright had asked him to do nothing. Confronting Purcell would shock the whole edifice of headquarters. Everyone would learn the truth about the Jar Boys and Doktor Glass.

For the first time since leaving the army, Langton felt truly and completely helpless, no longer master of his own actions. Sister Wright owned him now. She controlled him. He saw how far he'd sunk. But the reward for his silence . . .

Sarah. Oh God, Sarah.

Standing there in the hall, Langton rubbed at his eyes and forced himself to concentrate. Like a man learning to walk after an accident, he placed his thoughts one after the other. Work would see him through this. He needed tasks.

First, to bathe and change. He lit the back boiler in the kitchen and brewed coffee while it heated. After a tepid bath and shave, he found clean clothes and checked his appearance. He looked like a walking corpse, ashen and gaunt, but at least presentable. He had to play his part well on this day of the Span's inauguration. He couldn't afford to arouse any suspicion, especially among headquarters staff.

His composure crumbled in the hansom cab taking him to Victoria Street. He tapped on the ceiling hatch and told the driver, "Take me to the Pier Head instead."

"Don't know if I can, sir," the driver said, still looking at the road ahead. "The police have got it all roped off."

"Get me as close as you can to the encampment."

"The camp? Do me best, sir."

As the hansom crawled and cursed its way through streets thronged with decorations, Langton considered the wisdom of what he was about to try. Mrs. Grizedale might have fled the camp. She might not want to cooperate. Almost certainly she would not want to. But Langton needed answers, or at least reassurance. If only he'd had the courage to grasp the connectors of that jar in Doktor Glass's storeroom, then he would have known for sure.

The hansom made it as far as Islington before Langton had to climb down and walk. Even now, at eight in the morning, people flocked toward the Pier Head and the Span. Young, old, poor, well dressed; loafers sidling along with hands in their pockets and caps pushed back. Children in thin clothes. Middle-class matrons carrying wicker hampers. A microcosm of Liverpool life. All streaming toward the inauguration like iron filings to a magnet.

Langton pushed through the crowd and headed for the camp. Heavy timber barriers now blocked access to the Mersey's banks; Langton showed his warrant card to the constables on duty and then headed across the concourse. Stalls for food and souvenirs had been set up here in front of the half-finished Liver Guaranty Building hiding behind its temporary painted hoardings. Band music drifted over from the TSC compound. It turned the Pier Head into an ersatz fairground waiting for customers.

A line of policemen guarded the camp entrance. "Can't let no one in or out, sir."

Again, Langton produced his warrant card but had to wait until the sergeant went away to check. The cold shadow of the Span's soaring entrance ramp threw the camp's gates into twilight. The first support tower reared up above Langton like a monument. Mist or low cloud hid its apex.

The sergeant returned. "Major Fallows said to let you through, sir, and he asked if you'd see him soon as you could. He's over with the main party."

Langton slid through the police line and made for the camp gates. He searched the faces of the guards but couldn't see Mr. Lloyd. One of the men went to fetch him but made a show of not hurrying. After ten slow, painful minutes, Lloyd appeared. "Inspector. You come to check up on us as well?"

"I need to see someone inside the camp."

Lloyd stuck out his chin. "Business?"

"No. Personal."

When Lloyd hesitated, Langton said, "Please. It's important."

Lloyd stared at him a moment and then told the guards, "Let him in, boys."

Once inside, Langton tried to orient himself. He recognized the main street and the narrow alleys that led down to the rocky base of the Span's first tower, where he'd almost captured Durham.

"Who are you looking for?" Lloyd asked.

Briefly, Langton described Mrs. Grizedale, then started down Main Street, trying to find the window where he'd seen Meera's face.

Beside him, Lloyd coughed and said, "Mr. Dowden told me about your wife. Sorry to hear it."

Something twisted in Langton's side. "Thank you."

"Been a sad century, this one," Lloyd said, as if to himself. "Be glad to see the back of it."

A sudden loud groaning made Langton stop and look around. It sounded like a great metallic beast in pain.

"It's the Span, Inspector. Listen."

A cold wind brushed Langton's face. A second later, a grinding and creaking came from the enormous structure overhead. Then a long, haunting wail that Langton felt in his teeth. It seemed impossible for something so immense and solid to flex and move.

"Frightening, isn't it?" Lloyd said. "You want to hear it in a storm. No wonder the kids have nightmares."

A little farther along Main Street, Langton recognized the shack where he'd seen Meera. A gaunt woman in a frayed red shawl opened the door. She nodded to Lloyd and looked up at Langton, who asked for Mrs. Grizedale.

The woman pursed her lips. "What's she done?"

"Nothing. I just need to ask her—"

A movement behind the landlady, then Mrs. Grizedale's tired face appeared. "I recognized your voice, Inspector. It's all right, Mrs. Miller. I know this gentleman."

"I'll be outside," Lloyd said as Langton entered the shack.

He followed Mrs. Grizedale up rickety stairs and into a front room that leaned and tilted like something from a fairground fun house. Against one wall, a pair of bunks ripped from some ship. A fire burned in a small grate and leaked half its smoke back into the room.

"Mrs. Grizedale, I didn't want to trouble you again—"

"I'm relieved you came back."

Langton, still standing in the doorway, stared at her. "Relieved?"

Mrs. Grizedale sat at a crooked table. "She won't leave me alone."

"Sarah?"

She nodded. "I keep having the same dream: trapped, no air, no room, the sides closing in all around me. It's horrible. Horrible."

Langton thought of the jar standing on the zinc table.

Mrs. Grizedale pulled her shawl tighter around her shoulders and said, "I've never suffered these visions before. Not like this. She must have been very strong willed, your wife. Very strong."

"She was," Langton said. "I'm sorry. I didn't mean for this to happen. I didn't expect—"

Mrs. Grizedale stopped his words with her upturned palm. "The risk was mine to take. I knew what I was dealing with, but it's never been this powerful before. She doesn't want to leave."

She stared straight into Langton's eyes and said, almost as an accusation, "You must have loved each other very much."

Langton sagged against the door frame. When he closed his eyes he saw Sarah laughing, running across a green lawn in her yellow dress. Sarah in his arms. Sarah lying there, pale and wan, looking so small in that great wooden bed.

Then he opened his eyes and saw Mrs. Grizedale slumped and tired, exhausted. He couldn't put her through another ordeal. He couldn't ask her to contact Sarah again.

He turned away. "I'm sorry. I shouldn't have come."

"Wait." She crossed the room and rested one hand on his arm. "You should know: She's confused, like a child. I don't think she knows what has happened. And her spirit is becoming tainted."

"By what?"

"Every time someone connects with the jar, they take away a little of the energy within, but they also give a little of themselves. The transaction works both ways."

How many "clients" had sampled Sarah's essence, her memories? Had Sister Wright connected with her?

"Tell me what you've seen," Langton said. "Please. Anything that seems out of place, or strange."

Mrs. Grizedale smiled. "Strange? As if any of this is normal?"

"Please."

"I'll try." She closed her eyes a moment, then spoke of mismatched fragments of memories, like images from a child's scrapbook: forest walks and candlelit parties; a dress billowing in a summer breeze; lazy Sunday breakfasts; the sting of cold rain. These were recognizably Sarah's. Others were not: cigar-filled rooms; red and black cards on green baize tables; raucous music hall songs and lodge receptions.

And the strangest of all: "I see towers and a tall bridge dancing."

"Dancing?"

Mrs. Grizedale, eyes still closed, struggled to find the words. "It was shifting . . . sort of rippling, twisting from side to side as well as up and down. Dancing."

"Is it the Span?"

"I'm not sure . . . it could be, but . . ." She opened tired, bloodshot eyes. "Did I help?"

Langton didn't know, but he thanked her anyway. On the way through the jerry-built shack, he wondered which of Sarah's "clients" had passed on that image of a bridge in motion. Standing on the boardwalk, he looked up at the Span. Difficult to imagine that dancing.

As he turned back to say good-bye to Mrs. Grizedale, she spoke first: "I hope you find peace. Both of you."

"So do I," Langton said, wondering how she'd react if she knew of Sister Wright's plans for bringing Sarah back. He hoped Mrs. Grizedale never found out.

Langton took a step toward Lloyd. At that moment, a snarl erupted behind him. He turned and stepped aside, narrowly avoiding the hissing, spitting whirlwind of Meera. Before she could attack again, Lloyd ducked beneath her arms and grabbed her waist.

"Why don't you leave her alone?" Meera said, fighting Lloyd's grip and trying to reach Langton with clawing hands. "You hurt her enough."

"Meera, please," Mrs. Grizedale said. "It's all right."

But Meera seemed intent; her hand slid inside her jacket and reappeared with a short, fat, gleaming knife.

Lloyd knocked it from her grip and pulled her tight to him. "All right, my girl, less of that. You don't want every copper in the city around our necks, do you? That's right."

Then, to Langton, "You'd better make yourself scarce, Inspector. She's a right little bundle, this one."

Langton hurried toward the main gate. Behind him, curses and oaths poured from Meera, some of them not in English but none the less meaningful for that. He paused outside the gate and looked around at the stalls waiting for customers, the lines of police, and the crowds lining the approach to the Span. The Queen would receive quite a reception.

Langton rubbed his eyes and tried to concentrate, but the noise of the practicing brass bands, the stallholders, the waiting crowds, and the traffic all combined to overwhelm him. Perhaps he should just return home. Climb into that big wooden bed and let sleep obliterate everything. Sister Wright would approve; he would be doing exactly what she'd wanted. Nothing.

And what would he find when he opened his eyes? If Sister Wright kept her promise, would Langton find a stranger standing beside him? A young woman with a stranger's face but the eyes and soul that Langton had known for so many years? God forgive him.

No. Push that thought aside. Langton knew he still had much to do. Check on McBride; cooperate with Fallows; go through the motions of Kepler's investigation. What happened after today was another thing.

Then, as he started back to headquarters, Langton asked himself why Sister Wright wanted the Kepler case forgotten. McBride said that Purcell was his contact; if Sister Wright owned Purcell, there was no reason to silence Langton. She could simply tell Purcell to quash the case. Unless Purcell was not the problem.

Langton glanced back to the Span. Major Fallows? Was he the one?

Hesitating between headquarters and the Span, Langton turned for the city center. He'd been warned away from the Span; if he wanted to hold his wife again, he couldn't go against Sister Wright's orders. Just go through the motions. Do nothing. But Langton didn't know how long he could resist.

Nineteen

FTER FIGHTING HIS way up bedecked Victoria Street, Langton used the desk sergeant's phone to call the Infirmary. Eventually, a nurse told him that McBride was still in surgery; no, she didn't know which surgeon, or where Sister Wright was—did Langton wish to contact her? He set the phone down instead and climbed the stairs of a headquarters strangely quiet and empty; every officer must be out and on duty for the Queen's visit. Apparently only the clerks and office boys remained.

Up in his own office, Langton sat behind the empty desk and stared straight ahead. Even though McBride had betrayed him, and unwittingly the force, he didn't deserve to die. No, Purcell was to blame here. And, as yet, unpunished.

Harry opened the door and froze in surprise. "Sorry, sir. Didn't expect you in. I'll get you a pot of coffee."

"Just a moment, Harry. Sit down."

Already halfway through the door, Harry turned and shuffled to the desk. He stared at the visitor's chair as if it might bite him. When Lang-

ton motioned for him to sit, he perched on the very edge, as though
about to take flight.

Langton said, "How much did the newspaper pay you?"

Harry blushed scarlet and opened his mouth to speak.

"I know it was you," Langton said, raising his hand to stem Harry's
protest. "Too many times I found you at my desk. I have to take some
of the blame, for leaving the case files in view, but I didn't expect a spy
in the office. How much?"

Conflicting emotions contorted the boy's face. His hands gripped
the chair. Then he looked down at his boots. "A pound for every piece,
sir. I'm sorry."

"So am I, Harry. So am I. At least you made good money out of it.
A pound a go, eh? I suppose you have a good reason."

Harry shook his head. "I just wanted the money, sir."

Langton looked at the miserable boy, and any trace of anger disappeared. Harry's betrayal dwindled when compared to Purcell's or Mc-
Bride's. But it was still a betrayal. "What to do now, Harry?"

Glistening eyes glanced up. "Will I go to jail?"

"If you carry on like this, maybe," Langton said. "Look on this as a
warning and you might be all right."

"You mean . . . You're not telling on me?"

Langton almost smiled at the childhood expression. "No, I'm not
'telling on you,' but you can't work for me anymore, Harry. I don't like
having to look over my shoulder."

Harry stood up. His shoulders slumped and he still seemed about
to cry as he said, "The fourth floor is looking for an office boy, sir. Do
you think they'd have me? I promise I'd never do anything like this
again. I swear, sir."

"Go and ask them, Harry."

"Thank you, sir. I won't let you down." The deep blush returned. "I
mean, not again. Sir."

As the office door closed behind Harry, Langton slumped in his
chair, feeling suddenly very old and tired. He wondered if he'd been

too lenient. Half of the blame had to rest with him, though, and how could Langton lecture Harry on morals? Not after his agreement with Doktor Glass.

No, he had no right to lecture anyone.

He opened Kepler's case file at the last page and unscrewed his fountain pen. What could he write? Certainly not the truth. No mention of Sister Wright, Purcell, McBride, or Sarah. Nothing that might point to Doktor Glass. In short, nothing.

What had happened to Kepler? Sister Wright said she murdered only when she had no choice. If Langton could believe her word—and he had to admit that he still did—then what had Kepler done to justify his death and mutilation? Yes, he bore the tattoos of the Orange Free State Irregulars, so Sister Wright could hate him for that. She said she'd recognized the tattoos only *after* Kepler's death. So why had he died?

The fountain pen, almost touching the file sheet, leaked a jagged stain of ink. Langton cursed, blotted it, and glanced back through the earlier sheets. Here, where Langton and McBride had found the money and passports in Gloucester Road. Or here, where they'd found the destination address of so many of Kepler's telegrams: the Foreign and Commonwealth Office.

Major Fallows worked for the FCO and tacitly admitted that he worked in the secret services, with Kepler and Durham his agents in Liverpool.

Despite himself, Langton arranged and rearranged facts, trying to fit them together. It would be child's play for the government to place two of its agents inside the Span Company, either with or without Lord Salisbury's knowledge. Then, Kepler and Durham had frequented the dockers' pubs, asking around for hints of any Boers or malcontents. That made sense: Fallows would want them to sniff out anything that might endanger the Span.

Kepler had discovered more than he knew. Through either accident or carelessness, Kepler must have tipped his hand. Doktor Glass had realized he was casting around for information and decided to silence him.

Doktor Glass; Sister Wright. If she had feared Kepler, it meant she had a plot that she hadn't wanted him to discover. That business with his face, with the deliberate placing of his body where she knew it would be found, and quickly—they would have to be explained later. No, the main thing now was that plot. What had she wanted to hide?

The Span.

Langton looked through the window, along Victoria Street with its fluttering ribbons, garlands, and flags. He checked his pockets and desk drawers. Kepler had had a key from the Span; so had Jake. Kepler's was part of his work, but Jake's meant one thing: Sister Wright had a plot that concerned the transatlantic bridge. And she'd told Langton to avoid the Span. She'd been trying to save his life.

Then Langton remembered the words of the manager of Irving and Long: Doktor Glass had collected that massive copper coil, the component perhaps for an immense attractor. How many souls would that machine deal with? A hundred? A thousand? Two thousand?

Langton was already halfway up the stairs to Purcell's office when he thought of Sarah. His steps slowed. He'd promised Sister Wright. If she knew he suspected her hand in a plot against the Span, he might lose the chance to be with his wife. Forever.

He stood there, clutching the stone balustrade, half-turned to go back to his office. Step by slow step he descended the stairs. What could he do, anyway? It was too late. If Fallows and all his teams of agents couldn't identify a plot against the Span, what chance did Langton have?

He stood in his office, deliberately avoiding the window. All he had to do was go through the motions of his daily life. Pretend that nothing had changed. Then, tomorrow . . .

He couldn't do it. He thought of the crowds waiting to see the

Queen; he thought of the workers on the Span, the electric trains packed full of hopeful passengers waiting to start out for America, for new lives.

Langton pocketed Kepler's and Jake's keys for the Span, grabbed his coat, and ran out. At the landing, he hesitated, then decided that Purcell would be of no use to him. He ran down the stairs and into the city's noisy, festive atmosphere.

And Sarah? If he had to, how would he choose between her and the Span?

Langton pushed that thought to the very back of his mind and concentrated on forcing his way through the expectant crowds.

THOUSANDS OF PEOPLE packed the Goree and the approach to the Pier Head. Water Street, the artery leading straight down to the river, remained open only because of the lines of constables keeping back the waiting onlookers. Time and again, Langton had to show his warrant card to get through. Eventually he filtered through the main gates leading to the site of the inauguration ceremony.

A guard in crisp uniform of red and gold returned Langton's card. "No invitation, sir?"

"I need to see Major Fallows," Langton said.

"Sorry, sir. The major's too busy. Can't let you through."

As the guard turned away, Langton grabbed him by one gilded lapel. "If you don't let me talk to Fallows, there won't be any ceremony today. Or Span. Do you want to take that chance?"

The guard stared at Langton, then at the security guards waiting nearby. He pulled his lapel from Langton's grip, smoothed the wrinkled material, and nodded toward the freshly painted guards' hut. "Wait in there. Sir."

Inside the hut, Langton paced the small room and watched the lines of honored visitors arriving. Men in formal suits, top hats, silk waistcoats. Shivering women in fine gowns carrying parasols and winter bouquets fresh from orangeries and hothouses. Langton tried not to imagine them lifeless and inert. God, what was keeping Fallows?

Then he saw the major hurrying against the tide of arriving guests.

"What the hell's going on, Langton?"

"Close the door."

"Just tell me—"

Langton slammed the door of the guards' hut and set his back to it. "Kepler and Durham were your agents. You sent them down here to sniff out a Boer plot, but when Kepler discovered too much, the plotters killed him and frightened off Durham."

Fallows made for the door. "This is none of your concern."

Langton still blocked his path. "I'm concerned about the deaths of these people. There is a plot. I don't know what it is yet, but I have no doubt it exists. None."

Fallows stared at Langton for a moment. "We heard rumors of Boers planning to attack the Span."

"So you sent Kepler and Durham? Or whatever their real names are."

"I arranged posts for them inside the Span Company," Fallows said, checking his fob watch. "They kept their eyes and ears open, visited the pubs and workingmen's clubs, the shebeens and whorehouses. They sent regular updates."

"And?"

Fallows looked at the crowds beyond the glass. "There was something planned. They were sure of it, but they had nothing definite. That's why Kepler died; he overreached himself trying to get proof."

"Is that what Durham says?"

"Durham has not contacted me since Kepler's death."

Langton almost told him of Durham's visit in the early hours; the fugitive had said he trusted no one, not even Fallows. Did that work both ways? "You suspect Durham, don't you, Fallows? You wonder whether Durham killed Kepler and joined the plotters."

"I cannot discount it, Langton."

From the concourse outside came a sudden ragged fanfare as the military band practiced. Langton tried to remember all he could about Durham and Kepler. "Kepler was an Irregular."

"He was many things, both for the Boers and for our country. He'd been one of my best agents before he started drinking. Still, he was ideal for this; he had a history with the Boers. The plotters would trust him."

But the plotters weren't Boers, Langton said to himself. *It was Doktor Glass. And she hates the Boers.*

"Now, what's going on, Langton?" Fallows said. "My men have found nothing, no explosives or Boers or anarchists. What makes you think something will happen today?"

Langton looked at the immense first tower of the Span. How much could he tell Fallows without giving away Sister Wright, and Sarah? "Reefer Jake, one of the Jar Boys we caught, had a complex key from the Span."

"So? What does it fit?"

"I don't know. I'd like to find out."

"What does this Reefer Jake say?"

"Nothing. He died in the cells," Langton said. Fallows would never believe what happened after that, or Langton's theory about the massive attractor machine possibly assembled nearby. "Jake's key is no coincidence."

"It's hardly proof, Langton."

"I spoke with someone inside the gang, and I'm sure that something will happen here today unless we prevent it."

"What, Langton? Tell me. Give me details, specifics. Something my men can watch out for."

"I can't, Fallows. I don't even know what to look for myself."

Fallows stared at him for a few seconds like a constable gauging a drunk or street madman. "I wonder whose side you're on, Langton."

How could he answer that? He wasn't even sure himself. "I just don't want any more murders."

As Fallows glanced through the window to the waiting guards, Langton slid one hand to the Webley. He wondered if he could knock Fallows unconscious before the man called in the guards. Langton shifted his weight and edged a little closer.

Fallows turned to him and nodded. "I'll tell my teams to increase their vigilance. Although how they can stop something you only hint at . . . If you see anything definite, Langton, give three short blasts on this."

Langton took the strange device from Fallows. Heavier than its small size implied, it had a stubby aerial connected to a waxed voltaic battery cell no bigger than a matchbox. "Why don't I simply use my police whistle?"

"Because this emitter is ultrasonic," Fallows said. "It sends out a signal slightly above the usual range of hearing."

"Then how will your men hear it?"

"Sympathetic vibration," Fallows said, and took out from his right ear a small metal drum the size of a pea. "This is keyed to the sound waves from the device. Something to do with the diaphragm resonating at a certain frequency. The important thing is, any of my teams hearing this will be able to respond quickly."

Langton pocketed the device. "And none of the public will hear it and panic."

"Exactly. Now, put this pin in your lapel—it will identify you as one of my team. There." Fallows checked his fob watch for the sixth or seventh time, then made for the door. "If you see anything suspicious, anything at all, let my men know."

Outside, Langton stuck the gilt-and-red pin in his lapel, looked around, and wondered where to start. In front of the Span Company offices stood the temporary tiered seating and the royal family's enclosed booth. Most of the arriving guests milled about the area between the two, greeting acquaintances or just being seen for the sake of it. Everywhere Langton turned he saw newsreel cameramen, the *cinématographes*: on scaffolds, on the backs of wagons, on roofs, and even on boats in the nearby docks. The whole world would see this day. Would they watch a triumph or a disaster?

The international cameramen, leaning over their metal boxes on tripods, resembled strange five-legged hybrid creatures from mythology. Could Sister Wright have passed off one or more of her gang as newsmen? It could be anyone: guests, guards, servants, policemen . . .

Langton still thought of her as the dedicated nurse he'd first met in the Infirmary. He had difficulty seeing her as cold, ruthless Doktor Glass. Did she have trouble splitting those two halves? Everybody had some contradictions within them, Langton knew, but was it actually more severe with Sister Wright/Doktor Glass? Had she fractured into insanity?

Langton pushed through the crowd, not bothering to murmur apologies. He tried to look everywhere: at the dockside, now clean and scrubbed; at the smiling guests; at the curving sweep of the Span's entrance ramp, the suspended road and rail deck, and the serried ledges of the tower above. The thump and bray of the brass band distracted him, as did the smells of cigars and cigarettes, and the traces of a hundred perfumes.

He froze. A delicate hint of an odor gave him an almost physical momentum, a rush of movement back through the years. Sarah had used that perfume. The hint of orange blossom and freesia. She liked to dab it behind her ears, at the curve of her long, slender neck . . .

Langton shook his head as if drunk. He forced himself to pay attention to his surroundings. He had to concentrate. His hand found the key in his pocket. Jake's key. And up ahead stood the Span Company head office. Langton pushed his way to the building's lobby and saw the doors open, uniformed commissionaires standing either side. "I need to speak to someone in your administration. Anyone who deals with keys."

The commissionaire, a burly bruiser with the barely hidden tattoos of an ex-seaman at his wrists, glanced at Langton's lapel pin. "I'll see if anyone's in, sir."

While the man leaned into the switchboard cubicle, Langton paced the echoing marble lobby. He checked his watch. Eleven forty. Just over three hours until the Queen opened the Span.

The commissionaire returned. "Mr. Harrison from engineering is on his way down, sir."

Harrison, a grey man of less than thirty years, shook Langton's hand and asked how he could help. He examined Jake's key in the light of an electrolier, squinting along the barrel and feeling the jagged notches. "Very strange."

"What do you see?"

"Well . . . off the top of my head, I'd swear it looks like one of our caisson master keys. But I thought—I'm sure—they were all locked away. Very strange."

"What would it open?"

Harrison looked up. "Open? Why all the doors in the caissons. Every last one of them."

Langton took a deep breath. "What exactly are the caissons?"

Harrison led him to the lobby entrance and pointed to the nearest tower, the first of so many that stretched across the Atlantic. He pointed to the stone base that disappeared into the water. "You see there? The caissons were the wood and metal structures—like great bells hundreds of feet across—that we sank onto the seabed. After the masons dropped inside and built the foundations for each tower, we peeled away the caisson's outer shell and reused it, but the core remains. The original masons' access passages and stairwells were never filled in. This key fits the pressure doors to those."

Could that be the way Sister Wright would destroy the Span? Get into the tower's base and . . . what? Plant explosives? Undermine the foundations?

Langton tried to imagine the immense weight of the Span bearing down on its squat tower bases, each one a hundred feet across where it entered the water. Millions of tons of steel, granite, brick, iron. As well as the decorative stone panels flanking the soaring steel structure.

From this distance, the angular Egyptian figures looked monolithic and faintly threatening.

Harrison continued, turning the key in his hand. "This gives the workmen access to the inner maintenance corridors and ladders, right up from the bottom levels to the top of the towers. She needs a great deal of care and attention, the Span."

Again, the use of the female. "So, with this key, someone could attack the Span from inside?"

Harrison looked horrified. "I should hope not."

"But it's possible."

"Major Fallows's men have been all over the Span," Harrison said. "They've checked for sabotage and explosives, even for gas. I myself walked every foot of the first and second towers this past week. There's no sign of interference."

Or the signs are so strange or subtle that we don't see them, Langton thought. He held out his hand. "Could I take that?"

Harrison clutched the key. "I should lock this away with the others. Do you really think you'll need it?"

"Honestly? I don't know."

Harrison hesitated, glanced at the Span's first tower and then dropped the key in Langton's palm. "I'll have to tell Lord Salisbury."

"Of course." Langton shook Harrison's hand and dropped down the steps, but turned when the engineer called him.

"Do you think there's a threat to the Span, Inspector?"

Instead of answering, Langton said, "Major Fallows and his teams are confident they've checked everything."

Langton made for the freshly painted iron railings that guarded the edge of the quay. Beyond them, the sandstone blocks dropped away to the grey water of the dock. And fifty yards away stood the first tower. Solid. Immense. Apparently immovable.

Langton gripped the cold railing and felt the military band music vibrating through the iron. A chill wind skimmed the water. He remembered Mrs. Grizedale's vision, absorbed by Sarah from one of her jar's "clients": the dancing bridge. If it meant anything, how could that solid structure warp and shift? How could Sister Wright contort steel and stone?

A hand on Langton's shoulder made him spin around. He'd found the butt of the Webley before he recognized the man. "Professor."

"Inspector. I'm glad to have spotted you. I thought we should talk." Professor Caldwell Chivers didn't appear too happy; in fact, his expression, his hands clasped behind his back, and his rigid stance all made him look like a headmaster about to punish a pupil. "I believe you forced your way into my house without any provocation or good cause, threatened my staff, and left without any explanation for your behavior."

"Professor, I—"

"I don't take offense easily, Langton, but this is beyond the pale. I've a good mind to bring this up with the Chief Constable. Only Sister Wright vouching for your character prevented me from doing so already."

Langton stared at the Professor. "You've seen Sister Wright?"

"Of course. She's here as chairman of the nursing guild, and as my guest. Now, sir: an explanation."

Langton nodded. "You deserve one, but this isn't the time."

"Look here—"

"Someone means to harm the Span," Langton said, lowering his voice and taking a step closer to the Professor. "I thought it was you— that's why I burst into your house. I'm sorry."

The Professor gaped at Langton. "Me? How could you even think that?"

Langton waved that away; he didn't want to expose Sister Wright. Not yet. Perhaps never.

Instead, he said, "You designed part of the Span, didn't you?"

"Only the cladding, the bas-reliefs and such. Why?"

Langton took a deep breath. "If you wanted to destroy the Span, how would you do it?"

"Are you mad?"

"Possibly, but humor me. How?"

The Professor looked at the tower, at the milling guests, then back at Langton. "There are so many ways; the crudest would be explosives at the base or on the support lines. Gas, methane or natural, piped into the caissons. Sabotage, such as cutting through the cables . . . these have been anticipated and checked, surely?"

"They have, but what about something more subtle?"

"What do you mean?"

"Something out of the ordinary, something we wouldn't expect . . ." Again, Langton thought of Mrs. Grizedale. "What would make the bridge dance?"

This time, the Professor stared at Langton as though sure he was insane.

"Think, Professor. What could twist the Span out of shape?"

A pause, then the Professor smiled. "Galloping George."

"Pardon me?"

"A suspension bridge over the Charles River in New British Columbia," the Professor said. "Even in relatively low winds, the bridge used to ripple and sway. The locals nicknamed it Galloping George. And they weren't surprised when it shook itself to pieces in only a moderate gale. They had time to clear the bridge and call in a newsreel camera. I've seen the footage; the whole structure oscillated horizontally and vertically. An amazing sight."

Now sure he'd found the answer, Langton needed more information. "How? What caused it?"

"Poor design. Henry Marc Brunel could tell you all the details, obviously, but I think the prevailing winds took hold of the light bridge's solid plate girders, which offered too tempting a profile. At a certain frequency, the oscillation became torsional."

"Pardon me?"

The Professor flexed his hand like a sea wave. "The bridge started to twist. The oscillation increased in amplitude—became stronger—

under its own momentum, until eventually the phenomenal stresses tore the bridge apart."

Langton looked up at the Span. "Then the same will happen here. Today."

"In beautiful, calm weather like this? With no wind? Besides, Langton, the Brunels know what they are doing. See the latticework of open girders that line the entire length of the road and rail deck? Not only do they give the deck strength, they also break up the prevailing wind. No, the same could not happen here."

Langton sagged with fatigue. He'd believed he'd found the answer, but the Professor must be right. Not even Doktor Glass could conjure up a wind on a calm day like this, especially a wind at just the right frequency to shake the bridge. No, it was fanciful, the stuff of yellow-back fiction, something out of Louis Stevenson, Wilkie Collins, or Rhodes James.

So were the Jar Boys. And they existed.

"There must be another way," Langton said, rubbing his eyes. "Think, Professor; how else could someone destroy the Span?"

"Please, calm yourself, Langton." The Professor stepped closer and looked at Langton as if evaluating a patient. "You're obviously exhausted and overwrought, ideal conditions for a man to lose perspective and jump to the most outlandish conclusions. Fatigue drains more than our body—it affects our judgment."

"But, the Span—"

"Rest, man, that's what you need." The Professor laid a hand on Langton's shoulder and used the tone of voice he no doubt saved for his patients. "The Span is safe. The Brunels designed it to withstand earthquake, disaster, and sabotage. And I've seen almost as many security guards and policemen as guests. Trust me, Langton: Nothing will happen today."

Langton went to argue, then saw the reason and logic behind the Professor's kind words. Fatigue did sap logic, and the past week had drained Langton of everything. He looked up at the immense solidity of the Span and had to agree that it seemed impregnable. Permanent. Immovable.

"Perhaps you're right," Langton said. "I should rest."

"Absolutely. A few hours' sleep will make all the difference. And don't worry about the little, ah, incident at my house."

"Thank you, Professor." Langton shook the man's hand and then, as he turned away, said, "If you see Sister Wright, will you not mention that you saw me? That I've been here today?"

The Professor seemed about to ask why, but simply nodded. "If you wish."

Alone at the edge of the crowd, Langton leaned on the black iron railings and let the chill of the water below wash over him. Had he jeopardized Sarah's soul by coming here today? He'd had no choice; he'd really believed Sister Wright threatened the Span. Madness upon madness upon . . .

He shook his head to clear the detritus of thoughts and headed back for the main gates. The crowd thinned around him as guests climbed up to their waiting seats in the tiered grandstand. The military band struck up a jaunty march, one that Langton remembered from the Transvaal; the dusty, weary musicians had played it on the way into battle in the Natal, to lift morale. And there was something in that; music did have the power to affect a man's spirits.

Since he kept close to the edge of the Span Company concourse, near the railing separating it from the dock, Langton could see across the water to the camp and some of the sandstone bank of the Pier Head and George's Parade. Holes, sewer outlets, and tunnel entrances punctured the massive blocks and made Langton recall Durham's escape. Had the FCO agent suspected Professor Caldwell Chivers also? Was that why he'd exited the tunnels at Toxteth?

Less than a hundred yards away, a man's head popped out of a dark tunnel, looked around, then disappeared again. Langton stared at the spot, sure he had imagined it. The man's small, glistening skull appeared once again for a second, then ducked back inside the tunnel.

Langton hesitated. His hand reached for the warning device in his pocket. He could see the main gates to his right; to his left, where the dock wall met the sandstone bank of the Pier Head, lay the tunnel with its strange inhabitant. Langton turned left, ducking beneath the temporary wooden barriers and showing his lapel pin to the guards. He followed the railings at the dock's edge until he heard a familiar thudding sound like the heartbeat of a great animal. Then, skirting a low brick storehouse, he saw the steam wagon with its air pump wheezing on the cargo bed.

Sapper George, undressing at the side of the wagon, pulled his rubber suit up when he realized someone was approaching. "Oh, it's you, Inspector. Thought one of the guests had found us."

Langton looked down the open shaft nearby where a ladder descended into darkness. Two pulsing rubber hoses, one yellow, one red, slid over the brick coping. "I saw someone look out of one of the tunnels."

"That'd be young Eric," Sapper George said, still only half dressed. "I was just getting some decent clothes on; Major Fallows said to report anything strange, so—"

Langton stepped forward. "What did you find?"

Sapper George scratched his chin. "I don't rightly know, sir. Deep down, close to the Span's first tower, someone's built a great metal machine that looks like nothing on earth."

Twenty

L ANGTON COULDN'T BELIEVE the temperature of the tunnels beneath the Pier Head. Within minutes of climbing down the ladders, the cold had drilled into his bones, and his numb hands
and feet seemed to belong to someone else. He wished he'd accepted
Sapper George's offer of an insulated rubber suit; instead, impatience
had driven him down the shaft dressed as he was in his thin formal
clothes. As he splashed along the dank tunnels, water dripped from
the curving roof, trickled down the back of his neck, and soaked his
shirt and jacket.

Langton remembered looking up from the bottom of the access
shaft. The square patch of sky up above had seemed so small and distant. He'd had a sudden and absolute conviction that he'd never see
daylight again.

Now he could see Sapper George's light up ahead, the butane gas
lamp filling the brick-lined tunnel with a greasy yellow light. Sapper
George's distorted shadow climbed the walls and writhed as he waded
through a stream of thick, foul liquid. Familiar with the cramped tun-

nels, Sapper George had settled into a well-practiced half-crouch, shoulders slumped and head down, that made him resemble a shuffling ape from the penny dreadfuls. Langton still scraped his head against the low ceiling and blundered into the curving walls until his knuckles and forehead bled.

As he sank into a cold brook that reached his knees, Langton wished he'd simply waited for Fallows and the search teams to arrive. What could he have told them? He couldn't be sure that the machine deep in the tunnels belonged to Doktor Glass.

"Careful, sir," Sapper George said. "Mind the drop."

In the yellow light of the gas lamp, Langton saw a perfectly round hole in the floor. The water rushed into this sluice and sent back a roaring echo from deep below. Although roped to Sapper George with stout hemp, Langton took careful steps around the shaft. His boots slipped too easily on these slimy, crumbling bricks.

"Not too far now, sir. You'll soon be out in the dry again. Well, what passes for dry down here."

"Where are we?"

Sapper George looked up, as if he could see through the tons of earth and sandstone and bricks. "I reckon we're just at the edge of the bank, sir. Another few yards and we'll be under the Mersey."

Langton shuddered. Millions of cubic feet of cold grey water. Tons of silt and detritus. All kept at bay by a few courses of aging brickwork.

Struggling behind Sapper George, keen to distract himself, Langton asked, "Who built these tunnels?"

"Good question, sir. Smugglers built some of them, centuries back; they used to bring in tobacco and liquor, sugar, slaves too, even after the abolition act came in." Sapper George stopped for a moment to brush a couple of cockroaches off his shoulders. "There's older tunnels and shafts. Much older, built by the Romans, according to the records. Or more likely Roman slaves. And you can believe it when you look at the quality of the brickwork here."

He slapped the wall in passing, sending out a spray of cold water.

"Sewers, most of the tunnels, and waste channels. But there's others, weird passageways that don't seem to make any sense. They go up, down, across; they meet each other and branch off. Chains in the walls, and hooks, and old bones on the floor. Some say monks built them; others say devil worshippers."

Regretting having asked the question, Langton shuddered again. He tried to forget the Mersey River overhead. A sound stopped him a moment, made him search the darkness beyond the lamp's gleam. "Did you hear that? Someone sobbing. There."

Sapper George shook his head. "Sound travels strange paths down here, sir. Someone talks a mile away, you'd swear they was standing next to you. We had a young fella from the university come down to research some book he was doing, something called *acoustics* he said. Strange acoustics in these shafts, apparently. He didn't know the half of it."

Sapper George came to a three-way junction: One shaft went straight on; one dropped down; another curved right. He chose the right-hand tunnel and continued, "Different world down here, sir, isn't it?"

As the butane lamp sent a herd of glistening cockroaches swarming up the walls, Langton wondered how anyone could work down here. Not just work, but obviously *enjoy* being here. When Sapper George smiled at Langton, with the yellow light reflecting from his eyes and his small, sharp teeth, he looked like he belonged in this underworld.

For a moment, Langton wondered if Sister Wright was behind this. Did she control Sapper George too? Would he simply cut the rope and leave Langton down here in the scurrying dark? Langton's right hand patted the Webley.

Sapper George climbed a short flight of rough-hewn steps and shone the light through a skewed doorway. "Here we are, sir. Don't know if you can make anything of it . . ."

Langton had expected no more than a room, but the cavern stretched beyond the limit of the gas lamp. Even when Sapper George turned up the pressure, the hissing light barely reached the tall, barrel-vaulted ceiling and distant corners. Langton could just make out neat, regular brickwork. Complicated chains and rusting pulleys hung from the ceiling; the atmosphere made them resemble instruments of torture instead of the light fittings or cargo hooks they had probably been. Probably.

And on the dry, swept floor of the chamber, row after row of earthenware jars. All exactly the same size and exactly the same design. Laid out like glazed seeds waiting for a sun that would never reach this deep.

"I swear these weren't here two days back, sir," Sapper George said. He pointed back to the doorway they had come in through, and the neat pile of new bricks beside it. "The Span Company blocked up this room, but someone came along afterward and knocked it through. Can't make out why, though."

With careful steps, Langton walked between the rows of jars. On each one, green wax sealed the gap between the jar's lip and the lid. And from each lid emerged a pair of braided, cloth-covered electrical wires, one wire to each copper connector. The braided connectors lay on the dusty floor in neat lines, all heading in the same direction, toward another door in the far wall. After each row of jars, more cables joined the common braid until it looked as thick as Langton's thigh. Whoever had laid the cables had done a neat job, tying them together with waxed twine. But some of the outer wires lay clean and copper-bare where rats' teeth had recently gnawed.

Langton followed the bunched, braided cables across the floor. Up ahead, a new metal frame and doorway, the door itself like something from one of Levallier's submarine ships: heavy with rivets and cross-bracing steel bars operated by a central wheel.

"That's one of the new hatches the Span people put in, sir. Supposed to be watertight and closed at all times."

The door couldn't close, not with the braided cables climbing over its rubber-flanged threshold. Langton saw the mouth of a lock and tried the complex key he'd found on Reefer Jake; the lock mechanism turned and eight radiating brass bolts emerged gleaming with oil from the door's edges. Langton clicked them back into place and pocketed the key again before he opened the massive door fully.

A flickering white glow and the smells of damp earth and white flowers drifted from the second room, overlaid with a slightly acrid smell like burning rubber. Something else deterred Langton from crossing the threshold: a sensation at the back of his mind, an almost audible whisper conjuring dread. He turned to see if Sapper George felt the same effect; the tunnelman rubbed at his temples as if wishing away a headache.

Before he stepped inside, Langton took out his revolver, motioned Sapper George into the shelter of the wall, and then thrust the man's butane light into the second room. A score of rats' eyes gleamed black before the animals swarmed into the shadows. No human life appeared. Only the massive apparatus in the center of the room showed how recently people had worked down here.

Langton could remember the attractor machine he'd found in Redfers's house, and the more recent version the Jar Boys had used in Plimsoll Street: portable though heavy, and small enough to sit on a table.

The great apparatus now before him stood taller than his head. Gleaming cylinders of copper and steel. Convoluted pipes as stout as his arm. Irving and Long's wound copper coil hummed and shimmered slightly as if a great current passed through it. But the glowing center of the machine drew Langton's eye: fantastic whorls and spheres of clear glass linked by slender tubes, fluted pipes, curving arteries. The pulsing essences within that glass vortex never halted; every particle seemed in constant, silent motion. They swirled through the chambers like agile white mist, and their luminescence filled the cavern with a flickering pale glow.

The image of young Edith's soul leaving her body and flocking to the Jar Boys' attractor reared up in Langton's memory. He imagined the essences of all those jars in the adjacent cavern, all those charged particles channeled along the braided cables and into the vast machine. Hundreds of souls writhing inside that glass prison. What did Sister Wright plan for them?

Langton stepped over the braided cables that disappeared into the machine's innards. He tried another few steps; the air seemed to thicken and push him back like a hand pressing against his chest. His throat tightened as the whispering in the back of his mind grew louder, more urgent.

"What do you make of it, sir?" asked Sapper George. "Looks like some kind of engine to me."

"It does, at that," Langton said. An engine to drive the passage of souls? Or to use their power? And how had Sister Wright's men brought it down here?

Then Langton realized that no component was larger than six feet in length, not even the copper coil; small enough to manhandle through doorways and down narrow corridors and shafts. Even the diverse glass vessels connected together to form one unit. He could see lengths of rough wood in the corner, pallets and frames used to transport the individual pieces. The planning and operation must have taken months. The manufacture, years. How long had Sister Wright and her accomplices worked at this machine?

Langton had to destroy this device before Sister Wright activated it. He must release those essences trapped within, even though a part of him balked at causing them more pain than they endured already. Thinking of the thousands of guests waiting above, and of Her Exalted Majesty herself, he raised the Webley and took another step forward.

The keening at the rear of his skull climbed in pitch. As if sensing his intention, the gaseous cloud inside the apparatus flocked to the side facing him; Langton swore he heard the sound of something colloidal slapping against the inside of the glass structure.

He took another step. The cloud writhed in its prison. Emotions engulfed Langton: fear, pain, sorrow, envy, hatred, love. Like the pat-

terns in a childhood kaleidoscope, the emotions fragmented and seg-
mented, merged with each other at random to form new, unnameable
feelings, hybrids with a greater potency than the sum of their parts.

The Webley shook. He gripped the weapon in both hands and
tried to focus on the fragile glass whorl. The keening in his skull became a roaring, a pounding of almost physical intensity. And one emotion coalesced out of all the white noise: fear.

"I can't do it." Langton lowered the revolver and stepped back. He
dragged his sleeve across his sweating face and gulped damp air. "I
can't."

"You want me to have a shot at it, sir?" Sapper George asked.
"Maybe if we moved back to the doorway?"

Langton looked at the agitated cloud and caught the echoes of
the turmoil. Even though trapped and helpless, they feared release.
He couldn't harm them, but there had to be another way to disable the
machine. "Where does that cable lead?"

Sapper George pointed the butane lamp at one thick wire maybe
two inches across, bound in rubber and cloth. It met the far side of the
machine in a great gleaming brass connector the size of a shovel and
screwed down with a nut like something from a steamship. Langton
followed the unfurled cable into the darkness, with Sapper George
struggling behind.

Across the floor, through another great steel pressure door, down
a short passage and into a confined shaft that gave off stale air. As
Langton went to step inside, Sapper George pulled him back. "Careful, Inspector. Watch and listen."

Sapper George took a fragment of brick from the tunnel floor and
dropped it into the shaft. Langton counted. He gave up when he
reached twenty. Then came a distant splash.

"It's one of the Span's test boreholes," Sapper George said. "Deep,
they go. They should have filled them in, but that costs money. Besides,
who'd have business down here?"

A cold draft came from the ragged entrance. In the light of the butane lamp, Langton saw the thick insulated cable leading up and fixed to the rough-bore sides of the shaft with fresh steel screws. "What's above us?"

"The caisson, Inspector, and the foundations of the Span's first tower."

Langton stared up into the darkness beyond the reach of the butane lamp. What had Sister Wright planned? All those souls combined in the great machine, all that power concentrated and waiting. Waiting to destroy the Span.

He checked his fob watch: ten minutes after one. Far above him, in the world of daylight, the Queen's stately procession would be threading through the Liverpool streets. Soon she would arrive at the Pier Head and take her place among the guests. In the shadow of the Span's graceful entrance ramp and the enormous first tower.

"I need to get up there," Langton said, already leaning into the shaft and searching for handholds.

"Don't even think of it, Inspector."

Langton didn't answer; he wondered if he could find handholds in the rough walls of the shaft. He could almost make out the spiral of the Span Company's huge drill-bit auger. They might give enough purchase.

"Please, Inspector. I've worked down here nigh on twenty years and I wouldn't chance it. Suicide, I tell you."

Langton looked back at Sapper George, hesitated, and finally nodded. "You're right. We'll go back."

But as they retraced their steps toward the second chamber with its humming machine, Langton said, "Will you go back and find out what's keeping Major Fallows and his men? I'll wait here."

Sapper George stopped in the passageway and stared at Langton, his eyes glistening like jet in the butane light. Down here, more than ever, his sleek compact features made him resemble some strange burrowing animal. "You wouldn't be thinking of going up that tunnel, would you sir? Tell me it isn't so."

"We're wasting time, Sapper. Fallows will need your guidance."

Sapper George laid one grimy hand on Langton's arm. "There's one way to destroy that machine, sir. The Cromwell sluices."

He detoured Langton down another short passageway and up three steps. The walls here looked older, with crumbling bricks in uneven sizes. The wooden door at the end of the passage looked like something from an old man-o'-war: thick beams and rusting iron nails with heads an inch across, and all black with generations of bitumen and caulking. The bottom half of the door had a bulging iron plate held fast in vertical runners.

Sapper George held the butane lamp close to the door. "Some reckon they're older even than Cromwell's time. I don't know how old they are, but I know what's behind them: the Mersey."

Langton looked from the door to Sapper George. "That's all there is between us and the river?"

"Oh, she's stout enough, sir. Look at them crossbeams, and them fixings. She'll hold. She's held for centuries."

Langton knelt close to the iron plate in the door. He thought he could hear water swirling outside but put it down to imagination. "This is the sluice?"

"One of them, sir." Sapper George knelt beside him, switching the lamp from one hand to the other so Langton didn't get burned. "Used to be cables going up through iron pipes all the way to the Pier Head. Man up there could turn a wheel and the sluices on these deep levels would open; the Mersey would pour into every cavern, every passage. Well before the Span, this was."

"Why would you want to flood down here?"

A scraping noise from the dark passage behind them made both men turn and stare. Sapper George kept his voice low: "Witches, sir. Satanists. They used to love these levels. Dark and secret, and closer to him that they worshipped. People heard screams and chanting from the deep shafts, and found bones and things you wouldn't credit. Story goes that Cromwell himself got wind of the sects and had these gates put in. 'Let good cold water douse the fires of hell,' they reckon he said. And maybe he did at that."

Langton, cramped and shivering, stood up. "I'm glad we don't have that in this age."

Sapper George went to speak but shook his head instead.

Langton grasped the handle of the rusting metal wheel set beside the door. "You believe this still works?"

"Can't say for sure, sir. I wouldn't like to be the one who finds out."

As they walked back along the passageway, Langton glanced at the sluice door. A last resort, certainly, and one with no guarantee. But if it did work, the Mersey would reduce the machine to crumpled steel. Langton might have no choice.

In the second chamber, the machine still hummed and sent out its swirling, vaporous light. Langton watched it a moment and then said, "Tell Fallows all we've seen, Sapper George. Warn him."

Sapper George held out his right hand. "Good luck, sir. And be careful."

Langton shook the man's hand and found a small oblong of metal pressed into his own.

"You can have my backup light, Inspector. It might only last half an hour, but it's better than nothing. Just flick that switch there to turn it on."

"Thank you. For all your help."

Sapper George scuttled toward the first cavern, keeping to the edges of the room close to the wall and avoiding the machine. His voice echoed: "Young Eric has probably taken the wrong turn. Good lad, he is, but got his head filled with too much nonsense, not like it was in my day . . ."

Langton waited until Sapper George's voice had faded and the yellow glow of the butane lamp had disappeared into the darkness. Then he clicked on the electric light. It threw out a white globe of illumination barely a yard across. Enough light to enable Langton to select two planks of wood from the machine's discarded pallets and carry them back to the deep borehole. Setting the light down, he wedged the planks across the narrow shaft; they might not save him if he fell, but they at least offered some reassurance. He clipped the light to his jacket, took a deep breath of foul air, and climbed into the shaft.

The Span Company's auger had been slightly wider than Langton's shoulders. He found he could wedge his back against the shaft and find footholds in the rising spiral cut into the sandstone. As he climbed, he tried not to think of the drop beneath him, nor of the water above and around. At least a steady draft swept down the shaft and cooled his body as he sweated with the exertion.

He settled into a routine: left foot braced, then right, push and slide his back up another few inches. Then repeat. And again. Soon the muscles in his thighs burned. The rough serrations dug into his spine. He concentrated on the smooth cable screwed to the sides of the shaft like a sleek black snake climbing beside him.

Left foot, right foot, push and slide. How far did this shaft go? He must have been in it for an hour. The electric light still burned bright. Left foot, right foot, push and slide, with his hoarse breath echoing in the shaft.

Then his left foot found a weakened ridge: The rock crumbled. As he fell he spun to the left, where his head cracked into the wall and sent jagged white pain through his skull. His hands tore at the shaft, trying to grip the damp rock. Like a bucket in a well, he plummeted.

The cable saved him. His right hand clutched at a distended loop standing proud of the shaft. Langton hung there, exhausted, his right arm almost wrenched from its socket. The electric lamp swung on its short clip and sent distorted shadows climbing. From below Langton came an echoing thud and then a distant splash. He grasped the cable with his left hand and hung on, gasping in air. Then, slowly, he twisted his body and braced his legs against the other side of the shaft. He didn't let go of the cable.

How far had he fallen? How much time had he wasted? He looked down, saw nothing but darkness. The same darkness as that above.

As he began to climb again, slow and careful, he couldn't escape the certainty that he dreamed all this. The shaft, the pathetic sphere of light, the darkness and the smells: all imagined. Soon he would wake in his own bed. But the exertion was real; the pain was real. His bleeding knuckles, the throbbing in his left temple, his jaw, and burning muscles. They all proved it wasn't a dream. When he looked up, he began to see reflected light. At first a pinpoint, it grew to a dim metallic moon above him. A thought froze him for a moment: What if the Span Company had barred the head of the shaft?

Left foot, right foot, push and slide. Almost there. Almost.

No bars blocked the head of the shaft. Instead, a circular, convex metal hatch with a wheel at its center, again like something from a submarine. Langton could smell the fresh grease used in the mechanism. The black cable snaked up from below and through a fresh hole drilled through the arching brickwork surrounding the hatch. Langton braced his body, spun the wheel, and thrust the hatch open.

A small room awaited him, clean save for the upturned bodies of mummified cockroaches. Fresh brick dust ringed the cable jutting up from the borehole shaft, and more brick dust, red and fine, showed where that same cable continued and bored through the bricks surrounding the massive steel pressure door set in the far wall. Langton hauled his body over the hatch rim and looked through the pressure door's thick porthole quartz. Beyond the door lay darkness. Langton held Sapper George's fading backup light up high and saw a bank of switches on the opposite wall. He flicked them all.

The caged electric bulbs blinded him. He saw the confines of the small service room he stood in, a brick chamber built like an airlock. More light came through the door's porthole window, and this time when Langton looked through he saw the inside of the caisson shaft itself.

As beautiful and perfect as a cathedral nave, in alternating bands of red and yellow brick, the hexagonal core of the caisson thrust up from the Mersey's bedrock and converged at some invisible point far above Langton's craning neck. At least twenty yards across and cross-braced with interlacing steel joists a foot square and painted with red lead. Langton wondered how many men had seen this finished paean to Victorian engineering, intended like the rooftop statues on medieval cathedrals—invisible from the ground—for the eyes of God alone.

Somebody more mundane had visited the shaft, and recently. A strange device filled most of the caisson's white tiled floor like a vast metallic flower: Unfurled blue petals of thin sheet steel surrounded a central core of wound copper wire. Langton could see where the thick cable, after boring through the wall, terminated at the base of the device. He could even see the delicate petals tremble in some unseen draft.

Langton imagined the combined essences traveling up the cable from the machine below and into that bizarre device. Could the attractor, or whatever version of that strange machine it was, really cause the bridge to dance? To sway and twist and contort itself until it failed? Those heavy steel beams and solid bricks said not. Even so, Langton tried to open the massive pressure door and investigate the machine. The knurled wheel would not turn. He tried Reefer Jake's key in the mechanism, but it made no difference.

As he returned the key to his pocket, his hand reflexively patted the Webley. The revolver had gone. Langton remembered his fall in the shaft, and the distant sound of something heavy hitting the braced planks. He wasted no time in cursing the lost weapon.

Instead, he searched the service room for something to damage the cable, since he could not reach the machine itself. Only a few short lengths of wood remained, and they made no more than a shallow dent in the heavy copper cable. The metal casing of the electric lamp did little better.

Langton dragged his sleeve across his face and checked his fob watch: only six minutes before three. The Queen would have taken her seat. No doubt the military bands filled the Pier Head with martial airs. And thousands of people watched and waited in the Span's shadow.

Already hauling open the floor hatch, Langton knew he must shatter the glass heart of the transfer machine in the caverns, no matter what frantic remnants of emotion sliced through his mind. The Cromwell sluices had to remain the last resort—he cared not so much for himself but for Sapper George, Fallows, and all the men who might be caught out by the Mersey's power released into the tunnels.

A distant trembling stayed his hand. He stood at the open hatch and felt the floor vibrate under him, as did the cold metal in his grip. Like the heartbeat of a slow giant waking or the pounding of God's own engine at the center of the earth. Langton ran to the porthole window in the pressure door and saw the petals of the strange machine shake with each cycle of the vibration; they flexed and shimmered like a thing alive.

Then Langton realized that he caught only a small fraction of the transmitted signal. Other notes and echoes oscillated behind the initial coarse pounding. At the edge of hearing writhed weird harmonics, the shapes of notes shifting in and out of synchronization. What would happen when those various waveforms washed over each other and achieved synchronicity? When they combined themselves together just as the essences in the machine down below had combined?

Langton ran to the deep borehole and jammed his body into the shaft. He hesitated, then reached up and hauled the convex hatch into place; it slammed onto its rubber flanges with a heavy thud. Langton spun the wheel and looked down, then wished he hadn't; the foulsmelling shaft disappeared beneath his wedged, outspread feet. In the weakening light of the electric lamp, he stared straight ahead and gripped the loose furls of cable. Immediately, his head exploded with fragmented shards of memory and emotion; a hundred voices screamed inside him; white light blinded him.

He recoiled from the vibrating cable and almost fell down the shaft. Slowly now, with the voices still echoing in his head, Langton eased his body down the trembling borehole shaft. Despite the many slips and sudden scrapes, he avoided the black cable as if it were a thing alive. By the time he reached the braced planks and the jagged entrance into Sapper George's tunnel, blood poured from grated knuckles, elbows, and knees. As he stumbled from the shaft and collapsed onto the passage floor, he looked for the Webley but saw only crumbled brick and mud. Then the electric lamp gave out.

As darkness engulfed him, Langton held his breath. The pounding of the nearby machine obliterated all sound save Langton's own racing heart. He stood up in the narrow passage and tried to gain his bearings. One false step and he might find another borehole shaft or the intersection of lost corridors.

The cable helped him. As his eyes forgot the electric lamp, they detected a vague white glow from the cable itself. Half-crouched, Langton followed the ephemeral line back along the passage and soon saw a greater white glow framed by the pressure door ahead. He stepped over the high doorsill of the second chamber.

Sister Wright stood close to the glass nexus of the machine. The pale white light washed over her outstretched hand and gently smiling face. She gazed into the swirling cloud as if transfixed, like a small child intent on her first rainbow.

With the hesitant, apologetic steps of an interloper, Langton moved closer. "Sister Wright. Sister?"

She turned to him and drew back her hand. Her smile faded. "Oh, Matthew. You have no idea how sad I am to see you here."

As if justifying himself, Langton said, "I had no choice. I realized that you planned to attack the Span."

"You should have thought more like a husband than a policeman," Sister Wright said as she placed her body between Langton and the machine. "I asked you to stay away. I did ask. Do you remember?"

"I remember." Langton looked around the room but saw only shadows; the pale light from the glass vortex gave the only illumination and it did not reach the chamber's walls or corners. The muted pounding covered all sound of footsteps.

Moving to one side, slightly closer to the machine, Langton said, "Do you really think you can destroy the Span?"

Sister Wright nodded. "I believe so. Has the Professor explained to you about Galloping George, the American bridge that shook itself to pieces? He gave me both the inspiration and the science for this resonator."

"I doubt that the Professor would accept that honor," Langton said, trying to keep her talking while he sidled closer to the wooden stave on the ground next to the machine. "Would he want to carry the guilt of so many deaths? Of all those people above us?"

Sister Wright glanced away a moment. "I wish it could be otherwise, Matthew. Really I do. But I have no choice."

That halted Langton. He had concentrated on getting close to the stave and the machine, but he really wanted to discover what drove Sister Wright to do this. "Do you hate the Boers so much that you'd damage the Span and kill hundreds, maybe thousands, just to disgrace them?"

"I detest the Boers and all they've done, but they are not my target in this and never have been. They provide a useful scapegoat."

Langton stared at her.

"The Span will steal men's souls," Sister Wright said, her eyes gleaming. "What is it but an enormous metal aerial grounded at each tower, permanently charged by the electric railway, a magnet for the lost souls of the dying. Instead of gaining peace they will flock to this massive aerial and drain into the dead soil. Instead of freedom, imprisonment. Instead of peace, contamination. As soon as I realized the true horror of this, I knew I must destroy the Span."

Again, Langton remembered the empty birdcage in Sister Wright's office at the Infirmary and her story of releasing the captured animal. Now Langton looked into her intense gaze and saw madness. Sister

Wright's experiences in South Africa might have planted the seeds of insanity, but the years since had seen them grow out of all control.

"It's a bridge," Langton said. "No more than that."

She shook her head. "Are those jars simply glazed containers? No. Science has brought us to this, Matthew, and science is a wonderful servant but a dangerous master. Now is the time to regain control."

As if responding to her words, the swirling essences inside the glass vortex spun faster. The pounding faded, almost replaced by a high keening note like a buzz saw in the back of Langton's mind. The very air of the chamber seemed to thicken and grow heavy, so that each breath demanded concentration.

Langton wondered if Major Fallows's warning device would be heavy enough to shatter that glass; he felt the metal cube in his jacket. And he remembered Fallows's explanation: *sympathetic vibration.*

"Well done, Matthew," said Sister Wright, staring at the vortex. "Harnessing the charge of all these poor victims, the resonator's diaphragm will pulse the key frequency up the caisson chamber and through the Span itself. Every brick, every beam and cable will propagate the wave and amplify it. The Span has no choice—it must obey the laws of physics as laid down by God himself. The Professor's cladding will dampen any harmonics. One true waveform, pristine and pure . . . In time, the Span will shake itself to pieces.

"I swore that I would release every trapped soul I could find, but first they must fulfill one final task." Sister Wright leaned closer to the glass but did not touch it. Her lips moved, but her words seemed to take seconds to reach Langton. "Soon enough. You'll have your revenge as well as your freedom. And you'll save so many others."

Struggling against the dead air, Langton stepped forward, reached for the stave and raised it high over his head. Before he slammed it down onto the glass powerhouse of the machine, he felt it torn from his grip. He turned and saw pale hands emerging from the shadows; pale hands like shovels. Then a face without color, without expression.

"Forgive me, Matthew," Sister Wright said. "Jake."

Reefer Jake broke the stave like matchwood and hurled the pieces into the darkness. Langton ducked under the closing embrace, but a hand gripped his collar and yanked him back. Jake hauled Langton up off the floor and stared with impassive eyes. He drew back his right fist with almost deliberate delay.

Langton rained blows on Jake's chest and face, to no effect. His collar dug into his throat and cut off the air. Even as he kicked and punched and struggled, Langton couldn't take his eyes off Jake's fist pulling back like the piston of a steam locomotive.

Langton focused his one last thought. Sarah.

Jake's fist reached its farthest point. As Langton raised his arms to try to deflect the mammoth blow, he finally saw a change in the expression of Jake's face: surprise. The man's eyes opened wide; his mouth hung slack. Then, with Langton still clutched hard in his left hand, Jake toppled forward.

Langton tried to scramble out of the way before Jake's weight pinned him to the floor. As Langton clawed at the viselike fingers around his twisted collar, he saw the haft of a knife sunk up to its hilt in Jake's neck. Another man stepped out of the shadows. Durham.

The past two days had treated the agent badly. His torn clothes dripped mud and foul water; bloody cuts framed his filthy face. He limped to Jake's body, grasped the knife, and levered it out. He ignored Langton and made for Sister Wright.

"The machine," Langton said, still struggling to free himself. "For God's sake, Durham. The machine!"

Fallows's man did not turn or even register the words. He limped through the thickening air with the knife held down ready at his right side. He glared at Sister Wright as his left hand retrieved something from his pocket. "You left me a little keepsake on my pillow. I'm here to repay the kindness."

Sister Wright backed away from Durham but kept her body in front of the machine. "A true Brother Boer, I see."

Langton recoiled when he saw the object in Durham's outstretched hand: leathery, tanned, surgically removed from Kepler only days before.

"You should have heeded the warning," said Sister Wright, still backing away. Then, glancing between Langton, the machine, and Durham, she turned and fled down the passageway that led to the borehole and the caisson shaft. Durham went after her, his limp magnified by haste into an almost comical gait. There was nothing comical about the expression on his face or about the knife he carried.

As both quarry and pursuer disappeared into the passageway, Langton tore his clothes from Jake's grip. Stumbling to his feet, Langton dragged in mouthfuls of colloidal air and grabbed a section of wood. The ground shifted beneath his feet like the deck of an ocean liner. The keening in his mind threatened to sever all thought. Before it did, Langton raised the wooden club above his head and slammed it down in a savage arc.

Time seemed to slow. He felt the rough splintered wood in his hands. He saw the jagged corner slam into the glass. Fracture lines sped along the vortex like frost along a bough. Then it blew.

The explosion threw Langton back against the walls of the chamber. Pain lanced through him. He collapsed to the floor and curled into a ball even as waves of noise washed over him. Numb and battered, he waited for the screams and laughter and fractured words to fade. When they did, swallowed by the dark passages and chambers, Langton stumbled to his feet.

The ground still trembled. The keening in his skull seemed a little weaker, but not fading. When Langton touched the cable leading up to the strange apparatus in the caisson, he felt the power within. The machine still worked.

Langton had acted too late. The souls within the glass vortex must have already given up their power. In the light of Sister Wright's discarded lamp, he saw masonry dust drifting from the roof of the chamber. If the destructive resonance appeared so deep underground, what effect did it have on the Span above?

Langton snatched up the lamp and ran into the passageway. He tried to remember Sapper George's route back to the Cromwell sluices, but every turning looked the same, every passage seemed like the last. Panic reinforced the beat of the machine and activated some deep part of Langton's psyche, something atavistic and primeval; it made him want to flee, to run as far and as fast as he could. He fought the terror and concentrated on searching the tunnels.

There: that oval passageway with ankle-deep muddy water. At the end, a stout wooden door with a rusted metal hatch and a pulley wheel set into the frame.

Langton splashed down the channel and set the lamp on a ledge. He grasped the iron pulley wheel in both hands, took a breath, and turned. Nothing happened. He tried again. The mechanism defied him. He kicked and punched the metal sluice door, yelled at it, screamed and cursed. It ignored him.

Then he saw the locking pin in the wheel. He kicked the rusted pin loose from its hole and tried the wheel; this time it moved. Creaking and whining with reluctance, the wheel turned a quarter of a revolution, then half. Cogs meshed and the metal sluice gate set into the door lifted perhaps half an inch.

Langton put all his weight to the wheel handle. He felt the attractor machine's vibration in everything around him: the wheel, the floor, the door. He thought of the power of those combined essences, all tuned to the one true note that would resonate throughout the entire Span. He pushed harder.

Something cracked and grated inside the mechanism. The wheel spun free in Langton's hands and dropped him to his knees. The sluice gate shot upward in its runners and locked open.

On all fours, Langton looked into the open sluice and saw black silt. Compacted over two centuries until it resembled rock. Hard and solid.

Langton hung his head and felt the machine's resonance course through him. He could do no more. No more.

"Matthew . . ."

Langton looked up and saw Sister Wright leaning against the side of the passageway. She splashed through the shallow channel with her left hand pressed tight against her side. The fading lamplight made her face look pale and greasy. The smile on her face became a wince as she stumbled.

Langton jumped forward and caught her as she fell. He saw her left hand fall away from her dress in a bloody red arc. "Oh, God. I'm sorry."

"I deserve it," Sister Wright said, her words barely audible over the machine's pulse. "I killed his partner . . . even though . . . even though I—"

Langton held Sister Wright close to his chest until the wet coughing subsided. Then he picked her up in both arms, grabbed the lamp's hook and staggered back toward the entrance shafts leading up to the Pier Head.

"Leave me here, Matthew . . ."

"Save your strength."

Sister Wright looked up at him. "Please . . . leave me with the others."

Langton stepped over Jake's body in the second chamber and stumbled into the first. Here, the ranks of interconnected jars were now no more than that: earthenware containers emptied of their essences. Langton barely looked at them as he carried Sister Wright. He concentrated on trying to remember the route that Sapper George had showed him.

"Matthew . . . I only wanted to set them free."

Again he remembered the empty birdcage in the Infirmary office. "I know."

"I never meant—"

More coughing racked the body in Langton's arms. He hesitated and then continued along an unfamiliar corridor.

Sister Wright mumbled into his chest, "As soon as I saw Redfers, I knew . . . He had that look about him . . . I shed no tears at his death . . . At least he helped destroy the Span."

So Redfers's soul had been one of those essences powering the machine. Had Langton caught an echo of the doctor's fragmented thoughts from among the others? It didn't matter.

And why argue with Sister Wright? She honestly believed she'd acted for the best, like all fanatics. To her the Span was evil. And now it was too late.

Langton stood at a complex interchange and acknowledged to himself that he was lost. Sister Wright lay heavy and cold in his arms. He found a ledge above the waterline, wrapped his jacket around her, and held her in his arms. "We'll wait here awhile. There's plenty of time."

As the lamplight faded to a dim glow, Langton closed his eyes and rested his head back against the passageway walls. The machine's vibration seemed muted here but still persistent. The voice from the bundle wrapped in his arms could have come from miles away; it lulled him.

". . . All those poor people trapped . . . Even I had no idea until we found the first collection . . . So cruel, Matthew. So cruel . . ."

Langton remembered the basement room at Redfers's house, with its shelves that had held a hundred or more jars until Sister Wright—as Doktor Glass—had removed them. Were all those spirits now freed?

Then Langton opened his eyes. "What did you say? About Sarah?"

"She's safe, Matthew," Sister Wright said. "I promised you she would be . . . I kept my word. She's the only one left."

Langton could see the storeroom at Sister Wright's warehouse as clearly as if he stood there. The single jar standing on the zinc table. Sarah.

Before he could ask the questions that rushed to his lips, another sound joined the cycling pulse of the transfer machine: a deep rumbling like elephants stampeding through the lower caverns and passages. The floor and walls shook—not in time with the machine but rather to their own uneven rhythm. The roar of chaos.

Langton remembered that plug of silt and mud, all that had stopped the Mersey's waters.

Scooping his leaden arms under Sister Wright and staggering to his feet, he splashed through the channel's detritus, blind and confused, his only thought to get away from the rumbling destruction rising from below. He stumbled into walls, rebounded from unseen projections and lintels. The roaring intensified and a strong draft pushed Langton from behind and carried with it the smells of silt and river water.

Then, up ahead, lights and voices. Boots clattering against brick floors and ladders. At the head of the column, Sapper George, his face pulled taut by fear. "Inspector? God, sir, I never expected—"

Fallows pushed George aside and raised a revolver. "You're under arrest, Langton. You and your accomplice."

"We have minutes, if that, to get out of these tunnels," Langton told Fallows, then turned to Sapper George: "I opened one of the Cromwell sluices."

Sapper George's face turned even paler. He turned and waved the column of policemen and guards back toward the ladders like a frantic shepherd. "Back! Everybody back to the surface. Run, for God's sake."

The men hesitated, looked at Sapper George and Fallows, then listened to the rumbling from the lower caverns. Almost as one, they turned and rushed back along the passage.

"You'll give me an explanation," Fallows said, still pointing the revolver at Langton.

Sapper George replied for him, saying, "The Mersey is on its way up here, sir. If you don't believe your ears, just smell it."

Langton pushed past Fallows and carried Sister Wright in the glow of Sapper George's lamp. The sound seemed so close it must be just behind them; they'd never make the surface. Langton hoped that Sapper George was right about the tunnels' strange acoustics.

As he ran, half crouched, Langton looked down at Sister Wright's face. Quite unconscious now, she lolled in his arms with her head back, her mouth open. His exhausted body told him to drop her, to leave her here in the tunnels; after all, Doktor Glass had killed so many, and not all of them members of Jar Boy gangs.

Langton couldn't just leave her down here. Half of him wanted her to see justice, to see the damage she had done to the Span; half of him saw her as an injured woman who needed help. Either way, he wouldn't drop her.

Sapper George helped Langton maneuver her body up ladders and a section of broken stairs. Then Langton saw a different kind of radiance ahead: daylight. Young Eric stood at the bottom of the access shaft ladder, his eyes wide with panic. The last of the policemen and guards clambered up the ladder; Langton saw their muddy boot heels disappearing upward.

"Up you get, Eric," Sapper George shouted, slapping the boy on the back. "Move it, lad."

The roaring filled the tunnel now. Langton ushered Fallows forward with a nod of the head. "Go."

Fallows ran for the ladder and clattered up the rungs. Even before his feet were out of sight, George climbed up and then reached down for Sister Wright; he took her slack shoulders while Langton supported her weight from below. Langton's hands slipped from the greasy rungs, and he had to force his complaining body to cooperate. He pushed Sister Wright up the ladder while the roaring grew in his ears and reverberated through his bones. He could no longer separate the transfer machine's pulse from the Mersey's rushing force. Surely the machine could not survive?

"I have her, sir," Sapper George said. He sat on the edge of the access shaft coping with his arms around Sister Wright's inert body. "Eric? Give us a hand, lad."

Langton lifted Sister Wright to safety, then looked up and saw daylight framed by the edges of the entrance. He had only a few more rungs to climb. He could smell clean air.

From behind and below, a savage wind screamed past him and forced him from the head of the access shaft. Langton sprawled beside

Sapper George and Sister Wright, then rolled away with them as a plume of water blasted from the access shaft. The geyser erupted fifty feet into the air until gravity pulled it to earth; the grey water, fringed with dirty white foam, formed a ragged arch and then crashed down onto the pavement.

Langton covered Sister Wright's body with his own. Falling water pounded his back like lead and cut off all sound. He tasted foul silt and Mersey water. When the noise subsided, he looked up and saw Fallows and his men scattered around the head of the access shaft like discarded toy soldiers. Rivulets of muddy grey water rolled back toward the hatch like slow rain.

Then Langton saw the Span: The bridge danced. Towers of solid brick and steel shimmied and flexed in time to the machine's generated pulse. The road and rail deck rippled like a schoolgirl's skipping rope or a cabdriver's whip. Langton could see perfect oscillations racing along the contorted bed of concrete and steel. The support cables strung between the deck and the support pipes thrummed like harp strings; some of them snapped and whipped their lethal, braided strands.

People raced away from the Span, their screams drowned out by the complaining groans of steel under stress. Bricks and chunks of masonry splashed into the choppy River Mersey below. How long before the Span shook itself to pieces?

Langton had failed. He'd been too late.

Sister Wright opened her eyes and stared up at Langton. Her lips moved but he heard no words. He brushed the matted hair from her face and wondered if she knew she'd succeeded.

A change in the note of the twisting steel made Langton look up. Like a bow drawn across a violin's strings, the stressed steel's reverberations began to fade. The towers' motion gradually slowed until they sat back on their foundations like a photographer's subjects settling into focus. The road and rail deck's motion grew fainter; the waveforms weakened as their amplitude bled away. Like dying ripples on a pond, the oscillation faded.

Still a few chunks of masonry hit the water below, and the Span's deck swayed from side to side under its momentum. But it had survived. The silence left behind seemed deafening.

All around Langton, men sat up and stared at the Span. From the distance came the ringing bells of fire engines and ambulances. From the nearby grandstand, now canted to one side like a drunken thing, came weeping and cursing. People climbed to their feet and brushed the brick dust and debris from their clothes. Even the stampeding horses stopped in their tracks.

Langton reached down and gently closed the lids of Sister Wright's blank eyes. Before he hid her face beneath his jacket, he crossed her arms over her stomach; as he reached for her left hand, something metallic fell to the floor. A key. Langton pocketed the key and then drew his jacket up over Sister Wright's vacant, tranquil face.

Twenty-one

L ANGTON ESCAPED FROM the Pier Head and Fallows's questions at
six the next morning. Exhausted and wearing borrowed, mismatched clothes, he hailed a hansom cab and told the driver to
head along the Dock Road. He looked back for a moment at the men
swarming over the Span; the gas arc lights picked out the engineers,
navvies, cablemen, and hordes of Span company officials. Henry Marc
Brunel swore that the Span would be open within weeks. The thousands of people waiting to emigrate seemed to believe him.

Langton settled back into the cab's worn cushions. Every muscle
hurt; every part of him cried out for rest, but he knew he had so much
yet to do. McBride still waited in the Infirmary with Elsie at his side.
Fallows and Purcell had demanded his full report, although Langton
doubted that Purcell would welcome what he had to say. Langton still
had to officially close the case of Kepler and the missing—presumed
lost—Durham. And Queen Victoria herself had asked to see Langton,
to thank him in person.

All that must wait.

At Langton's shout, the cab stopped outside the entrance to Gladstone Dock. Langton walked down the empty steps to the dockside and the tall sides of dark warehouses. He could hear the Mersey slapping the wooden pilings and sandstone quays beneath him. How soft and pleasant that sound seemed now. How deceptive.

Sister Wright's warehouse reared up at his right. He found the rough wooden door standing ajar. The interior lay dark and apparently empty. Langton clicked on the electric lamp he'd borrowed from Sapper George's wagon; the beam of white light showed dancing dust motes, an empty hallway, and the darker outlines of open doorways. In the first side room, Langton found the bunks empty and the chairs overturned. A mosaic of bright playing cards spilled from the table and onto the floor.

Deeper inside the building, Langton found the bizarre sitting room quiet and cold. No embers glowed in the hearth. Only the ticking clock broke the silence. The lamp's beam picked out polished wood, chintz couches, a sparkling decanter. The room waited for an owner who would never return.

Langton stood outside the storeroom door and took deep breaths. He retrieved the key he'd found clutched in Sister Wright's hand and turned it in the lock. The massive door swung open without a sound. Langton found the light switch inside the entrance and flicked it on.

Caged bulbs filled the room with light and showed shelf after empty shelf. Every jar that Sister Wright had collected, bought, or "rescued" from other gangs had gone into the maw of the machine buried deep in the cavern beneath the Span. Every jar save one.

Sarah's jar stood in the center of the zinc table. The copper ring and green wax seal glinted. Dwarfed by that cavernous room, it seemed lost and out of place. Alone. Vulnerable. Langton circled the table and ran his hand over its cold metal surface. Then he reached out and picked up the jar in both hands. A ripple of recognition drifted up his arms and made him blink back tears.

Like a priest with a chalice, Langton carried his wife's jar through the warehouse and along the wharf to the water's edge. He set it down on the cold stone surface and knelt beside it. He worked the green wax loose with his pocketknife until the gleaming copper seal lay exposed. He gripped the seal, then hesitated. Would Sister Wright have kept her word? Despite her death in the tunnels, would she have ensured Sarah's resurrection?

Even now, if he kept the jar safe, he could bond with Sarah whenever he wanted. Nobody else would know. He could delay saying goodbye; he wouldn't have to feel so alone, so bereft. He could connect with her right up to the moment that her depleted essence finally faded to nothing.

How long would that take? Days? Weeks? Possibly months for Sarah trapped inside her prison.

Langton bowed his head a moment before turning the seal in his hand and releasing the lid.

The bright mist within swirled from the jar and enveloped Langton. Soft and warm, it set his skin tingling. He closed his eyes as a thousand overlapping memories surged through him: Sarah laughing before they kissed, dancing to soft music, running through the rain, her eyes locking onto his over a candle's flame. The feel of her hand resting in his; her skin gliding under his hand; the warmth of her lips on his neck; her words whispering in his ear; the smell of her perfume . . .

And then she was gone. Langton stood on the wharf and watched the bright mist rise and dissolve into the pink light of dawn over the Mersey. Hand outstretched, he tracked every particle before the sunlight absorbed them. He breathed cold morning air and let the moment settle through him like rain. Then he smiled good-bye and turned back toward the street and the waking city.

Behind him, golden in the new day, rose the waiting towers and cables of the Transatlantic Span. And beyond the Span, America.